＃ ALMOST MAYBES

ANNA P.

Almost Maybes is a work of fiction. Names, characters, places, and incidents either are the product of the author's imagination or are used fictitiously. Any resemblance to actual persons, living or dead, events, or locales is entirely coincidental.

ALMOST MAYBES Copyright © 2022 Anna P.

All rights reserved.

No part of this book may be reproduced or used in any manner without the prior written permission of the copyright owner, except for the use of brief quotations in a book review.

ASIN: B09VQX7WZW (Ebook)

ISBN: 978-93-5627-540-9 (Paperback)

Edited by Sarah Elliott

Cover Illustration & Design by Akshaya Raghu

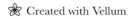 Created with Vellum

*For my grandmothers—Amy and Velliamma.
Thank you for inspiring me to write Baby.
I miss you both deeply.*

AUTHOR'S NOTE

Content and Trigger Warnings: *Homophobia, fat shaming, racism, bigotry, gaslighting, physical assault, attempted rape*

This is an open door romance, so the content may not be suitable for some readers. There are multiple scenes depicting consensual sex and intimacy. There are scenes with a vibrator as well. There is also the presence of coarse language and swearing spread across the book.

There are also scenes of racism and hate, where a white character confronts the Indian lead about her skin color and her presence in her house. These scenes might be hard for some to read, so if you do not wish to read them, please skip chapters 32-34.

While I have not suffered as much racism as Oleander does in the book, having lived in predominantly white countries over the course of my life, I have encountered racist comments and hate. I have also used inspiration from a friend who suffered similar situations and I hope I have handled these subjects and topics with care.

AUTHOR'S NOTE

I know there's value in writing a story set in India about an Indian character, but I wanted the writing process to be an escape for me from what life is like here. To Americans reading this, I apologize profusely if I've butchered the locations I've picked. I closed my eyes and pointed at a random spot on the map and picked the state of Delaware and created a small city of my own, Wildes.

ONE

Oleander

T*-Minus 30 minutes till orgasms and sleep.*
 Oleander repeated this in her head like a mantra to distract from the fact she'd been on her feet for eight hours.

That didn't include the four hours of dance lessons she worked that morning.

And she'd done it all while slinging drinks and being polite to customers even though she was running on no sleep and no orgasms. All she wanted to do was go home, drown herself in a bottle of wine and soak in the tub before passing out for the rest of the weekend.

T-Minus 30 minutes till orgasms and sleep.

Ollie was halfway into her locker at the Hazy Barrel, the bar she'd been working at for the last eight years, taking a few deep breaths before she could clock out. Cassie, the worst coworker ever, came crashing through the doors and grabbed onto her shoulders. Ollie groaned at the contact, already aware of what came next.

"Ollie, I *need* you to take my shift."

"Nope. Grant is waiting for me at home and I'm tired." Ollie snapped, refusing to let Cassie know *Grant* was her vibrator—because he *granted* her multiple orgasms without talking. Everyone at work thought *Grant* was a new boyfriend and Ollie used that to her advantage.

"There's an emergency at home. You need to take my shift."

"Oh well, because it's *another* emergency." Ollie responded as sarcastically as she could given her exhaustion. Cassie had an emergency *every* Friday evening.

"I'll even give you my paycheck, nobody else can cover for me."

"Cass…."

"Thanks doll, you're the best." In an intoxicating haze of whatever perfume she was wearing, Cassie was gone. It was a miracle she still had this job, considering Ollie took home most of that money since she worked all her shifts without complaint.

Okay, *some* complaint.

There was absolutely nothing glamorous about this job, but in a small town like Wildes, Delaware, you took what you got. It helped pay some of her bills, but on nights like this when other staff members found lame-ass reasons to run out early, Ollie *hated* her job. The Hazy Barrel had been an empty warehouse 15 years ago before Killian Graham turned it into a bar. Some called it a dive bar, some called it the best place to drink in town. Ollie called it work.

When Ollie walked out of another desk job, she'd walked into the Barrel with her best friend and proceeded to get very drunk. A few hours into their binge drinking, Ollie decided working at a bar would be fun. Sure, her traditional Indian grandmother would lose her shit, but it was a paying job. She was 29, unemployed and unable to save any money to pay her parents back, so she practically begged Killian to give her the job. For the first six weeks, he trained her and then set her up behind the bar. And Ollie had stayed.

Eight years later, much to her grandmother's disappointment, Ollie was still there. Sure, she got a promotion and she was the head bartender, but it wasn't great. Even though she taught dance every weekend, her grandmother wanted more from her. How else could she brag about her only granddaughter to her friends? Ollie was never going to sit behind a desk again. It was confining, boring and not satisfying enough.

Besides, where else could she wear vintage tees, cuffed jeans and comfortable sneakers all day?

Granted, bartending wasn't her ultimate goal. Ollie wanted to dance. That was her *thing*. Her brothers wanted to play cops and robbers, and beat each other up, but not Ollie. Her mother signed her up for ballet when she was little, but when she started to grow up and gained weight, her ballet teacher very *politely* told her mother Ollie was too big-boned to be a ballet dancer.

Of course, her grandmother liked to remind Ollie that she could always learn *Bharatanatyam*. While an ancient and legendary dance form from her home country, that wasn't what Ollie wanted to do. Ballet wasn't even her first choice, but it was so rare for people to teach freestyle. She decided to find a way to do it herself. This was before YouTube existed and you had to rely on MTV to play a Janet Jackson video so you could learn the moves. And it wasn't like there were a lot of job postings looking for choreographers, but Ollie knew her way to get there was to learn from the best.

So, she started auditioning. Ollie kept getting told she wouldn't fit—she was too brown, too chubby and too….something else offensive. No matter how thick your skin was, after a point, the words started to hurt and Ollie gave up.

Now, she worked six days at the Barrel and taught dance on two days, so she could pay her bills and pay her parents back for college.

"What are you still doing here?" *Killian*. The man in charge.

Ollie sighed, looking up from cleaning tables. "Cassie had a family emergency, so I'm working her shift *and* taking her paycheck."

"That's not how it works, Bow."

"You can make it out to her, give me the cash."

"Baby, you know I can't." Killian replied, his voice cloyingly sweet.

Ollie gritted her teeth and inhaled sharply through her nose. "Do you need something?"

"Table 12," he said with a smirk, knowing he'd won this conversation. "Champagne. They're celebrating."

Ollie nodded and waved him off as she returned to the bar, adjusting the apron around her waist. Ollie stepped behind the bar and smiled at the new faces. "Hey there, what can I get you?"

And so it went—one fruity cocktail after another and a bottle of champagne with sparklers causing havoc. While the other bartenders kept their heads down and pocketed their tips, Ollie watched everyone. People watching was an underrated pastime. You could tell so much about someone by watching them for 30 seconds. Like the redhead in the jeans; she didn't want to be there but she was sucking it up for her drunk friends. Or the trio of young men at a standing table, drinking beer and ignoring everything around them.

As a bartender, you met all kinds of people. Some of them treated you like a shrink, wanting to tell you their life stories and relationship woes, others sat at the bar quietly and moped until you had to get them a cab to go home. *This* was one of five things she enjoyed about her job.

Smiling to herself as she wiped down another glass, Ollie was distracted by her own thoughts when a soft voice purred her name. She'd know that voice anywhere. Looking up, Ollie was greeted by a purple-haired woman leaning over the bar, displaying her delicious cleavage and stunning smile.

"Becca," Ollie greeted her. "What can I get for you?"

"A screaming orgasm."

Ollie snorted as she watched the woman. "And your friend?"

Becca flipped her hair over one shoulder and smiled. "Just me tonight."

Ollie nodded and made the drink, aware of Becca watching her every move. This was exactly how they met a year ago—Becca leaning over the bar top, with flaming orange hair, asking for a screaming orgasm she chugged in one breath. And when her shift was over, Ollie went home with Becca and they both had more screaming orgasms that left her satisfied for a few days. The next time she saw Becca, she had her arms wrapped around another woman and Ollie laughed it off. One night stands were great and it worked on nights when she didn't want to go home alone or she forgot to charge Grant. If Becca was back for a repeat, Ollie wasn't interested.

"Here you go, one screaming orgasm."

"Maybe later I can give you one?"

Ollie offered a smile she hoped conveyed she wasn't interested, "Have a good one."

Becca pouted, still flashing Ollie her cleavage as she seductively toyed with the straw in her glass by curling her tongue and wrapping her lips around it. Ollie *was* horny, it was bound to turn her on. But, Becca wasn't what she was looking for.

"Brent," Ollie called out to one of the other bartenders, forcing her eyes from Becca. "I'm gonna take five." Brent nodded and Ollie smiled at Becca as she walked off.

STEPPING INTO THE LADIES ROOM, Ollie stifled a groan when she found a group of women hogging all the sinks and mirrors. They were touching up their makeup and hair, chattering and giggling. Usually, Ollie didn't judge women for the kind of lifestyles they wanted to live. Everybody liked something different and you couldn't judge them based on their likes always. But at that moment, in the terrible mood she was in, her brain conjured up an image of her going Uma Thurman in *Kill Bill* on those women to get them out of the way.

She *should* dislike these women—they were the ones that ruined every relationship. Well, not these women specifically, but the ones who looked like them. Tall, leggy, with shiny hair, expensive clothes, perfectly applied makeup and shrill voices that were a siren's call for men and women alike.

It wasn't her fault her Indian mother was born in America and it wasn't her fault she was curvier than she was thin. Okay, maybe that second thing was on her. But Ollie didn't hate her body. Till she graduated high school, Ollie had looked like those women. She was *skinny* and had legs for days, her curves were accentuated by tight dresses and tiny tank tops. But, it was the 90s and everyone looked the same, no matter the color of their skin or their sexual preferences.

But when she left home and went to college, junk food became an easy solution. Obviously, Ollie and her best friend, Frankie, started piling on the pounds. While they partied occasionally and ran across campus almost every day, it wasn't enough to lose weight. By the time she graduated college, depression over the demise of her first real relationship set in and food became her best friend.

For a while, she hated the way her body changed, but the older she got, the more she came to appreciate her body. She might have been raised to believe that women of a *certain size* were unappealing, and it took Ollie a *long time* to look in the mirror and see a woman who was confident and comfortable with her size. There were always going to be those who used the word 'fat' as an insult, but to Ollie, being fat wasn't a bad thing. She wasn't unhealthy, she wasn't *settling* for her new shape—she loved who she was. Every inch of her body was the way she liked it, from her wide hips to her breasts and even her slightly larger ass. If people didn't like what they saw when they looked at her, that was their problem.

Her maternal grandmother, fondly called Baby, lectured her on her weight, hair and face her whole life. Ollie knew the basics of what Baby had gone through in her South Indian hometown and running away to America to meet and marry a man was her way of escaping it. Baby had also grown up in a society where women were meant to look, dress and behave a certain way, so when Ollie was growing up, she went above and beyond with making sure she knew what was *expected* of her.

Sadly, the running away and falling in love was only applicable to Baby. Ollie had to lose weight, straighten her wild hair and marry an eligible South Indian bachelor. Not even her mother marrying a half-white man could change Baby's mind. Hell, one of her brothers had married a white woman and Baby adored her. But Ollie? She had to marry an Indian man. Being bisexual? Not something Baby would ever be able to wrap her head around, so Ollie kept the secret.

These thoughts usually sent her down an unappealing spiral, but Ollie had a long shift ahead of her. So she decided that the women deserved to touch up their makeup and look good for whoever they were trying to impress, but she wasn't going to stand around and wait.

Sighing heavily, she stepped out of the ladies room. Ollie eyed the men's room and pursed her lips. Nothing she hadn't seen before and besides, when she first started at the Barrel, Killian put her in charge of cleaning the restrooms, so she figured she could get away with it. Hand on the door, Ollie sucked in a deep breath in case another drunk patron had relieved himself on the floor instead of the urinal and started to push. But the door swung open and she almost fell onto the sticky floor.

"Gah!"

"Holy shit, I'm sorry. Are you okay?" Hands moved to help her straighten up and Ollie shook him off, taking a minute to catch her breath before regretting that decision instantly.

Fighting back a gag, she shuddered, "Who opens doors like that?"

"I didn't know there was a right way to open a door."

Ollie huffed, scuffing her feet against the sticky floor, "Yanking it open like you're mad at the door is not the right way to do it."

"You do realize this is the *men's room* right?"

"Yeah, so?" Ollie pushed her shoulders back and looked up at the door police. A playful smirk, messy dark brown hair, a faint blush on his cheeks and hazel eyes greeted her and Ollie fought the smile tugging at her lips in response. Her eyes dragged down his frame, taking in his brown and green plaid shirt with a Chewbacca t-shirt underneath, dark jeans and sneakers. *Cute nerd.* Ollie bit back a smile and gestured for him to step aside, putting on her best-exasperated face, "Do you mind?"

"Warning, there's a drunk dude under the sinks, one in the stalls and one serenading the urinal."

"What's his song of choice?" Ollie heard herself chuckle and mentally kicked herself.

He offered her a wider smile as he spoke, "*I Will Always Love You* by Whitney Houston, of course."

"So cliché," Ollie made a face and stepped past him. "You may leave."

"This place looks dangerous, you could use the help."

Ollie narrowed her eyes, "Do I look like a damsel in distress?"

"Sounds like a trick question."

"Smart boy. Goodbye." Ollie glanced back and waved him off, getting a laugh and a quick nod in response before he walked away, closing the door behind him, trapping the smells in there with her. *Sweet baby Jesus.*

TWO
Jackson

Jackson had a love/hate relationship with his job—working 16 hours, hunched over a keyboard, designing something you knew the client was going to trash once they saw it. It wasn't that Jackson was bad at his job—this client was difficult to work with. And Jackson had worked four long days coming up with the perfect visual pitch only for it to get thrown out the window. *Again.*

Advertising was a soul-sucking job, but it was one that kept him employed, paid and allowed him to use his talents the right way. This is what he went to college for and he was finally able to do something with what he had learned.

While he could not kill his clients or burn the house down, he could get absolutely drunk. And drag his two colleagues-slash-friends down with him.

They were two pitchers of beer down, but it wasn't numbing the stress making his shoulders clench and his stomach ache. Trevor and Carson, his two friends from work, were chatting and looking around for women to flirt with, but Jackson's head was still fixed on the project they'd been working on. It was better than moping about being single, so he considered this an improvement.

"This beer is terrible." Carson muttered.

"This round's on you, Jack," Trevor told him with a hard thump on the back.

"Every round has been *on me* tonight—next time, you're buying." His friends shrugged and Jackson rolled his eyes as he headed towards the bar.

As always, the Hazy Barrel was packed for a Friday night. People were clinging to every inch of the space and Jackson groaned as he moved through people congregating in the middle, trying not to brush up against anyone.

Then he saw *her*.

Earlier, when he'd opened the door to the men's room, the last thing he expected to see was a woman on her way to a very disgusting face plant. He'd tried to help her up, she shook him off and laid into him about opening doors weirdly. But Jackson had also been too captivated by her husky voice to produce a smart comeback.

As he stood at one end of the bar, waiting for people to move out of the way so he could place his order, Jackson took a minute to catalog this woman. He'd gotten a brief look at her outside the men's room at the same time she was sizing him up, but this was an even better view.

She was a few inches shorter than him, with thick dark hair that looked naturally unruly, or maybe unbrushed. The ends of her hair had blonde streaks and her outfit told him she didn't give a shit about being fashionable—dark jeans clung to her wide hips and thick thighs paired with a vintage Metallica t-shirt she'd tied up on one side, showing off a little bit of her stomach. He also got a glimpse of a tattoo in the space between her shirt and her waistband.

And her eyes. Man, her eyes pierced him. Brown, but darker than his, with a hint of gold. Thinking about it now, Jackson didn't even realize how close they'd been standing until he registered the gold flecks. Her mouth had been turned down in displeasure, but he could tell her bottom lip was plumper and she had the pinkest and most kissable lips he'd ever seen.

Tearing his eyes away from her, Jackson stepped forward to set the empty pitcher on the bar and ordered three IPAs. While the bartender went to fetch his drinks, his eyes drifted back to the brunette. She was laughing, head thrown back and Jackson swallowed at the beautiful sight. Three bottles of beer were set down in front of him and Jackson handed the money over, dropped the change in the tip jar, grabbed his beers and returned to his friends.

JACKSON WAS NOW on wingman duty, something he sucked at majorly. Apparently, his friends chose to ignore that, because they expected him to deliver. Jackson had always been considered an *awkward turtle*—because he had been a weird looking kid, a lanky and dorky teenager, and his favorite thing to do in school was read comic books and discuss *Star Wars*. Girls didn't care for scrawny boys who fumbled over their words or didn't have any *street cred*.

Jackson had stuck out like a sore thumb—because he wore hand-me-downs from his older brother, took the bus and his older siblings left him to fend for himself. When he wasn't with his only two real friends, he'd spent every free moment at school doing his homework to become the best student. Sure, it helped him graduate at the top of his class and get scholarships to anywhere he wanted to go, but Jackson wanted a different experience in college.

Until his first girlfriend, he didn't even think he was worth a second look. But she found a way to make him feel attractive. And the awkward turtle turned into a slightly less awkward guy and he made a *few* more friends.

Even now, Jackson collected everything to do with the Ninja Turtles and had *Star Wars* things on his desk at work.

Hell, he was wearing a Chewbacca t-shirt under his flannel shirt. Jackson was never going to apologize for liking pop culture and being a nerd—these were the things that made his life bearable.

But, to other people, that was boring and unattractive.

Women wanted bulky athletic guys who could bench press all of Jackson's weight. Jackson didn't even know what *bench press* meant. And the most exercise he got was teaching karate on the weekends.

"Okay," Carson said as he faced Jackson. "What the fuck is going on with you?"

"What do you mean?"

Trevor snorted from his other side. "You're supposed to be our wingman. So, why aren't you helping us score?"

Jackson looked around, noticing some of the women glancing their way. And he realized he'd been off in his own world this whole time. "I'm clearly not a good wingman tonight."

"But your cute, awkward and dorky personality always brings the hot women in."

Carson put his hand on Jackson's shoulder, "Haven't you heard, Trev, women don't care for cute and awkward anymore."

"Fuck off." Jackson said with a laugh, gently shoving Carson aside as he reached for his beer.

"Incoming," Trevor muttered and they straightened up as two pretty women stepped up to their table. Jackson smiled tightly, watching his friends from the corner of his eyes as their grins broadened

"Hi," one of the women said as she set her things on their table. "I'm Mia and this is Lily."

"Nice to meet you ladies." Trevor greeted them and Jackson watched in absolute fascination as his friend turned on the charm. "I'm Trevor, and these are my friends Carson and Jackson."

There was a chorus of *hi*'s around the table and the ladies launched into talking about how they were new in town and looking for someone to show them around. They were pretty, no doubt—one had glossy blonde hair and the other had jet black hair, they had on a whole lot of makeup and wore tiny dresses. They were clearly out to get attention and Trevor and Carson were eating out of the palm of their hands. Jackson was less interested. Not that he wasn't attracted to them—you'd have to be blind to not notice them—but he was definitely not the kind of person to indulge in one night stands or flirt with women at the drop of a hat.

While he convinced himself he was over it, Jackson was still a little sore over his last break up. Honestly, he thought Ursula would be *the one*. Despite her evil Disney queen name, she'd been the perfect girlfriend. They met through a friend at a party and he'd teased her about her name, she'd teased him about his because she was obsessed with *Sons of Anarchy* and expected everyone named Jackson to look like Charlie Hunnam. After they'd spent the whole night talking, he'd driven her home and she'd pinned him against her front door and kissed him goodnight and walked away.

A week later, they flirted over text before she agreed to meet him for drinks. And one thing led to another and they were tangled up in her sheets. Jackson had been single for a long time before Ursula and he'd indulged in one night stands when he had the courage, time and patience for it, but she completely took him by surprise.

One minute he was Jackson, the guy from Afocus Designs and the next minute he was introduced as Ursula Banner's boyfriend. And for two whole years, he basked in the title. Till she got bored of his witty banter and pop culture references and invited someone else for drinks and let them get tangled up in her sheets. The crazy part was, Ursula didn't apologize for cheating on him. She said, *"Things were getting so...boring, right? So I figured I'd save you the trouble."*

Jackson didn't get his favorite t-shirt back, lost his Ninja Turtles toothbrush and the girl he thought he was going to marry.

It had been six months and his friends were still unsure if Jackson was okay. Somedays, *he* wasn't sure if he was okay. He was chugging along and doing the best he could. But on nights like this, he missed knowing when he was done, he could go home and curl up with someone. The only person he went home to was his turtle, named after his favorite Ninja Turtle —Raphael.

Ursula told him his unrealistic expectations of relationships came from all the romantic comedies he watched. But he didn't think any of it was unrealistic. Look at his dad. Sure, he'd married one woman and had three kids before she abandoned them. But Callum Huxley finally found his soulmate. Mindy, his stepmother, was incredible and she loved his dad with abandon. Mindy put a smile on his father's otherwise drawn face and she brought joy into the Huxley house. Witnessing that, as well as every romantic comedy on the planet told Jackson if his father could find love again, why couldn't he?

He wanted to find his *person*. Sure, Jackson had a bad habit of falling in love too fast and forgetting you had to gradually infuse yourself into the lives of people, but was it so bad that he let himself go with Ursula? She seemed to think so. And like every other woman on the planet, she didn't think his *Star Wars* and Turtle love was healthy.

Apparently, those were meant for kids and not adults. That should have been the first sign Ursula was going to leave him for someone else.

"Earth to Jack!"

Jackson blinked and looked at his friends, noticing their worried expressions, "Sorry, what were you saying?"

"You okay, bud? You zoned out there for a long time," Carson frowned and Jackson shrugged.

"Just got lost in my head."

"Yeah, Mia and Lily noticed that too," Trevor pointed out with a frown of his own and Jackson's shoulders sank.

"Shit, guys, I'm sorry."

"It's cool, they were worried about you for a minute there, but we convinced them you do this often."

"I take back my apology."

Carson laughed and gave Jackson's shoulder a squeeze, "Besides, they seemed more interested in us than you, so you're fine."

"Let's not rely on me to be a wingman next time, okay?"

"Fine," Trevor said as he grabbed their empty bottles. "Only because you have sucked at every wingman attempt since we became friends."

"I don't know what made you think I'd be a good wingman in the first place."

"Because of your approachable face and disarming smile." His friends laughed and went off to get them more beers. Jackson rubbed his face and headed to the restroom, trying to think of anything but how much his ex-girlfriend had messed him up.

THREE
Oleander

Bathroom run complete and another round of spilled drinks cleaned up, Ollie silently cursed Cassie for saddling her with this dumb shift. *It's for the money*, she repeated, replacing her earlier orgasm mantra for this one. If that wasn't enough, a patron so very politely said she'd look beautiful if she smiled, so Ollie pasted on a terrifying smile to keep everyone at bay.

She was definitely not the most pleasant person working at the Barrel, but she *tried*. Some days, she flirted with everyone who stepped up to the bar, she went home with a pocketful of tips and phone numbers and came back the next day to do it again. But on other days, after an exhausting session with toddlers in tutus, she couldn't deal with adults.

She'd been at the Barrel long enough that Killian stopped trying to change her. He accepted that she did a damn good job, didn't sleep with *all* their customers and was a quick teacher when it came to new bartenders. He would prefer it if she smiled more and wore something more revealing. But he knew she'd punch him in the nuts if he kept on about it.

She was squatting behind the bar to get a break from

human interaction with her face stuck in one of the tiny fridges when she heard Brent call her name.

"We're running out of glasses. Could you check in the back?"

"Ugh, no. I've been on my feet all day."

"It's just a few more hours, Ollie."

"Fuck me, this day never ends." Ollie groaned and straightened to her full height and pressed her hands into her lower back to soothe an ache.

Walking through the doors leading to the kitchen, Ollie found her face stretching into her first real smile of the day. The guys in the kitchen were her favorite people; they fed her consistently and let her hang with them on slow nights. There were five of them—two on dish duty and three chefs. They'd been at the Barrel almost as long as she had and Ollie knew they survived because they banded together.

"There's our favorite girl!" Harry, the main chef, called out, blowing her a kiss.

"I hope you're saving some of that for me, Harry. You know I'm a sucker for chicken wings."

Harry laughed, "Everyone seems to be in the mood for my wings tonight."

"I'll save you some." Joey, one of the guys on dish duty, told her and winked as he leaned in to kiss her cheek. Joey and Ollie shared one hot weekend when they first met, and instead of it being awkward after, they seemed to fit together really well.

"Thanks, handsome. But first, I need all the clean glasses loaded up."

"Almost done." Joey smirked and went off to load up the tray with the glasses and Ollie took a minute to admire the way these guys worked. None of them put up with Killian and his bullshit and they all worked their asses off daily. Most nights, they left last, once the kitchen was cleaned up and inventory was taken, and showed up the next day to do it all over again.

As Joey started to slide a tray of clean glasses over, Ollie felt her phone vibrate in her back pocket. Frowning, she pulled it out and saw her parents number on the screen. Gesturing to the phone, she patted Joey on the arm and walked farther into the kitchen and away from the sounds of the cooking to answer. Her parents never called this late, so if they were calling her now, it must be serious.

"What's wrong?" She said as she answered the phone, using her free hand to massage her scalp.

"Why must something be wrong for me to call?" Ollie closed her eyes and resisted the urge to groan at the sound of her grandmother's voice. She loved Baby, she truly did, but her grandmother was a traditional South Indian woman and she believed things must continue to happen the way she knew best. Also, she kept speaking in her mother tongue of Malayalam in hopes that Ollie would one day learn the language as well.

"*Ammachi*," the South Indian name for grandmother rolled off her tongue in a heavy accent and Ollie sighed softly. "What are you still doing awake?"

"My favorite granddaughter doesn't call me enough, so I'm calling her."

"I'm your *only* granddaughter."

"And that is why you must call me once a week."

"Okay, I'll keep that in mind," Ollie said, leaning against a counter, causing steel dishes to clatter behind her.

"What is that noise? Where are you?"

"I'm still at work."

"Tsk." Baby made *that* sound judgmental and Ollie had to fight a smile. "You should not be working so much. Your parents have lots of money, just take it."

"I want my own money, Ammachi, you know this."

Baby switched to English, "Yes, but can't you make money somewhere else?"

"I like working here!" Ollie protested and heard how

ridiculous she sounded.

"Is that why you're still there at..." There was some rustling on the other end, "Close to 11pm?"

"Yes," Ollie cleared her throat. "Was there a reason you called?"

"We found you a boy."

Ollie groaned and started to pace, fingers pinching the bridge of her nose. "Another one?"

"He is very handsome, very wealthy, fair and also very tall." Baby ignored Ollie's tone of frustration and went on. "He works at NASA."

"So he's in Houston." Ollie sighed.

"We've got lots of family in Houston. And you like space!"

Ollie waved at Joey, needing an escape from this call. But the idiot smiled and shook his head.

"I used to like space, when I was a *child*."

Baby hummed and continued, "He's going to be in Wilmington next week and I have told your mother to set up a meeting."

"Okay, Ammachi, I'll speak with mom."

"You know I only want you to be happy." She said it in an annoyingly sweet tone Ollie hated. "I would also like to see you get married before I die."

"You've been saying that since I was 21. It doesn't work on me anymore."

"One can only hope." Baby said in Malayalam, making Ollie laugh. Like always, without saying 'goodbye', she hung up and Ollie put her phone away with a groan.

"Here you go, beautiful." Joey slid a tray over and wiped his hands. "Come back in an hour and I'll get you another tray."

Ollie smirked at Joey, "How about in an hour you take a break and we slip out for a bit?"

"Get outta here! Don't distract the kid from his job."

Harry called out from the front of the kitchen. Ollie laughed and she used her hip to push open the door.

SHE'D ONLY GOTTEN a few steps out of the kitchen when someone bumped into her and made the tray wobble, dropping a few of the glasses to the floor in a loud crash. "Watch where you're going!"

"Shit, I'm so sorry."

Ollie straightened the tray, growling as her heart raced and made note of the fact she'd lost only a few glasses. She set the tray on the counter closest to her and bent down to gather up the bigger pieces. "Please step back so I can clean this up."

Male hands reached for the glass shards, "Let me help."

"Sir, please…" she lifted her head, groaning quietly when she recognized the guy. "*You, again.*"

He smiled wide, "I feel like now is not the right time to say 'hello'."

"And yet, you did. Seriously, return to your table. I'll get this cleaned up."

"I don't mind, it's the least I can do." His hands were moving around in her periphery and Ollie bit back a huff of frustration.

"Be careful, there are some really tiny pieces that could—"

"Ah fuck!" He cursed. Ollie's head snapped up and she noticed the blood dripping from his hand.

"Why couldn't you just do what I told you?"

"Are you seriously giving me shit for trying to help you?"

Narrowing her eyes at him, Ollie nodded, "Yes! Because I told you not to help me. Now, you're bleeding everywhere and that's another thing to add to my list."

"Look, I'm sorry, I…I didn't want to get you into trouble. Or whatever it is your boss would do."

Ollie sighed, because shit, Killian was *definitely* going to take this out of her paycheck. Standing up, she called out to Brent, and turned to the bleeding guy, "Come on, there's a first aid kit in the back, let's clean it up."

"Uh, it's okay, I'll get one of my friends to take me home."

"You're bleeding all over the place and I honestly don't want to clean up after you, so come with me."

"Anyone ever tell you that you're a little terrifying?"

"Every single day." Ollie said with a fake smile and led the way to the locker room.

This guy wasn't the first to tell her she was terrifying, sarcastic or rough. She had little patience for idiots and assholes. Ollie had been using sarcasm to hide her true feelings and moods for years and she wasn't going to stop. And when paired with her lack of filter, it sometimes came out all wrong. She knew it, but she couldn't stop herself till the words were actually out of her mouth.

Gesturing to a bench, she opened her locker and grabbed the first aid kit. Ollie pulled out the tweezers, antiseptic, cotton swabs and tape. Setting everything down, she straddled the bench and held her hand out to him, "I promise, I won't bite."

"I'll be the judge of that."

She smirked, flashing him her teeth, "I could bite, if that's what you're into."

"I don't know where your teeth have been, so I'm going to pass."

"Lots of places, really. You'd be lucky to have my teeth on you."

He cleared his throat, "I feel like we should exchange names if we're going to continue this conversation."

"Ollie," she grunted and quickly added. "Oleander."

"Jackson," he said and wiggled his injured hand. "It's good to meet you, Oleander."

Ollie used the tweezers to pull out the glass, covered cotton in rubbing alcohol and gently wiped it over his wounds and wrapped it up. "All done."

She straightened up and took a proper look at Jackson. He was young. Well, younger than her, that much she was sure of. He was handsome. Sharp nose, wide smile, light scruff that hugged a strong jaw and his hazel eyes were sparkling. Ollie always thought people said that in books for the fun of it, but Jackson's eyes really *sparkled*.

His youth was also evident in his clothes. Ollie had noticed his casual outfit earlier, her eyes lingering on his Chewbacca t-shirt, which made her giggle. It was a sketch of Chewbacca drinking beer and underneath it read 'Brewbacca'. And paired with his plaid shirt, jeans and sneakers, he looked very young. But the thing that really got her attention this time was he'd folded up the sleeves of his shirt to reveal strong forearms dusted with dark hair. Why did that look so good on men?

Ollie blinked when she realized she'd been staring at Jackson and he was smiling because he'd caught her in the act. She laughed as she put everything away.

"You look too young to be in a place like this, Jackson."

"How old do you think I am?"

Ollie pretended to think about it as she closed the box, "Twelve."

"You've been hanging out with strange kids if you think twelve year olds can have facial hair."

"You call that facial hair?" She snorted and shook her head.

"Hey! I'm a slow grower."

"That's a great pick-up line. I bet all the teen girls love that."

"I'm not going to touch that."

"First smart decision all evening," Ollie added with a chuckle and put the box in her locker.

"I'm 26, if it really matters to the age police."

"I wanna make sure I'm not crossing any illegal lines letting my team serve you or be in this locker room alone with you."

"This conversation got out of hand really fast." Jackson said with a soft laugh.

Ollie glanced at him, her heart stuttering when she caught Jackson looking at her. And he was *looking*. His eyes brushed over her body and down to her incredibly comfortable sneakers and back up to her face. When he met her eyes and realized she'd caught him in the act, Jackson blushed.

"If you're done checking me out, it's time to go."

"Right." Jackson nodded, looking at his hand.

"Don't crash into anybody else tonight, okay?"

"I'll try. Thanks, Oleander."

"Good night, Jackson." She caught the smirk on his face before he stepped out of the locker room, leaving Ollie's heart racing faster than it had in a really long time.

FOUR
Oleander

After a weekend of no accidental alcohol spills, broken glasses or former one night stands, Ollie was back at the Barrel. She'd spent most of Saturday dancing with the kids and on Sunday, she'd visited her best friend and they ate their weight in chocolate cookies while binge watching *Parks & Recreation* for the millionth time.

She'd spent all of Monday morning sleeping and woke up in time to shower, change and make it to the Barrel for her shift that evening. Shockingly, Cassie was there, already wiping down the bar and helping Brent organize glasses before they opened.

When she was ready, Killian called her to his office. "I heard you broke some glasses."

Ollie dropped into the chair in front of Killian's massive table. "Wasn't looking where I was going as I stepped out of the kitchen, dropped about four."

"You know what this means, right?"

"Yes," she said with a sigh. "You're taking it out of my paycheck."

"What's with the attitude?"

"What attitude?" Ollie frowned. Killian shook his head.

"Also," he started, making Ollie stiffen in anticipation of something she wasn't going to like. "Cassie is on thin ice. One more *family emergency*, I'm going to have to fire her."

"You should ask her about these emergencies before you fire her, maybe they're legit."

"Every Friday night, really?"

Ollie shrugged, because who knew what went on in anybody else's homes. Everyone at the Barrel thought she was dating some guy named Grant, for crying out loud.

"Look, whatever her reasons are, you should ask her what is going on," Ollie insisted.

A creepy smile spread over Killian's mouth, "Or *you* could ask her. You know, woman to woman."

"Fine," Ollie growled and got to her feet, ignoring the way Killian's eyes moved over her body. "And while I'm here, we're gonna need more hands on deck."

Killian mumbled something, but Ollie stopped listening as she walked out of his office and down the stairs to where people were already starting to fill up the Barrel.

AFTER BABY DROPPED the news about this NASA boy on her, Ollie had been silently fuming that her family was still doing this. Sure, it was not what her mother sanctioned, but whatever Baby said happened. No matter how many times Ollie tried to convince her grandmother she wasn't like other Indian women, Baby didn't get it.

From the day she turned 21, Baby had been dropping hints. There was a document created—a *biodata*, her grandmother called it—with all of her information: height, weight, skin tone, education and more circulated to other Indian families. And in turn they would send the biodata of their sons to see if there could be a match. Ollie had never liked it and even though she came out as bisexual to her parents pretty early on, they kept that secret from Baby.

Last Saturday, when she got home after her dance lessons for the day, her mother called to remind her about her *date*. With her parents living in her hometown of Huntington, West Virginia, she didn't see them as often as she'd like. Ollie gave her mother grief about this boy, because she thought they were done with it.

"It's to make your Ammachi happy, Annie." Her mother had said in a sweet voice, using the nickname only she was allowed to use. You'd think after bestowing her with the name *Oleander*, her mother would actually use it. But 'Annie' was one in a long list of nicknames that had no connection to her actual name.

So okay, they were lying to Baby about her sexuality, about her lack of interest in marriage. It was *very* healthy. She knew it was for the best. Baby could be a tad bit dramatic and if they told her she wasn't looking to get married *now*, her grandmother might actually have a heart attack. Or do something drastic. She wouldn't actually do anything to jeopardize the family, but everyone knew whatever they did was to keep Baby happy.

So Ollie took the number of this eligible bachelor and sent him a text on Monday to meet on Friday. She could give her grandmother this much. It was a simple date, it didn't have to mean anything. She'd spend the evening with him, let him pay for her food and drive herself back to her apartment and go to sleep with Grant between her legs. Simple.

OLLIE HAD BEEN on her feet non stop for hours before she took a break. And that meant squatting behind the bar and sneakily drinking a bottle of beer. It's what they all did and it worked—you found a quiet space and fit yourself in there for fifteen minutes, hydrated and got back to work. Since it was a Tuesday, she was counting on being able to go home on time. She had dance class in the morning and she didn't want to show up exhausted and not be able to teach yet again. Honestly, it was a miracle she'd survived her Saturday lesson.

When her fifteen minutes were up, she tossed her empty bottle in the bin and got to her feet. Smoothing down her shirt, Ollie grabbed her apron and wrapped it around her waist as she turned to face waiting customers and her eyes met familiar hazel ones paired with a crooked smile.

"Hi, again."

Ollie arched an eyebrow, "Jackson."

"Don't sound so excited to see me." His smile widened and Ollie rolled her eyes

"I'm trying to contain myself, I guess it's not working."

"Lucky me."

"What would the lucky guy like?" Ollie huffed out a laugh.

"Three beers, please. And maybe your number?"

Ollie's eyes widened as she opened the beers, "Wow, *I'm* also lucky tonight."

"I'm going to take all of that sarcasm as a no."

"And he's adept at reading sarcasm. You *might* be my dream man."

"Really? My luck skyrocketed," Jackson snorted and Ollie rolled her eyes again.

"Three beers, anything else?"

"A coffee?"

Ollie shook her head, "We don't serve coffee."

"Would you like to go out and drink some?"

She gave him a flat stare, "You're serious."

"As a heart attack."

"Those are quite dangerous."

Jackson chuckled, "So you could save me the trouble and say yes."

"But I hate coffee," Ollie shrugged.

"I'm sorry, I thought I heard you say you *hate* coffee?"

"Yeah, it makes me sick."

"How can anyone hate coffee?"

Ollie stopped what she was doing and glared at him, "The same way someone can love it."

"It's *coffee*."

"Jackson."

"Oleander."

"Don't say my whole name like that." Ollie frowned at him and Jackson held his hands up.

"Let me buy you a non-coffee, somewhere outside of here and I'll call you whatever you want."

"Why?" Ollie was genuinely confused.

Jackson looked perplexed as he leaned against the bar, "Why does anyone ask a person out for coffee or non-coffee?"

"Fuck if I know. I don't get asked out for coffee."

"Would you prefer it if we weren't drinking at all?" Jackson tilted his head.

"I would prefer it if you weren't asking me out."

"Why not?"

"Christ." Ollie huffed, trying to understand how to let this guy down. It had been a long time since a guy had been this vocal about asking her out. Some would slip her their number, others would hit on her and walk away when Ollie turned her glare on them. Not Jackson. He was either not good at reading her glares, or he didn't care.

"Seriously, why not?"

"You're too young to be asking me out."

"We already established I'm not 12."

Ollie gestured for Jackson to move aside to let another customer through, "I'm not interested."

"Will you kill me if I ask why?"

"Yes." She sighed, opening a beer for the other customer. "Look, I'm not interested in dating or romance. I don't have the time or the desire to fall in love and whatever else is going to happen here."

"Why do you think that's what it is?"

"Because Jackson, you have *romance* written all over you. You look like the kind of guy who wants to woo a woman and charm her. I'm not that girl."

Jackson frowned and Ollie hated that she was being so honest and brutal. When he spoke, his voice was soft, "What kind of girl are you?"

"The kind that likes to fuck and walk away."

Her words clearly had the desired effect, because Jackson's face fell and he took a step back, taking his beers with him. Ollie watched him turn around and head for one of the tables, her heart racing. She hadn't meant to be so harsh, but given that Jackson wasn't getting the hint, Ollie felt like she needed to be honest and maybe a little assertive.

As HER SHIFT came to an end, Ollie caught sight of Jackson and his friends walking out. He met her eyes and offered her a small smile which Ollie returned on instinct. There was nothing wrong with Jackson, but more with his gender. Ollie had her issues with men stemming from her first serious heterosexual relationship and ever since, she struggled to connect with men without worrying about everything else that came with it.

Sure, she'd hooked up with Joey, but it had been one weekend—what he didn't know was Ollie had a panic attack in the bathroom afterwards. She'd brushed away her tears and smoothed down her hair before crawling back into bed with him.

Her first serious relationship with a man had ended badly. When she got emotional, he teased her. When she put on a little more weight, he mocked her. When she worked long hours, he berated her. But Ollie assumed it was because she wasn't able to split her time and prioritize properly. That it was *her* fault.

And when Pierce started mocking the obviously sensitive topic of arranged marriages and forcing Indian women to marry men for their money or their wealth, Ollie started getting frustrated with him. As always, Pierce believed being well educated meant he could criticize an old Indian tradition with big impact words—archaic, ridiculous, pathetic. The whole time they were together, she never once told him horror stories of her arranged marriage meetings, because he would have used that against her too.

Ollie didn't hate men, she didn't trust them or herself when she was with them. She didn't trust women either. All of her relationships had left her feeling empty, lonely and unworthy. While she knew going on one date with Jackson wouldn't do anything, it was the awareness that Jackson was the kind of guy who liked relationships that made her hesitate.

He was younger, but Ollie knew that age was just a number. He was old enough to make his own decisions and know what he wanted. And apparently he wanted her. Ollie had seen the determination in his eyes when he came to the bar and the sadness when she shut him down. Ollie needed to get through this date with the dude from NASA, tell her family it wasn't going to work and get back to her life.

And do all of it without thinking about what it would feel like to give Jackson a chance.

FIVE
Oleander

J oseph, like all good South Indian boys who were born and raised in America, was well educated and quite handsome. He was a whole foot taller than her, was incredibly well-groomed with shiny straight white teeth that dazzled every time he spoke. Ollie noticed all of this in the 30 seconds as the hostess led her to their table.

Joseph was early, earning a point in his favor. He also stood up when she was escorted to the table and offered to pull her chair out which was another point. Of course, Ollie said she could pull out her own chair, because it was always so awkward trying to sit and match the pace at which someone else was adjusting your chair.

Once they were seated, Ollie and Joseph pondered over the menu and settled on a bottle of Riesling and starters before thanking the waitress.

"Thank you for taking the time to meet me."

Ollie smiled as she crossed her ankles, smoothing her soft peach dress over her thighs, "I should be thanking you for coming all the way to Wilmington and making this easier."

"I'm glad it all worked out." Joseph told her with a smile before reaching for his water.

"So, NASA. How on earth did you get there?"

Joseph laughed and Ollie was glad he didn't frown at the way she put the question across to him. "Didn't all of us grow up wanting to travel amongst the stars?"

"Totally. I built myself a spaceship out of empty cartons one time in the driveway before my dad destroyed it by accident."

"Ouch." Joseph touched his chest like he was hurt for her. "I think you beat me in the desire to travel the stars, but I had a telescope to watch satellites and the planets. All I wanted to do was be there."

"I hear a but…"

"But…" Joseph laughed, Ollie smiled when she noticed his blush. "I have an insane fear of flying."

"That's a logical fear, but you'd think NASA would have a way to make the whole experience easier."

"Right? I hoped they would; they are *literally* rocket scientists. But no, I could not travel to the stars." Joseph smiled as their waitress came back and poured out their wine. "I could, however, work on the ground and be part of the team that makes better spacecraft."

"So that's what you do now, I assume?"

"Yup, I'm a rocket scientist."

Ollie grinned, raising her glass of wine to cheers him, "Here's to being an actual rocket scientist."

"Thank you, I appreciate it."

The waitress came back with their appetizers, served them both before vanishing again. Ollie ate a piece of the gnocchi and looked up to find Joseph watching her. She covered her mouth with her free hand and arched an eyebrow as she looked at him. "What?"

"Nothing…you're a lot more beautiful than the picture I saw."

Ollie swallowed her food and leaned back with her glass of wine in hand, "I definitely don't do well in photographs."

"Don't get me wrong, you looked beautiful there too. But in person, you're…"

For a brief moment, Joseph's words and the way he was talking to her reminded her of Jackson and it made her heart stall. No, she should *not* be thinking of Jackson or the handsome face she'd put a frown on the last time they saw each other. Instead, she focused on Joseph.

"Gorgeous. Stunning. Spectacular. Breathtaking. Am I close?"

Joseph laughed and Ollie smiled, "All of the above."

"Sadly, I can't say the same for you," Ollie told him, watching the color drain from Joseph's face. "Because your family didn't send me a picture."

"Oh god," Joseph gasped, making Ollie chuckle. "For a moment, I thought you were going to break my heart."

"The night's still young."

ONCE THEY'D FINISHED their appetizers, Joseph and Ollie spent another few minutes going over the best dishes on the menu. She liked the rapport she was forming with him, but it was more of a friendly connection. Sure, he was handsome, smart and charming, but the spark was missing. She'd met tons of guys like this, set up through their families, and all of them expected something from her. But there were a few like Joseph, who enjoyed being teased and could keep up with her banter, who joked and laughed with her.

And yet, there was still something missing.

"Okay, it's a toss-up between the crab cake and the fish tacos."

Ollie pursed her lips, "So you're a seafood person."

"I see food and I eat it person, yeah."

"That is terrible." Ollie laughed. "As a rocket scientist, you should do better."

"Once it was out of my mouth, I couldn't take it back."

She chuckled, "While you choose between the seafood, I think steak is calling my name."

Joseph nodded and called the waitress back. He gave her their order, let her top up their wine and ordered another bottle. Ollie would need to sober up before she drove back if she was going to have any more to drink.

"Now that we've gone into detail about me and my life as a rocket scientist, let's talk about you."

"Oh god, let's not." Ollie laughed, reaching for her water before more wine came along.

"Come on, I know you studied English and got your bachelor's degree, what came after?"

Ollie smiled down into her lap and thought about how to say this. "I worked with a magazine for a bit, but it was pretty boring and I was mostly unimpressed with the job."

"Did you want to go into journalism?"

"At the time, I thought so, yeah. But sitting behind a desk, spending 16 hours staring at a computer screen? Not what I wanted."

Ollie tucked her hair behind her ear as Joseph hummed before speaking, "So you quit, I'm assuming, and went on to do what?"

"I teach dance to little kids," Ollie beamed, loving being able to talk about this with someone new. "I take classes in the mornings and I bartend in the evenings."

Joseph went still and Ollie watched his smile twitch before fading slightly. Pierce had this same look on his face when she'd said that she wanted to teach kids how to dance and he'd been around when she first got the job at the Barrel. He looked down on her for her choices and it seemed that Joseph was doing the same thing.

"Bartending..." The word came off his tongue like an insult and he cleared his throat before continuing, "Your family didn't mention that."

Ollie laughed to lighten the mood, "Imagine knowing everything about a person before meeting them for the first time."

"But why bartending?" Joseph now looked puzzled and Ollie inhaled deeply.

"Why not bartending? I get to meet some of the most interesting people, I get to be their confidante and their friend for the evening, I get to experience lots of incredible things that are unique to bars…" she explained with a wide smile, trying to hide how she was annoyed with Joseph.

"Is it something you're doing as a temporary thing?"

And there it was.

Ollie blew out a breath and shook her head. When she opened her mouth to speak, the waitress came back with their food and the wine. Ollie turned to Joseph once she was gone, "I don't think I should drink anymore, I have to drive back home."

"Yeah, of course, you must remind people of that a lot in your line of work, right?"

Ollie offered him a tight smile and focused on her food. He wasn't being rude, but there was so much he wasn't saying and Ollie fucking hated it. While her parents had raised her to be independent and do whatever she wanted, others would never understand her life choices. Hell, Baby didn't even understand what she was doing with her life. It irked her that Joseph brushed past her teaching kids how to dance, but he focused on her being a bartender.

Joseph kept making small talk through their meal, but Ollie was done. She should have known this would happen. Indian families had this *thing* about their kids working in minimum wage jobs. Back in India, Baby used to tell her, upper-middle-class families raised their children to become doctors and engineers, not work at coffee shops or pubs or teach dance. Those were jobs for the middle class or lower-middle-class, not families like hers. Clearly Joseph believed that too, because he was stiff and unimpressed. And compared to his *rocket scientist* job, hers probably sounded really *pathetic* to him.

Wasn't that what Pierce said to her too?

DINNER WAS OVER, the bottle of wine was returned and when Joseph asked if she wanted dessert, Ollie *politely* declined. Her frustration and disappointment over Joseph's behavior had helped sober her up pretty quick. Once he'd paid the bill and walked her outside, Ollie knew what she was going to tell her family. She thanked him, refusing to touch him in any way. His words hurt because she had so much faith in him being decent. While she had no plans to marry him, Ollie figured meeting one decent guy through her family wouldn't hurt. But Joseph had let her down and now, she had to tell her parents to stop bending to Baby's whims and fancies because she was the matriarch of the family.

"Can I walk you to your car?"

"God no," Ollie spat the words out, closing her eyes to stop from saying anything else. "I mean, no thank you. I am more than capable of finding my way."

"Right, okay."

"Thanks for dinner, Joseph. I hope you find the woman you're looking for eventually."

He frowned, "Did you not have a good time tonight?"

"Are you kidding me?" Ollie scoffed.

"I was actually going to ask you out again."

Ollie stepped away from Joseph and shook her head, "Why do you want to take me out again? You spent the last half of our dinner judging my life choices."

"I didn't judge, I feel like you could be doing so much more."

"But that's not up to you. I love what I do and I wouldn't change it for anyone else."

"Don't you want more out of life?" Joseph genuinely looked confused.

"Like what? Become a rocket scientist?"

"For example, yeah."

Ollie blew out a breath and held her hands together as she looked at Joseph properly, "I'm never going to be the good Indian wife you or your family want. I hope you find her, though. Because you deserve to be happy and be in love, but it can't be me."

"Oleander, don't…"

She held one hand up, *hating* the way her name sounded on his lips, "Thank you, Joseph. You picked a great restaurant, but our relationship…our *friendship* ends here."

Joseph started to open his mouth to speak, but Ollie shook her head and turned around, walking away from him as she dug out her keys.

As she slid into her car, Ollie found texts from her grandmother about more boys coming into town to see her. One even requested she fly out to some small town in California to see him instead of him coming to her. The drive home took her an hour and the whole time, Ollie was thinking about how she had fallen for this bullshit again.

Walking into her apartment, Ollie groaned when her phone started ringing. *Baby Calling* appeared on her screen, accompanied by the most adorable picture of her and her grandmother from when she was a kid. Ollie shrugged off her jacket and answered, putting her grandmother on loudspeaker as she went about getting ready for bed.

"How is Joseph?"

"Self-centered and looking for a good Indian *housewife*."

Baby *tsked* like Ollie was being ridiculous, "Once he gets to know you, he will understand housewives are not important."

"Ammachi, we know I'm not the kind of girl these guys need."

"No such thing. I sent you more biodatas and let me know how the meetings go."

Ollie stripped off her dress as Baby hung up and collapsed backwards onto her bed, her head pounding from all these ridiculous *dates* her grandmother kept setting her up on.

SIX
Jackson

Jackson would be lying if he said he hadn't thought about Oleander since their last interaction. She filled up a lot of the empty spaces in his head. During a boring meeting, Jackson sketched her in his notebook and stared at it for days. What was so special about her?

His friends said it was because she rejected him. Jackson thought it was because she was the first woman he was able to have a normal conversation with in a really long time. And yes, she was captivatingly beautiful. Outside the men's room, at the bar—she'd made him stop and stare. And even though she'd rejected him pretty publicly and a little harshly, Jackson couldn't stop thinking about her.

However, he was glad for Saturday to distract him from all thoughts of Oleander—because he spent six busy hours at the dojo. Karate had been an escape from the age of 12. When he was being bullied in school, his stepmother had helped him find himself. And it happened through karate. Like a lot of people who watched *Karate Kid* growing up—the original one with Ralph Macchio and Pat Morita, of course—Jackson wanted to be a karate kid too. Mindy took him down to the dojo near their house, signed him up. Every alternate day after that, Jackson trained and strengthened himself, and got smarter when dealing with bullies.

Now he was older and not afraid of bullies, he figured it made sense to help other kids out. When he moved to Wildes with his boys, Jackson looked for a dojo first. And he was surprised to find one between work and his apartment. It was a small dojo, with two instructors and mostly teenage kids. But when Jackson joined and slowly worked his way up to becoming a sensei, they started bringing in younger kids. And at the dojo, everybody was safe. Much like it was when he was a kid.

Every weekend, Jackson worked with different groups of kids to help them strengthen every part of their body. His first day as a sensei, Jackson had been so nervous. He didn't look like he could teach anyone karate, but when the kids walked into the dojo, he knew he was going to make a difference in their lives. All of them were small, skinny and helpless, just like he'd been as a kid. They looked scared, hunched in on themselves and didn't make eye contact. Traumatized was the only word that came to mind, because it was exactly how he felt when he'd first started karate.

For him, karate had never been about fighting back or hurting those who hurt him. It was about giving him the confidence to look his bullies in the eyes and show them he wasn't afraid. Fighting back did nothing good in the long term, but if you stood up to your demons and you showed them you weren't afraid, they backed off.

THAT SATURDAY, like every other, he left his apartment early to go sit at Better Latte Than Never, a coffee shop close to the dojo before class. With his *gi* packed into his duffle bag, Jackson pulled off his cap as he walked through the doors of the coffee shop. At this time of day, the place was relatively empty, a few tables were occupied and the low buzz of conversation and soft music soothed his overworked brain.

The baristas were already working on his order, so once he paid and waited for it to be ready, he looked around the coffee shop and found a familiar face. Jackson turned away quickly, pressing his eyes shut like he was imagining her being there. When he looked again, Oleander was sitting in his favorite spot, with a large cup and a book open in her lap.

The sight of her took his breath away.

He was still staring at her when his name was called. Oleander lifted her head and their eyes met. She smiled and Jackson felt his heart leap out of his chest. Instead of smiling back, he slapped his free hand over his chest, as if that would stop his heart from running away. The action made her laugh and the guy at the counter said his name again. Jackson finally found the strength to smile back as Oleander pushed out the chair across from her.

Okay, you can do this. She's just another woman, nothing *to get nervous about.* With his coffee in hand, Jackson moved towards Oleander's table and carefully set everything down.

"Hi," he mumbled as he finally dropped into the chair across from her. "I thought you didn't drink coffee?"

"I don't. This is the best hot chocolate in all of Wildes."

Jackson peered over the table to look in her cup and smiled, "Hot chocolate, I'll keep it in mind."

Oleander smiled and he felt it *everywhere*. This was a different woman from the one he'd spoken with that night. And he liked this version better, a million times better.

"What are you doing here anyway?"

Jackson shrugged and lifted his coffee to his lips, "Drinking coffee, like most people in here."

"Hilarious," she deadpanned. "You know what I mean."

"I teach at a karate dojo a few blocks from away every Saturday, so I come in here before my sessions."

"Karate?"

Jackson nodded, smiling as he took another sip of his coffee, "I know I don't look like a martial artist, but it's mostly karate for self-defense and conditioning your body. It also improves mental strength."

"Karate can do all of that?"

"Oh yeah, karate is so much more than just kicking people around and being Jackie Chan all the time."

"Shut up." Oleander looked so amused. She closed her book and dropped it off the table. He leaned back, slightly concerned about where the book went when she spoke up. "I have a giant bag under the table that holds my whole life."

"Like Mary Poppins."

Oleander nodded and gestured at him. "Hold on, we're still talking about this karate thing."

"Right, okay, so…" Jackson sat up straighter, excited that someone wanted to know about his other life, and smiled across at Oleander. "Karate is about strength conditioning, it's about building muscle and power, but it's also really good for mental health. Much like yoga, you have to be one with yourself, one with your mind and focus on inner peace and all of that."

"Wow."

Jackson found Oleander staring at him and he blushed, realizing he'd blabbered on about karate. He so rarely got to talk about what he did or liked, so it felt nice to have someone be interested.

"What are *you* doing here?"

"Drinking my hot chocolate, duh," she said with a grin and lifted her mug to her lips. Those eyes twinkled at him and he melted into his chair.

"I've never seen you here before."

"Do you own this place?"

"Well, I'm here every Saturday," he countered, arching an eyebrow and Oleander narrowed her eyes at him. The action reminded him of their first interactions and how different this was to that.

"Fine," she sighed heavily and Jackson chuckled as he wrapped both hands around his mug. "I usually don't have time before my classes, so I have my drinks on the go. My morning classes got canceled, so I was able to step in for a bit."

"What classes? This seems pretty far from campus."

"Oh! Dance classes," Oleander corrected him and Jackson's eyes widened, which made her narrow her eyes again. "What's that look?"

"You're a dancer."

"I'm a dance *teacher*."

"Sure, but you have to be a dancer to be able to teach someone else to dance."

"I guess…" she trailed off and Jackson let his eyes wander over what he could see of her. She had on a top that read *Brown Girls Do it Better*, with a light denim jacket on over it.

"What kind of dance do you teach? Ballet?"

Oleander made a *pfft* noise and leaned back as she waved at herself, "Do I look like a ballet dancer?"

Jackson's eyes dropped to the sliver of skin between her top and her pants. "What do ballet dancers look like?"

"Not this," she told him, rolling her eyes as she adjusted her crop top.

"Okay, so not ballet, what do you teach?"

"Well, it's a mixture of everything. I learned some ballet, so I mix it up with hip-hop and some freestyle stuff. And because they're kids who have smartphones, lots of popular dance moves too."

"Like the ones they do on TikTok?"

Oleander made a face and Jackson laughed, "I had to download the app the other day, just to learn some of the moves and it's a mind-melting platform."

"It's okay once you get used to it, though."

"I don't want to get used to it. I want life to be the way it was with MTV playing music videos and the radio stations dedicated to heavy metal."

Jackson just stared at her in amusement. "You are fascinating."

Oleander laughed and tossed a napkin at him, "I'm old school, I like keeping things simple. I can't keep up with the new shit."

"I'm happy to teach you how to keep up with the new shit."

Jackson was the last person to tell if he was flirting or not, but given how many words she'd said to him, maybe he was on the right track. He never wanted to stop talking to her, because there was something blooming in his chest and it felt so good, he never wanted it to go.

"This might seem odd, but the woman from the bar the other night and the one sitting in front of me are very different. This is a kind of test, right?"

"What are you talking about?" Oleander looked confused and Jackson winced.

"Last time we met, you basically told me to fuck off," Jackson explained and saw the blush rise on Oleander's cheeks as he continued. "But today, you *insisted* I sit with you. What's changed?"

"I dunno." She mumbled something else, but Jackson wasn't sure if he'd heard her right.

"What's that?"

Huffing, Oleander shrugged off her denim jacket and tossed it onto her bag. She raised her arms to run her fingers through her hair and Jackson watched all of this in slow motion. She was distracting, but also intriguing. The fact that Oleander was spending time with him was a big deal. He didn't want to say or do anything that would make her end this time together. Jackson looked away and found two guys at a neighboring table look at Oleander appraisingly. And it irritated him.

He didn't want her to notice other guys when he *finally* had all of her attention.

"Look, I'm not always the most pleasant person to be around, okay?"

"Oh yeah, I got that from every single one of our interactions," Jackson said with a straight face and got a glower in return, which made him smile.

"I take time letting people in and getting to know them. And you…"

Jackson leaned forward, curious to know what he'd done, "I what?"

"You took me by surprise."

"I'm confused."

Oleander inhaled deeply, pushing her shoulders back and her chest up and Jackson's eyes dropped to where the text on her t-shirt was stretched across her breasts before blinking away.

"You're cute, you know that, right? A girl could get used to your attention and forget about everything else."

"Right…" Jackson said, blushing because that was unexpected. But also confusing.

"And I haven't…" Oleander blew out a frustrated breath and Jackson frowned. "I don't do well around men, attractive ones especially."

"Oh."

Hot damn, she thought he was attractive. Jackson looked at himself, his black t-shirt, brown chinos, Vans and back at Oleander. She nodded when their eyes met and he blushed, looking away again because holy shit, she thought he was attractive.

Not just *cute*, but attractive.

Jackson cleared his throat, "I make you feel something?"

"Sure, let's call it that. And my instinct is to react in the opposite way, like a defense mechanism."

"Defense against my attractiveness?" He couldn't help himself.

"Ugh." Oleander dropped her head into her hands, but Jackson just smiled.

"Oleander."

"No, don't do—" she lifted her head and shook it at him. "Don't say my name like *that*."

"Like what?"

"All charming, sexy and ugh, *that*. Stop it."

Jackson pressed his lips together to fight back a smile. He cleared his throat, "I'm sorry. Can I call you…Ollie, was it?"

"Gah, no keep calling me Oleander. It sounds nice when you say it."

Jackson just nodded and lifted his coffee to his lips. They smiled at each other as they sipped and the moment was ruined by Oleander's ringing phone. She answered it with a huff and Jackson tried not to listen, but heard her apologizing for being late and that she would be there in 15 minutes.

Jackson arched an eyebrow when he saw the dejected look on her face, "You have to go."

"Yeah," she said softly, twisting her lips to the side. "I lost track of time and now my first class for the day has already arrived and I'm not there."

"Is it close by?"

"Not really, but I've got my car, so I'll get there in time," Oleander told him as she stood up, lifting her Mary Poppins bag. Jackson took a moment to look at her properly and smiled at her worn-out gray sweatpants and the flannel shirt tied around her waist. He stood up and finished his coffee before bending to retrieve his bag as well. He stepped aside and let Oleander move around him, biting his lip as his eyes drank in the sight of her in baggy clothes. He liked it. He'd seen two different sides of her and he liked both.

"It was good to see you again, Jackson."

"You too, Oleander," he said with a smile, holding the door open for her. He stepped out after her and raised a hand to gesture in the direction he was going and she gestured the opposite way. They laughed and nodded, starting in their respective directions. Jackson got a few feet and turned around to find Oleander walking backwards with a smile on her face. She waved at him and Jackson did the same before turning in the direction of the dojo.

SEVEN
Oleander

It was only after Ollie got into her car that she remembered she forgot to get her usual cup of tea to go. She dropped her things in the car and rushed back, hoping to see Jackson again, but he wasn't there. She grabbed her tea then drove to the studio. And in her excitement, she dropped hot tea all over herself. Which was as pleasant as it sounded.

"You're late," Kristen at the front desk of Tiny Dancers announced when Ollie walked in, tapping her smartwatch. "And you've got something all over you."

"Thank you, Captain Obvious."

"You're lucky all your kids aren't here yet."

"Can you set up for me? I'm going to swap clothes." Ollie asked with a smile and hurried into the back to change.

Melody, Kristen's sister, started Tiny Dancers years ago when she realized there were people in town who wanted to learn how to dance but had nowhere to go in Wildes. When Ollie showed up for her interview, she'd asked Melody if she was an Elton John fan and the woman looked at her puzzled. Ollie had memories of her parents dancing to *Tiny Dancer* by Elton John in the kitchen, and she'd been raised by a man who lived for the classics. Apparently, Melody just liked the way it sounded and it stuck.

Dancing was therapeutic. When she was young, she would walk into dance class and forget about everything else—all the annoyances of her family and school drama. It might have started out with ballet, but eventually as her body changed, Ollie found other forms of dance to embrace.

She might have had dreams to go places, to work with a dance school in New York or California, or even become a choreographer on some big stage, but teaching kids dance was comforting. They weren't as enthusiastic as she was, but once they got down to it, they were always happy to learn. And with TikTok creating new dances, Ollie was learning something new from them too.

When she first started at Tiny Dancers, Ollie had considered making it her full-time job. But Melody couldn't afford to pay her. It was why she juggled two jobs—both exhausting her to the point of delirium some nights. To most people, having the kind of education she did with all the opportunities at her fingertips, Ollie could work any job. But she didn't like sitting still for too long. Dancing helped her deal with all of her frustrations and working at the Barrel allowed her to make more money. It wasn't like either job paid her a lot, but she was able to save quite a bit every month.

One day, Ollie would quit working at the Barrel and put all of her focus into dancing. She wasn't a ballet dancer or a professional dancer, but she was passionate. And she saw the impact she was making with the kids she taught. When Jackson talked about how karate helped mental strength, Ollie realized that on some level, dance did the same. It taught you coordination, balance, focus, strengthened your memory and how to use your body to tell a story.

Thinking about her morning with Jackson made Ollie smile. She *had* been different. And it felt good.

Pulling her hair up into a messy bun on top of her head,

Ollie smoothed her hands over her t-shirt and clean leggings, and walked into the studio.

"Miss Bowen, you're late!" The tiniest of dancers called out, dressed in a purple tutu, hands on her hips and her little ponytail swaying as she shook her head.

"I'm sorry, Claire, being an adult is hard."

"Mommy says that too, but she says *mommy juice* helps."

"Of course she does," Ollie snorted and smiled as Claire twirled back into formation.

Ollie let the kids wear whatever they wanted during her classes—some of the girls wore colorful tutus, others wore leggings and t-shirts, there were also some boys who came straight from whatever sport they were into that year and danced while sweaty and gross. In the beginning, Ollie had told parents their kids needed to wash up or at least change clothes before showing up for dance, but they clearly ignored her request.

"Places! We've got an hour and I want to see if you remember everything from our last class."

Hours later Ollie was sitting on the floor, her back against the wall of mirrors. The kids had danced their little hearts out and insisted Ollie dance with them too, so she had. The little ones left and the next batch came in, made up of slightly older girls. They were the bane of her existence. Every single one of them wore new sparkly clothes to class, they all did their hair the same way, wore shiny lip gloss and talked with a weird lilt in their accent.

When they left, her final group came in. This was her favorite group—it was made up of women, mostly between the ages of 25 and 40. While Tiny Dancers mostly catered to young kids, Ollie had convinced Melody that giving moms and other women a place to go to let loose would be a great idea. They didn't expect so many women to sign up. It was also her largest class with over 25 women packed into her standard studio room. But they were all so enthusiastic and knew the classic dance songs from the 80s and 90s. They even remembered dance moves by their favorite boy bands.

Dancing was also a way for her to come to terms with her body. Ollie was a confident woman who wore tight jeans and t-shirts, who flaunted her curves and her large ass. That morning, under Jackson's gaze, she'd felt *beautiful*. She liked that he enjoyed what he saw. Ollie had been pretty upfront about her attraction to him too, which was unlike her. But what was the point in pretending she didn't feel something? Especially after how she'd treated him the first few times.

But still, people didn't seem to enjoy watching women who weren't *skinny* dancing. In a time when Lizzo was alive, how was the world still behaving like that?

Teaching kids was good that way. They didn't judge her size, didn't comment on her shaking thighs or the fact her boobs were dancing when she was. They danced and let their troubles fly free. And for someone like Ollie, to be around kids who were so positive and adorable was a treat. But there were always going to be mothers who didn't understand these classes wouldn't turn *their* tiny dancers into professional dancers.

"Oleander, do you have a minute?" A nasally voice interrupted her thoughts and Ollie glanced over at the woman standing in the doorway of her studio.

Speaking of mothers...

"Hey, Candice." Ollie forced herself not to roll her eyes and stood up.

"I know we've talked about this before, but I don't think you should mix the boys and girls together for your classes."

"Forgive me for not remembering your reasons behind it."

"Those boys aren't here to learn dance seriously, and they distract all the girls."

Ollie frowned. "I'm not sure what you mean."

"Please consider doing separate classes for boys and girls."

"Candice, I appreciate your concern, but as you saw today, the boys are incredibly well behaved," Ollie responded, trying to keep frustration out of her voice. "The most you could have an issue with is they smell like a locker room when they show up."

"I do have other issues, but you don't seem to acknowledge them."

Sighing heavily, Ollie arched an eyebrow. "Care to remind me of these issues?"

"You don't look like someone who would inspire confidence in these little girls. With your clothes and your tattoos and your…" Candice waved in her direction and Ollie gritted out a smile.

"My body?" she asked, adjusting her t-shirt, accentuating her curvy stature. "The sooner you accept that people come in all shapes, sizes and colors, the sooner your kids will also realize that."

Candice shook her head, looking offended by this conversation. "I have no issue with your body, Oleander, you are not who I imagine as an inspiration for my daughter."

"I'm sorry, what?"

"For a school assignment the other day, Claire told her teacher *you* were her hero."

Ollie stared at Candice in shock. "That's…wow."

Candice sighed. "I understand you're teaching my daughter dance, but I would appreciate it if you weren't teaching her anything else."

"Candice, honestly, I don't spend too much time with the kids outside of class."

Candice didn't look convinced and she took a step back, smoothing down her neatly pressed clothes. "Maybe a little less attention will help."

And then she was gone.

It took Ollie a minute to wrap her head around what had happened. Some little white girl thought *she* was an inspiration. And her mother didn't appreciate it. Ollie understood Candice's concern—*she* wanted to be her daughter's hero and inspiration. But at the same time, she hated that Candice didn't think Ollie was good enough to be Claire's hero. Laughing to herself as she accepted everything that had happened, Ollie wished she could tell someone about this.

Not just someone, but *Jackson*.

AFTER DANCE CLASS, Ollie picked up dinner on her way home. Since she wasn't working that evening, it meant she could spend some time with Grant. The whole way home, her brain filled with thoughts of Jackson—he *was* attractive and charming. Ollie had never been the kind of girl who liked beefy, athletic guys and wasn't attracted to athletes or jocks. Not because they were more popular than her, but because they were so stereotypically attractive. *Everyone* wanted them.

Even though she knew she was bisexual at a young age, Ollie's first real relationship had been with a scrawny boy. He took her virginity and woke up popular one day. Then there was Nina, who wasn't scrawny or athletic, but she was beautiful. Ollie believed she had a type in women too, but apparently Nina wasn't the right woman. Not when Nina broke her heart into a million tiny pieces after graduation by returning to her high school sweetheart. Her *male* high school sweetheart.

Pierce was the game changer. He was tall, attractive and incredibly smart. He looked good in suits, jeans, sweatpants and naked. Pierce was the kind of man every woman wanted. He came off the pages of a romance novel, until he showed his true colors and became the monster of her nightmares.

Moving on from Pierce had been hard, but Ollie started

therapy. The first few sessions left her feeling hollow and worn out, but the more she talked about him, the more she realized how badly he treated her. For so much of the relationship, Ollie had been gaslighted and she had to remind herself that it wasn't *her* fault.

While therapy helped, Ollie hated being called out on personality traits she'd always been so proud of. It also made her realize she was always settling for easy, instead of being with someone who truly deserved her. That was partly why she refused to get involved in a relationship, because she never knew if she was meeting the right person or accepting every man and woman that threw themselves into her arms. Ollie had made enough bad relationship choices to know she deserved better than the people she picked.

The silence in the apartment told her she was alone—her roommate and friend, Lachlan, was most likely at a 'writing retreat' or warming the bed of someone new. In her bedroom, she set the food on the nightstand and checked if her vibrator was charged before stripping down to nothing.

Ollie filled up the tub, tossed in some bath salts and let the water fill. Bringing her phone and vibrator into the bathroom, she turned on one of the soft metal playlists, letting the bathroom fill up with her favorite scents and sounds. When the tub was full, Ollie turned off the water and got in, sinking until her head was submerged and stretched as she surfaced.

There was absolutely no doubt who was taking over all thought processes, because once she turned on her vibrator and pushed it under the water and between her legs, her brain filled with Jackson's face. In the past, she'd gotten off to celebrities and random people she'd met, but this time, it was Jackson. A few weeks ago, he would have been considered random, but now, he was so much more.

Ollie swung one leg over the side of the tub as she rubbed the tip over her clit, causing her body to jerk slightly. Biting down on her lip, she turned up the setting and pushed the vibrator in, a soft gasp escaping her lips. Ollie closed her eyes and slowly fucked herself, letting the vibrator do most of the work as she moved her hips slowly, adding a little friction. Her head swam with Jackson's face—his smile, the way he blushed, his long fingers as he held his cup, his eyes twinkling and *of course*, the way he said her name.

Oleander.

It seemed to echo in the bathroom and Ollie's back arched as she pressed against her g-spot and cried out, her other hand slipping between her legs to touch and soothe her swollen clit. Whimpering, she continued to fuck herself as she played with her clit, pushing herself to the first of many orgasms that night. Crying out as she came, Ollie smiled and settled back into the tub. That's when she noticed in all her writhing and moving, she'd splashed water over the edge of the tub.

Laughing softly, Ollie turned off her vibrator and sat up to unplug the tub. There would be no more sitting in bathwater, not when she'd built herself into hunger. Standing up, she used the shower and quickly washed herself, washed her vibrator, and with a towel wrapped around her body, stepped outside to plug it in. She turned the music off, put her phone on charge as well and tugged on an old t-shirt and shorts before going to get herself the box of sushi and a tall glass of wine.

EIGHT
Oleander

Three days after the accidental date with Jackson, and the evening spent with her vibrator and his face in her head, Ollie was worried about herself. It had been fun talking to him, but she'd said way too much. Talking about karate and dance had been fine, but Jackson asked the *big* question and Ollie fumbled. But, she'd *also* given Jackson hope, which might be a problem.

It was all because of her *date* with Joseph—and those disastrous dates with the other men Baby had found. He'd turned her inside out with his predictable reaction and his need to find a wife. She actually couldn't even remember what was written in his biodata about why he was still single at 38. Now that she thought about it, it was silly she got so worked up when *he* was the one who was the mess. Sure, he had a job at NASA, but she was happy with her life. She had the most incredible friends and she was content. And Joseph fucking up that evening sent her mind spinning to Jackson and how he didn't judge her. Except to point out her treatment of him, which was fair.

When she came charging out of her bedroom, she hoped to find Lachlan there to ease her nerves. Her friend kept the weirdest hours while he wrote yet another bestseller, and that meant that he was always cooking up a storm when Ollie was asleep. That morning, there was evidence of Lachlan's cooking but no sign of him. Needing a little TLC, she grabbed her bag and drove to Frankie's apartment.

Frankie and Ollie met when they were 10, when the former moved in next door in her neighborhood of Huntington. Ollie was the oddball at school, so when Frankie was brought into class one day, they instantly connected. Frankie had lost her parents, and she'd come to live with her grandmother. Ollie had always been fond of Nana Willows—she was best friends with Baby and the two women would sit on the porch to cackle and gossip about their neighbors.

Nana Willows was white, but she behaved like a typical Indian grandmother thanks to Baby's influence. Frankie and Ollie not only bonded over idiots at school, but over the fact their grandmothers were absolutely insane. And they'd been inseparable since.

Except for a stupid fight their senior year of high school, there wasn't a time in their lives when Frankie and Ollie didn't speak a minimum for three times a week. They'd moved to Delaware together for college and found their way to Wildes together.

♡♡♡

"I'M SO FUCKED!" Ollie yelled as she barged into Frankie's apartment, slamming the door shut behind her. When she didn't hear a response, she stopped and frowned at the silence. "Frank?"

Ollie heard her friend talking to someone, the sound coming from the spare bedroom that Frankie sometimes used as an office. She tip-toed and pushed the door open to find her best friend and assistant sitting in front of their laptops while on a conference call. Ollie made an apologetic face and backed out of the room, closing the door behind her.

Ollie kicked her shoes off and walked into Frankie's large kitchen to find something to eat. Or drink. It was happy hour somewhere in the world.

Francesca Willows was one of the most sought after wedding planners in Delaware—but don't you dare call her *Francesca* if you wanted to keep breathing. She worked for a Cruella de Vil meets Miranda Priestly type of woman who took all the credit, and made Frankie do all the work. It allowed her best friend to afford this gorgeous two bedroom apartment.

Seated on the couch, Ollie was halfway through a bag of Doritos and drinking wine straight from the bottle when the door opened. Ginny, Frankie's assistant, waved awkwardly and rushed out of the apartment as her best friend dropped down beside her.

"You could have called. Or texted," Frankie said before taking a swig of the wine. "Instead of startling the fuck out of my new client."

"If they can't handle me, you shouldn't be working for them."

Frankie chuckled. "So, who did you kill and how much longer till the body starts to stink?"

"Great questions, this is why we're friends," Ollie mumbled through a mouthful of Dorito crumbs. "I killed myself and I think I'm already stinking."

Frankie leaned in, sniffed and gagged before ripping the bag of Doritos out of Ollie's arms. "Into the shower with you. My garbage smells better and I forgot to take it out last night."

Ollie got to her feet, whining and groaning as she followed Frankie to the bathroom. She'd been run off her feet and thanks to dry baths and lots of deodorant, Ollie managed to get through dance classes during the week and shifts at the

Barrel. And that morning, a shower was the last thing on her mind when the panic attack woke her up.

While her friend went to retrieve clothes and a towel, Ollie stripped and stepped into the shower. The cold water hit her and she didn't even flinch; she was numb at this point. Between Joseph's behavior, all the Pierce flashbacks, and the warm feelings she got from being around Jackson—it was all *too much*.

"Okay, start from the beginning." Frankie called from the other side of the shower curtain.

Ollie sighed and lathered shampoo into her hair. She told Frankie about her disastrous date with Joseph, other uneventful dates and the morning with Jackson, then getting off to thoughts of him all night and when she finished, her best friend hummed.

Ollie pulled back the curtain to glared at Frankie. "Really, after all that, I get a fucking *hum?*"

"I don't even know what you want me to say."

"Give me advice, you nincompoop."

Frankie grinned. "We're name calling now, I like where this is going."

Ollie growled and finished washing up. She grabbed the towel and wrapped it around her body before reaching for a smaller one to wrap around her hair. She dried her body as Frankie handed her a full glass of wine and pulled on the baggy clothes left on the sink. With her hair wrapped in a towel, Ollie joined Frankie on the couch.

"Let me see if I got all of this right," Frankie started, sipping from her own glass of wine as she shifted on the couch to face Ollie. "You think Jackson is cute, but he's got 'relationship' written all over him, so when he asks you out, you shut him down *hard*. Then you go on *more* Baby sanctioned dates and almost lose your shit with this handsome guy because he judged your job choices. *Then*, oh I'm not done yet, you spent a morning with Jackson, used his existence to give yourself multiple orgasms the very same night and now you have butterflies in your stomach. What did I miss?"

"The part where I said I'm going to kill you if you rehash all of this again."

"Right, whatever. I'm like a cat, I've got nine lives."

"Why are we friends again?" Ollie shifted, sloshing wine onto herself. She lifted her t-shirt to her lips and sucked on the wine spreading there before taking a sip from the glass.

"Seriously, Anders," Frankie said, using a nickname she'd picked up when they were kids. "You're not interested in Joseph and you're *definitely* interested in Jackson. What is the problem?"

"Remember Pierce? That's the problem."

"Jesus fucking Christ." Frankie rubbed the bridge of her nose and Ollie frowned. "You walked away from someone who reminded you of Pierce and it *wasn't* Jackson."

Ollie scrunched up her nose. "I haven't *dated* a guy since Pierce. I've slept with a few and they've all felt like shit. Jackson, in case that wasn't clear yet, is a guy."

"A very cute guy, from the sounds of it."

Ugh. "Yes, he *is* cute. He's also got this whole Ralph Macchio thing from *Karate Kid* going on with wanting to help the little guy."

"Oh, Ralph Macchio was a babe."

"He was *okay*," Ollie said with a shrug, dropping more wine on herself.

"Totally not what we're supposed to be discussing," Frankie told her, nudging her gently.

"My track record with men before and after Pierce has been...shit, to keep it simple. I don't want to get into a relationship or sleep with someone and have to constantly worry about what they're going to say about me one day."

"Babe," Frankie sighed and shook her head. "Are you planning on staying single forever?"

"That's what one night stands are for," Ollie said with a huff. "Don't be in a relationship, but don't be lonely either."

"I know better than anyone how much this scares you, but you're not even giving yourself a chance."

"I don't have it in me to go through heartbreak or a panic attack every time a guy touches me naked."

"Have you ever thought about…" Frankie started and when Ollie opened her mouth to speak, she held her hands up. "Let me finish. Have you ever thought about talking to your *fun* buddies about these things? Set boundaries."

"As if any of them care what I've been through or how I feel."

"You're not even giving them a chance to understand what you've been through."

"Self-preservation."

Frankie sighed. "So you're going to fuck everyone that comes your way and walk off without any attachments till the day you die?"

"Doesn't sound so bad when you put it like that."

Frankie arched an eyebrow. "When was the last time you had sex?"

"It was two…no, three….wait," Ollie frowned and pinched her lips together as she thought about it. "Fuck me."

"Exactly what you should be telling this Jackson guy."

"Six months, Frank. I haven't had sex for *six months*."

Frankie emptied her glass of wine. "It's been more than a year for me, so you're fine."

Ollie stood up when her best friend did and they moved to the kitchen where Frankie rummaged around in her fridge for leftovers. "Hypothetically, I say yes to a date with Jackson. And hypothetically, it turns into more dates. And sex. I'm going to completely freak the fuck out."

"Anders," Frankie said with so much exasperation, Ollie felt like she was being punished. "Talk to Jackson when you think sex is going to be on the table. Or wherever, you know what I mean. Just…don't run away from it."

"It sounds so easy when you say it like that, but it's not. People aren't always going to be understanding."

"Women can be pretty selfish too," Frankie pointed out as she emptied leftover Chinese food into her wok and set it on the stove.

"Can you imagine me telling him I have something horrible to say before we have sex?"

Frankie sighed. "It's not *horrible*, it's what happened to you. And nobody said he needs all the details, let him know what you're comfortable with."

Ollie made a face, trying to figure out how that would go over. If she was being honest, Ollie didn't even know if she was looking to date or sleep with him. This was exactly why she'd chased him off the first time he asked her out. Because she didn't trust herself to be with someone of the opposite sex without having a panic attack.

"Do you remember what you said to me before I went on my first date after I got over what Trent had done to me?" Frankie asked, leaning her hip against the kitchen counter. Ollie shook her head and her friend continued. "You said, 'Frank, if this guy can't see how great you are, he doesn't deserve even this one date. Go out there, show the world the actions of one asshole is not going to stop you from living your best life.'"

Ollie blinked back tears, staring at her bare feet as she thought back to that day. Frankie had gotten pregnant by her high school boyfriend who forced her to get an abortion because he didn't want to be *trapped* by her. She didn't tell her grandmother, but Ollie went with her to the clinic, held her hand as she went through the procedure and watched her best friend collapse in on herself for months afterwards. It wasn't so much the abortion that hurt her, but the way Trent treated her and the news of the pregnancy.

"And," Frankie continued, chuckling when Ollie gave her *the look*, "I also remember what I told you after Pierce was gone."

Ollie wiped her tears and smiled as she repeated what Frankie told her all those years ago. "You said, 'We are badass women who can't be put down by any man, no matter what they call us. You, my friend, will rise from this and like a phoenix you will slay everything in life.'"

When Ollie finished speaking, they were both sobbing messes and they wrapped their arms around each other, holding on tight as their sobs turned into laughter and they were screaming when the fire alarm started blaring because Frankie forgot to keep an eye on the wok.

They finally settled on ordering food and finished two whole bottles of wine before Ollie was able to think straight. And she realized Frankie was right—she was punishing Jackson based on his gender and not based on the kind of person he was. She already used his existence to give herself quite a few orgasms, and besides, he seemed like a good guy. He was funny, charming and a little awkward. She liked the way he made her feel and Ollie knew if she didn't give him a chance, she might regret it later on.

NINE
Jackson

Even before he'd met her and become enamored with Oleander, Jackson had liked coming to the Hazy Barrel. It was close enough to work that they didn't have to drive far when they needed a break, their drinks were great, and the space was reasonably large. Once he'd met and flirted with Oleander, Jackson was addicted. He'd told his two best friends about Oleander, letting them know he was finally ready to move on from Ursula. They had been surprised at first, but then decided they needed to meet her. So they agreed to meet at the Barrel at the end of the work day.

When Jackson stepped into the bar, his eyes clashed with a pair of brown eyes and his heart and feet stopped. He saw the slight twitch at the corner of her lips as he was nudged forward.

"Why did you stop?" Gavin nudged him harder and Jackson blinked out of his thoughts to glance at his best friend in slight confusion. "You okay, Jack?"

"Yeah, sorry, thought I saw someone."

"Ugh, it's not *her* is it?" Gavin was obviously referencing Ursula, but it still took Jackson a moment to understand who he was talking about.

Shaking his head, he shuddered slightly and looked at his friend. "I would have probably turned around and walked out if I did see her."

"I'd burn this place down if she came here," Gavin added with a grin. "I'll get us a table and check in on Milo, you get us drinks."

Jackson blew out a breath as Gavin walked away and he turned back to the bar to see if he could spot Oleander. She was gone. But, she'd been there *minutes* ago, those beautiful eyes settling on him as he walked through the door. Almost like she was waiting for him.

Smiling to himself, Jackson walked over. After not seeing Oleander for a few days at the Barrel, he'd actually given up hope of ever seeing her again. Stepping up to the bar, he nodded at one of the bartenders and opened his mouth to give him the order when Oleander popped up in front of him.

"Jesus," Jackson said with a laugh, his hand over his chest as he shook his head at the brunette. "Don't scare me like that."

"*Jackson.*"

"Oleander, fancy seeing you here."

She offered him a smile and looked around. "I know, what are the odds?"

"Haven't seen you around for a few days," Jackson said, mentally kicking himself for letting those words slip out.

"Oh, you've been keeping tabs on me."

"Just like coming to a place where I know a familiar face who also knows my order."

"Of course." Oleander smirked at him and then turned away to get his favorite beer. When he held up three fingers, she grabbed two more bottles and popped them open before setting them on the bar. "Stay out of trouble."

"I should be saying that to you."

"Well, you know me, trouble follows me everywhere," Oleander told him with a grin and Jackson took a moment to look her over as she turned away. She had her long hair in two braids, one lay over her shoulder while the other down her back. And instead of a vintage band tee like before, she was wearing a powder pink one with the words 'Brown Girl Power' printed across the front in bold font. A hand appeared in his line of sight, snapping at him and Jackson blushed as he lifted his eyes back to Oleander's.

"Sorry, I like your t-shirt," he said with a sheepish smile.

"Oh yeah? What do you like about it so much?"

Jackson rubbed the back of his neck and laughed softly. "The font is great. I appreciate a good font."

"Is that what the kids call it these days?" She laughed and Jackson's blush seemed to spread everywhere as he reached for his beers.

"Thanks for these," he said with a smile, waving the bottles as he stepped away from the bar. "I'll see you around."

Oleander nodded, offering him another smile before turning away, leaving Jackson staring at her a moment longer. And then he blew out a breath and turned around to find his two best friends grinning at him. Rolling his eyes, he walked over, set the beers down and dropped into the extra chair at the table. Only after he was seated did Jackson realize that his back was to the bar, so now he couldn't see Oleander, but his two best friends could.

"Damn, Jack, she's gorgeous," Milo whispered as he reached for one of the beers, his eyes on Oleander.

Sighing heavily, Jackson nodded. "I know."

"Wait, you were flirting with the bartender?" Gavin looked so confused, Jackson laughed.

"That's *the* woman I was telling you about."

Gavin snorted. "She's way out of your league, Jack. I hope she knows that."

"Fuck you," Jackson said.

"Oh, you've got it bad."

"He's got *something*, that's for sure," Milo added with a chuckle and Jackson flipped them off.

Jackson behaved himself most of the time—he only glanced over his shoulder once or twice. The rest of the time, he was talking with his friends, catching up on their lives. But Jackson started to zone out. It wasn't that his friends had boring jobs—Milo was an underwear model and Gavin worked with his family's veterinarian clinic—they were extremely physical jobs and as two guys who were incredibly fit and muscular, the jobs fit them. Jackson wasn't skinny anymore, thanks to all the karate he did. But he was definitely the lamer of the three of them and it sometimes puzzled him how they ended up being best friends. But these guys were truly the best part of his teenage years and Jackson knew that if it wasn't for Milo and Gavin, he might not have survived.

"Jesus, Jack, just go talk to her."

Jackson startled, releasing his beer bottle. "What did I miss?"

"Nothing of importance, clearly."

"What?" Jackson looked between his friends in confusion, trying to understand what they were saying. Milo chuckled and shook his head, gently shoving Gavin.

"It doesn't matter. What does matter is you going over there and talking to this woman who clearly has you completely whipped," Gavin responded, tipped his beer back to finish it and swapped bottles with him. "Now go, get yourself a fresh drink."

"I am not whipped," Jackson said softly and scratched the back of his neck as he added. "I don't want to chase her away again."

Gavin nudged the bottle. "You won't know what'll happen if you don't go talk to her."

After a few minutes of hesitation, Jackson was on his way to the bar when he noticed a dark-haired woman talking to Oleander. He knew that if he went back to the table, his friends would never forgive him, so Jackson gritted his teeth and continued his trek to the bar.

Standing behind the woman who was talking to Oleander, Jackson offered a tight smile and gestured to his empty bottle.

"Hey," Oleander said with a grin. "Another round?"

"Just one, thanks." Jackson nodded as Oleander pointed at the woman and then at Jackson.

"Frank, this is Jackson. Jackson, this is my best friend Frankie."

Frankie grinned wide. "So, you're *the* Jackson."

His eyes widened and looked between the two friends. So Oleander was talking about him. "I must be. It's nice to meet you, Frankie."

"Don't listen to her," Oleander told him, handing him his beer.

Frankie waved Oleander off and turned her attention to Jackson completely. "For the record, she has *not* been talking about you for the past week."

"For fuck's sake, Frank." Oleander looked embarrassed and Jackson felt smug.

"*What?* The boy clearly didn't come here just for a refill."

"I'm uh…" Blushing, Jackson felt his heart pound so loud he was sure the two women could hear, but he was also so embarrassed to be in this position at all. "I'm gonna go."

"No, stay," Frankie told him, patting the bar. "I'm leaving. I just came by to give her a hard time."

"Deep breaths, Frank."

"Be good to him, Ollie," Frankie told her friend and then turned to him. "You seem like a nice guy, but if you hurt her, I will hurt you."

"*Really* nice to meet you, Frankie." Jackson forced a smile on his face and when she was gone, he turned to Oleander with wide eyes. "She's...interesting."

She laughed. "That's not the word I would ever use to describe my best friend."

"So...you've been talking about me?"

Oleander rolled those gorgeous eyes and Jackson got a glimpse of a smile, which made him smile as well as he leaned forward against the bar, his beer forgotten as he watched her. "I might have mentioned you...like, *once*."

"*He's* mentioned you more than that," Jackson heard Gavin say from behind him, followed by a slap on the shoulder. Why did he invite his best friends again?

Oleander grinned and stuck her hand out when Milo stretched his hand over the bar. "It's nice to finally meet you. I'm Milo and that's Gavin. We're heading out now—you'll get yourself home, right?"

"Yes, *dad*, I know how to get myself home," Jackson sighed and Milo ruffled his hair as he walked away.

"*You've* been talking about me."

Jackson turned to face Oleander and the smile on her face...fuck, he felt like he'd earned that smile. Rubbing his mouth with one hand, Jackson shook his head. "I might have mentioned you a couple of times."

"Did you mention that I was a bitch in the men's room?"

"Obviously," Jackson laughed, reaching for his beer.

"Of cou—" Oleander started only to get cut off when an annoyed male voice cut into their conversation. "Jesus, Bow, no flirting with the customers. How many times do I have to tell you?"

Jackson heard the growl come out of Oleander and noticed the tight expression on her face. That shouldn't have been as hot as it was, but now that he'd heard the sound of her growling, it was stuck in his head.

"You're on lock-up duty today. Harry and the boys are

checking out early, so you need to get everything squared away."

Oleander huffed and Jackson looked between her and the man who'd interrupted them as she responded, "That's four times this month."

"Which means you've been breaking my rules a lot. Lock up and we'll call it even." He tossed Oleander a bunch of keys, glared at Jackson and walked away.

"I'm sorry, I should probably go."

"Stay," Oleander whispered, turning to look at him. "Might as well keep me company since you got me into trouble tonight."

"Uh, that sounds like grounds for more trouble."

Oleander shrugged and twisted the towel in her hands, like she was nervous about what she was asking him to do. "Probably, but it's no fun doing it on my own. Besides, I can score you free food."

"Why didn't you lead with that?" Jackson chuckled and picked up his beer, gesturing to the table he'd been at earlier with the boys. "I'll wait over…there."

Oleander nodded and smiled at him. He returned the smile and walked backwards a few steps before she broke eye contact and then he made his way over to the table and sat down, blowing out a shaky breath. *Holy shit, he'd scored an evening with Oleander.*

TEN

Oleander

It took almost three hours before the bar closed. And once the kitchen staff were gone, the remaining staff helped Ollie clean up before leaving. She forgot how long it took to wrap up the bar and by the time everyone was gone, she was exhausted. And hungry. But also very aware that she was alone with Jackson.

And he'd waited, nursing beers and watching her the whole time. Had it been anyone else, Ollie would have felt uncomfortable having eyes on her. If anything, she liked the way he saw her. He smiled whenever their eyes met and it made her focus on getting through the few hours left of her shift. While Jackson's smiles told her he wasn't like the other guys, her brain wasn't allowing her to see things that way. She was worried she'd let him in too far already.

She'd been unloading the register when Killian stepped onto the bar floor. Ollie lifted her head to watch him glare at Jackson before he turned to her. He looked pissed and Ollie didn't know if it was because she'd been flirting with a customer or because said customer was still sitting there. Killian gave her a *look* and walked out the door.

In the time it took for Killian to leave and Ollie to lock up,

Jackson had already started piling one of the bin trays with dirty glasses. Smiling, she came around the bar and put the keys by the register.

"I wasn't expecting you to help."

"Do we need to wash these before you lock up?" Jackson asked, ignoring her comment as he picked up the tray.

"Toss them in the dishwasher in the back and they'll run it in the morning."

"What else do we need to do before locking up?"

"Well, I promised you free food, so we need to eat." She smiled and got a beautiful grin in return. It distracted her for a few minutes. "Uh, glasses, empty bottles, everything goes in the back."

"Okay, I'll start on the glasses. Do you wanna do the rest?"

"Sure," Ollie nodded, chewing on her bottom lip. "Thank you."

"For what?"

"For staying. For helping."

"You asked me to."

"I didn't think you'd actually wait." Ollie laughed.

"I've been coming in every day for the last week in hopes of seeing you again," Jackson told her. "Waiting five more hours didn't seem like such an ordeal."

Ollie's heart pounded hard. There was something earnest about Jackson that told her he wasn't looking to hurt or take advantage of her. If anything, he was being honest and his interest in her hadn't waned. After their coffee/hot chocolate morning and her conversation with Frankie, Ollie felt like *maybe* this could be fun. She wasn't expecting a marriage proposal or anything, she liked the way Jackson made her feel—the word that popped into her head was *safe*.

She hadn't felt safe with a man in a long time, so it was a big deal.

"I'll get started on these," Jackson told her, and Ollie realized she'd been staring. Nodding, she looked away to hide her blush.

SHE FOUND them both full body aprons, and after showing Jackson where to load up the glasses and dishes, Ollie dragged empty bottles into the back and separated everything into their respective bins. They went back and wiped down the bar, swept and mopped the floor, and locked up. After they'd shed their aprons in the kitchen, Ollie pulled out the leftovers and spread them out on the table. Tugging out an extra Tupperware dish with a grin.

"Lucky you, Harry even left us some of his famous tiramisu."

Jackson's eyes widened, "That's not on the menu, is it?"

"Nope," she grinned. "He makes it for the staff when it's a slow shift."

"All of this smells really good, I can't believe I've never eaten any of this food before."

Arching an eyebrow, Ollie looked at Jackson over the food. "You've been coming here every day for the past week and you haven't eaten the food?"

"Before I met you, my friends and I came here to drink after work," Jackson said with a shrug. "And after...well, my focus wasn't on the food or drinks."

"Why?"

"Why what?" Jackson picked up a piece of chicken and popped it into his mouth and Ollie watched in fascination as he chewed. "Oleander?"

"Shit, sorry, what were we talking about?"

"You said 'why' and I said 'why what' and then you spaced out on me."

"Right," Ollie laughed, taking a bite of one of the bread rolls. "Why did you keep coming back?"

"To see you again."

"But *why*, Jackson?"

"Because…" Ollie arched an eyebrow at him and he laughed softly as she took another bite of the bread roll. "You fascinate me."

"I terrify and fascinate you?"

"Yeah, you really do," Jackson responded, licking his fingers. Ollie was clearly missing sex, because the simple act of his tongue sliding out to lick sauce off his fingers made her quiver. Her mind conjured up an image of his tongue doing that to her body and Ollie felt heat pool between her thighs. She even noticed his long fingers with neatly cut nails and bit back a growl at the thought of those fingers sliding inside her.

Jackson's voice interrupted her thoughts. "The first time we met, you scared me. The second time, it was like you were a different person."

She rolled her eyes, "Well, your hand was bleeding all over the place."

"Sure, but there was something else. I can't remember the last time I was drawn to someone the way I was drawn to you. It's so cliché, but you were like the sun and everyone was rotating around you. And I wanted to be part of your orbit." Jackson paused and Ollie bit her lip at his words. "Then you told me to fuck off because I was too young."

"Oh my god, you're an asshole," Ollie laughed, chucking the rest of her bread roll at him. Her eyes widened when Jackson opened his mouth and caught the piece. "Impressive."

"Thank you, I'll be here all week."

"You *have* been here all week." Ollie teased.

She saw Jackson's eyes darken as he spoke, "You took my breath away when I opened the men's room door. I would have stood there and stared at you for the rest of the evening."

"If I remember correctly, I was scowling and looking like something the cat dragged in."

Jackson shook his head, the corner of his mouth tipped up

in a smile, "You did look angry, but your eyes were twinkling and you had this thing about you that drew me in. I wish I had crashed into you on purpose. I wanted you to keep sassing me, except glass got stuck in my hand and that was a mess."

"I was not sassing you."

"I've never met anyone who sasses more than you do."

Ollie laughed. "Frankie is definitely the queen of sass. I would not want to get too close to her."

"I would like to get closer to you, though."

"Oh, *Jackson*, that is a terrible line."

"It's not a line, Oleander."

She stared at him, eyes wide and heart pounding. This whole time, he'd been cautious, awkward, polite and cute; the man sitting across from her now was a different person. And it was shockingly hot. Ollie swallowed the food in her mouth and licked her lips, watching Jackson's eyes dip to her mouth to follow the action. She bit her bottom lip and fought back whatever sound was trying to make its way out of her throat.

"That day," Jackson broke the silence. "At the coffee shop, I didn't know how to approach you or what to say. If you hadn't initiated the conversation, I might have stared at my coffee the whole time."

"Do I make you nervous?"

Jackson nodded, "We barely know each other, but I like you. Or I like the person you've let me see. But you've also got this wall up and that's fine—you can't trust everybody you meet—but I constantly feel like I need to be better than myself around you and that makes me nervous."

"Fuck, that sounds awful. *I* sound awful!"

"No, fuck," Jackson cursed under his breath and shook his head. "That's not what I meant. I've never met a woman like you and I want you to give me a chance, so I'm working really hard to earn it."

Ollie made a face and she realized Jackson was right—she *had* been making him work for it, but it was the only way she could decide if he was worth it or not. He'd come by the bar a few times after their first messy interaction, but it was the coffee shop morning that really changed everything. Ollie now understood how important that day was to him. It was important to her too.

"I still feel bad for the way I reacted. It's been…a long time since I've been interested in *this*."

Jackson leaned forward slightly. "What is *this*?"

"You know…doing something that is clearly *not* going to lead to a one night stand."

"Ah," was all Jackson said before he went back to his food and Ollie huffed, because he'd managed to make *her* feel awkward about herself for a change.

They continued to eat in silence and every so often, Ollie would lift her head and find Jackson watching her, but instead of looking away, he'd smile and keep his eyes on her. Men did this often—stare at her till she responded to them, and it usually led to lewd remarks and suggestions for them to hook up. With Jackson, it was almost like he didn't expect anything from her. Well, other than a chance to be around her. Which was another new thing. Ollie didn't know how to behave around Jackson when he liked being in her company.

Ollie dropped her fork, making it clatter against the counter. Jackson startled, looking at her in confusion. She sighed heavily, "I hate silences, they're awkward and long and frustrating."

"Are you sure you're talking about silences?"

Ollie sputtered out a laugh as she replayed her sentence, "I have met awkward and frustrating penises too, yes."

He smiled and pushed his food away, reaching for a bottle of water and Ollie watched. Was drinking water supposed to be erotic? Jackson lifted the bottle to his lips, tipped his head back and chugged. His Adam's apple bobbed as he swallowed and his jaw tightened with the same action and Ollie found herself licking her lips and tilting her head to watch the whole thing unfold. Just as he lowered the bottle, she blinked and shifted her attention to the tiramisu.

As Ollie cut the giant chunk of tiramisu into half and put one on a plate for Jackson, he cleared his throat to get her attention, "Tell me about your name."

"What about it?"

"I don't think I've ever met an Oleander before."

Ollie smiled, really starting to love the way her name sounded rolling off of Jackson's tongue. "My parents were somewhere in California when they came across a shrub. My mom liked the flowers and my dad was going to pluck a few when someone told them it was poisonous. But my mom loved the name and stuck with it."

"You're named after a poisonous shrub?"

"I'm beautiful and deadly and you won't know it until you touch me."

"I can attest to that." Jackson smirked, playfully reaching across the table to touch her arm, hissing as he pulled away. "Unlike you, I inherited my name from my dad's grandfather."

"And a fine name it is. At least it's a common name, kids at school called me all kinds of things."

"Kids are assholes anyway. Who cares what they said about you?"

"I did! Well, at the time I did. It felt good to meet Frankie, who didn't use her given name and we got clubbed as the girls with boys names."

"Ollie and Frankie. You should have started a band."

Ugh, she even liked the way he said her nickname. "And kill people everywhere since neither of us can hold a tune."

Jackson laughed. "That's why they invented auto-tune."

Ollie smiled and shook her head, finishing off her tiramisu before sliding off the stool to rinse everything out. She turned around to reach for the other dishes and found Jackson watching her again. "What?"

"Can I take you out this weekend?"

Ollie arched an eyebrow at him. "You're not going to stop until I say yes, are you?"

"I will stop if you want me to stop, I feel like we're having fun together and it would be a waste to not even see where this could go."

"Where do you see this going?" Ollie arched an eyebrow and rinsed out the plates and carried everything to the dishwasher and loaded it up.

"A couple more dates, maybe?"

"No coffee date, though."

Jackson nodded, a wide smile splitting his face. "I was thinking more like a food truck festival."

Ollie was very excited at the thought of food trucks. "That is so cool. I say yes to a food truck festival."

"And a date with me."

Ollie rolled her eyes and smiled. "A date with you at a food truck festival."

"Should I pick you up?"

"I'm still not sure you're not a serial killer, so no."

Jackson snorted. "Do I get your number instead?"

"That seems less dangerous, so yes." She nodded and rattled off her number. As she washed her hands her phone beeped in her back pocket and she looked back at Jackson.

He held his hands up with a smirk. "I had to make sure you weren't giving me a fake number."

"You're ridiculous," Ollie laughed and waved him off.

"Thanks for tonight, Oleander," he told her, pocketing his phone as he moved backwards to the kitchen doors with a smile. "I'll see you this weekend."

"Good night, Jackson."

He winked and stepped out through the swinging doors, leaving Ollie alone in the kitchen for a moment. Her phone beeped again and she fished it out of her pocket to find two text messages waiting from Jackson.

ANNA P.

Unknown: *Please let this be you.*
Unknown: *Thank you for giving me a chance, I'll make it worth it.*

ELEVEN

Jackson

For as long as he could remember the Wildes Food Truck festival happened twice a year—during spring and summer. When he was growing up, the Huxley family would drive down from Middletown, eat everything they could get their hands on, and drive back in a food coma.

This year, they promised there would be close to 80 trucks, live music all day and a fully stocked bar. It sounded like the perfect kind of place to take Oleander.

Ursula had never cared for food trucks or street food, always wanting Jackson to spend lots of money at fancy restaurants where they didn't include the price on the menu. She liked dressing up, being seen in public and flaunting the fact that she visited all these places. She would even make Jackson pose for a million pictures all night. Only to spend the rest of the evening uploading everything to Instagram.

Jackson *hated* Instagram. Sure, it was a big part of advertising and they had to always pay attention to the trends to make the right kind of communication plans. But if he could, he'd avoid Instagram for the rest of his life. Ursula had ruined a lot of things for him, but he was going to make sure this food truck date was one that would stay with Oleander forever. Even if nothing more came from this, Jackson truly believed it would be memorable.

Since they agreed to meet at the park instead of him picking her up, he got there 10 minutes early to scope out the place. However, showing up early didn't mean he got an easy spot to park, because all of Wildes had turned up for the food trucks.

As Jackson waited in line for tickets, he spotted a group of teenagers ahead of him. They were on a quadruple date and he realized that he'd never done that in high school, let alone go on a regular date. But the guys looked excited to be out with the girls and Jackson understood that feeling.

He had that look on his face when he was getting ready as well, because he was so damn excited. It was unlike Jackson to worry about his clothes, but he spent 15 agonizing minutes staring at his wardrobe of punny t-shirts and shirts before he settled on khakis, a dark tee, and his most comfortable flannel.

Jackson had also spent far too long trying to decide what kind of flowers Oleander would like. At the florist, he said he only wanted one flower and went on to explain his date and why he wanted to keep it simple, so she gave him a coral peony. The florist even told him peonies symbolized good luck, love and honor—he could definitely do with some luck.

He knew it was weird to appreciate a woman who ate everything, but after dating women who picked at their food, insisted on expensive restaurants, or women who only ate kale everywhere they went; it was refreshing to meet a woman who didn't hold back. He'd told Oleander to bring her appetite, because he intended for them to drink and eat everything they could get their hands on.

As he waited, Jackson replayed the whole conversation about him asking her out, a small smile tugging at his lips. When they spent the evening together, talking and getting to know each other, Jackson discovered he really did like that version of Oleander—she was funny, sassy and incredibly sexy. Plus, she was drop dead gorgeous when she released all the tension in her body and let herself laugh. Every laugh he pulled out of her felt like a tiny victory and Jackson loved it.

Loud music blasted through the speakers and Jackson blinked away the haze. When he looked up, the crowd heading his way parted to reveal Oleander. *Holy shit.* The whole thing felt like a scene out of a movie, and he stopped breathing at the sight of her.

Jackson had gotten so used to seeing Oleander in jeans and tees, so to see her in a dress with her legs and cleavage on display knocked the wind out of him.

She had a light sweater on, covering up her arms. The dress fluttered around her thick thighs, exposing gorgeous legs that ended in a pair of white Converse. He was very aware of the fact that Oleander was a plus size woman, but now that he could see her legs without denim encasing them, he was in awe of the shape and the length. Oleander had her hair down —it was messy and ruffled and looked like she'd *just* rolled out of bed. Jackson wanted to drag her back into bed right away.

When Jackson finished looking her up and down, he found her watching him while talking on the phone. And the smile on her face made his heart race. Everyone else around them faded away as she reached him. Jackson couldn't stop staring as she said goodbye and dropped her phone into the tote on her shoulder before turning her stunning smile on him. "Hi."

"You look incredible."

"I do, don't I?" Oleander grinned, taking a small step back to twirl, causing her dress to flare out and flaunt those thighs before she stopped and turned back to him. "I pulled this one out just for you, so I'm glad you appreciate it."

"I *do* appreciate it," he told her, his eyes drinking in the way the dress cinched at the waist while hugging her breasts and hips. He wanted to run his hands over her body desperately.

"You clean up nicely," Oleander smiled, tugging gently on

his jacket. "And I'm glad you didn't brush your hair, this messy look is working for me."

Jackson was sure his heart stopped, but he was aware of enough to hold up the flower. Oleander's eyes lit up and her smile widened as he twirled the short stem between his fingers, "The florist said peonies symbolize things that probably don't apply to us yet. But, I felt like the color would look good against your skin, so…" Jackson knew he was rambling, but the look on Oleander's face made it hard to pay attention.

"Thank you," Oleander whispered and took the flower from him, lifting it to her nose and sniffing as she smiled. "I'm guessing it's for my hair?"

Jackson nodded. "May I?"

She handed the flower back to him and Jackson stepped closer as he lifted his hand to tuck her hair back behind her ear and with the other hand, he slid the flower over her ear and smiled as he adjusted it.

"How do I look?"

"Beautiful," he whispered, hand lingering against her ear. Oleander stared up at him and Jackson hesitated, moving his hand farther to cup her cheek. She nodded as they leaned in closer, her warm breath brushing against his mouth. Jackson took that nod as consent and slanted his mouth over hers. A soft sound came out of her as their lips fit together and when he teased the seam of her lips with his tongue, she opened up for him.

Oleander's arms wound around his waist as he used his other hand to tug her closer, careful not to crush the flower, his tongue sliding past her lips to tangle with hers. He felt light headed, every inch of his body coming alive and heard someone growl before realizing the sound came out of him.

After what felt like forever, he broke the kiss and rested his forehead against Oleander's. She chuckled and Jackson smiled, stroking his thumb along her jaw.

"I promise I'll do my best to behave now."

Oleander whispered, "Don't you dare, I like this side of you."

"You bring out this side of me," he said.

"I like that," she grinned. "I'm *starving* and you promised great food."

He blew out a breath and smiled. "I can't believe you're here."

"Well, you made it sound like life or death if I said no," Oleander teased and Jackson narrowed his eyes.

"You could have said no."

"And miss out on a kiss like that?"

Jackson grinned and held a hand out to Oleander. "I was really nervous, in case you couldn't tell."

"You were not." She made a *pfft* sound and slid her hand into his, their fingers locking. "You were definitely thinking about it as I walked over."

"I was actually thinking about how beautiful you are."

"Stop it," she whispered and Jackson noticed that she was blushing.

Jackson smiled when Oleander squeezed his hand. "I'm glad you agreed to go out with me. Today is going to be a lot of fun."

"I'm looking forward to you popping my food truck cherry."

"Right." He stared at her a moment, the words making him blush as he looked away. "We're hitting up every single truck, unless it says vegan or organic on the side."

"Don't knock vegan food, some of it is good!"

"Most times I've eaten it, I've wanted to scrub my mouth out with soap."

Jackson chuckled at the expression on Oleander's face, "We're going to find a good vegan food truck and change your mind."

TWELVE

Oleander

Her first encounter with Jackson had been a mess and Ollie knew she was being tough on him, but her experience with men and their behavior made her gun-shy. She didn't have the patience to deal with another man child and his feelings if it meant putting herself out there. But in the time they'd met, and the night he stayed back to help her clean up, Ollie realized Jackson was different.

Jackson was also really easy to be around. He was young, but after that first moment of frustration about his age, she got over it. Age was just a number, wasn't that what she'd told herself every year since she was 25? They might be 10 years apart, but age didn't make a person more mature or interesting—the person was responsible for it on their own. And so far, Jackson was proving to be far more interesting than most of her exes, men and women.

What you saw with Jackson was what you got, and Ollie liked it. He was charming and funny and whenever he smiled, her heart stopped. On top of that, he was persistent. Which should have scared her—but Jackson didn't come on too strong. He almost seemed to know she would push him away, so he took baby steps to get to where she was. Ollie appreciated that.

Pierce had broken her in ways Ollie wasn't sure she was ever going to be able to fix. It started with emotional trust and ended with physical trust. Ollie had told herself that after Pierce, she wasn't going to get emotionally involved with anyone.

Apparently Jackson didn't get that memo. Because he made her smile and even worse, made her look forward to this damn date. She hadn't wanted it, but he'd found a way under her armor.

Thanks to Frankie, Ollie always thought only lumberjacks wore flannel. Jackson was no lumberjack, and she was pretty sure he didn't know how to chop wood. But he looked so good. Ollie had an image of her wearing his shirt and nothing else, and it made her blush as she took in the sight of Jackson. She'd noticed his face the first time they met, but now she was noticing the sharpness of his jaw, the way his hair curled around his ears—it was incredible to *watch* him. And when he'd tucked the flower behind her ear, Ollie even got a whiff of his cologne, which left her knees shaking.

Then there was *the kiss*. When he was tucking the flower into her hair, stroking her ear and jaw with his fingers, Ollie knew exactly what she wanted Jackson to do. He even *asked for permission*, which was something nobody did anymore. Did Jackson sense her panic or was he decent enough to know that asking before taking was the right thing to do?

"Okay, that's terrible. We're never going back there again." Ollie gagged, spitting the food into a napkin.

"I told you vegan food was weird."

"That's not accurate, since you inhaled that veggie burger," Ollie teased as she looked up and spotted something on his chin. Using an extra napkin, she wiped it off Jackson's face.

They'd been at the park for an hour and thanks to all the walking and talking they were doing, she wasn't too full yet. They'd definitely encountered some really weird food choices, especially since they discussed trying one dish from every truck.

"I need something to wash this out of my mouth." She gagged again and used a napkin to scrub at her tongue, like it would help. "We passed a dessert truck, wanna circle around and go find it?"

"Or," Jackson grinned, making Ollie frown as she dumped the offending food in the bin and wiped her hands, "we let these guys surprise us with their concoctions."

Ollie glanced at the truck Jackson was pointing to and frowned, "I abandoned a plate of food because they wouldn't tell us what was in it and now you want *more* surprises?"

Jackson snorted. "Live a little, Oleander. How can milkshakes be disgusting?"

"I'm not going to hold back when they give you something gross," Ollie shot back, but let Jackson tug her towards the food truck with a unicorn painted along the side.

There weren't a lot of people standing at the truck, but whoever had cups in their hands looked pretty pleased with what they were drinking. The giddy look on Jackson's face told her he was going to be just as happy.

"Hey there, lovebirds, welcome to Shake For a Surprise, do you know how this works?" A wide smile greeted them and Ollie tried to straighten her face but failed when Jackson squeezed her hand.

"We place our order and you make it for us?"

"With a twist!" They laughed and Ollie fought back a groan, leaning into Jackson's side as they were handed scraps of paper. "Fill this out by ticking off the things you like and we'll whip up something magical."

Ollie shook her head, already preparing to watch Jackson throw away another terrible food choice. But he was right, how could dessert be disgusting?

"This sounds really dangerous."

"Do you trust me?"

"Yes, but I don't trust them. They're too happy," Ollie said with a frown.

"Live a little, babe," Jackson told her with a chuckle and with his paper against the side of the truck, he started ticking things off his list.

"Wow, we're at the *babe* point of the day already," Ollie teased and stepped up beside him, ticking things off her list before stretching up to see what he'd selected.

"If you're not a fan of it, I won't use it again."

"Never been called babe like *that* before, so I don't know how I feel about it yet."

Jackson arched an eyebrow, "How have you been called babe?"

"When guys at the Barrel want my number or grab my ass or want my attention," Ollie said, passing their papers through the service window. When she turned around to look at Jackson, she noticed the expression on his face. "What's wrong?"

"They grab your ass at the Barrel?"

Ollie shrugged. "It's a *bar*, Jackson, with every kind of drunk person."

"But grabbing your ass…that's harassment."

"I'm a big girl, I can handle it."

"Ollie," he said her name with a frustrated sigh and she smiled. "What? Why are you smiling?"

"You called me *Ollie*."

"Because I'm annoyed. Not with you, but the circumstances."

"Hey," she reached for his hand and stepped closer. "I like that you want to defend my honor, but it's not a big deal."

"When was the last time someone grabbed your ass?"

Rolling her eyes, Ollie huffed, "Seriously?"

"Humor me, please."

Ollie stepped closer to him and guided his hand around her waist. She slowly tugged it down to rest on her ass and tilted her head to smile up at him. "Today was the last time someone grabbed my ass."

Jackson's eyes widened as he smoothed his hand over the curve of her ass and moved it back to her hip. "I sound like a tough guy, but if I was around and someone grabbed your ass, I don't know what I'd do."

"You'd do nothing, Jackson. Like I said, I don't need you to be my knight in shining armor."

"I wish I could be."

Ollie was starting to realize she would be okay if Jackson *was* her knight in shining armor. He seemed genuinely distressed knowing she got grabbed at the bar quite often. It was amusing to her, but she understood that for someone who'd never worked in that kind of environment, it was probably shocking. Even Killian docked her pay when Ollie slapped the first customer that grabbed her ass. For all of her history with men and being manhandled, Ollie had realized in the real world, people didn't give a shit as much as you wanted them to.

If it wasn't for the physical proof, her report about Pierce would have gone unheard. Ollie realized comparing Jackson to her ex wasn't beneficial. For so many reasons, but starting with the fact that Jackson was a decent human being where Pierce wasn't.

Then again, Ollie didn't know enough about Jackson to judge whether or not he'd protect her in any situation. Would he think she was disgusting for having been with a woman before? Would he think she was ugly once he saw her naked? Her fears and worries would plague her for the rest of her life, but if she didn't let herself go and drop her guard, she would never get to enjoy the little things in life. Though, she didn't think Jackson would get so worked up about her ass being grabbed.

Ollie opened her mouth to respond to him when their names were called. She turned to the truck and found two disposable cups with lids, straws and spoons.

"Before you look inside, take a sip and let me know what you think."

Ollie reached for the one with her name and handed Jackson his cup. She stuck the straw through the hole and took a sip, her eyes widening as her tastebuds were treated to the most incredible flavors.

When she looked up at Jackson, he had the same expression. "Holy shit."

"Tell your friends to stop by, we'll be here all weekend." They announced before vanishing.

Ollie handed Jackson money for their drinks and took another sip, laughing as she shook her head. "This is a cup of magic."

"Let's swap, I wanna see what you got."

Ollie handed her cup over and took a sip of Jackson's, a quiet moan falling from her lips. "What did you put on your list?"

"Strawberries, dark chocolate, salted caramel, apple crumble, ice cream and coffee," Jackson led them to a picnic table and as she sat down, he straddled the bench beside her. But his eyes widened and he started to reach for his drink in her hand. "Oh shit, babe, there's coffee in there."

She loved how easily he called her *babe*, like he'd always been saying it. Ollie had never been a fan of terms of endearment, because they always sounded forced and unappealing. But coming off of Jackson's lips, she knew he wasn't doing it to flirt with her.

"Eh, it won't kill me," Ollie said and took another big sip before handing his drink back. "I also had dark chocolate, salted caramel and ice cream on my list, but also asked for red velvet, brownies and Oreos. I can't taste any of those ingredients specifically, but somehow, it's all there?"

"This *is* magic in a cup. I don't know why there aren't more people at his truck."

Ollie shrugged, "Maybe he wants to take it slow and win people over gradually. I mean, he's tucked away this far back, he's got a strategy."

"Whatever it is, I like this."

"We should come back around later and see if he can whip up something as good the second time around."

"That's a great idea," Jackson said and leaned in. Ollie smiled as she met him halfway, kissing him softly.

"This is the most I have kissed or smiled with someone in a really long time."

"You deserve to be kissed and made to smile always." Jackson said the words softly.

See, he wasn't doing it with a purpose. His end goal might be to get her naked, but there was *more* to what he wanted and it felt good. They turned their focus to their drinks and when she looked up, she found Jackson had managed to smear some of his shake in the corner of his mouth. Pulling her mouth off of her straw with a soft pop, she lifted a hand and swiped her thumb over his mouth. Jackson's eyes met hers and she bit down on her bottom lip as he pressed a soft kiss to her thumb.

Ollie laughed and shook her head, "Okay, where to next?"

THIRTEEN
Jackson

Jackson knew it in his bones—he was going to fall in love with Oleander and it would break him when she didn't feel the same.

After the shakes, they wandered around the park hand-in-hand. Jackson spent so much time watching her that he kept tripping over his own feet. He was awkward *without* screaming kids tripping him up, so with them everywhere, Jackson was surprised he didn't fall on his face. He'd never been confident when it came to women, whether he was dating them or in a friendship—he always felt like those women could do better—but with Oleander, none of that filtered into his mind. The only thing he thought about with her was how he never wanted their date to end.

Armed with donuts, Oleander led them to a bench that had just been vacated by a family. She sat down, adjusting her dress and Jackson sat down beside her, straddling the bench. It was distracting, watching her in that dress. Jackson had never cared what women wore, but he liked what *she* was wearing. The dress was *flowy*—there was no other way to explain what it looked like—and he fucking loved it. When she moved, the bottom twirled around her thighs and he got a chance to stare at her legs. It also hugged her delicious curves and stretched over her ass.

And Jackson was definitely in love with her ass.

The few times Oleander got ahead of him in their search for the next best item, he found other people staring at her too. She was so confident that it exuded off of her and Jackson was captivated.

This is how it always happened—he got hooked and addicted, fell in love and everything fell apart.

Jackson didn't want that with Oleander. For one, she was far more mature than the women he'd been with. And she'd clearly experienced more in life than he had. And while she had a lot to teach him, she had a lot to offer by existing in his life.

Oleander made a noise between a moan and a growl, and Jackson snapped out of his thoughts to look at her. A group of guys passed them as she moaned and they gave Jackson a 'thumbs up' paired with disgusting smirks and he rolled his eyes at them.

"You should know this now, I can get addicted to donuts."

He laughed. "I got that from all the noises you made and how you bought one of every flavor."

Oleander made a face, "I was ready to buy out all of them, but Brea gave me *that* look."

"First name basis with the owner?" Jackson smirked, wondering where he'd gone when she'd chatted up the woman at the truck.

"She was telling me the story of how she and Ben met—that's her partner—and ugh, I'm not someone who cares for romantic things, but it was perfect."

"You're not a romantic?"

Oleander shrugged. "I mean..I like romance, but I also don't?"

"That sounds like an interesting story."

"It's a very long one."

"We've got nothing but time."

Oleander scrunched up her nose and Jackson chuckled. "Must we?"

"Isn't that what people do on their first dates, get to know each other?"

"You've had your tongue in my mouth and your hand on my ass. Aren't we already getting to know each other?" Oleander smiled at him sweetly and broke a donut in two pieces and handed one half to him. "Fine, ask away."

Jackson grinned, proud of himself for wearing her down as he took a bite of the donut. If he was really interested in the donut, he would have been able to enjoy the flavors that filled his mouth. But he was so distracted by the way Oleander was eating that he had to force himself to focus on what they were supposed to be doing.

He was also very distracted by the memory of his hand tracing the shape of her full ass and their tongues dancing together when he greeted her. The thoughts made his brain wander and his pants tighten, which was definitely not family friendly at all.

Clearing his throat, Jackson took another bite of the donut before speaking. "What's the most underrated alcoholic beverage?"

Oleander's eyebrow arched up. "That's not how this game works."

Jackson laughed. "We're doing things differently. Now, answer the question."

"In my opinion?" she asked and Jackson nodded. "Tequila shots. People talk about it in books and you see everyone knocking them back in movies, but so few people order it at the Barrel. Frankie is single-handedly finishing our stock."

"I, personally, know that tequila makes people do stupid shit," Jackson said with a smirk.

"Now I need to know more, so let's go with…something stupid you've done while drunk."

Jackson rolled his eyes. "I once confessed my undying love to a cactus, thinking it was the woman I was flirting with and proceeded to throw up in her handbag minutes later."

Oleander burst out laughing. The only other person who knew about this was Gavin and he had been the one to drag him away from the party. And since then, he'd avoided tequila if he could. It *really* did make him do stupid shit.

"I regret bringing up alcohol. Moving on." He waved his hand, like he was erasing the conversation, but Oleander was still laughing. "If you went to the Olympics, what would it be for?"

"Oh good one!" Oleander bounced, drawing his attention to her breasts. Jackson blinked quickly so she wouldn't catch him in the act. "I'd say swimming. I used to swim a lot, but maybe not Olympic level, but I loved it so much."

"Why did you stop?"

Shrugging, Oleander picked up another donut. "My body started changing and I was coming to terms with it, and those swimsuits hug you like a second skin and I wasn't ready."

He nodded, his eyes drinking in her curves. To know she hadn't always been this confident comforted him. Before karate became his means of fitness, Jackson had been a scrawny and lanky kid and he'd hated his body.

"What is the worst color in the world?"

Oleander's question caught him off guard and he blinked, frowning at her. "Is that because I'm a designer?"

"You're a designer?"

Jackson laughed. "A graphic designer, yeah. I feel like that is something I should have told you already."

"Nope," she smiled, taking another bite of her donut. "You told me about karate."

"Weird," he said with a snort, trying not to get distracted by her donut eating again. "I'm actually very against the color *yellow*."

"What did yellow ever do to you?"

"First, my karate level at yellow belt was the worst. Then, Pikachu happened and it was like everything around me was yellow."

Oleander snorted, Jackson smile at the sound. "Wow, I better hide all my yellow clothes."

"If anyone could change my mind about yellow, it would be you."

Jackson didn't mean for the words to sound so serious, but when he saw Oleander smile, he couldn't stop the blush from creeping over his face. She could make him change his mind about *anything* and that was scary.

"Right." He cleared his throat and reached for a donut, but changed his mind. "What's the most overrated movie you've ever seen?"

"This might get me killed, but," Oleander whispered and leaned in as she spoke, her eyes fixed on his, "*Avatar.* I still don't understand why everyone liked it so much."

Jackson pressed his lips together as Oleander's eyes darted everywhere. She was fucking adorable and he didn't know if he'd survive this date with her. All he wanted to do was wrap her up in his arms and press his face into her neck.

"I agree with you," Jackson said, using his thumb to wipe icing from the corner of Oleander's mouth. He didn't even realize he'd done it till he pulled his hand away. And to cover that up, he spoke quickly. "James Cameron also made *Titanic,* which in my opinion, is the most overrated romantic movie ever."

"Oh my god, you're a fan of rom-coms, aren't you?"

Jackson frowned. "They give you hope, okay!"

"So, what's your favorite one?"

"Uh," he paused and narrowed his eyes at Oleander. "This feels like a trick question."

"I am not so silently judging your movie genre preferences, but I'll try not to go too overboard."

It was his turn to snort. "I'm going to get so much grief for saying this, but *Pretty In Pink*."

Oleander shrugged, like she didn't feel the same way, "I'd pick *10 Things I Hate About You*."

Jackson barely heard her because he was watching her stuff the donut into her mouth, making a mess with crumbs and sprinkles. When her tongue darted out, Jackson snapped back into reality.

"I like that you don't watch rom-coms and you probably think *Die Hard* is a Christmas movie."

Oleander pushed the donuts aside. "I love John McClane, but is it really a Christmas movie?"

"I'm impressed. Most action fans *insist* it is."

"I like to break the mold."

Jackson smiled because everything about Oleander broke the mold. "Your first relationship?"

"*Now* we're getting personal. But fine, her name was Nina," Oleander said it with a sigh and looked up at him. "I'm bi."

Jackson wasn't *shocked*, if that's what she was thinking, but he was surprised. However, he wasn't going to judge Oleander based on her sexual preferences.

"I figured. So, tell me more about Nina."

Oleander hesitated and Jackson reached for a donut, breaking it in half to hand a piece to her. A smile tugged at her lips as Oleander took a bite, chewed and swallowed.

"We were in college, and we hooked up once, twice and it became a *thing*. All four years together, we made it work. Then after graduation, she was gone. Our relationship ended without a word," Oleander paused. "A few years later, she popped up all over social media with a brood of kids and a *husband*. Apparently, I was a four-year experiment."

"Ouch." Jackson winced.

"I got really picky about my relationships after that. And still…"

Jackson frowned, donut halfway to his mouth. "Still what?"

"I got fucked over a lot. I'm starting to think maybe the problem is me."

"Or you just picked the wrong people."

"Does that include you?" Oleander asked.

"Are we headed in that direction?"

"Are we?" Oleander sounded cautious and Jackson wondered what she was thinking.

"I hope so. I know you're wary, so I'm not rushing you into anything."

"What are you expecting out of this, Jackson?" She asked and Jackson remembered her asking this when they were sitting in the Barrel kitchen.

"What does anybody expect out of a first date?"

"Stop answering my questions with a question."

"Okay," Jackson laughed and brushed a hand through his hair, weighing his answer carefully before speaking. "I'm the kind of guy that falls for a woman right off the bat. I always worry I come on too strong and any chance I have of something more with them is gone before we even get ahead. I like you and I barely know you, so imagine what it would be like if I did get to know you."

"You'd probably like me less, if I'm being honest."

"I doubt that. But, I know you've got this wall up because of your past relationships and I respect that. But I also want to get past those walls. I want to see *you*. I want us to be more than two people who eat, kiss and flirt at a food truck festival."

"You want to be my boyfriend." Oleander said it as a statement and turned slightly on the bench to face him properly.

"I want to be your boyfriend," Jackson nodded, finishing off the donut. "I want to be the person you turn to on a rough day, be someone who can text you at stupid o'clock and put a smile on your face. I want to get to know you, as much as I can, because what I've seen of you so far? I like that person a lot."

"How are you still single?"

He shrugged and licked his fingers, watching Oleander's eyes drop to his mouth. "Apparently women don't like it when guys are open about their feelings?"

"You're flirting with the wrong women, Jackson."

"Do you fit into that bracket too?"

"God, no. I like people who are in touch with their feelings and acknowledge them."

"I know we're still getting to know each other, but I really hope you'll give me a chance."

She smiled. "I'm here, aren't I? I don't know what this is, but I like the way you look at me and the way I feel when I'm with you."

As Oleander spoke, explaining her thoughts and her mind, Jackson realized she knew exactly what he felt for her. But instead of using that to her advantage and taking him for a ride, she was making him aware he was too much of an open book. Strangely, she seemed to like that about him.

"I don't have to pretend with you, Jackson, and that's a big deal. I'm always putting on a show for people," Oleander explained, smoothing her dress over her thighs. "I don't trust easily, but I project my hard shell, because it's easier than letting people into my life. And with you, I find myself doing that a lot less."

Nodding, Jackson smiled. "You said you like the way I look at you. How do I look at you?"

"Like you've seen a rainbow after days of darkness."

"You *are* a rainbow, Oleander. Don't let anyone tell you otherwise."

THEIR CONVERSATION KEPT CHANGING TOPICS, but Oleander did most of the talking and Jackson discovered that he was okay with it. The sound of her voice was so soothing as she gave him a full education on her obsession with action movies.

They even talked about *Star Wars* and whether or not it was important to watch it in chronological order or in the machete order—machete won, obviously. He'd never dated a woman who even knew the basics of *Star Wars*, let alone anything about the machete order. Oleander surprised him at every turn.

The best part was that everything about them fit—from the food they liked, to the size of their hands and the fit of their mouths, to the way her curves molded against his straight lines perfectly.

It had been so long since he'd been with someone who didn't expect him to be everything at once, it felt good to be *himself* without all the weight of being perfect all the time.

FOURTEEN

Oleander

Ollie had no fucking clue who the band was. But they were playing music she didn't listen to, and they'd been at it for an hour already. Everyone else was singing along and cheering, but Ollie didn't particularly care about it. However, it was clearly winning Jackson over, because he was singing along and smiling at her when she caught him in the act. It was fucking adorable.

He was fucking adorable. And sexy. And charming. And insanely distracting.

They'd finished their second set of shakes and, like the first round, it had been glorious. Ollie didn't know what Mr. Chipper did and how he managed to create something out of their favorite items, but it was damn good.

When the band announced they were taking a 15 minute break, Jackson turned to her. "I can tell this isn't your kind of music."

"Was it because of my heavy sighing or because I was slurping my drink so loud?"

"Both." He laughed and slid a hand over her bare knee, making it seem like the most natural thing to do. "Do you wanna leave?"

"Nope," she took another sip of her drink. "You look like you're having fun and there's nowhere else I want to be."

"Good," Jackson mumbled, his eyes falling to her lips as she swiped her tongue over them and he quickly looked up into her eyes. Ollie didn't know how to react to the fact that Jackson was distracted by her, so she was glad when he quickly followed it up with a question. "What's your favorite color?"

"Aquamarine. What's your least favorite food item?"

Jackson made a face. "Mushrooms. I tell everyone I'm allergic, when in reality I can't stand the idea of eating *fungi*. Dream vacation destination?"

"Don't hate on mushrooms, they're delicious," Ollie laughed and poked his side before answering. "Bali. Drink you like the most?"

"Craft beer is a big win in my book, but I like a glass of whiskey now and then. Movie you can watch over and over again?"

"*Armageddon*. Makes me cry every single time." Ollie grinned. "Favorite job?"

"Being a designer at an advertising agency, basically what I'm doing right now." Jackson said and Ollie nodded. "A secret talent?"

"I can bend myself like a pretzel." She wiggled her eyebrows.

A growl came out of him and Ollie couldn't help but smile as Jackson's eyes glazed over before he blinked. "You did that on purpose."

"What?"

"Don't look at me like you're innocent." He pointed at her and Ollie laughed.

"You asked and I told you."

"Fuck." The word came out so soft, but Ollie heard it in his growly tone. "I need to do something else to stop thinking about it."

"Okay, how about this," she said, lowering her drink as she

smiled at him. "You tell me how you got into karate, and we move on past my random fact?"

Jackson narrowed his eyes and Ollie gave him her best angelic smile, which clearly won him over. But his body language changed, his face tightened and his shoulders seemed to rise to his ears and Ollie frowned. Instead of stopping him, she reached for his hand, linked their fingers together and set it in her lap. Jackson watched the action and let out a shaky breath.

"I was bullied as a kid," Jackson started. "My mom left soon after I was born and my dad checked out because he was depressed. My older siblings were too young to really raise me, and of course without adult supervision, I was messy, so the older, bigger kids would get pretty aggressive."

Ollie squeezed his hand when Jackson paused, this time he lifted his eyes to hers and smiled softly. "Then my dad met Mindy. She and her baby became part of our family. She was a great mom to me and saw how much shit I was getting at school, so she would stepped in and helped. Mindy knew of this guy who worked at a karate dojo and signed me up. I was maybe 12 or 13 and I went every day after school and I got tough. At first, I was getting picked on there as well, but I kept fighting back and eventually, I made it stick."

She remembered what he said at the coffee shop, how doing karate wasn't just about physical strengthening, it was also for mental strength. It clearly helped him as a bullied kid get stronger in every way. And looking at the man in front of her now, Ollie was glad he'd overcome it all.

"That's incredible, Jackson. So that's why you're teaching other kids?"

He nodded. "Bullies don't stop existing in the world, they get bigger and bolder. And there are so many kids who look like me…scrawny, underfed and unloved who are great targets. I want to help them the way Mindy and my sensei helped me."

"*You* are incredible," Ollie whispered, their eyes meeting as she gave his hand another squeeze. "How many kids do you work with?"

"Right now, I have about 12 students in my class."

"I'm sure you're a superhero to those kids."

"They hate my guts," Jackson laughed. "But, that's just the start. I hope I'm actually able to help them get out of the cycle and protect themselves."

"Did you ever get into fights after you started learning karate?"

"At school? Oh yeah. Mindy got called in a lot, but she was always proud of me for standing up for myself."

"Do you think you might start classes for adults or women?"

"We've talked about it," Jackson mumbled. "Would you sign up?"

"Hell yeah," Ollie grinned and performed what she thought was a karate chop. "Frankie and I would love to learn some moves. So far, we know what Sandra Bullock taught us in *Miss Congeniality* and holding our keys between our fingers."

"Have you ever had to use it?"

"Maybe once, but it's better to be prepared, right?" She lifted a hand to cup Jackson's cheek. "You continue to surprise me, Jackson."

"I'm glad, otherwise I feel like you'd be bored of me really soon."

Ollie gently shoved him, making Jackson laugh. "I haven't gotten bored of you yet, so…there's still a possibility."

"Oh, so there's a chance we might not ride off into the sunset together."

Nodding, she took another sip of her shake and pouted when nothing came through. "Well, now that my shake is over, there's even less chance of that happening."

"Come on," Jackson chuckled, hand out as he got to his feet. "Let's get more shakes for the road."

Ollie took his hand and arched an eyebrow. "Where is this road taking us?"

"Wherever you want it to go."

She stretched up onto her toes to press a soft kiss against his lips before dropping back to her feet. "Lead the way, *padawan*."

Jackson made the growly sound again and Ollie smirked, loving that a casual mention of something *Star Wars* related would get him so wired up. Such a nerd. She loved it.

FOLLOWING him to Shake For A Surprise, Ollie replayed the whole day in her head. When they met, she'd been so reluctant to let him in. If they hadn't seen each other at the coffee shop, Ollie knew Jackson would not have flirted with her on his next visit. And now, she was holding his hand, kissing him, being seen in public with him…this was how relationships started.

And instead of absolute panic, she was feeling something else—she was really comfortable with Jackson. Not once did he make her feel nervous around him or uneasy for any reason.

Ollie didn't even realize they'd reached the food truck till Mr. Chipper interrupted her thoughts to announce they knew exactly what to make them and vanished into the truck. Ollie leaned against Jackson as he wound an arm around her shoulders, tucking her into his side.

That was another thing that felt normal—she leaned into him and his body knew exactly what to do. Ollie felt safe in Jackson's arms and that was a big deal since she so rarely felt safe outside of her friends circle anymore.

Snuggling into him more, inhaling his scent Ollie whispered. "We should find out their name and spread the word."

"We should petition to be brand ambassadors."

Ollie loved the way their brains were working together. "Yes! Put that advertising brain to good use, cutie."

"I like that, though I hope I'm more than cute."

"Right now, you're fucking cute. We can revisit this later and see how I feel."

"No pressure whatsoever," Jackson chuckled.

"You got me this far, Jackson. That says a lot about how much further we could go."

"Now I want to say fuck it to these shakes and go home."

"If you did that," Mr. Chipper announced and presented two large cups, "you'd miss out on this delicious creation. I figure after all the things you've tried so far, you could use a little bit of the same thing."

"You made us the same thing?"

"Damn straight. You two look good together and you keep trying each other's creations, so I figure, why not combine all of it and create something awesome."

"Thank you, that's…you might have helped me score a second date," Jackson laughed and Ollie rolled her eyes. But she had to agree, there was something about these shakes that made them both so comfortable coming back repeatedly. "I'm Jackson, this is Oleander."

"Good to meet you two. I'm Niles. If you're ever near Bethany Beach, come visit us."

"Thanks Niles," Ollie said, handing Jackson a cup.

"You two have a good weekend and I'll see you soon." Ollie watched him walk away and realized they hadn't paid.

"Niles, wait, we need to pay for these!"

"On the house!" He called out and vanished into the truck. Jackson was already slurping on his shake, making all kinds of inappropriate noises that made Ollie laugh.

"Come on, let's head out and get away from all these people."

"Can't wait to get me alone, huh?"

"Yes ma'am, that's exactly what I want to do," Jackson

said with a straight face, Ollie couldn't help but laugh. While she might have been ready to go home with Jackson, there was a part of Ollie felt like they couldn't rush this. Kissing, touching and holding hands was one thing, but sex was a really big deal. As someone who struggled to connect with men in the bedroom after Pierce, Ollie didn't want to go home with Jackson because it was an option.

She wanted every single time they were intimate to mean something more than sex. Which was why when they reached her car, Ollie turned around and leaned back against it.

At Jackson's frown, Ollie smiled. "We're not going home."

His eyes widened as he looked around. "You want to do it here?"

Ollie laughed. "We're not having sex tonight, Jackson."

"Oh."

"Not that I don't want to have sex with you, I'm not sure we're there yet."

Jackson nodded. "But you're up for more dates?"

"Absolutely," Ollie grinned and watched Jackson's face transform.

"That's good enough for me. I really enjoyed spending time with you, Oleander. Today was...different."

"What does that mean?"

"In a good way, obviously, because I've never gone on a date like this before. It's usually dinner or drinks or something with lots of people I know," Jackson explained and Ollie nodded. "But this felt good. There were lots of people, but it was also just you and me."

"I really enjoyed today too, this might be one of my favorite dates of all time." she smiled.

"So now whatever we do next, I have to top this."

Ollie grinned. "No pressure."

Jackson laughed as she took another big sip of her shake. He watched her, moving in closer and Ollie smiled around her straw. One hand landed gently on her hip and Ollie pulled her drink away.

"May I kiss you?" Jackson's voice was soft, but almost desperate.

"Of course."

The words were barely out of her mouth before he was kissing her. Unlike their kiss from earlier, this one was deeper and more passionate. Ollie sighed softly against his mouth and pulled away.

"Sorry, did I do something wrong?"

"No, no, I wanted to put our drinks down so we could use both hands."

Jackson laughed as he took her drink and set them on the roof of her car. Ollie smiled and curled her hand into the front of his shirt and pulled him back towards her, their mouths crashing hungrily. The kiss was amazing and Ollie felt it everywhere. Jackson's hands slid down her sides and pulled her against him, she wrapped her arms around his neck, opening her mouth as his tongue swept inside.

He growled, she moaned and her fingers slid into his hair as she held him close for a deeper kiss. Ollie felt Jackson's fingers curl into her sides and she whimpered as she stretched up, needing more of him.

"If we don't stop, I won't be able to let you go," Jackson whispered as he pulled away, his breath warm against her lips.

"Fine," Ollie grumbled and leaned back against the car, her hands sliding down to rest on his chest. She gently pushed him backwards and Jackson smiled.

"I'll text you about our next date."

"Don't make me wait too long, okay?" She whispered.

Jackson nodded, reached for his drink and walked backwards till someone honked. She watched as Jackson jumped and moved aside. When he looked back at her, he was blushing and Ollie grinned, waving him off as she slid into her

FIFTEEN

Jackson

Jackson hated that he sounded like a *guy* when Oleander said they weren't going to have sex. Sure, he was hoping he'd get laid, because he knew the food truck festival date was a special one. But he wasn't actually that disappointed they weren't going home together. No that was a lie—he was mildly disappointed. But it had been his best date *ever*.

His feelings for Oleander sometimes felt overwhelming. When he thought about her, Jackson's heart would race and he'd feel his face stretch into a smile. Whenever she texted him, he'd drop everything he was doing to reply. There was something about the way she made him feel that he couldn't put his finger on, but he didn't need to identify it.

She made him feel *alive*.

But here lay the problem: Jackson had played his best hand with the food truck festival and now he was all out of good ideas. Jackson knew that Oleander wasn't going to be the kind of woman who wanted luxury—she liked eating with her fingers, loading up on sugar and having a good time. She might have worn a beautiful dress, but she paired it with sneakers, because she was ready to spend time on her feet.

And he didn't know how to date women who liked the simple things.

Thankfully for him, his friends had a poker night a few days after his date and Everleigh was coming. Everleigh had gone to school with the boys in Middletown, she and Milo had a brief relationship and when that ended, she'd become part of their bi-monthly poker nights.

As soon as Everleigh walked through the door of Milo's apartment, poker was abandoned in favor of helping Jackson plan dates. She asked questions, made notes and discussed different places to go. By the end of the night, Jackson had a month worth of dates in hand and all he had to do was pick the best ones.

Jackson: *Are you ready for my dates to rock your world?*

Oleander: *I'm actually kinda nervous now.*

Jackson: *I think you're going to love them.*

Oleander: *Wait, you've actually planned a whole bunch?*

Jackson: *I got some help and enough ideas to last me a while.*

Oleander: *Wow, you weren't kidding about wanting to go on dates.*

Jackson: *I want to spend as much time with you as I can and if that means multiple dates, so be it.*

Oleander: *That's really cute.*

Oleander: *Do I get a hint of what I'm in for?*

Jackson: *Lots of fun stuff and a chance for us to get to know each other really well.*

Oleander: *Didn't we already do that on our first date?*

Jackson: *Oh, this is a different kind of method.*

Oleander: *I'm excited!*

Jackson: *Meet me at the park where we had our first date, this Sunday, 9am. All will be revealed.*

THE FIRST OF those dates was paintball and because he didn't know too many people, he invited Milo and Gavin to come along and told Oleander she could invite Frankie if she wanted. So at least they had a team of their own. He booked them a game and after picking the girls up at the park, Jackson drove them over to the venue. Oleander and Frankie had been far more excited than he expected, which was good. Because their team won effortlessly.

After paintball, they went to a bar close by and filled themselves up with food and beer. The five of them looked like they'd been through the wringer and were covered in paint, but they didn't care. Even when other patrons glared at them for making too much noise or looking the way they did. Milo and Jackson challenged the girls to a round of pool, which ended with the boys losing. Oleander was competitive, but Frankie was a whole other level. Jackson liked that even though it was a group *date*, he got to see a different side of Oleander.

Dressed in shorts that flaunted her gorgeous legs and a faded t-shirt, she was aggressive, loud and so incredibly sexy. If he was being honest, he'd never noticed these things about women before, and Jackson was pretty sure he was never really interested in women with big personalities. But Oleander had him wrapped around the pinkie.

After the successful first date, Jackson had to shuffle his ideas. He found out when Oleander had her next evening off from the Barrel and signed them up for 'Sangria and Strokes' at a small art gallery in town. He didn't care for wine, but it was the only drink they were offering. Besides, he figured they'd have a good time.

Oleander showed up in another dress and this time she'd paired them with heels and Jackson had to bite his fist at first sight—those legs, *fuck*, she was trying to kill him. After a quick walk-through of the gallery—where Oleander and Jackson kept touching and teasing each other—each couple was handed a jug of sangria that would be topped up as they finished it, and asked to sit in front of easels. The easels were angled in such a way that they couldn't see what the other person was drawing, which was great, because despite being a designer, he wasn't always confident about his art.

The theme for the evening was to paint something that represented your partner and all Jackson could think about was painting Oleander as she was. He had never done anything like this before, and he knew the idea was to paint her without painting *her*. She poured them both a glass of sangria and tied her hair up as she got to work. Jackson's eyes followed the shape of her neck, imagining what it would feel like to press his lips to the spot where her neck met her shoulder. It took everything in him to turn away, even though all he wanted to do was stare at her some more. The lady hosting the evening announced they had 30 minutes to do their paintings, after which they could all mingle and drink some more.

At the end of the 30 minutes, Oleander flipped her easel around to show him a splash of colors. It was a mix of browns and blues and greens and some red.

"It's kinda hard to paint you when I'm still figuring you out."

Jackson smiled. "What do all these colors mean?"

"These are colors I think of when I think of you."

"You think of me?"

Oleander rolled her eyes and turned her canvas away. "Show me yours."

Unlike hers, Jackson had actually drawn elements that described Oleander in his mind. sneakers, peonies, stars, a unicorn and all of it laid over watercolor, with Oleander's name woven through the paint.

"Wow," was all she said as she slid off her stool and came to stand beside him.

"It's…" Jackson was at a loss for words as he watched her.

"I agree with what you said about not knowing each other well enough for this assignment."

"And yet, you managed to capture the little things about me."

"Like you used my favorite colors."

Oleander's eyes widened. "Those were your favorite colors?"

Jackson gestured to his green Henley and smiled. "I think every time I've seen you, I've been wearing one of those colors."

"Okay, we're not doing too bad."

They didn't stay for the mingling, they left their sangria half finished, grabbed their canvases and slipped out before anyone could stop them. Jackson suggested a walk and Oleander pulled off her heels as they walked hand in hand along the promenade. At the end of the night, Jackson drove to Oleander's apartment and walked to her front door. He set the canvases just inside her front door, not entirely sure what she would do with them. Then said good night and took a step back, resisting the urge to kiss her. Jackson moved towards the elevators, then changed his mind, rushing back as Oleander started to close the door. He nudged it open gently and stepped inside her apartment, his hands moving to frame her face as he lowered his lips to hers.

Oleander laughed against his mouth as she tugged him closer till her back was against the wall. The kiss was hot and sweet, and he fought the growing desire to press himself against her, so Oleander would know what she made him feel. But he finally pulled away, kissing her once more, and walked out of her apartment.

The following weekend, they attended a cooking class at a pizza place in Newark, where Jackson and the boys had been frequent customers for years. To say Oleander was excited was an understatement, because as soon as they walked in and were handed their aprons, gloves and hairnets, she was squealing about how she wanted to learn to make pizza.

The owner, an older Italian man, gave them instructions and made them watch as he prepared the dough, kneaded it and tossed it around to get the perfect shape and size. It took both Jackson and Oleander a million tries to even flip the dough the right way, but it never came down the way it was supposed to. And after so many failed attempts, they were asked to focus on the sauce. Jackson was glad other than the owner and his youngest son, nobody else was there to watch their absolute disaster. The sauce wasn't their strong suit either, but at least they didn't burn it. However, Oleander did steal a lot of pepperoni before they could spread it out across the pizza.

When Jackson parked under her building afterwards, Oleander climbed into his lap in the front seat and they made out till she leaned back and hit the horn, startling them. He walked her to her door and instead of walking away, he kissed her right there. Pressed up against her front door, their hands wandered and her mouth trailed along his jaw and neck till a neighbor chased him off.

Jackson was really proud of what he was able to do and how much Oleander seemed to enjoy all the dates. While he would have liked to take her back to Better Latte Than Never, he knew Saturdays were always a mad rush to get to class, so he opted for a different approach.

Armed with a tall cup of hot chocolate and a bag of danishes for her, Jackson waited outside her building early the next morning. She stumbled out through the main doors, rummaging in her bag, but all Jackson could see was how beautiful she looked. Oleander had clearly rolled out of bed and into her clothes because she was rumpled, messy and cute as fuck. Her hair was pulled up in a messy bun and she was frowning until she looked up and saw him.

When their eyes met, Jackson grinned, watching the frown vanish and her eyes widen.

"What are you doing here?"

"I know you have an early start, so I figured I'd bring you some sustenance."

Oleander grinned and walked over to him. "You brought me hot chocolate and a croissant?"

"And a few other things, yeah."

She stretched up and kissed him before settling on her feet to take the drink from him. Oleander closed her eyes and Jackson's heart stuttered as she sipped on her hot drink. A soft whimper escaped her lips and Jackson laughed.

"I'm also offering chauffeur services, if you need it."

"Don't you have class?"

"Not an early one like yours."

Oleander narrowed her eyes. "How late?"

"My first class isn't till 11."

"Why are you awake?"

Jackson smiled. "Because I wanted to surprise you with a little treat."

"Is this part of your dates?"

"I wanted to take you back to where everything changed."

Oleander tilted her head like she was thinking about it. "Oh, the coffee shop?"

"Yeah," he grinned. "I know we've been busy and rushed, so this seemed like a better idea."

Oleander smiled. "I can't believe you've been planning so many dates."

"Like I said, I really wanted to spend all my time with you."

"I love it," she whispered and took another sip. "I feel like I'm being wooed."

Jackson's eyes widened at the word. "Why didn't I think of it that way?"

She laughed and leaned her head against his chest. "I don't know why I decided to take this early morning class."

Jackson rubbed a hand down her back, his lips pressed to

the top of her head briefly. "Are you working with kids this early?"

"No, thank god," she laughed and nuzzled into his chest. "I have an older group that comes in on some weekends and early mornings on other days."

"That actually sounds fun."

Oleander straightened up, and took another sip of her drink. This time, she let out a tiny moan. "It's a great workout, but when I'm so sleepy, it's not fun."

"Did I keep you out too late?"

"Absolutely. This is totally your fault."

Jackson laughed and kissed Oleander's forehead, "Come on, let me give you a ride."

"You're sure you're not going to be late?"

"I promise, now get in." He opened the passenger side door and once Oleander was in, he walked around to the other side and slid in behind the wheel. Jackson turned on the car and handed his unlocked phone to Oleander. "Put in the address."

And for the next twenty minutes as he drove her to work, they talked about her dance classes, about working with different age groups and why she enjoyed it so much. Oleander gave him a lazy kiss when he dropped her off and Jackson drove back home, where he proceeded to fall asleep fully clothed till his alarm woke him up for his class at the dojo.

Even though he was tired, Jackson felt like it was worth it.

Because he got to spend his morning with the woman who was slowly working her way into his life. And his heart.

SIXTEEN
Jackson

For their next date, Jackson found a new bar that was close to both their places, and because he was planning on drinking, Jackson didn't take his car. He got them a cab and picked Oleander up on the way. It had been two weeks of these dates and he was loving every single minute. They saw each other regularly and when they weren't together, they were texting and once, they attempted to FaceTime, but between her schedule and his, it was impossible to talk for long enough to make it work. He didn't care as long as she kept giving him the chance to woo her.

From the minute Oleander used that word, Jackson realized that's exactly what he was doing. He was wooing her and he was going out of his way to prove to her that their relationship wasn't a passing thing and he wanted this.

"I can't believe I gave up my night at my *bar* job to go spend it in another bar."

Jackson rolled his eyes. "The difference is, someone else is serving you drinks."

"What are you doing checking out the competition?"

"Is it *really* competition?"

Oleander arched an eyebrow. "It's competition if it has your attention."

Jackson smirked as she nudged him, settling into his side in the cab as they made the 20 minute drive. Oleander had her hair pulled back in a tight bun and she was wearing a black dress that stopped at the knees. The neck was wide open, and showing off enough cleavage for him to be distracted. The sleeves were long and poofy and on her feet, she was wearing those same heels from a few nights ago. Her legs looked incredible.

Jackson had told her to dress up, because he wanted this to be a sit down, drink and eat kind of date. The kinds where you splurged on an expensive alcohol and ate finger food that cost more than you could afford. If she was going to dress up, so was he. He had on black trousers, a black shirt with the top two buttons open and a casual black blazer over it. When he picked her up, Oleander whistled before adding: "I'm gonna have the hottest date tonight."

Walking through the doors of Swirled Spoon, Jackson put his hand on Oleander's back and guided her towards a high table. He helped her into her chair as a waitress came over with the menu. Unlike the Barrel, this place was decked out to be fancy with all the dim lighting and expensive decor. Oleander looked around, taking in all the details, which gave Jackson time to admire her.

"This is a really fancy date."

He shrugged, "We've done the fun stuff and I figured it's time for the fancy stuff."

Oleander tilted her head. "You know I don't need any of this, right?"

"I know," he nodded. "That doesn't mean I still don't want to spoil you."

"So this is all part of your wooing plan?"

"Absolutely."

Oleander laughed and picked up a menu to peruse it.

Once she'd decided what she wanted, Jackson went to order it. As he stood at the bar, waiting for their drinks, he looked over at his date. When they first met, he never would have imagined being on a date with someone like Oleander. Because she was truly out of his league—she was so fucking beautiful, staring at her made his heart race and his trousers tighter.

With their drinks in hand, he returned and set her whiskey sour in front of her. Jackson sat down and raised his drink in a toast.

"To wooing."

Oleander laughed and clinked her glass against his before taking a sip. Her eyes popped open and Jackson chuckled as she stared at her drink and took another sip.

"Holy shit, this is *good*. Better than the ones I make."

"I've never had a whiskey sour before."

Oleander took another sip. "Next time, I'll make you one. But right now, I need to figure out what they've done to make it taste so good."

THE REST of the night went on like that. Oleander tried a few of their whiskey cocktails and joked about Killian finding out she was at another bar.

Then the DJ played music that made her groove. Oleander slid out of her chair and made her way onto the dance floor and Jackson sat there, hypnotized. When he was finally able to tear his eyes off of her, he realized he wasn't the only one captivated by the way Oleander was moving.

He should have known someone would try their luck. A tall, beefy guy from a table across the dance floor was moving towards Oleander, like an animal stalking its prey, and Jackson gritted his teeth as he watched this unfold. He knew that he should be staking his claim, but Oleander wouldn't appreciate it. Even as the thought crossed his mind, Oleander was looking at him, a sexy smirk tugging at her lips.

Jackson slid off his chair and moved towards her, his eyes drinking in the sight of this woman who was all curves and all *his*. He'd miscalculated the distance he had to cover, because before he was close enough, the beefy guy smirked at Jackson and grabbed Oleander at the same time—one arm sliding around her waist as he yanked her back against him. A second later Oleander shook out of the guy's grip and spinning around to face him. The sound of her hand hitting his face filled the bar as the music slowed down, rendering the guy speechless.

"Don't fucking touch a woman without her permission," she spat, anger and venom dripping from every word. The guy had the audacity to smirk, rubbing his cheek as he shrugged at her. The guy looked like he was going to reach for her again, so Jackson stepped around Oleander and he finally got the hint and backed away.

Jackson blew out a shaky breath and turned to face Oleander. He released the tension in his jaw as her arms slid around his waist, pulling him closer to her. Their lips brushed briefly as Jackson set his hands on her hips and pulling back so he could look at her.

"You're my knight in shining armor." He whispered.

Oleander laughed. "Well, I'm definitely no damsel in distress."

"I was mostly jealous that you might dance with him."

Shaking her head, Oleander cupped his face. "I'm here with *you*, therefore, I dance with you."

"I'm not a good dancer."

Oleander moved closer. "Sway with me and you'll be fine."

And Jackson did. His hands moved over her back, down to her ass and around to her hips as Oleander spun in his arms, her back to his chest, ass to his dick, and back to face him. He lost track of the number of songs they danced to, but eventually, she got tired and dragged them back to their table. And after countless drinks, Oleander wasn't entirely steady on her feet. But she seemed to be aware of her surroundings and the fact that she'd had too much to drink. A soft giggle escaped her lips as she smoothed a hand over the front of her dress.

"Maybe it's time to go home."

Jackson chuckled and patted his pockets for his wallet, but Oleander was faster and held out her card. He stared at it a moment and smiled, getting a wink in return.

"I'll go pay the bill and be right back, don't go anywhere."

She nodded, "I won't."

Once he'd paid with her card, Jackson walked out and helped her into the cab. They weren't too drunk, but they were definitely tipsy and Jackson knew that he would feel better if she was with him. He gave the cab driver his address and helped Oleander untie her hair, his fingers brushing through the soft strands as she nuzzled into his shoulder.

When they reached his apartment, they used each other for support out of the cab. He was really glad that his roommate, Carson, was gone for the weekend, because he had no idea what was going to happen.

Jackson let them into the apartment and Oleander leaned against the wall to kick off her heels. He sniffed the air and made a face at the smell of old garbage. Jackson opened a window, dug out one of Carson's Bath & Bodyworks candles from his secret stash and lit it. As Oleander looked around, Jackson took the trash out and came back in time to hear her squeal.

"You have a turtle!"

"Meet Raphael," Jackson said, coming up behind her. His pet turtle had been like an emotional support animal, except Raph did nothing but sit there and stare at him. "He's named after my favorite Ninja Turtle."

"Shut the front door!" Oleander turned to face him, her hands landing on his shoulders. "You're a Ninja Turtles fan?"

"Fan is an understatement."

She fanned herself. "You *are* perfect."

"What's going on here?" Jackson frowned, seeing wonder and awe in Oleander's eyes. Not a single woman had been excited about Raph before. Hell, even his friends thought Jackson was crazy to be obsessed about talking reptiles. Oleander was practically bouncing as her fingers curled around his biceps and Jackson couldn't help but smile at her excitement.

"Growing up, I would get all of my brothers' old toys and the most precious of the lot were the Turtles. One Halloween, I dressed up as April O'Neil and every year after that I went as a different Turtle."

Jackson's eyes widened, because there was absolutely no way that this woman standing in his apartment was saying those words. "You might be my perfect woman."

"How did we never talk about this?"

"I think you were too busy stuffing your face to ask the important questions."

"Hilarious," Oleander deadpanned and Jackson laughed. "Other than Raph, who is your favorite?"

"Master Splinter, of course. He was the coolest dad-slash-sensei. I sometimes imagined that *he* was the one teaching me karate, instead of my actual sensei."

"That is fucking adorable."

"When I was 18, I got this…" Jackson trailed off, shrugging out of his jacket and rolled up the sleeves of his shirt, going as high as he could to show her a bit of his tattoo. Oleander swayed slightly, with a dreamy look in her eyes and Jackson chuckled "It's the only tattoo I have, but it felt like the right thing to get done."

"I can't see it—your sexy forearms are distracting me."

Jackson pulled out his phone, found the picture and held it out to her. "There you go."

"Whoa, Jackson, this is beautiful. Did you draw this?"

"I drew this pretty early on—it's *my* rendition of Splinter. And when I finally found the courage, I went out and got it done." He'd been 16 when he first started sketching the tattoo. It was a basic rat at first, then he graduated into the details and put the *gi* on Master Splinter. He did lots of research and found the perfect way to draw it. By the time he turned 18, he had the tattoo done and perfected. His father had been so impressed that he'd gone with Jackson to get the tattoo.

"It's amazing. I always wanted to get a Turtles tattoo done, like one of their colored masks or something."

Jackson reached for Oleander's arm, rubbing his thumb over the watercolor and line drawing of a unicorn on her wrist. "I think the unicorn is pretty symbolic of who you are too."

"Damn straight it is. I'm fucking magical."

"Yes, you most certainly are," Jackson muttered and as Oleander reached for him, he did the same, tugging her into his arms.

OLEANDER'S HANDS were everywhere and Jackson carefully moved them through the apartment, trying not to let her bump into any of the furniture as he guided them down the hallway to his room. Pushing the door open, he backed them up against the bed before bending down to scoop her up in his arms—it was only a few seconds before he tossed her onto the mattress.

"Impressive," Oleander whispered, shifting onto her knees as Jackson stayed on his feet.

"Not tripping over anything or carrying you to bed?"

"Both." She brushed her fingers over his chest and down

the line of buttons as they faced each other. "I don't think I've ever been carried to bed before."

"I'll try to do that more often."

"As long as you don't break those arms doing so."

"Hey," he scolded her softly and Oleander started undoing the buttons on his shirt.

"What? You're a skinny guy."

"*Hey!*" Jackson protested, pushing his shirt off. "I am not skinny."

"*Oh.*" Oleander's mouth formed a perfect O, her eyes never leaving his chest. Jackson blushed, head to toe. He watched her reach out, brushing her fingers along his chest and down to his stomach where he had a *hint* of abs. Crunches were less fun than eating donuts and drinking shakes all day. Jackson wasn't weird looking or scrawny anymore, but he was definitely not fit and shapely like his friends.

The way Oleander was looking at him? It was enough.

He was awkwardly trying to curl in on himself—he was like a turtle in some situations. But Oleander wasn't done staring. She let her fingers trail down the smattering of hair on his stomach and Jackson shivered, watching her face as she gently tugged at his belt.

"Wait, wait," Jackson breathed, his hands circling Oleander's wrists to pull her hands away.

"What, why?"

"I feel like I'm going to blow my load even before I'm inside you."

"I'm really good at helping get it back up," Oleander said with a naughty smirk.

"*Oleander.*"

"Fuck, that should not be as hot as it is." She growled this time and Jackson stared at her in shock.

The first time he'd heard her growl, he'd been so caught off guard. The second time he'd been turned on. This time, he was already so unbearably hard he was almost bursting at the seams and he wanted to be better prepared before she made him come undone.

Jackson released her wrists and took a step back, putting space between them. Oleander didn't like that and moved to the edge of the bed, trying to close the gap. Jackson realized that it was pointless trying to run away from her. Oleander smiled and Jackson gave up the fight, taking a small step back towards the bed.

"It's been a while since I've…you know…"

"No, Jackson, I don't know. What?"

"Since I've been with someone. Since I've had sex. Since I've let someone else touch me."

Oleander nodded. "What do you think about when you touch yourself?"

"I don't want to talk about this."

"Why not? I mean, it's not like I'm *not* going to touch you, I just want to know."

Jackson closed the gap between them, his hands falling to her waist as she leaned into him, her chest pressed against his. He'd never told a woman that he got off to thoughts about her before. Jackson had used various muses to get off, but to actually talk about it and admit it to someone? That was a whole new feeling.

Jackson curled his fingers against her sides, bunching up her dress, watching it rise up over her thighs, his cock now straining against the front of his pants. By the way Oleander's eyes glazed over, he could tell that she felt it too. He was bolstered by that look in her eyes, the desire to be with him— it drove him to hold on and not let go.

Licking his lips, Jackson leaned in slightly and brushed his mouth over Oleander's as he whispered. "I think about you, Oleander. It's been you for weeks."

SEVENTEEN
Oleander

"*I think about you, Oleander. It's been you for weeks.*"

And just like that, any chance she had practicing self-control went out the window. He got off to thoughts of her. In some part of her mind, she understood it was completely shallow. But that was the thing she held onto. It was also sobering, to know this guy was so turned on by her he used her as inspiration to jack off whenever he could.

Ollie knew she was attractive, but this kind of desire, this kind of raw need for her was new and she felt breathless. Relationships didn't mean anything about your desirable factor—it was about feelings and emotions and connections. One minute he was blushing and hiding himself, and the next he was sliding her dress up, telling her she consumed his thoughts as he jerked off. Ollie liked that she was getting to see all the different sides of Jackson, because it was insanely hot.

If Jackson moved his hand a few inches inwards and between her legs, he'd feel how wet she was for him. Ollie was *dripping*. Sure, he wasn't muscular and ripped, but Jackson was fit. He had definition and those arms…good god, she'd been drawn to his forearms already, but with the Splinter tattoo and muscles, she was completely captivated. And now that he was shirtless, his arms flexing and tattoo staring back at her, Ollie felt like she could come just by staring at Jackson a little longer.

Clearing her throat, Ollie wet her lips and lifted her eyes to Jackson's as she spoke softly. "What am I doing in these thoughts?"

"Oleander, *please*..." his words made Ollie quiver, rubbing her thighs together.

"Jackson...it's been a while for me too." His eyes met hers and it was like he was checking to make sure she wasn't lying, so Ollie nodded, wanting him to know she was in the same boat.

"Like this, really. Except you're wearing a lot less."

Ollie slid her hands down his chest. "What about you, what are you wearing?"

Jackson blushed, looking down at himself as he mumbled, "A condom?"

"Okay," Ollie nodded and moved off the bed, watching as Jackson lifted his eyes to hers. She reached for the bottom of her dress and pulled it up over her head. She had on a sexy black lace bra and the most uncomfortable pair of Spanx. But Jackson didn't take his eyes off of her.

Bending over, she pushed the Spanx down her thighs, groaning and wiggling at the frustrating struggle. She hadn't expected them to end up in bed together, so Spanx wasn't a well thought out thing. After all the dancing, she'd definitely sweated enough to cause her Spanx to roll up at the bottom and stick to her in all the wrong places. Once she got it off, Ollie kicked it aside as she straightened up, hands on her hips.

Oh yeah, she was *definitely* glad she'd worn these lucky panties. Because Jackson's eyes widened as he looked at crotch. With anyone else, Ollie would have been a little nervous about how they'd react to her stomach curling over the waistband of her panties, but Jackson's gaze never made her feel like she was *disgusting*.

"Holy shit, are those…"

She nodded. "Ninja Turtle panties for every day of the week? Yes, they are."

"You're wearing the wrong day, though."

Ollie chuckled. "If you do it right, I won't be wearing anything at all today."

"You are truly the most perfect woman."

"I do all right," she said and gestured at his mostly clothed frame. "Now show me the rest of *your* perfect body."

Jackson blushed, muttering 'bossy' under his breath. Ollie watched, completely distracted by his broad shoulders and arms flexing as he undid his belt and zipper, pushing his pants off. Her tongue swept over her lips as she took in his torso, not too bulky, but perfectly muscular and followed his happy trail to where it vanished into his boxers.

"Oleander."

"Mhm, what?"

He sighed. "My eyes are up here."

"What eyes? I only see a happy trail."

Jackson laughed and it made her look at him, smiling at the blush spreading across his chest. "Do you plan on getting the rest of your things off?"

"In a minute, I'm watching something. Go on, don't stop."

"*Babe.*" Her eyes met his and Ollie shivered at the way he said the most random term of endearment coupled with the way he looked at her. She reached behind her and unhooked her bra, letting the straps slide down her arms and onto the floor. "*Welp.*"

Ollie huffed out a laugh, "Take your boxers off already."

"Bossy."

"Horny," she corrected him.

"Together."

"*Fine.*" Ollie was being dramatic, but she hooked her fingers into the waistband of her panties and nodded at Jackson. "On the count of one."

"One." And they both dropped their underwear at the same time.

Ollie whistled as she stared at Jackson. Without his boxers providing protection, Ollie was able to stare at his dick. She'd seen her fair share—some of them were ugly, some were okay and some were pretty damn gorgeous. Jackson? He had a great dick. It was long, thick and hard, twitching as she stared at it. Ollie licked her lips and lifted her eyes to Jackson's, watching him as he seemed to catalog all of her body too.

"That's a pretty great penis," Ollie said, making Jackson blush. She could see that he was dying to cover up, hands itching to move over his dick. Instead, his eyes met hers with a smile.

"You have a pretty great body."

"Thanks, I did it all myself."

"Yeah…shit, you don't do justice to what was in my head all this time."

"Come here," she whispered, loving the way his words washed over her. It was so simple and didn't mean anything other than what he intended for it to mean. Ollie climbed back into bed and held a hand out to him. "Let's try and outdo your imagination."

IT HAD BEEN a long time since she'd been naked with a man and as she climbed into bed, she started to get nervous. The last thing Ollie wanted was to have a panic attack, so she lay on her side, eyes following Jackson as he lay down beside her.

"Are you okay?"

She nodded, swallowing hard. "Yeah…*no*. There's something I should tell you."

Jackson propped himself up on his elbow and looked at her. Instinctively, she wanted to cover up for this conversation, but she forced herself to stay calm and breathe.

"I haven't been with a man in a *really* long time," she explained, fingers playing with the sheets. "Someone I was with a long time ago hurt me, physically. And now, I can't have a man on top of me."

"Fuck, Oleander, I'm sorry."

"I don't usually tell people about it, but since we're...you know..."

"I don't know, what are we?" Jackson threw her words back, smiling.

She narrowed her eyes. "Since we're naked and about to have sex, I figured you should know."

"Do you want to be on top?"

Chewing on her lip, Ollie nodded. "Yes"

"Have you ever been on top?"

"Maybe once?" she mumbled.

"Hey," he whispered, laying down and moving closer to her. "We can take as much time as you need, okay? Just tell me what is and isn't comfortable for you."

"Okay," she whispered, smiling as she moved closer to him.

Jackson returned the smile and brushed his fingers along her side, tracing her waist and hips. Ollie shivered at the touch as her back arched slightly, her nipples rubbing against his bare chest. It felt so normal and natural to be laying there naked with this man. She liked the way it felt to have Jackson's eyes and hands graze over her body. And before she could take another breath, their mouths were connecting. Ollie moaned into the kiss, her fingers sliding into his hair as she held him against her.

She liked that he was being careful with her, and when his hand slid over her ass, gently pulling her towards him, Ollie felt him hard and hot against her stomach. She shifted against him and Jackson moved his hand over her ass and down to her thigh, guiding a leg over his hip, lining them up so his dick rubbed against her, making Ollie gasp.

They broke the kiss and Ollie dropped a hand to Jackson's chest, smiling when she felt how fast his heart was beating. He moved his hand up to her back and they held onto each other lightly, like they were afraid what would happen if they let go.

Jackson muttered something about a condom and reached into his nightstand and pulled out a box, which proceeded to fall and scatter across the floor. Ollie laughed softly, feeling the worries in her chest ease as she watched him fumble around. Jackson had managed to grab one before the incident and he was blushing from head to toe all over again.

Ollie took the condom from Jackson as his mouth moved along her neck while hands cupped and teased her breasts. Quivering, she tore open the packet and managed to snag her nail on the condom, ripping it. The tear wasn't visible, and Ollie felt like maybe she was imagining it, but given how erratic she was with taking the pill she didn't want to take any chances.

"Um…"

"What happened?" Jackson pulled back to look at her and Ollie laughed, covering her face with one hand while holding the ripped condom with the other. "We might need another one."

"Good thing I have a whole box, huh?"

Jackson kissed her and Ollie moved at the same time he did, because she knew the condoms were all on her side of the bed. Because they were moving without any coordination, they tumbled, falling to the floor. Jackson groaned and she laughed at how ridiculous this whole evening was turning out to be.

"Are you okay?" Ollie asked, half on top of Jackson and half on the floor, her hip stinging from the fall. "Did I break your penis?"

"God no, but everything else hurts."

"I think we're cursed." Ollie shifted, curling into Jackson's side as she tilted her head to look at him.

"Maybe we're meant to take it slow."

"How much slower can we go?"

"*Really* slow," he mumbled.

Ollie smiled as Jackson cradled her head in his hand and leaned in to kiss her softly. Sighing against his mouth, Ollie wrapped one leg around his waist and sank into the kiss.

Jackson pulled back and mumbled. "Thank you, by the way."

"For not breaking your penis?"

"For going out with me." Jackson playfully tugged on her hair. "For letting me woo you these last few weeks."

"You're welcome," she whispered, tracing shapes on his chest with the tip of her finger. "These dates have really been some of the best I've been on. I can't remember the last time I had this much fun on every date."

"Me too."

She smiled, "I'm also impressed you got me naked and in your bed this fast."

"I thought you'd be a lot harder to crack given how much you made me work for everything."

Ollie poked him in the side. "I had to make sure you were worth it."

"And what's the verdict?"

"You'll do."

"Thanks," he deadpanned, fingers still playing with her hair.

It felt good, being with Jackson without having to fill the silence. Finally when she felt her hip go numb, Ollie groaned and sat up. "Can we get back into bed now?"

"Fuck. Yeah."

Ollie pushed herself to her feet and tugged on an abandoned t-shirt—it barely covered her ass and hugged all of her curves, so Ollie tugged her panties on and brushed her hands through her hair. "Where's the bathroom?"

"First door on the left."

Once in the bathroom, she refused to look at her reflection as she washed her hands after peeing. For as long as Ollie could remember, mirrors were not her best friend. She used them during dance classes, but when it came to looking at herself for anything other than getting ready, she avoided them. And now, with almost sex hair and a flush on her cheeks, Ollie didn't want to look at herself and jinx it. Ollie closed the bedroom door behind her and grinned at the sight of Jackson sitting up in his bed, shirtless, with his covers settled around his waist as he looked at his phone.

"What are you doing?"

Jackson tapped his phone, "Setting an alarm."

"What for? I don't plan on going anywhere tomorrow."

Jackson's eyes widened. "Really?"

"Yeah, I hope to pick up where we left off before I tore the condom and we collapsed on the floor."

"All right, alarm is off." Jackson tossed his phone onto the nightstand and sank into the bed. She climbed in and curled up beside him, fluffing a pillow and sinking into it with a happy sigh.

"You look really good in my t-shirt, by the way."

Ollie blinked up at Jackson sleepily and smoothed a hand over the t-shirt. "Thank you. I feel really good in it too."

"Good night, beautiful," Jackson mumbled, tugging her against him, his lips brushing over her forehead as Ollie yawned and closed her eyes.

EIGHTEEN
Jackson

He couldn't remember the last time he'd slept that well. The night started out with Oleander tucked into his side and at some point with her hand dangerously close to the waistband of his boxers. He startled awake early in the morning and shifted them so he could spoon her. In her sleep Oleander guided Jackson's hand under her shirt. With the warmth of her body and his thumb brushing against the underside of her breast, Jackson fell back asleep.

Despite not setting an alarm, his body woke him up like clockwork while Oleander snored and drooled into the pillow. He realized it was creepy to watch her sleep, but he'd cataloged every detail of her face. He'd never done this before, sleeping with someone *before* sex. If she hadn't ripped the condom and they hadn't fallen off the bed, would Oleander have left soon after sex?

His thoughts were also consumed by her confession. Someone in her past had hurt her really bad that it made her uncomfortable to be with a man. When she said the words haltingly, he'd been shocked. Oleander hadn't told him to gain sympathy—she told him so he'd be aware of what she was comfortable with. The last thing Jackson wanted was for Oleander to feel obligated to fuck him. Because he liked her enough to wait.

Startling when his phone vibrated, Jackson frowned. He picked it up and slid out of bed when he saw Mindy's name on his screen. Stepping out of the room, Jackson pulled the door closed and answered the phone. "Hey Mindy."

His stepmother sounded cheerful, as always. "Hey honey, I expected the voicemail to pick up."

"My body didn't get the memo that it's a weekend."

"Why are you whispering?"

"Sorry." Jackson cleared his throat before speaking. "What's up?"

"It's Keleigh's eighteenth birthday in a couple of weeks and I'm planning a party. She doesn't want it, I know, but my baby is turning eighteen!" Jackson chuckled at Mindy's dramatic sigh. "I was hoping you could drive up for the party. Also, don't bring her any gifts, she's doing this fundraising thing and she'd prefer contributions."

"Of course, Mindy, I'll be there. Wouldn't miss a chance to torture my baby sister."

Mindy's voice lifted at his confirmation. "Good! She'll be really happy to see you."

"I'm looking forward to it," Jackson assured her and asked about his older siblings. "Are Brandon and Lisbeth coming?"

"Beth and Carrie said they'd come with the kids. I don't think the boys will make it," Mindy explained, calling out Lisbeth's husband and Brandon for always being the antisocial ones. "But having you here will make up for it."

"I wouldn't miss it for anything."

"I know, sweetheart. I'll let you get back to bed, call me soon okay?"

"I will. Love you," Jackson told her, smiling when she returned the love and blew kisses into the phone before hanging up.

Blowing out a breath, Jackson watched Raph peek out of his shell and tuck himself back inside. His siblings didn't care for Mindy, but they did like Keleigh. His brother was always going to pick some 'work' related event over being with the family. At least his wife, Carrie, loved hanging out with the Huxley gang. Then there was Lisbeth. His sister was a character unto herself and sometimes he was confused how they were related when they were all so drastically different.

WHEN JACKSON CAME BACK into his bedroom, he couldn't help the snort that escaped him. Oleander was in the middle of the bed, with the covers kicked off. Her hair was wild and spread out over the pillow she had been drooling on moments ago. And the t-shirt was bunched up around her waist, leaving her Ninja Turtle panties exposed. She was still snoring, but Jackson couldn't help but smile at the sight. Lifting his phone, he took a picture and set it on his dresser. Climbing into bed, he let his eyes take in the rest of her body.

Oleander wasn't skinny, but Jackson didn't care about that. He might have dated skinny or thin girls before, but Oleander's curves and extra body fat didn't bother him. He'd never paid attention to a woman's body the way he looked at her. Her thighs were thick and soft, with dimples in her hips and her stomach was the same, with tiny rolls above the waistband of her panties. He'd definitely noticed that before, but when she was standing in front of him in just Turtle panties, he'd lost all focus on anything else.

But what he did notice and did love about Oleander's body were her *curves*. Jackson had traced them last night, but actually seeing them in the soft light of the morning was something special. The night before, Jackson had most certainly noticed the curve of her back where it met her ass and how her dress rode up slightly because of it. Then there were her full breasts—he couldn't wait to hold them in his hands again.

Smiling, he stretched a hand out and brushed it up her leg, moving up her knee and to her thigh. At his touch, she stirred and turned onto her side. It took Oleander a minute to realize Jackson was no longer beside her, because she turned onto her back and looked around.

When she finally focused on him, Jackson grinned. "Morning."

"Were you watching me sleep?"

"I was actually checking out your underwear."

Oleander gave him a lazy smile. "Hot, right?"

"The hottest," Jackson nodded as Oleander yawned, stretching her arms and legs.

"Why are you awake?"

"I got used to early mornings, so sleeping in is out of the question."

"Poor baby," Oleander pouted and sat up, "I'll spoon you back to sleep if you want."

Her hair was wild and Jackson loved how untamed it was. He'd seen it in so many different forms, but this was definitely a favorite. She stretched her arms out and pressed her hands on either side of his face.

Jackson laughed, pressing his mouth against one of her palms. "I think I got enough sleep."

"Well, since neither of us is going back to sleep…" She wiggled her eyebrows and moved closer to him, sliding into his lap. "Maybe we can stay awake together."

"I'd like that," he whispered as Oleander leaned in and kissed him, her body pressed flush against his. Jackson slid his hands up her bare thighs and around to her ass, tugging Oleander closer to him. And that slight shift and pressure made him harder, pulling a groan out of him. He felt Oleander smile against his mouth and Jackson held her tight as her tongue pushed past his lips to tangle with his.

He would never tire of kissing this woman; her mouth was devastating. As was the rest of her and Jackson knew once he'd been inside her, he'd never be the same again. Oleander's fingers slid through his hair and the minute his fingers dug into her ass, she started rocking against him. Groaning at the feel of her warm center pressing against his hard dick, Jackson shifted on the bed and stretched his legs out.

Oleander broke the kiss and leaned back slightly, aligning their hips perfectly that his eyes almost rolled back in his head. She smirked, clearly amused by his reaction, and whipped the t-shirt off, leaving her in just her infamous panties.

He'd never be able to watch a Ninja Turtles cartoon or movie the same way again. Jackson moved his hands from her ass to cup her breasts, eliciting a soft gasp from Oleander. With his eyes on hers, Jackson traced the curve of her breasts with his thumbs and bit his lip at how hard her nipples were. He finally tore his eyes away from her face to stare at her breasts. They filled his cupped hands, a lighter shade of brown than the rest of her body with dark nipples pebbled for him.

Oleander shifted her hips, rocking back and forth against his aching cock and Jackson growled. He needed to be inside her, but Jackson also wanted to drag this out and taste every inch of her. Dipping his head, he kissed her breasts. He cupped them and lifted them to take one breast into his mouth. Her fingers were back in his hair as he sucked and twirled his tongue around her nipple. While his tongue lavished one breast with attention, his fingers teased and tugged at the other. He could hear Oleander panting, and all of the sounds coming out of her made him throb. She obviously felt it, because she ground against him even harder, making him grunt around her breast.

Jackson seriously hoped he wouldn't come before he was inside her. When he moved his mouth to the other breast, Oleander's head fell back, the ends of her hair brushing against his thighs. She whimpered his name and Jackson opened his eyes to look up at her, gently biting her nipple at the dazed look on her face.

He slid his hands to grip her ass, guiding her as she rubbed against him. Even through the thin material of their underwear, he could feel her heat and it was intoxicating. Releasing her nipple, Jackson licked a trail up the valley between her breasts and kissed along her collarbone. He kissed her neck and shoulder as Oleander's fingers tugged on his hair, the movement of her hips getting more desperate.

Panting, Oleander opened her eyes to look at him, "More, Jackson, *more*."

"More what, babe?"

"More of your mouth. More of your hands. More of *you*."

Jackson prided himself on being good at foreplay, but he was *aching* to be inside her. Clearly Oleander felt the same way, because when he slid a hand into her hair and pulled her mouth back to his, she let out one of those delicious growls.

His tongue swept into her mouth, making them both moan. And as her hands wandered over his chest and down to his boxers, Jackson let his free hand skate down her spine, over the curve of her ass and into her panties. Oleander gasped into the kiss and he squeezed her ass as she wrapped her hand around him.

"Fuck, wait." He mumbled.

"No more waiting. *I want you.*" Oleander whined, gripping him tight in her hand.

"Go slow, or I'll explode right here." Jackson explained, his heart racing.

Oleander slid off his lap and Jackson frowned, reaching for her. But his fingers grazed her calves as she lay down and slid her panties off, tossing them over the side of the bed. Oleander watched him, a small smile on her face as she spread her legs, giving him a proper look at her pussy for the first time and Jackson swallowed.

She was pink and *dripping*, and Jackson was blown away

that *he'd* made her feel that way. As he stared, Oleander slid a hand between her legs and slowly touched herself. Jackson wrapped his hand around his cock and tugged gently, easing the ache as he watched her. Oleander pulled her hand away, wiggling her wet fingers at him.

"If you don't hurry up, I'll do it all on my own."

Jackson moved faster than he ever had in his life, jumping out of bed, pushing off his boxers and retrieving a condom from the floor. He tore it open, rolled it onto himself and looked up to find Oleander watching him with hooded eyes as she continued to touch herself. He wanted to be the one touching her, tasting her, dipping his fingers into her wet pussy.

"Stop." The word came out of him as a growly command.

Oleander arched an eyebrow at his tone, like she was challenging him, but she didn't stop. She slid two fingers in and her body arched, his eyes trailed down to where her fingers moved inside her.

"Make me."

Christ, this woman.

Jackson clenched his shoulders to stop himself from jumping onto her and climbed back into bed. Moving onto his knees between her thighs, he gently tugged at her hand and lifted it to his mouth. Licking his lips, he parted them and with his eyes on Oleander, slipped her fingers into his mouth and sucked.

The taste of her exploded on his tongue and Jackson had to fight back a growl as he focused on her. Oleander's eyes were wide and lips parted as she watched.

Releasing her hand, Jackson got some of his confidence back as he smirked. "Delicious."

NINETEEN
Oleander

Oh yeah, Jackson was intent on killing her. How did this man go from shy and awkward to a sexy stud teasing and tasting her? Had she simply assumed he was an awkward turtle, when he was actually an incredibly confident and sexy man? The thoughts circled her mind as Jackson licked her fingers and grinned.

Jackson watched her—his eyes seemed to drink in her curves, folds, and rolls, he didn't look disgusted. It was a new feeling, to have someone *want* to stare at her. Ollie had always been uncomfortable when it came to her stretch marks, stomach rolls and love handles. But Jackson touched and traced every inch of her, like he wanted to memorize her body. Ollie watched as he slid his hands along her legs, his eyes fixed on her pussy.

She nudged him with a foot. "Jackson?"

"Hmm?" His eyes lifted to hers, "Just processing this."

She laughed. "Usually what happens is you slide your penis inside my vagina and make me come."

"What happens before that?"

"Slide your fingers inside me if you'd like."

Jackson made a face. "What if I don't last?"

"Trust me, baby, you'll last."

"We're at the *baby* stage of the relationship, huh?"

"We won't be if you keep staring instead of putting your dick inside me," Ollie said, fighting back a smile.

His head jerked in a gentle nod and before he moved, Jackson paused. As if he just remembered what Ollie told him the night before.

She waited till he was sitting up, his legs stretched out, and then climbed into his lap. Ollie pressed her knees into the mattress, her hard nipples brushing against his chest as she wrapped her arms around his neck. Jackson's hands coasted over her sides to rest on her hips and she leaned in to brush her mouth against his gently, feeling his warm breath against her parted lips. Cupping the back of his head, she pulled his mouth to hers and their breaths mingled when their tongues moved together. Ollie felt Jackson's dick twitch between them, so she brushed a hand down his chest and gripped his condom encased cock. Jackson's hips jerked into her hand and she smiled into the kiss.

"Now," Jackson said in a playful tone, "I put my penis in your vagina and make you come."

Ollie laughed and gripped him harder, Jackson's laugh turned into a grunt as he dropped his forehead to her shoulder. His fingers curled into her hips and Ollie looked down between them before lifting her hips. Their eyes met and Jackson nodded, silently encouraging her to keep going. His hand covered hers on his dick and Ollie angled her hips to line them up. Biting down on her bottom lip, Ollie rocked allowing the tip of his dick to brush through her folds. She pulled her hand away and set them both on his shoulders, sliding down on Jackson's cock.

"*Fuck.*"

Ollie breathed out the word, tensing for a moment before she moved her hips slowly to take him deeper. She watched him, loving the fact that this was affecting him just as much.

With every shift of her hips, he slid deeper into her and Ollie's eyes fluttered shut. Jackson lifted his hips, thrusting up into her and the room echoed with their moans.

"Don't move," she muttered, clenching around him.

"Babe, *you* need to move."

Hearing the strain in his voice, Ollie looked at Jackson and started moving. Slow at first, their bodies adjusting to each other and when she tugged his mouth back to hers, his hands on her hips helped her move smoother. The kiss broke, his mouth wandered to her neck and shoulder as he guided her faster. Ollie cried out, clenching around him and she felt Jackson groan against her chest.

"Don't do that, Oleander."

Ollie muttered. "Do what?"

Even as she spoke, she was clenching around him again. Jackson moaned loudly, his fingers digging into her ass to move her hips faster. In this position, Ollie was in control. Her nails dragged up his back and into his hair, scratching against his scalp as their lips reconnected. She rocked against him faster, moving her hips in messy figure eights—every single shift of her hips making Jackson moan under his breath.

Jackson buried his face in the crook of her neck and Ollie continued to ride him, getting lost in the haze of Jackson filling her up. Pressure against her clit made Ollie's hips jerk and she looked down between their bodies to watch as Jackson rubbed her. He pulled back to look at her and the desire in his eyes made her clench around him again.

A strained moan came out of Jackson. "Let go, Oleander."

Their mouths connected in a messy kiss—tongues, teeth bumping—as Oleander did what she was told and came, her orgasm shaking her entire body. Seconds later Jackson came as well, his hips thrusting up into her as their arms tightened around each other.

Ollie leaned into Jackson, her breathing ragged and

pressed her lips against his shoulder. Jackson's chest was rising and falling out of sync with hers, their hearts beat at the same rhythm. After a long moment, Ollie slid off Jackson and collapsed backwards on the bed in a satisfied heap. Jackson collapsed face first beside her and Ollie laughed. "That's definitely a good way to wake up,"

"So that was good for you too."

"It was pretty great," she admitted. "I've never been on top with a guy before; I have messed around with my vibrator in this position, but with you…it feels different."

Ollie smiled, brushing her hair out of her face. Every other time she'd been with a man, she'd panicked. With Jackson, the panic had set in early, but she'd also been open with him. So this morning's adventure wasn't stressful. It had been, as she told him, *pretty great.*

"Maybe next time you can show me how you use your vibrator."

Ollie grinned, thinking back on the night when she gave herself multiple orgasms because her brain was filled with Jackson. Now that she'd had the real thing, would her vibrator still do the trick?

"It depends on how I feel about you next time."

"Ouch."

Ollie sat up with a laugh, smoothing her hair back and swung her legs over the side of the bed. Jackson reached for her, his fingers curling into her thigh.

"Where are you going?"

"I need to wash up."

Jackson nodded, stretching and turning onto his back. "Hurry back."

Ollie tugged on the t-shirt she'd worn earlier, watching as Jackson peeled off the condom. Biting her lip, Ollie took one more full look at his body and rushed to the bathroom.

She peed, washed herself and as she cleaned her hands, Ollie looked at her reflection—she was flushed and looked well fucked. When was the last time she looked this happy about sex? Ollie might have been hesitant about Jackson at first, but he'd found a way to wear her down.

She ran her damp fingers through her tangled mane and straightened it out the best she could. She felt fucking beautiful. Since Pierce, she hadn't felt that way around a man. Men made her nervous when she was naked. Jackson looked at her like she was the only woman in the world and Ollie basked in it.

It might have been almost 10 years since Pierce walked out of her life, but the scars were still there. And sometimes they felt *real*. Jackson had been so gentle and she'd also connected with Jackson outside of the bedroom. They'd touched, teased and tortured each other for weeks before giving each other what they really wanted.

There was also the fact he made her come through penetration.

Outside of her vibrator and her own fingers, Ollie rarely came during penetrative sex. Men sometimes didn't even care if you were wet or lubricated enough, they pushed into you and took what they wanted. And she'd hooked up with a few of *their kind*, only to end up in hotel bathrooms or bathrooms in their apartments washing off the disgust while she breathed through another panic attack.

It was why Ollie stopped hooking up with men at the bar and settled for women. Although, women were also sometimes pretty ridiculous with their demands and expectations.

Ollie had put too much stock into sex, so when she first slept with a man, it didn't measure up. Pierce tried, there was no doubt, but Ollie orgasmed maybe once in every three times they had sex. And worse, he didn't even know she was faking it.

With Jackson, the orgasm was real. The fact that feelings and a connection were present made it much more special. She hadn't lied to Jackson, she felt great. One orgasm was sometimes all it took to unravel everything knotted up inside of you. A sense of relief coupled with the fact that she'd been with a man without needing a paper bag after made it special. Something told her Jackson would make her come every single time he was inside her and *that* was what she had to look forward to.

OLLIE OPENED THE BATHROOM DOOR, smiling to herself but at the sight of an unfamiliar face staring at her, she yelped loudly. The guy in front of her jumped backwards when Jackson rushed out of his room, buck naked. When he realized they had company, he quickly dropped his hands to cover his dick and Ollie swallowed back a laugh.

"What the fuck, Carson?"

Carson had his hand over his eyes, gesturing around the apartment with his other hand. "Dude, I *live* here."

"You're not supposed to be *here*." Jackson huffed and Ollie looked between them.

"Well…plans changed. I didn't know you had company, or I'd have texted," he said and smiled at her. "I'm Carson. You're the hot bartender from the Barrel."

"And you were leaving?" Jackson spoke, his tone all rough and pointed.

Carson shrugged. "Sure, I can be leaving. Any idea when I can come back?"

"I'll text you."

"Right, okay, nice to meet you, bartender from the Barrel. *Jackson*." He said his friend's name with a touch of something and walked out the front door mumbling under his breath.

Jackson sighed, stepping past her into the bathroom. "I'm glad you put that on."

Ollie looked at the t-shirt that barely covered her. "I'm not sure it protected me from anything."

"What was that sound?"

"Reflex?"

Jackson chuckled, lifting up the toilet seat to take a leak and Ollie let her eyes drag over his body. Jackson might have been a lanky guy, but his thighs and calves had muscles that clenched. She bit her lip, her eyes drinking him in properly before lifting to his face to find her watching him.

"Are you done checking me out?"

"Not even close. This is the first time I'm getting to stare at you."

Jackson smirked, turning in a slow circle. "Is there a particular angle you like?"

Ollie smiled, shaking her head at how silly he was being. Jackson winked and moved to wash his hands at the sink. She stepped up behind him and gave his ass a squeeze. "This is a good angle."

"I knew you were an ass person." Jackson laughed.

Ollie pressed herself against his back, kissing between his shoulder blades. "I think I'm a *Jackson* person."

Jackson looked over his shoulder at her. "Really?"

"You don't believe me?"

"I do," he nodded. "It's still so strange to have you saying that while wearing just *my* t-shirt."

"If you're lucky, I'll do more than *say* things."

Jackson chuckled and Ollie grabbed his ass again, before walking back to his bedroom. Her stomach rumbled loudly as Jackson walked in, still gloriously naked, and closed the door.

"What was that?"

"I get really hungry after sex," Ollie told him, turning to sit on the edge of the bed.

"How do you feel about pancakes?"

Her eyes widened. "Oh my god, do you cook?"

"If you're okay eating them undercooked or burnt."

"You *almost* went up a few notches."

Jackson laughed. "There's a diner down the street. Or I can run down and get us some food while you stay like this."

Ollie smirked as Jackson ran his eyes over her. "We can always go and come back. I have nowhere to be until this evening."

"Back at the Barrel tonight?"

"Another late shift, but it'll be worth it after today." Ollie nodded, picking her dress off the floor. She swapped the t-shirt for her dress before picking up her panties and making a face.

Jackson cleared his throat, gesturing to his hamper. "We can put in a load when we come back."

Ollie tossed her panties into the hamper and slipped on her pumps. Her eyes followed him as he pulled on jeans and a t-shirt, sitting down beside her to pull on his own sneakers. Once they were dressed, Ollie used his mouthwash while Jackson brushed his teeth and they set out for breakfast.

All with the promise of returning to his apartment and climbing back into bed together.

TWENTY
Jackson

The whole time they were out of his apartment, Jackson could only think of one thing—Oleander wasn't wearing panties. Her cleavage was also distracting him, but she wasn't wearing *panties*. And the knowledge distracted him from everything. She kept talking, but now that he'd seen her completely naked and he'd *tasted* her, he couldn't focus.

At some point, they'd finished their meal and Jackson realized he'd probably nodded along and smiled at all the right moments. It wasn't that he wasn't interested—his brain was unable to focus on everything at once. All he wanted to do was take Oleander back home and strip her naked again.

"You know," her voice interrupted his thoughts as he unlocked his front door, "you've been checked out all morning."

"Have I?"

Oleander stepped inside and toed off her pumps. "Do you know what I was talking about?"

"Sure, uh…it was…" Jackson trailed off and dropped his head, chin to his chest as he chuckled. "No, I do not."

"Well, at least you're honest. Because for a while there I

was talking about bondage. You kept nodding and agreeing, so I figured you might be interested."

"I've never tried it," Jackson said. "Totally not the point."

"What's going on?" Oleander frowned.

"It's going to sound really silly when I tell you…"

She crossed her arms over her chest, pushing her boobs up and Jackson bit back a groan. "Try me."

"Halfway to the diner I realized you weren't wearing panties and it's been on my mind the whole time."

Oleander grinned, keeping her eyes on him as she took a small step closer. "What have you been thinking about?"

He let out a shaky breath. "What it would be like to climb under the table and press my mouth between your thighs."

"You want to go down on me."

Jackson nodded. "It would be my honor."

"Okay," she whispered, her hands sliding up his chest, over his shoulders and around his neck. Jackson watched Oleander, his eyes searching hers. But instead of saying anything, she pulled his mouth to hers and Jackson relented.

The kiss was soft and slow, their lips fitting together perfectly before her tongue swept over his, encouraging him to part his lips. Jackson moved his hands down to Oleander's waist and tugged her closer to him, erasing any gap between their bodies. Moaning softly into the kiss as her tongue slid past his lips and over his, Jackson's hands slid down to Oleander's ass and gave it a squeeze. She growled against his mouth and Jackson chuckled, pulling away to look at her.

"We should take this back to the bedroom."

Oleander nodded, extracting herself from his arms. "You should probably let Carson come back."

"Are you sure you can stay quiet?"

"I wasn't that loud!" She poked him.

Jackson smirked. "But we haven't really done a lot of the good stuff yet."

"Promises, promises." Oleander mumbled, leaving him in

the hallway. Jackson pulled out his phone to let Carson know he should come home.

Carson: *If you're still going to be sexing up the hot bartender, I don't want any part of it.*

Jackson: *She's still here, but I feel bad that I kicked you out.*

Carson: *She guilted you into calling me back, didn't she?*

Jackson tilted his head back and took a deep breath. Because *of course* Oleander made him feel guilty about sending his housemate out earlier.

Jackson: *Just come back home, asshole. We'll be in my room.*

Carson: *Don't get too loud, I don't need you rubbing your joy in my face.*

Jackson silenced his phone and walked into the bedroom where he found Oleander sitting in the middle of the bed, typing away furiously on her phone.

"Whatcha doing?"

"Letting Frankie know I'm about to have a man voluntarily go down on me."

Jackson's eyes widened. "What?"

"I'm kidding!" Oleander laughed, leaning over to put her phone on the nightstand. "Just letting her know I'm okay."

"Was she worried I kidnapped you?"

"Absolutely."

"Seriously?"

Oleander rolled her eyes. "Like I said, it's been a while since I've been out with a guy and we do this thing where we check in on each other during dates, to make sure everything's okay."

"You guys are really close, huh?"

"Best friends, but also sisters."

Jackson rounded to his side of the bed. "That's pretty cool. Milo and Gav are basically family too."

"I'm glad. Everyone needs friends that are family."

Jackson unloaded his pockets and turned to find Oleander smiling at him. "What?"

"I can tell you're nervous."

"I'm not nervous." He said as he sat down.

Oleander leaned against his back, her chin on his shoulder. "You are and it's okay."

"I'm...it's not nerves, it's something else. Something I can't entirely identify."

"Is it bad?"

Jackson shook his head and adjusted himself so he was facing her. "No, not bad. I like this...you and me. I like that you trust me to be with you."

"I've spent so much of my life being afraid of *this*; that's why I was hesitant at first. But now that I've spent so much time with you, seen you naked and shown you my Ninja Turtle panties—" Oleander paused and they both laughed, "— I do trust you. I even trust myself with you, which is a bigger deal."

"Thank you."

"You're amazing, Jackson."

They stared at one another, hands moving to link their fingers, the corners of their mouths tipping upwards into small smiles—and Jackson *felt* it. This woman was going to do more than change his life and he was looking forward to it. He always fell too hard too fast and he knew it would happen with Oleander as well, but he didn't care.

As long as he didn't say the words too early.

"Should we take our clothes off?"

Jackson blinked at Oleander's question and nodded. "That's a good place to start."

They moved apart as Jackson stood up, tugging off his t-shirt and pushing off his jeans before turning to find Oleander kneeling in the middle of the bed completely naked. *Fuck*. Of course she'd stripped off her dress and bra in record time. Their eyes met once he'd gotten another good look at her body and Jackson smiled as Oleander lay back, her dark hair spread out across his pillow.

Oleander didn't speak—she watched him, her legs spreading open slowly as Jackson climbed into bed. He couldn't take his eyes off of her.

"May I?" Jackson asked, his voice soft.

"May you…what?"

"Move over you?"

Oleander smiled, licking her lips as she lifted herself onto her elbows. "I thought you were going to do something else?"

"Eventually," he whispered, hands moving up her legs and thighs, curving over her hips as he moved closer. Oleander's breath hitched and Jackson lifted his eyes to make sure she was okay. A soft nod was all he got in response. He was still wearing his boxers and the realization only hit him as he moved over her fully, hands pressed into the mattress on either side of her. Their hips lined up and Oleander rocked up against him. Jackson groaned and dropped his head to her chest.

"I'm sorry." She whispered.

"No, you're not."

Oleander laughed. "I'm *kinda* sorry."

And before he could say anything else, she pushed her fingers into his hair. Jackson had always liked having his hair played with, and when he was stressed or nervous, he made a mess of his hair too. It was comforting. And Oleander was doing it without knowing the effect it would have on him. A shiver raced up his spine at the way her short nails scraped against his scalp and Jackson moaned.

"Your fingers in my hair might be my new favorite thing."

"Oh yeah?" Oleander smirked, brushing the tips of her fingers over his scalp and Jackson quivered, his hips pressing against hers.

Instead of speaking, he grazed her mouth with his and kissed along her jaw before moving to her neck. Oleander continued to play with his hair as his lips reached her breasts.

His elbows settled on either side, pressing into the mattress as he twirled his tongue around her nipples, sucking them into his mouth. He took his time, smiling when Oleander started squirming, her fingers in his hair getting rough with the tugs and pulls.

Jackson took his time kissing along her stomach, making Oleander giggle—he stored the knowledge that she was ticklish away—and spread her thighs apart as he settled between them on his stomach. His eyes met hers as he kissed his way down her mound and Oleander let out a breathy sigh.

"You okay, up there?"

She huffed. "I'm very impatient and you're testing me."

"I want to make sure you enjoy everything."

"I *am* enjoying everything, but I want everything else too." Oleander all but whined.

"What constitutes *everything else*?"

"Oh my god, Jackson, if you don't put that mouth to better use, I will take care of myself." Oleander glared and Jackson laughed. The crazy part was, he knew she'd push him away and do it herself. So, Jackson gave Oleander what she wanted.

Keeping his eyes on her, Jackson stroked his fingers through her folds and curled them to rub her with his knuckle. She quivered and he smiled, continuing to rub her with his knuckle until she glared at him again. Jackson looped his free hand around her thigh, guiding her leg over his shoulder. And before she could protest again, he replaced his hand with his mouth.

Oleander's hips pushed against his mouth and Jackson used both hands to steady her. He pressed her down against the bed as his tongue moved through her folds. He took his time tasting, sucking, twirling and he felt her body rise and shake, wanting more.

He lifted his eyes to watch Oleander's hands grip at the pillow, sheets and even her breasts, but never once his hair. Jackson reached up and tugged on her arm, silently begging her to grab at his hair. Using his other hand, he parted her folds and dipped his tongue inside her. Without his hands holding her down, Oleander arched off the bed, a loud moan echoing through the room.

Jackson smiled and slipped two fingers into her. Oleander cried out loud and grabbed at his hair. Growling, Jackson turned his head to rest against her thigh, watching as his fingers slid in and out of her. Jackson curled his fingers inside her and with his free hand he rubbed her clit. Despite her promise to be quiet, Oleander got louder with every stroke of his fingers. And before she could come down from that, he sucked her clit into his mouth.

And that was all it took.

Oleander bowed off the bed, her pussy clenching around his fingers as she hit her release. Her fingers in his hair tugged hard, but Jackson ignored the pain as Oleander rode out her orgasm, her legs going limp.

Pulling his fingers out, Jackson stayed where he was, head resting against her thigh as he licked them clean, completely intoxicated by the taste and scent of her. He kissed along her inner thighs, up her body and moved to lay beside her, smiling at the look of pure ecstasy on her face.

"You didn't tell me you were good with your mouth."

Jackson smirked. "I like to think I'm a good kisser."

"There's a good kisser and a good *kisser*. You do both pretty well."

"It's a superpower and I keep it a secret."

"You should definitely not share it with anyone else. *Ever.*"

"It's all yours, babe."

"Good," Oleander said with a satisfied smile and turned onto her side to look at him. "But, seriously, *you* were incredible."

Jackson blushed. "Thanks, I guess."

"And I'm gonna need more."

"Like I said, all yours," Jackson promised, laughing as

Oleander pressed against him, her mouth capturing his in a hot kiss that lasted forever.

Screw breathing, he'd live off of the taste of Oleander and her kisses alone.

TWENTY-ONE
Jackson

It had been almost a week since their weekend of sex and outside of a few texts, Jackson and Oleander hadn't seen each other. The first round of sex had been phenomenal and so had everything that followed. After he went down on her post-breakfast, they'd spent the rest of the day in bed. Jackson discovered Oleander was *very* ticklish and her laughter got really high-pitched when she couldn't stop herself.

It was an amazing feeling, seeing her completely unraveled that way. To watch this woman, who was always so tough and so stoic in public, let go and have fun was incredible.

He'd also discovered that kissing her was his favorite thing in the world. There was something about the way her mouth and tongue danced with his that did it for him. Plus, when she kissed him, Oleander always found a way to play with his hair. Until her, Jackson had never been impacted by hair play during sex. With Oleander, he was obsessed with the way her fingers felt against his scalp and tugging on his hair.

When Oleander left his apartment Sunday evening for work, she'd done so with promises to plan another date. But when she didn't bring it up during their texting, he wondered if she forgot. He didn't have time to go down to the Barrel either, because another project had landed on his plate. It wasn't an urgent one, but the first few days with strategy meetings and discussions, he knew it would be impossible to leave work before 9PM. And when he did wrap up, he went home and fell face first into bed.

The first night without Oleander, Jackson had fallen asleep with the scent of her filling his nose. But it also reminded him how dirty the sheets probably were, so he tossed them in the laundry before leaving for work. His sheets didn't smell like her anymore, but his head was full of deliciously distracting visuals.

Jackson also wondered if he'd come on too strong. His random confessions, the way he watched her...maybe it was too much for Oleander. There was also the possibility she was busy—Jackson knew she spent hours teaching dance even during the week and hours working at the Barrel.

JACKSON WAS in the middle of sketching out a logo in his notebook when his phone buzzed. The page he was working on had a million different iterations of the same thing and he was still unhappy about it, but at least he was starting to see the differences. Lifting his head from the page, he glanced at his phone and smiled at the text.

Oleander: *You miss me.*

Chuckling, he set his pencil down and leaned back in his chair as he opened up their chat.

Jackson: *Is that what this feeling is?*

He put his phone down and stood up to stretch his arms above his head, twisting his body to loosen his tight muscles. His phone buzzed and Jackson smiled at her reply.

Oleander: *Does your heart race really fast? Do you feel breathless when you think of me? Are you smiling so wide your face probably hurts?*

Oleander: *Then yes, you fucking miss me.*

Jackson picked up his phone and leaned against his desk as he replied, ready to give up this monotonous work of creating a logo.

Jackson: *You've got me all figured out. My cheeks hurt so much right now.*

Oleander: *I knew it. I mean, I would miss me too.*

Jackson: *I think my bed misses you too.*

Oleander: *Oh, now you're playing dirty.*

Jackson: *If we were in bed together, we most definitely would be...*

Rolling his eyes at his cheesy response, Jackson covered his mouth with one hand to hide his smile. This woman had him in knots. She also had him spending an insane amount of time on his phone.

Oleander: *I could make that happen...*

Oleander: *What are you doing in...an hour?*

Jackson: *Should my answer be YOU?*

Oleander: *Can that be your answer, truly?*

Jackson: *I honestly would love nothing more than to be with you right now, but...*

Jackson sighed heavily and looked at the time on the top of his phone before glancing around the office. He could take a 'lunch' break and nobody would miss him. Jackson had been showing up early every single day and leaving late too. His phone buzzed again and he realized he hadn't completed his message before hitting send.

Oleander: *...but what, Jackson? The anticipation is killing me!*

Jackson: *Sorry, I'm at work. And I'm trying to figure out the best way to get out of here.*

Oleander: *Well, you're not going to be able to get me naked if you get out of there anyway.*

Jackson: *I thought this was a booty call.*

Oleander: *I'm getting ready for an afternoon with toddlers in tutus.*

Jackson frowned and realized she'd probably taken on more classes before her shift at the Barrel.

Jackson: *I can spend time with you without getting you naked, even if that is all I want to do.*

Oleander: *I can call in sick at the Barrel tonight.*

His heart stalled and Jackson smiled. Oleander was willing to give up one of her shifts at the bar to spend the evening with him. How could he refuse that offer?

Jackson: *How about I come to your toddlers in tutus session and take you for an early dinner?*

Oleander: *I actually wanted to take you somewhere, but naked time after?*

Jackson: *Most definitely, my lady.*

Oleander: *Oooh, are we going to role play?*

Jackson snorted, but the image of Oleander dressed up like a bar wench was seared in his brain. Especially if she wore one of those dresses that pushed her boobs up.

Jackson: *I could be open to it.*

Oleander: *I know a place we can get costumes.*

Jackson: *I'm on my way.*

Jackson packed up his things, making sure to let Carson know he wasn't going to be home that evening. He stuffed his laptop into his bag, fully prepared to take on some more work later—it had happened too many times in the past. Thankfully, this project wasn't due till the end of next week, so he had enough time.

He wasn't going to lie, from the minute Oleander told him she taught dance, all Jackson was thinking about was watching her dance again. He didn't know the first thing about dancing, and she might have told him to just *sway* on their last date, but he had seen enough videos to know dancing was all in the hips and the confidence. Basically everything he did not possess.

When he pulled up in front of Tiny Dancers, Jackson noticed that Oleander's car wasn't there, which meant she had hopefully planned for his visit. He grabbed his phone and wallet, and walked into the studio only to be greeted by a whole group of women bent over their phones. But the minute the door slammed shut behind him, all those women were looking at him. A brunette behind the desk with the name of the studio printed across the front in the ugliest font arched an eyebrow at him.

"Hi, can I help you?"

"I..uh...I'm looking for Oleander?"

"You are?"

"Jackson."

"Are you a parent or a student?"

"I'm here to pick her up."

The brunette huffed and stepped out from behind the desk, waving him over. "Come with me."

Jackson followed, glancing over his shoulder at the women in the waiting area and found them all back on their phones. The brunette opened a thick door and the sounds of giggling girls and all the pink in the world accosted him. "Scream if you want to be rescued."

"Thanks?"

She rolled her eyes and walked away, leaving Jackson standing there absolutely clueless. It was a pretty large studio space, with mirrors along one wall and wooden bars attached from one end to the other. In the middle, a group of little girls in different shades of pink and purple were gathered around. Some had tutus on, others were wearing leotards, but they were all looking absolutely excited about something in the huddle.

Oleander popped up from the middle of it all and he chuckled as he looked her over. Of course she was wearing a tutu, but she was also wearing one of his t-shirts—*Pew Pew Pew* was written across the front in the standard *Star Wars* font. Her hair was up in a messy bun and she had no makeup on. As she stepped out from the circle of girls, he let his eyes trail down her body, drinking in her legs wrapped in dark lycra.

Jackson bit back the dirty words on the tip of his tongue

and smiled. "Nice tutu."

Oleander smoothed a hand over the misbehaving frills. "Thank you, kind sir. This is *just* for you."

"I appreciate it, my lady."

"Excuse me." A tiny voice interrupted them and Jackson looked past Oleander to find a little blonde girl with her hands on her hips glaring at them. "Are we going to dance or flirt?"

Oleander snorted and turned to look at the little girl. "Where did you get *that* attitude?"

The little girl rolled her eyes and thrust a hip out. "Miss Bowen, we want to dance."

"All right, Claire, no need to get sassy."

"Who are you, mister?"

Jackson stepped forward, but Oleander held a hand. "Claire, be nice."

"I just asked him who he is."

"I'm Jackson," he offered, as Claire looked him over. "Would it be okay if I stayed for today's class?"

Claire seemed to think about it, shrugged and turned back to her friends. Jackson and Oleander let out sighs of relief and looked at each other.

"Thank you," she whispered with a grin that made Jackson's heart race.

"Where do you want me?"

Oleander's eyes darkened and Jackson swallowed back a groan at his own question. She gestured to one of the chairs against the mirror and waved him off. It would be incredibly inappropriate to get hard in a dance class full of little girls, so Jackson thought of everything and anything that was not Oleander.

She clapped twice and the girls got into formation, looking to her for further guidance. Jackson smiled in complete awe at how easily she did her job.

"Let's start from the beginning. Does everyone remember what they need to do?"

A chorus of 'Yes Miss Bowen' went up and Jackson grinned at how enthusiastic these little girls were. The music started and they started moving—not a single one in the same direction, beat or rhythm. Some of them even sang along to the song, doing their own thing.

Jackson watched in amusement as Oleander weaved through kids to correct a few. Her focus never wavered, always making sure they were on the right track. When the song ended, she moved to the front of the class and repeated instructions before hitting play again.

For the next hour, Oleander guided the kids through two different dance routines and Jackson watched in complete fascination as she finally wrangled them all to follow the beat. By the end of the session, they were more or less in sync. When Oleander congratulated them, the group broke into shrieks and squeals, and Jackson plugged his ears because it was way too loud in an enclosed space.

But more importantly, he'd watched Oleander dance. At the bar, under the influence of alcohol, Oleander moved differently. But it had been sensual and distracting. Now, when she moved, she floated, her hips moving as her arms and shoulders did, her legs barely touching the ground as she performed complicated routines—well, they looked complicated to *him*.

Watching her, his heart was beating so fast, Jackson was sure it was echoing in the room.

"Bye Miss Bowen! Bye Miss Bowen's boyfriend!"

Jackson snapped out of his thoughts as Claire waved at him on her way out of the studio. He chuckled softly, watching as Oleander held the door open. Once all the kids were gone and Oleander had closed the door, Jackson got to his feet.

"That...was *insane*. How do you do this every single day?"

"I'm on autopilot most of the time, but these kids are so stinking cute, I love teaching them."

"I can't believe you taught them all of that in one class."

Oleander laughed as she reached around her back and her tutu fell to the floor. Now he could see her bottom half fully—the wide flare of her hips, her thick thighs and the way it tapered down to her feet. He had memorized every dip and dimple, and even encased in leggings, he could point them out.

"This is their tenth class and they *just* got it. It's a long road." She said with a sigh, bringing his attention back to her face.

"But still, they listened to you and did what they were told. That many giggling girls following orders is so rare."

"I should be offended, but it's very true." Oleander laughed. "But, today was a good day."

While Oleander gathered her things, Jackson watched. He moved to help and she frowned. Then dropped her things in his open arms.

"I'm only letting you do this while I change."

He smirked. "Okay."

"I'll meet you outside."

"And here I thought you'd invite me into the locker rooms."

"I hope those thoughts will keep you going till I'm ready." Oleander grinned, patted his ass as she walked out of the studio. "I'll meet you out front in 15."

Jackson carried Oleander's things and put them in the back of his car. He leaned against the side and scrolled through his messages as he waited for her. There was a text from Mindy, reminding him about the party and not to buy a gift. A group chat with his siblings had them bitching and moaning about Keleigh's party and Jackson sighed as he ignored their messages. Jackson set a calendar reminder and looked up as the door opened to reveal Oleander.

Today, she was dressed in cut-offs that were frayed at the edges, a faded blue band tee and classic Vans. Her hair was open and ruffled, unlike how it was during dance class, and she had a gorgeous glow. Jackson looked at his clothes—pressed chinos and full-sleeved shirt, rolled up to his elbows—and sighed. "I feel very overdressed."

Oleander smiled. "I like this look on you."

"It's called office chic," Jackson said, blushing at her compliment. "Where are we going?"

"Somewhere special."

"Did I tell you that I'm not a big fan of surprises?"

"Whaaaaaat?" Oleander gasped as she tossed the rest of her things in the backseat before climbing into the passenger seat. "How can you not like surprises?"

"They sometimes go wrong and make me really uncomfortable."

"It's not *that* kind of surprise, though."

"I'll take your word for it." Jackson buckled himself in and leaned across the console, smiling when Oleander met him halfway for a quick kiss. Like they'd done this a million times before.

It felt natural. And fucking great.

TWENTY-TWO
Oleander

To most people, this wouldn't be considered as a surprise, but she knew Jackson would appreciate it. It was a 30 minute drive to Wilmington, which was why Ollie had asked him to meet her during lunch. They'd get there with time to get food and see Niles.

Since she left Jackson's apartment on Sunday, Ollie had been texting Niles to ask where he'd be since the food truck festival was over. He told her they would be in Wilmington for a few days before the weekend took him somewhere else. So after Jackson agreed to spend the day with her, Ollie texted Niles to let him know they were coming.

"You could have said we're going to Wilmington."

"You would have asked me what's in Wilmington."

"And you could have deflected," Jackson chuckled and stretched a hand out to rest it on her thigh, his fingers brushing against her skin.

It really felt natural. Like spending all of Sunday with him despite how nervous she was at first. And now in his car, Ollie was half turned towards him, staring at Jackson as he drove. His shirt sleeves were rolled up to his elbows and Ollie found the dusting of hair on his arms and the muscles so distracting.

He'd chosen to play some classic rock station, but she wasn't listening to the music. She was focused on the beating of her heart and the warmth of Jackson's hand on her thigh.

Putting her hand over his, Ollie reminded herself that this could be good. Eventually, she'd have to tell Jackson the truth about Pierce. So he'd understand what it was about sex with men that made her so nervous. Jackson had been so good, listening and asking questions, doing things to make her comfortable as opposed to what *he* wanted.

Part of the reason why she took so long to get in touch with him was because she was coming to terms with what all of this meant. He'd wooed the fuck out of her and it had ended with them in bed all weekend. She hadn't done that in a really long time. After Pierce, there was a brief fling with a woman named Holliday which was the last time Ollie had spent a weekend with someone she had feelings for.

Until Jackson.

Being with him still scared her, because she was worried that once he saw the ugly parts, he would retreat. He didn't think her curves were too much or her rolls were ugly; Jackson seemed to like all the parts that Ollie took years to come to terms with. He'd spent hours on Sunday tracing her body, following her curves and licking along parts she didn't think about. And even now, he looked at her like she hung the damn moon.

Jackson turned his hand over, linking their fingers and squeezed. Ollie smiled, resting her head against the seat as the corner of Jackson's mouth tipped up in a smile.

"What are you thinking about so hard?"

"You," Ollie told him honestly, still smiling as he glanced at her. "Me. Us. All of it."

"Do you wanna tell me more?"

"I've never gotten this attached to someone before or this fast. It scares me."

"Why?" Jackson looked genuinely puzzled and Ollie

nibbled on her bottom lip as she thought about the right way to answer his question.

"We talked about my lack of trust in relationships, right? I don't ever feel like the person I'm with is actually *with* me. I always feel like I'm putting more into it," she sighed and looked down at his paler hand against her brown skin, the contrast so evident. "I don't feel that with you. And because it's this new feeling, I don't know how to handle it."

"To anyone else I'd say *don't overthink it*," Jackson admitted with a smile, "But, I know what you mean. It feels easy with us, it feels normal...like we've been in this for a while."

"Exactly." She let out a shaky breath. "And it scares me, because that means I've given you more than I've given anyone else and you could just...."

"I won't, Oleander." Jackson's voice dropped to a whisper and he gave her hand a gentle squeeze. "I won't make promises, but I will do everything not to hurt you."

"What if *I* hurt you, Jackson?"

"I'm a big boy, babe. I'll pick myself up again and do whatever it takes to get back to life before you." Ollie sighed, unsure if she should be upset he didn't say he'd fight for her, but she got what he meant.

"What if I hurt *both* of us?"

"Then we lean on our friends to help us get through the worst." Jackson said it so firmly, his fingers squeezing hers. "But put your trust in me, Oleander. Let's figure this out together."

"I *do* trust you, Jackson."

"And it scares you, I get it. I'm going to do whatever I can to earn that trust properly."

"Okay, baby," Ollie whispered, lifting Jackson's hand to her mouth, brushing her lips over his knuckles.

Niles had sent her directions to a free parking zone close to where he was set up, so Ollie made sure that's where Jackson went, still not giving him a single clue about what was happening. Once he'd parked the car, she grabbed her bag and slid on her sunglasses, grinning at Jackson. Ollie took his hand, linking their fingers and with the directions memorized, she led him to where Niles was parked, along with a few other food trucks. When Shake For A Surprise came into view, Ollie glanced up at Jackson and saw the wide smile split his face and knew she'd done the right thing.

"Hello again lovebirds!"

"Hey Niles."

"Your girl here has been planning this for days—you hold onto this one," Niles told Jackson, who laughed and shook his head and squeezed her hand. "My favorite taco truck is up front and there's a really good burger truck too. Why don't you fill up on grub and swing back for dessert."

"Thanks Niles," Ollie told him. "You've got the list I sent you, right?"

"Absolutely. I know *just* what you need." Niles vanished into his truck and Ollie turned to Jackson, who was staring at her with a smile.

"You did this for me."

"Obviously."

"Thank you," he whispered, leaning in to kiss her. "Watching you dance with kids and being here is turning out to be totally worth skipping out on work."

"I know. Now come on, I *am* starving."

Like in Wildes, they *indulged*. And it felt good to not have to think twice about what she wanted to eat. Pierce and Nina had always tried to get her to stop eating more than one taco, thinking it was what her mother would say. Her parents had always been supportive and when Ollie started to gain weight, her mother offered some advice initially and backed off when Ollie snapped. But Jackson didn't seem to care if she was eating her weight in food or drinking all the shakes. If Sunday was anything to go by, he was turned on by her body with all its rolls, wrinkles and stretch marks.

After Jackson had finished the fries she couldn't eat, Ollie decided they needed to go for a walk before letting Niles fill them up again. She let out an unladylike burp, eyes widening as she slapped a hand over her mouth in shock. Jackson released a burp of his own, which was ten times worse and Ollie snorted before bursting into laughter. This level of comfort was freeing and Ollie had to admit she only felt this way around Frankie and Lachlan. Not her exes, not her family; but somehow Jackson made her let those walls down.

Once they'd tossed their trash away and paid for their food, Jackson took Ollie's hand again. Apparently Jackson knew his way around Wilmington, so when she suggested using maps to find their way, he frowned at her. His old stomping grounds, Jackson said, and they set off.

After an hour of walking around Wilmington and soaking up the beautiful city, they were back at Niles' truck. He was putting the finishing touches on their drinks, so he directed them towards tables set up on the other side of his truck.

"This really is a great surprise."

Ollie smiled. "See, not all surprises are bad!"

"It was definitely not what I was thinking."

Ollie chuckled as Niles brought their drinks over. He set it on the table and smiled. "I got a list of things from your lady, I hope you enjoy it."

Jackson's eyes widened and Ollie bit her lip as she watched him. It had taken her one day to come up with the idea and when she'd spoken to Niles, he said he could do it, she made a list and now…

"Thanks Niles." Ollie said with a smile and Niles winked as he walked back to the truck.

Jackson looked at her. "Do I even want to know what was on the list?"

"First," she said and pushed his drink towards him, "take a sip and tell me what you think."

"And then you'll tell me what you listed out?"

Shrugging, she grabbed her drink. "Maybe."

Jackson narrowed his eyes and Ollie smiled, stretching one leg out to bump her foot against his knee. Jackson took a sip and closed his eyes as he swallowed, his jaw moving like he was trying to identify all the flavors. Ollie also took a small sip, sighing at the flavors. While she still hadn't *tasted* Jackson, if he was a dessert, this was what he would be.

Jackson's eyes opened and Ollie saw affection reflected back at her. Her heart raced as she stared at him, her bottom lip tucked between her teeth.

"It's incredible."

Ollie nodded, taking another sip as she kept her eyes on Jackson.

"Oleander, tell me."

"Tell you…what?"

Jackson growled and Ollie smiled. "You're still keeping me in suspense?"

Ollie grinned around the straw and took another big sip. She fished around in her bag for her phone and once she had it, set her drink aside to open the Notes app.

"Are you sure you're ready for this?"

"As ready as I'll ever be, smart ass," Jackson told her with a laugh.

Ollie smirked and read the note. "Jackson is, in short, a good person. He's kind, generous, honest, charming, but also incredibly awkward and shy. He's careful and open, he's understanding and patient. He's also absolutely dreamy."

"Dreamy, huh?"

"Hush." Ollie waved him off, smiling as she continued reading. "Jackson doesn't know it, but he's the kind of person everyone wishes they had in their lives. As a friend, as a lover, as everything. I hope these help you create something magical,

Niles, because I'm not always good with words, but maybe you can help me make him *feel* how being with him makes me feel."

Setting her phone in her lap, Ollie looked up and found Jackson staring at her.

"You think that much of me?"

"And then some."

"Oleander." His voice was shaky and she bit her lip as she watched him. "You are incredible."

She blushed, shaking her head as she toyed with her phone, unable to meet his eyes because it was a lot. She hadn't intended for everything to come out, but she was glad she said what she felt for him.

"You," he whispered, moving closer on the bench, "are everything I never thought I could have. You know the movie *Weird Science*, where they create their perfect woman on a computer and she comes to life? You're the kind of woman I've created in my head for years and being with you made me realize it."

"You *Weird Science*'d me?"

Jackson laughed. "In a way, I guess I did. I didn't even realize I was looking for a woman who was stubborn, sassy, sexy and smart, but also someone who is confident, honest, beautiful, funny, sexy and keeps me on my toes."

"You said sexy twice."

"Damn right, I did, because you are. You are so incredibly sexy, I hope you remember that forever. I don't think I've met a single woman who is everything that you are."

Instead of answering, Ollie leaned forward and kissed Jackson. Her hands moved to either side of his face and she smiled into the kiss before pulling back to look at him. "Let's go home."

TWENTY-THREE
Jackson

Despite texting Carson about coming home late, Jackson was actually glad Oleander agreed to go back to hers. He didn't want to sound eager, but he wanted to see her apartment. She'd seen the inside of his, spent a night there and bonded with Raph and now it felt natural that he saw hers.

The drive back to her apartment was filled with laughter and lots of hand holding. Jackson asked silly questions about her musical tastes and favorite ice cream flavors. They even played a game of identifying the song playing on the radio within 30 seconds of it starting. Despite her lack of interest in popular music, Oleander beat him by six songs. It was safe to say she was shocked too.

Oleander unlocked her front door and let them into her apartment. Jackson took in the white walls, mismatched furniture, colorful art on the walls and plants in fun pots scattered all over the main room. It was a much bigger space than what he and Carson shared, but it was homey.

"This is exactly the kind of place I imagined you'd live in."

"Really?"

Jackson nodded, smiling as he moved towards the bookshelves and brushed his fingers along the spines. One of his favorite authors was James Rymer and Oleander had every single one of his books, some had more than one copy or edition.

"Would you like a tour of my bedroom?"

"Absolutely," he said without hesitation.

"When I first moved in here with Frankie, we spent hours pouring over colors and themes we liked and what we wanted for our space," Oleander explained, leading the way to her room. "And we hit up every garage sale and thrift store and put this together."

"The amount of colors, the plants, the artwork, the books—it all really does feel very *you*."

Oleander pushed open the door to her bedroom, ushering him in. "It's actually more Frankie than me, but I'm glad you think I'm made up of colors."

"Every single color of the rainbow is in you," Jackson told her as he stepped inside her room and paused. While the main rooms were a mix of everything, Oleander's bedroom was a lot calmer. There were plants and books on two shelves, but her walls were plain and the only big pop of color came from her comforter, which was haphazardly spread across her bed.

He turned as the door clicked shut, but instead of looking at Oleander, his eyes snagged on the art hanging on the wall—their canvases from Sangria and Strokes had been framed and hung up. His heart stuttered at the knowledge that she'd kept it and when he glanced at her, Oleander was blushing.

"Like I said, those were the best dates of my life."

"I actually forgot about this," he admitted, moving towards the art. "*This* is a much better surprise."

"Good," Oleander smiled and slid off her sneakers, then reached for his hand and tugged him towards the bed. She released his hand and jumped into the middle, laughing as she stretched out and patted the space beside her. So Jackson did what she did—toed off his shoes, bounced over and collapsed beside her. He turned onto his side and looked at her, his heart threatening to leap out of his chest again.

This *was* love.

He'd never felt this with Ursula, but he *knew* what this feeling was. Oleander turned to face him and grinned, making Jackson smile wider. But her expression changed and Jackson frowned, as Oleander sighed softly.

"There's something I need to tell you."

His heart stalled. "Okay?"

"Before we started dating," Oleander paused and chewed on her lip, "I'd been going on dates."

"As one does."

"Dates with potential husbands."

"What?" Jackson's eyes widened.

"*Some* Indian families still believe in arranged marriages and that means introducing their eligible children to each other."

"You met eligible bachelors."

Oleander nodded. "I met a bunch and they were…not it. They wanted someone who wasn't me, someone who I would never truly be."

"What did they want?"

"A woman who would stay home and cook, raise a family and take care of him. Someone with a high paying job or a woman who was skinny and fairer."

Jackson nodded, swallowing back the curse on the tip of his tongue. Oleander reached out and put her hand on his chest, as if she could calm him down. It worked, actually.

"I was never actually going to choose any of them, but I was doing it because it was what my grandmother wanted, what was *expected* of me."

"Why are you telling me this?"

Oleander sighed. "Because I want you to understand that with me, what you see is what you get. I'm not ever going to be like women you see in magazines or movies or in porn and I don't even know if I want to get married or have a family."

Jackson leaned in slightly and kissed the tip of her nose. "Thank you for telling me. I'm not expecting you to be anyone else—I like you for who you are and that's not going to change."

"Promise?"

He nodded and Oleander smiled, making his heart gallop. And Jackson realized that he should be honest with her too.

"Earlier, in the car," he started, "I said that if we broke up, I'd get back to life before you."

Oleander nodded, walking her fingers across his hand.

"I lied."

"Oh?"

Jackson cleared his throat. "I don't think I could ever go back to life before you. I'd fight like hell to keep you in my life, because this feels good. I like who I am with you and I don't want to lose that."

"I know," she whispered.

"I'm afraid I'll do something to fuck it all up."

"One of us is going to do something stupid eventually, Jackson, we can't avoid it."

"I know, but I want us to have a painless relationship."

"That's a myth, they don't exist," Oleander whispered, sliding a little closer to him. "My parents have been together for close to 50 years and they still fight. My mother leaves home for a few days at a time to give them a break from each other."

"So you're saying in 50 years, you'll take days off from me because I'm driving you insane?"

Oleander laughed, cupping Jackson's face in her hand. "Exactly. Because no matter how many years we've been together, it's not always going to be painless."

"I feel like I've had enough heartbreak for someone my

age. Then I look at my dad and realize he's had it worse, *and* he had to raise three kids at the same time."

"Look at it this way," Oleander explained, stroking his cheek, "If your dad can get up and move on with his life and my parents can make a marriage work for so long, we can get through a little heartache and struggles."

"Moral of the story, if we fuck up, we put the pieces back together."

"And we do it together."

"I really hope I'm not the one to fuck it all up."

"Ass," Oleander laughed, gently poking him in the chest before she moved closer, pressing herself against him. "But can we stop talking now?"

Instead of answering her, Jackson leaned in and kissed her, his fingers holding her chin. Oleander sighed against his mouth, her fingers finding purchase in his hair, like they always did. Jackson's hand left her chin to stroke over her jaw and down her neck, to her shoulder and stopped at her elbow. Oleander leaned into him further, getting rid of any and all space between their bodies. She lifted one leg up over Jackson's side and smiled into the kiss as his hand slid down to rest on her ass.

The kiss grew desperate and Jackson groaned as Oleander slid her hands under his shirt, the cool tips of her fingers brushing against his warm skin. Jackson shivered and Oleander giggled against his mouth. But she wasn't done— her hands were moving, gently pushing him onto his back. Jackson lay back and looked up as Oleander straddled his hips.

His hands settled on her waist as Oleander lifted her t-shirt up and tossed it aside. And she did the one thing that made him laugh, but also fall completely in love with her right there and then. Oleander unhooked her bra and let out the loudest sigh of relief. Her body instantly relaxed as her hips pressed against his.

Jackson chuckled, bringing Oleander's attention back to him. "Don't laugh, those fuckers hurt."

"Can't you wear one of those...sports bra thingies?"

Oleander arched an eyebrow. "Sports bra thingies, for this chest size?"

"Yes?"

"In sports bra thingies, my boobs will be squished even further," Oleander said with a loud snort, bending to press her mouth to his. The kiss broke and they pulled away long enough to take off their clothes. Jackson couldn't get over how beautiful Oleander was and he loved that she was so confident in herself that she never once covered up under his gaze.

Once they were both naked, Oleander was back in his lap, guiding his hands to her bare breasts. She sighed as he cupped them, the weight perfect in his hands. He stroked her nipples with his thumbs and Oleander's head fell back, exposing her gorgeous neck to him. He watched her body respond and released her left breast to stroke his thumb over the tattoo inscribed against her side. "What's this one about?"

"I was heartbroken and angry, and I'd been talking about getting another tattoo for a while," Oleander explained, eyes downcast like she was embarrassed of the words on her body. "And I was always so fascinated by E.E. Cummings and his words. This seemed fitting at the time."

Jackson read the words out loud. "*'Be of love a little more careful than of anything.'* This one explains everything about you in a few words."

"I was angry with my ex, I was angry with myself, I didn't know how to channel my anger, so I took it out on my body instead."

"It's beautiful, even if it was done in rage."

"Now it's one of my favorite tattoos," Oleander told him with a soft laugh, her eyes meeting his. "Because I took my time and I was careful and look where it got me."

Jackson stared at her, his heart pounding at her words. A

small smile tugged at his lips and when Oleander returned it, Jackson slid his hand down her side to the tattoo on her hip, the one that had been teasing him from the moment he met her.

"What about this?"

"Why are we talking about my tattoos?"

Jackson shrugged. "Because it tells me so much about you."

"Haven't I already told you enough?"

"I don't think I'll ever have enough of you, Oleander." Jackson whispered her name and felt her quiver under his hand, making him smile. It was a minimal tattoo of a wave cresting, with the word *breathe* printed beneath it.

"It's a reminder to breathe."

"Breathing is important, sure," he said in a tone that told her he understood there was more to the story.

She sighed heavily and covered Jackson's hand with hers. "I tried to run away from home a few times, because I was so frustrated that my parents didn't understand my choices or that my grandmother kept forcing me to be someone else. At a time when everyone was getting birds tattooed on their skin, I wanted to be a wave, rolling in every day and rolling back out without letting anything stop it. I wanted to be able to live my life without letting anyone affect me along the way."

"Did you manage to make that happen?"

"Yeah," she whispered and looked into his eyes. "I lied to the tattoo artist and said I was 18, but I was only 16. After this, I went away to college and my life got easier."

"You're so strong, Oleander, and these tattoos show how much you have overcome to be where you are." Jackson said the words, noticing that her eyes were glassy as she stared down at him. But she quickly blinked away the tears and pushed her shoulders back.

"Before you ask, the unicorn tattoo was something Frankie and I did together."

"I figured," Jackson smiled, amused that Oleander was moving past the compliment he'd paid her. "I saw the matching one on her arm the other day."

"Her grandmother almost skinned us alive when she saw the tattoos, but she accepted that we were always going to do whatever we wanted, no matter what she thought or said."

Jackson nodded, his thumb still brushing over the tattoo on her hip as he smiled to himself.

"What's the smile for?"

"What smile?"

Oleander narrowed her eyes when he looked up at her. "You smiled as you stared at my tattoo."

"Oh, *that* smile." Jackson chuckled. "I'm really impressed by you and I'm really glad I was annoyingly persistent that you gave me a chance."

Oleander poked his chest. "Are you going to keep bringing up how mean I was to you?"

"Yes, because it'll make for a great story for our kids one day."

Sure, she'd said she wasn't sure if she wanted to get married to have a family, but that didn't mean she was completely against it either. Oleander rolled her eyes, her hips sliding against his in a slow and seductive tease.

"I am naked, wet and rubbing up against you and you're thinking about our non-existent kids." Oleander huffed and started to move away.

Jackson halted her movements with his hands on her hips and sat up, one arm snaking around her waist. He pressed his lips to the corner of her mouth, smiling when he felt Oleander's lips curve into a smile as well.

"I'm thinking about you. Like always," he whispered as their lips met again for a slow kiss, their hands wandering over each other, touching and teasing slowly.

TWENTY-FOUR
Oleander

"Good answer," Ollie whispered, shivering as Jackson's hands followed her curves down her sides before resting on her ass.

While she hadn't planned for an evening of sex when they got back from Wilmington, Ollie wasn't going to complain. It had taken her a long time to come to terms with her body after Pierce, so to have this man look at her like she was the most beautiful creature in the world made her pretty happy.

Besides, Jackson *definitely* liked her for more than just her body.

As they kissed, Ollie moved her hips onto his thighs so she could wrap her fingers around his dick. Jackson shivered and she smiled, breaking the kiss to focus on the job in hand. Licking the fingers on one hand, she wrapped it around his cock, stroked him from base to tip and released him, smiling as his dick lay against his stomach.

Moving further down his legs, Ollie smiled and Jackson frowned, so she gestured to his legs. "Spread 'em."

Jackson obliged, his brow furrowing further. "What are you doing?"

"Relax," Ollie mumbled and settled between his spread

legs and reached for his dick, lazily stroking him as she got comfortable. Jackson muttered her name as she rubbed his tip, spreading the bead of moisture down his length and before he could say anything else, she wrapped her lips around the head of his cock.

"*Fuck*, babe," Jackson groaned and Ollie hummed in response, swirling her tongue around the tip. "You don't have to do this."

"I really *want* to," she mumbled as she pulled her mouth away, "But, I want you to tell me what works."

Jackson nodded slowly, blowing out a shaky breath. Ollie could tell that he was trying to figure out what would work. When he spoke, she couldn't help the snort that escaped her lips.

"I know I'm supposed to *teach* you, but I don't even know where to start."

Circling his base, Ollie tilted her head. "So, I know the basics. I read somewhere that I should fondle your balls."

"Sweet lord," Jackson groaned. "The basic point of the blow job is to use your tongue whenever you can and your hands too. You can *fondle* my balls if you want. But if you touch them, I'll be coming in less than 10 seconds."

Ollie pursed her lips. "So mouth, tongue and hands. *And* if I want you absolutely wild, fondling."

Jackson nodded and Ollie licked her lips as she put her full focus on stroking him, feeling his dick twitch in her hand. Shifting into a comfortable position on her knees, Ollie slid her hand down to his base and took his tip into her mouth. Sliding her lips further down his dick, she sucked gently, causing Jackson to groan. Breathing through her nose, Ollie looked up and found Jackson pressing his eyes shut tight and took him deeper into her mouth. Twisting her hand around his base, she used her tongue, sliding it along the length of him.

"Fuck, just like that."

Ollie hummed in acknowledgement and Jackson's hips jerked, his tip hitting the back of her throat. Her eyes watered and he slid his fingers into her hair as he mumbled an apology. She noticed that the muscles in his thighs quivered as she moved her mouth along him, using her tongue whenever she could. As his fingers curled into her hair, Ollie cupped his ball-sack and massaged it slowly.

"Oleander, *stop*."

Pulling her mouth off him with a pop, Ollie swiped her hand over her lips and frowned. "Was it not good?"

"You're fucking *spectacular* at that, but I want to come inside you."

"Next time," she said with a smug grin and moved over him, "you'll let me finish that."

Jackson nodded, slightly breathless, "Next time, you can take however long you want."

Smiling, she moved off of him and heard the sigh of relief escape Jackson. It made her laugh as she glanced over at him, watching him grip his cock, grinding his teeth like he was trying not to get carried away.

Pulling open the drawer of her nightstand, she grabbed a box of condoms and Ollie winced when she saw how old they were and she heard Jackson chuckle.

He spoke softly. "I'm almost afraid to ask when you used them last."

"I don't think we should use these. Give me a minute."

Ollie rushed out of her room and into Lachlan's, grabbing the box of condoms in his nightstand and rushed back to her bedroom. She closed her bedroom door and held the box up to Jackson, her eyes widening when she noticed what he had in his hand. Considering how many times they talked about it, she wasn't surprised that he'd found *Grant*.

Ollie smiled as she climbed into bed, setting the box of condoms beside her. "That's Grant."

Jackson looked at her in confusion. "It has a name?"

"*I* gave it a name," she explained and took Grant from him. "Want to see how it works?"

"Yes." Jackson's response was instant, his voice strained. She'd never used her vibrator in front of someone before; she'd used the wand while having sex with an ex in the past.

"If you want a better view, move over."

Jackson nodded, his hand fisting around his cock as he shifted to the edge of the bed. She turned on the vibrator, smiling as the soft buzz filled the room. Ollie grabbed the lube from the drawer and fluffed up the pillows so she could lean back. Jackson watched intently as she squirted lube onto the vibrator and spread it over the head. He cursed under his breath and Ollie smirked when she watched him stroke himself slowly.

She spread her legs, keeping her feet flat on the bed and brushed her fingers through her folds. Jackson made another sound. She used the vibrator to repeat the action, making him grunt. Ollie bit down on her bottom lip and increased the speed of the vibrator and spreading her folds with one hand, guided the vibrator inside. Her body jerked and her head fell backwards, a moan falling from her lips. She was already so worked up from rubbing up against Jackson so she was squirming as she slid the vibrator in and out, switching the speed every so often.

Jackson mumbled and Ollie lifted her head to watch him. His eyes were glazed over, but he was completely focused on what she was doing.

"Touch me," she whispered and Jackson's eyes snapped to hers.

He moved forward and brushed one hand up a leg as the other moved between her thighs. When his thumb brushed against her clit, Ollie jerked and almost lost her grip on the vibrator. Jackson clearly noticed, because he took it and resumed what she was doing.

"Right there, Jackson, fuck…that's good." Ollie breathed

out, rocking her hips desperately. He rubbed her clit as he thrust the vibrator into her faster. Ollie reached out and grabbed his wrist as the vibrator hit the spot and she arched off the bed, screaming his name. Ollie tugged on Jackson's wrist as she rode out her orgasm, and she heard him chuckle softly.

"Is it always like that?" he whispered.

Ollie shook her head. "It's *never* like that."

He nodded, his eyes drifting between her legs as he slowly slid the vibrator out of her. Ollie whimpered at the loss and her body shuddered, sinking into the bed as she released his hand.

"Why do you call it Grant?"

Ollie smiled, her legs stretched out on either side of Jackson. "Because before you, he *granted* me all of my orgasms."

"Will Grant feel left out since I'm here?"

"I'm sure we can find ways to include Grant."

Jackson grinned and leaned in, Ollie met him halfway and their lips connected. It was such a rush, having Jackson watch her pleasure herself and have him be part of it. She scooted forward, his hands settled on her hips as she set her hands on his shoulders.

He mumbled about a condom and Ollie brushed her mouth over his bare shoulder, her teeth scraping along his skin. His muscles flexed under her teeth and she bit down on the flesh. He slid an arm around her waist and hauled her up into his lap, making Ollie growl as she pressed her mouth against his again.

Jackson was *really* good with his mouth and she loved how he didn't hold back when it came to kissing her. One hand slid into her hair and held her there as they kissed, tongues fighting for dominance and teeth scraping in their desperate need to have each other.

"Put it on," Ollie whispered, grabbing a condom as she broke the kiss. When he took it from her, she kissed along his clenched jaw and down to his neck. Ollie was going to mark him up because it felt good to know he was *hers*.

She heard the rustling of the condom wrapper and pulled back to watch as Jackson rolled the condom on with shaky hands. When he looked up at her, she smiled and leaned in to kiss him again. Ollie wrapped one hand around his tip as Jackson wrapped a hand around his base, she lifted her hips and slid down on him, her hand moving down till she bumped against his. They both pulled their hands away and she slid down, till Jackson was fully seated inside her.

She was already sensitive from earlier, it took absolutely no effort to get her worked up and ready for another orgasm.

"God, Oleander, you are...*perfect*."

"You..." she breathed out as she clenched around him, "Are perfect for me."

"*Move.*" Ollie saw the pained expression on Jackson's face as his fingers curled into her hips. She rocked against him and bit down on her lip to swallow the sounds that threatened to spill out. Using her hands on his shoulders as leverage, Ollie finally found the perfect way to move. Jackson's hands urged her on and Ollie moved her hips up and down, moaning louder with every inch he thrust in and out of her.

"Fuck, that's so hot," she whispered.

With Jackson's encouragement, Ollie moved faster. Every so often, she dropped herself back down so he was fully seated inside her and rolled her hips, causing both of them to moan loudly. Riding him faster, Ollie cried out when he hit the perfect spot. For a minute, she saw stars and it felt like she was spinning. Jackson had been patient, but he finally took charge and bucked up into her, causing Ollie to cry out, her clit rubbing against his pelvis with every thrust.

Ollie leaned away, her hands resting on his thighs as her head fell backwards. With this switch in angle, he was right where she wanted him. Ollie rolled her hips lazily against his, wanting all the friction, but not wanting to bounce or move too fast. She felt Jackson's hand move over her stomach and down between their joined bodies, but it was only when he stroked her clit that Ollie's hips snapped into quick movement.

Ollie gasped as she clenched around him, her nails digging into his thighs, head thrown back as she came with his name a whisper on her lips. Jackson pushed up into her again and she felt him come, emptying into the condom as he collapsed backwards, taking her with him.

They lay there for a long time, and Ollie blew her sweaty hair out of her face when she felt Jackson's fingers trace shapes along her back. Smiling to herself, she slid off Jackson and collapsed on the bed beside him with a satisfied sigh.

When she glanced at Jackson, Ollie found him smiling at her. "That was…*fantastic*."

"I repeat, sex has never been like this before," she whispered. "*You* are fantastic."

"I look forward to more time with Grant. *And* your mouth," Jackson said as tugged her into him and kissed her, making Ollie smile.

"We better wash up." Ollie kissed him once more and slid out of bed. When she didn't hear movement behind, she looked over her shoulder at Jackson. "What?"

He smiled, eyes sliding over her naked body. "You're incredible."

"*Jackson.*"

He smiled, sitting at the edge of her bed. Ollie knew everything had shifted, and she was more than okay with it. She might have been worried about dating him in the beginning, but Jackson proved he understood her in ways other partners hadn't. And there was all the sex they were having, which was absolutely mind blowing.

They were both completely naked, something that happened every time they wanted to have a *conversation*. Usually, Ollie felt vulnerable when she was naked and during serious conversations.

But, with Jackson, it was none of those things.

His voice dropped to a whisper. "I think my words might scare you."

"You won't know till you try," Ollie told him, faintly aware of what he was going to say.

"You already know you make me feel all kinds of things," Jackson started, rubbing the back of his neck. "So this shouldn't come as a surprise."

"I still want to hear you say it."

"I'm falling for you, Oleander. Even though it scares both of us and we literally just talked about it today," he explained and smiled. "But when I'm with you, I feel more like myself. I don't have to hide my nerdy side, I don't have to pretend. I can be *me*."

"I know what you mean," she told him, smiling as she cupped his face. "I also get to be *me* for a change. It's liberating. *You* make me feel like myself again and I love it."

"I agree," Jackson nodded. "With you, I want to do it all. I want to try new things and experience things I've only read about."

"Like what?"

"Use a vibrator during sex, bungee jumping…"

Ollie rolled her eyes. "No bungee jumping."

He chuckled, tugging her closer. "Does this finally make me your boyfriend?"

Ollie giggled, which made Jackson smile, rubbing her thumb over his cheek. "I guess it does."

"Every single date, every single adventure, it's been amazing because it's been with you."

Ollie pressed her forehead against his. "And now, the rest of our dates have to be even better."

"I'll make it work, trust me."

Ollie leaned in and kissed Jackson, smiling against his mouth as his hands slid down to her ass and tried to pull her back into bed. She groaned and broke away, muttering against

TWENTY-FIVE

Jackson

They'd been dating for about two months when Oleander suggested hosting a dinner for their friends. Jackson had been ready to refuse, but she'd seen it coming. He loved his friends, he wanted all of them to hang out together, but he was also nervous about this *formal* sort of meeting. He still hadn't met this elusive roommate of hers and other than Frankie, he didn't know if she had more important friends.

So, they were doing it.

To level the playing field, he invited Everleigh as well. When Gavin let it slip during a poker night, Jackson realized that having Ever there would probably help.

This still felt like meeting the family of a girlfriend—obviously Jackson was stressed as fuck. He'd changed his clothes *thrice* and had almost given up to settle on a *Star Wars* t-shirt when Everleigh had called, insisting he wear something nice.

He was dressed in dark jeans and a green and black flannel button down. Jackson had even put on his comfortable boots. Once he was ready, he met his friends at Milo's apartment, where they took a cab over to Oleander's place.

Seeing all of them looking flawless did stress him out a bit, but no matter who was around them, Oleander's eyes and hands always seemed to find him. That was the important thing to keep in mind. She wanted *him*. Not Gavin or Milo. She chose him and Jackson was so eternally grateful.

"Well hello, beautiful people." Frankie greeted them at the door. He took a moment to appreciate how beautiful she was, but behind her he saw Oleander grinning and his heart started to race.

"Ugh, it's impossible being in a room with you two."

Jackson laughed, leaning in to kiss Frankie's cheek. "It's always good to see you, trouble."

Oleander bit her lip as she stepped around the guy she was talking to and Jackson let his eyes sweep over her. They hadn't seen each other in almost a week; between work and planning this party, it seemed impossible to find the time. Their phones had gotten a lot of action though. Oleander had suggested they try phone sex, which sent her into a fit of giggles when Jackson tried on his seductive voice. Apparently he wasn't cut out for it.

Jackson moved towards her slowly, one hand gripping his overnight bag and the other itching to touch her. She was wearing a light blue-gray dress that fell mid-thigh and those gorgeous legs were on display. His eyes did another sweep of her beautiful body and smiled, still in shock that she was *his*.

Oleander laughed as she closed the gap between them, her arms winding around his neck. Jackson slid his free hand around her waist and tugged her against him as he kissed her back. He felt Oleander smile against his mouth and he finally pulled away from her.

"Hi."

Oleander pouted. "I missed you this week."

"I missed you too."

"At least you get me all to yourself this weekend." Jackson kissed the tip of her nose at the reminder.

"Speaking of the weekend, can I drop my bag off in your room?"

"Let me help you with that, in case you get lost." Oleander said it loudly, making everyone laugh. He grinned at his *girlfriend* and let her take his hand, leading him to her room.

Once inside, Oleander shut the door and leaned against it, one hand tugging him towards her. Jackson dropped his bag and lifted both hands to cup her cheeks as he dropped his mouth to hers. Her arms were around his waist and Jackson moaned softly as their tongues touched and teased. Oleander's fingers slid into his hair and he quivered, remembering the last time she'd done that and forced himself to pull away.

"We should get back out there, or they'll never let us live this down."

She huffed, tugging his mouth back towards hers. "I don't care, I just want more of you."

"Oleander."

"Ugh, fine." She rolled her eyes and before he could step away, she kissed him again. Her mouth covered his and Jackson growled when Oleander nipped at his bottom lip, tugging on it gently before releasing it.

As they pulled away, she whispered, "If I forget to mention it later, I love this look."

"Thank you. Everleigh picked it for me."

"Who on earth is Everleigh?"

He arched an eyebrow. "Am I sensing jealousy?"

"Uh, yes. Because this is the first I'm hearing of her."

"Babe, Everleigh is *just* a friend. She's never had my interest. Milo, however…" Jackson shrugged. "They used to have a thing back in high school, but not anymore."

"Why haven't you mentioned her before?"

"I don't know really, I mean…" Jackson shrugged, his fingers playing with her hair as he thought about why Ever had never come up in conversations. "She's really busy and barely has time to see us. But I figured that it would be good for her to finally meet you guys and for you to also may—"

"It's okay." Oleander put her hand over his mouth, stopping him from rambling and Jackson kissed her palm. "I've never been jealous of someone before, so that was interesting."

"But to be clear, you have nothing to be jealous of. I'm with you, completely and I don't want anyone else."

"Ditto," Oleander whispered and Jackson wasn't sure if he imagined it or if her voice actually quivered on the word. He kissed her till someone knocked on the door, breaking them apart.

THERE WAS a flurry of introductions and Jackson finally got his first good look at the elusive Lachlan. Oleander didn't say much except that he was a writer, and it made him curious why it was a secret. Everyone met Everleigh and exchanged pleasantries. Jackson watched Oleander as she shook hands with his only real female friend and bit back a smile, because she *was* jealous. And it was cute.

While Oleander and Frankie worked on everyone's drink orders, Jackson stood with Milo and Lachlan and talked about sports. Like every warm blooded American, he watched the Super Bowl, but beyond that he didn't care.

Frankie came around, putting drinks in everyone's hands and as the guys continued talking sports, Jackson let his eyes wander. Gavin said something funny that made Frankie tip her head back and laugh. He wondered if he imagined it, but he was sure he heard Milo growl. He also noticed that Everleigh was awkwardly standing in front of a bookshelf, eyes darting around before turning to stare at the books he'd admired not too long ago.

He had to admit that it felt good, having his friends mingle with Oleander's, it made their relationship more *real*. They already referred to each other as boyfriend and girlfriend, but this cemented it even more.

The apartment looked different—the light was low, there was soft music playing and there were also candles lit. Jackson watched as Milo broke away from their group, heading straight for Frankie and Gavin. He noticed Frankie's expression soften and wondered if he was missing something. But Oleander wrapped her arm around his waist and all other thoughts flew out the window.

He knew without a doubt, in that moment, he was going to admit that he was in love with her. He'd told Ursula he loved her pretty early on in the relationship, and she'd said it back six months later. Looking back, Jackson knew his ex hadn't actually ever loved him or wanted to be with him, but she probably stayed because he gave her something she wasn't getting anywhere else at the time.

"You done being hostess with the mostest?"

Oleander laughed, nuzzling into his chest. "It's all pretend. Lachlan did all the cooking and he wanted me to make sure it stayed warm."

"You're still *hosting* this party, babe, that's what counts."

He kissed the top of her head when Gavin joined their group, adding to the sports talk. Oleander made a frustrated sound and tugged him towards a wide single seater. He sat down and she slid in beside him, half in his lap.

"I'm glad we did this."

"Looks like my friends are getting along fine with your friends," Jackson told her, kissing the side of her head.

"Especially Frankie and Milo," she mumbled and Jackson followed her gaze to where their best friends were sitting pretty close.

"I noticed that too, but I'm not sure when or how they met."

Oleander shrugged, snuggling into him. Jackson set his glass on a table so he could hold her tighter. "So," he said softly, clearing his throat, "What's the deal with Lachlan?"

"What do you mean?"

"You got *very* creative with what he does for a living."

Oleander shrugged. "He likes keeping a low profile, so we don't divulge too much information."

"Not even to me?"

"Don't play that card with me, Jackson, I am sworn to secrecy."

"I should be offended that as your *boyfriend* I don't know these things."

"I'm extremely loyal and faithful." Oleander brushed him off with a smile. "So, *Everleigh*."

"She's really protective, so any woman that comes into the circle needs to get along with Ever."

Oleander nodded. "She doesn't seem too worried about you and me."

"Because the guys promised her we're good together."

"Aw," Oleander grinned and squeezed his arm. "We are good together, aren't we?"

"We're *great* together, babe," Jackson assured her with a soft kiss to her temple.

Jackson *was* happy. It had been a long time since he'd met a group of people he actually liked being around. He already enjoyed Frankie's company, and he felt like he would eventually get to know Lachlan better. Right now, he was soaking it all up, trying to get used to the idea of being in a relationship again.

One that made his heart race and his palms sweat, in all the good ways.

"Do you think we should make this like a once every few months kind of deal?"

Jackson shrugged. "I only agreed because I'll have you to myself for the weekend."

"Shut up."

Jackson laughed and looked at Oleander. She had the most beautiful smile lighting up her face. "But sure, I think it'll be nice for all of us to get together every now and then."

Oleander chuckled, pointing at Milo and Frankie. "I'm surprised I didn't see it before, they look really good together."

Jackson had to agree. Besides being unfairly attractive, they already seemed to have that *spark*. The very same spark Jackson felt when he was with Oleander.

On the other side of the room, Gavin, Everleigh and Lachlan seemed to have finally moved on from sports, both of them laughing at something Lachlan said. Despite not knowing *everything* about Lachlan, he seemed like a decent guy. Besides, Jackson knew it wasn't like Oleander and Frankie to be friends with someone who wasn't worthy.

Oleander's head was on his shoulder as she hummed along with the music, and he smiled. This was exactly what he'd always wanted. He thought he had it with Ursula, but that was a lie.

Sensing his eyes on her, Oleander lifted her head. "You okay?"

"Yeah, just enjoying all of this."

Oleander smiled. "Frankie has some games planned, so we don't all get stuck in our twosomes."

"I'd definitely like to be in a twosome with you right now."

She poked him in the side. "Behave yourself."

"I mean, we could sneak away and they won't notice."

Oleander shook her head and he chuckled. "You get me all weekend, so we must be social tonight."

"Fine. Only because it'll make you happy."

"This is why you're a good boyfriend."

"Is that the only reason?"

Oleander pretended to think about it. "I mean, your dick is glorious and you do that thing with your tongue I seem to enjoy."

"Ah, so it's all physical."

"Well, it's a bit of everything."

"I'm glad I could make your day and nights better."

She winked. "You do so much more than that, handsome."

Good, because I'm in love with you. Jackson said the last bit in his head as Oleander kissed him.

TWENTY-SIX
Oleander

When Ollie suggested this party, they knew it was because she was in love with Jackson. Ollie had never worn her heart on her sleeve and everyone she'd dated had to fight for her love. After Pierce, Ollie had stayed clear of introducing them to her best friends. But Jackson wasn't like Pierce or Nina.

Having everyone there felt good. She watched their friends mingle and despite having met for the first time that night, they seemed to get along like a house on fire. Ollie might have spent most of the time cuddled up against Jackson in her favorite chair, but that didn't take away from enjoying everybody else's company. Ollie also made a mental note to ask Frankie about Milo, because those two looked far too cozy for people who had *just* met.

Speaking of Frankie, her best friend was the best party planner on the planet. Not only did she have games for a little ice breaker, but when she was organizing the party, she'd designed name cards. If you gave Frankie the freedom to plan a party, she went all out.

Ollie was also glad they had invested in a larger table years ago and it fit everyone comfortably. When the drinks started running low and everyone started to get hungry, Frankie had led them to the table she'd decorated and set up so beautifully. There were flowers on the table, fancy plates and cutlery. She might have complained about planning a party on a rough day, but Frankie knocked this out of the park.

Thanks to the name cards, Ollie was at one end of the table, with Jackson at the other. On her right, at the head of the table, was Milo and on her left was Everleigh. On Milo's right was Lachlan, Frankie and Jackson. With Gavin closing out the group at the foot of the table.

Lachlan had been in charge of the food, so as it was passed around and everyone tried different dishes, she heard moans at how good everything was. But Lachlan refused to take ownership for the food. That had always been the case and Ollie was so impressed with how good he was when it came to food. Looking at him, you'd think he was a lumberjack most of the time, but he was so damn talented.

They were halfway through their meal when Everleigh said her name softly. Ollie set her cutlery down and reached for her wine as she turned to face Jackson's friend.

"I know this is really weird, especially since we didn't know the other existed, but I'm really glad Jackson met you."

Ollie laughed and took a sip of her wine. "I'm really glad he met me too. And also I'm glad *we* got to meet."

Everleigh chuckled "I'm going to strangle these boys later, I'm always looking for more girlfriends. You and Frankie seem to have a pretty good relationship going."

"Well, we've known each other for a while. And Lachlan fits into our trio somehow."

"I totally get his place in this group—that's how I am with the boys," Everleigh explained and with a quick nod at Milo, she smiled. "And it's only because we used to date."

"Honestly, it could have ended after your relationship was over, but it says a lot that they kept you in their circle."

"I guess?" Everleigh blushed. "But I'm only bringing it up because Jack's ex really pulled a number on him."

"Yeah..." Ollie nodded, pretending like she knew what Everleigh was talking about. Ollie realized she'd done quite a bit of talking about her past relationships, but Jackson never offered.

Everleigh was still speaking. "I think we all knew she was wrong for him. But to *cheat* on him and brush it off like it was nothing, that was harsh."

"I'm sure," Ollie agreed, her heart racing as she glanced at Jackson and found him laughing at something Frankie said. She turned to her food as Everleigh continued.

"She broke his heart and Jackson doesn't talk about it, because he believes saying her name will make her magically appear." Ollie snorted and Everleigh laughed. "But you're so much better than her. You seem pretty awesome and Jackson is so lucky."

Ollie made an *aw shucks* face, her eyes meeting Jackson's as she glanced at him, a small smile playing on his lips. Tearing her eyes away, she smiled at Everleigh. "I think we both got pretty lucky."

As everyone was finishing up dinner, Ollie escaped into the kitchen with the intention of getting dessert together. She hadn't been put in charge of food because she could burn everything, but she'd *assisted* in the kitchen. But honestly, Ollie wanted to breathe. She knew she was lucky with Jackson, but the fact that he hadn't told her about this woman, or any more details made her feel a little unsteady.

She was bent over, reaching into the bottom shelf of the fridge for the tiramisu when she felt hands on her waist. Jumping, she knocked her head against the side of the fridge and groaned.

"Fuck, babe, I'm sorry."

"It's okay." She winced, grabbing the dessert as she straightened up. Jackson was instantly there, his hand going to the spot on her head and touched it gently. When she flinched, he made a face and opened the freezer. He'd been in her apartment so much, it seemed so natural for Jackson to find a kitchen towel and empty ice into it, wrap it up and hand it to her.

"I didn't think I'd scare you. You okay?"

"Yeah, got a lot on my mind."

"Do you want to talk about it?"

Ollie sighed heavily, pressing the towel to her head as she moved around the center counter to grab the dessert plates and spoons Frankie had set aside.

But she changed her mind and turned to Jackson. "Why don't we talk about your exes?"

His eyes widened. "What?"

"We've talked about my past relationships, but never yours."

Jackson frowned. "Uh…I don't know? I never want to talk about them."

"But your last girlfriend hurt you really badly, and you never talk about it."

He sighed, crossing his arms over his chest. "What did Ever say?"

"That you were heartbroken over her for a while."

"I *was*, but I got over it and moved on."

"With me," Ollie frowned, adjusting the ice against her head. "Am I your rebound?"

"Jesus, Oleander, you are anything but a rebound." He shook his head. "That relationship had been over for six months when I met you. Sure, I was still a little bummed about how she ended things, but I wasn't hung up on her and I wasn't using you as a way to get over her."

"Why didn't you tell me?"

"Because I didn't want her to *contaminate* what we had. I was happy for the first time in a long time and I didn't want her to have power over that."

"She's not a witch, Jackson. She has no control if you say her name."

"I got into this habit of not saying her name, for fear of what would happen," he explained, sounding frustrated. "And when we met, I decided I didn't want her to fill up the spaces."

"Do you still love her?"

"Fuck, no." Jackson looked like he was hurt she would even ask him that. "I want nothing to do with her—she left me for someone else."

He looked so upset talking about his ex, but he looked even more upset that she would question him. Ollie wouldn't be *Ollie* if she didn't ask a million questions. She wanted to know everything about Jackson and this woman, she wanted to understand how he felt about her and whether it was something Ollie needed to worry about.

Granted, she hadn't told him *everything* about Pierce, but he had to have guessed by now. Their first night together, she told him about her trouble with being under someone and he hadn't questioned it. She vaguely talked about Pierce and how he made her feel, but he'd never once said anything about the woman that hurt him. That hurt *her* and Ollie wished she wasn't so worried about her place in Jackson's life.

Ollie opened her mouth to respond to Jackson when Frankie stepped into the kitchen, hands on her hips and glared at the two of them.

"You better not be letting the dessert melt, Anders."

Ollie rolled her eyes. "Relax, your tiramisu is fine."

"You lovebirds doing okay?"

"Yeah, I'll bring this out in a minute." Ollie nodded and her friend got the hint.

Ollie turned back to Jackson, who was staring at her. "I believe you. But I want us to talk about this later."

"Okay. She's a part of my past. Right now, it's just you. I only want *you*."

ONCE THEY CARRIED the dessert out, Jackson helped her serve the tiramisu and hand the plates out to the waiting masses and they returned to their assigned seats. Ollie knew she was jumping to conclusions and Everleigh meant no harm in bringing it up. But given Nina's lies and the way Pierce reacted to her history, being afraid and worried was expected. Jackson would never truly understand how scarred she was after Pierce, but he hadn't flinched at the first mention of Nina. He *accepted* her—bisexuality, curves, insecurities and all.

When everyone was done with dessert, Frankie stood up and smirked at the table. "Top up your drinks, young ones, because we're about to play an old fashioned college game to get to know each other."

Ollie snorted. "We're *not* getting drunk."

Milo frowned and looked around the table, "Wait, what are we playing?"

"Oh, you beautiful boy, we're going to play Never Have I Ever. And we're going to get really *deep*," Frankie smirked. "Back to the living room!"

Ollie pushed her chair back and started piling up the plates and without even her asking, Jackson stepped up to help. He rinsed every plate and Ollie loaded it into the dishwasher. He helped her put all the food away and once she was done stuffing the fridge with leftovers, she closed the door and turned, only to find Jackson *right there*. Ollie sucked in a sharp breath and leaned back against the cool door as she stared up at him.

"I'm sorry I didn't tell you about Ursula. I don't like thinking about her or how she hurt me, but I see not talking about it made it worse."

Ollie nodded. "I get it and it's okay. I wish I hadn't heard it from someone else."

"I know, but I *will* tell you everything."

Ollie lifted her hands to Jackson's face, her finger tips scratching against his scruff. "We have all night to talk about it."

"I was hoping for us to do so much more all night."

"We can find a way to do it all, I promise."

Jackson leaned forward and rested his forehead against hers, Ollie slid her hands down to his chest. "Since I met you, I haven't thought about her at all. You've consumed my every waking thought, Oleander."

"Jackson…"

"I want you to know *this* is what I've always wanted and I would never do anything to hurt you."

"I know, baby." She tipped her head back, her eyes searching his. "I know."

Their lips met for a soft kiss and Ollie parted her lips to deepen it when they heard Frankie call out for them. Jackson laughed as Ollie groaned, grabbing their glasses to join the gang for games.

TWENTY-SEVEN

Jackson

As was the case with playing *Never Have I Ever*, everyone got pretty drunk. Jackson was amused by how often Milo and Frankie asked the most sexual questions they could think of. Most of them sat there and watched as they rattled off statement after statement, knocking back shots of whisky and vodka. After a point, everyone got the hint that they weren't required for the game. Which prompted Frankie to get a little more creative.

It was close to 2AM by the time everything wrapped up. Oleander, Lachlan and Jackson booked cabs for everyone and bundled people off. The three of them cleaned up the mess, and filled up the dishwasher. While Lachlan finished cleaning up, Oleander suggested they go to the roof. And Jackson wasn't going to argue. With a blanket in her hands, he let her lead the way upstairs.

He was annoyed with Everleigh for running her mouth, but at the same time, Jackson understood why she did it. All of them had been worried when Ursula dumped him and seeing him happy with Oleander could be concerning—he wished they'd trust him, because she was nothing like Ursula.

Oleander looked so hurt by the fact that she'd had to learn

about Ursula from someone else, but Jackson didn't know how else to explain that he wanted nothing to do with his ex anymore. And that included talking about her. But they were going to talk about it.

Oleander deserved that much.

Stepping out onto the roof, Jackson saw a couch and low table. He followed Oleander and sat down, draping the blanket over their legs. She'd changed out of her heels into fluffy unicorn slippers. Jackson smiled when she lifted her feet onto the table and snuggled into his side.

"When Frankie used to live here, we'd come up almost every night and finish a bottle of wine while we stared up at the stars."

"And since she moved out?"

Oleander shrugged. "I started working late shifts and Lachlan is rarely here. It's no fun to do it alone."

"Next time you want to drink and stare at the stars, call me."

Oleander smirked. "Why do you think I brought you up here?"

"To talk?"

"Well, since we don't have wine and the stars are a little low on voltage tonight, I guess I'll make do." Oleander laughed and Jackson kissed the top of her head, his fingers threading through hers under the blanket.

They sat like that for a while, staring up at the stars and Jackson wondered if he could identify any of them, but gave up when it became clear he didn't know any of the stars except for Orion.

"So, you dated a Disney villain." Oleander's voice cut through his thoughts.

Jackson snorted. "When I first met her, she was the opposite of the Disney villain. She was beautiful and funny. She took what she wanted and it was a huge turn on."

"But then she turned evil?"

"Not the word I'd use, but the guys would agree for sure." Jackson twisted his lips to the side. "Apparently she got *bored*. She wanted more and I wasn't giving her that. But instead of talking about it, she…found someone else."

"What?"

Jackson sighed, "I was gone for the weekend on a work trip, she wasn't replying to my texts or answering my calls. And when I got back, I caught her fucking someone else."

"Did you…*wait?*"

"Because I was an idiot and I thought I was in love, yeah." Jackson sighed. "And she came out, disheveled and half-naked, and said she got bored and wanted more and it was fun while it lasted."

Oleander stayed silent and Jackson turned to look at her to see her frowning hard. Her mouth moved, but he couldn't hear what she was saying.

"What are you muttering about?"

She frowned. "I'm trying to find the words."

"There's nothing to say." Jackson chewed on his bottom lip as he thought about everything that came after. "I was a mess after that—I couldn't work, I could barely function. The guys did everything to help me, but I wasn't handling it well. I was so fucking miserable. And one day, I got out of bed and decided it wasn't worth it. And four months later, I met you."

"That is terrible," Oleander said, sitting up and brushing her hair out of her face. "Not the meeting me part, but having to accept that was how it ended."

"Maybe I should have seen it coming. Ursula was always a flirt and a little flighty, but I believed she loved me."

"Sometimes people are not what we make them out to be."

Jackson frowned at her words and reached for her hand. "That sounds like the *end* of a story."

Oleander sighed and shook her head, leaning back against

him. Jackson wrapped his arm around her and pressed his lips to the top of her head.

"We've all got a Disney villain in our lives, and it's okay if you don't want to talk about it."

"I definitely don't like talking about it, but I think it's important that I do."

"Who was it?"

Jackson felt more than saw Oleander shudder as she whispered his name. "Pierce."

And in that instant he knew whatever this guy had done to her, he hated him.

IT WAS OBVIOUSLY REALLY hard for her to talk about it, because once she said his name, Oleander was on her feet, twisting her fingers. Jackson stayed put and waited for her to tell him what happened. He *knew* it was going to be horrible, because she looked so small.

Jackson had seen Oleander nervous and uncomfortable, but he'd never seen this side of her.

She suddenly came to a halt, her wet eyes lifting to his. "He put me in the hospital."

"*What?*" The word came out in a breath and Jackson moved to stand up, but Oleander shook her head, so he stayed seated. He wanted to hold her, comfort her, but it was clear Oleander didn't want that. "We don't have to…"

"You deserve to know. Someone other than Frankie, Lachlan and my therapist should know," Oleander said softly. "And I want us to not have any more of these secrets."

"Okay, take your time. I'm right here." Jackson assured her, leaning forward and resting his elbows on his thighs as he clenched and unclenched his fists, trying to stay calm.

"Pierce was my first *serious* boyfriend. I thought he was the one," Oleander started, laughing sadly. "We'd been together for three years, but there were times when he would make me feel bad about myself. My job wasn't good enough, I was eating too much, I needed new friends, I had to be more ambitious. He called me *pathetic* and *silly* and *foolish*. I always thought he was in a *mood*."

Jackson shook his head, not understanding what that meant. Oleander met his eyes and sighed before speaking again.

"I loved him, so I looked past all the bad things. I had someone who wanted to be with me, *really* be with me and after Nina broke my confidence, I needed the ego boost."

He hated that she'd been made to feel like she wasn't worthy. While he didn't understand why Nina or this Pierce had hurt her, Jackson understood it wasn't his place to speak.

"We'd never talked about our past relationships and were foolish to think they didn't matter. But Nina wrote me a letter to apologize for college and everything that followed. I was at work, so Pierce found it and opened it." Oleander started pacing again and her eyes were moving everywhere, except on him and Jackson gritted his teeth as she continued.

"When I got home, he was sitting on the couch, fuming. I was in a good mood, so I didn't think much of it. But when I got to him, Pierce was on his feet, holding out the letter and spitting words at me. It took me a while to really understand what he was saying and when I reached for the letter, he shoved me." Oleander paused, her breath hitching.

After a long moment of silence, she turned to face him. "I fell on the floor. He towered over me and spat at me. Then he spoke, in a tone of voice I'd never heard before. Honestly, I was so shocked at the person in front of me, I didn't know what to do. He said, *'You little whore. You shared a bed with a woman for four years and you chose not to tell me? What will my family think when they find out the woman I'm dating has fucked a woman?'*"

Jackson quickly stood up and wrapped the blanket around her. Oleander turned to him when he took a step back, tears streaming down her face and Jackson felt his own eyes fill up. Blowing out a breath, Oleander tightened the blanket around her and turned away.

"He grabbed me by the hair and lifted me off the floor, stuffed the letter in my mouth and choked me. He pinned me to the couch and punched me, hitting me in the ribs. And he started to rip my clothes off. He was so angry, he was turning red in the face and spewing all kinds of ugly things." Oleander finally looked at him as she spoke the next part. "Every time I'm under someone, my brain flashes back to that night and I have panic attacks. I've *finally* gotten over the ugly words he's said about my body, but there's still so much that lingers."

"Did he…." Jackson swallowed, unable to get the word out. Oleander shook her head and he let out a sigh of relief.

"Almost," Oleander whispered. "Someone rang the doorbell, so he let me go to answer the door. While he spoke to whoever had showed up, I found the strength to grab my things and run into the bedroom." She paused and wiped away her tears. "I locked myself away from him, called Frankie and waited for her to arrive. Pierce had calmed down by then, but when Frankie showed up with Lachlan, he lost his mind again. I think Lachlan knocked him down as Frankie helped me pack my things and leave."

Jackson realized he was crying when Oleander moved towards him and cupped his face, smiling sadly. "I was supposed to audition for a part in a dance movie the next day—that's why I was in a good mood—but with my black eye, bruised ribs and neck, there was no way I could go. At the hospital, they called the cops and after much coaxing, I told them about Pierce. Frankie gave them his address and that was it. They took pictures, took down my statement and I never saw or heard from him again."

Leaning into her hand, Jackson kissed her palm. "I hate him for what he did to you, for what he made you feel."

"I hate him too. But," Oleander smiled sadly, "I feel like

that helped me get stronger and fight for what I wanted. It made me careful with every relationship. My mind was clouded with New Year's lust when it came to the woman I dated after him, but after that…it took me six years to let someone in."

"I'm so sorry, Oleander," Jackson whispered, cupping her face and lifting her eyes to his. "I'm glad you were able to get out of that, because you deserve the world, you deserve so much better."

"I have the world, Jackson. I have you."

"I hope I'm worthy of—" Jackson's eyes widened as Oleander put her fingers over his mouth and smiled, shaking her head at him.

"You are worthy, you are *so fucking worthy*." She traced his mouth with her thumb and stared up into his eyes. "I love you, Jackson."

Jackson stared at her in shock, his heart racing as his mouth dropped open. Oleander arched an eyebrow at him and Jackson blinked. "Fuck…Oleander, I was supposed to say it first. I had a plan."

"So did I."

Jackson laughed, leaning in to kiss her softly, his thumbs brushing away her tears as he pulled back to look into her eyes. "I love you too, Oleander. I think I fell in love with you when you wrapped my hand up in the locker room, when you called me a kid and made fun of my scruff."

"I know. You wear your feelings on your sleeve, remember?"

"Yeah, baby, I remember," Jackson smiled, pulling her in for another kiss.

TWENTY-EIGHT
Oleander

Ollie hadn't intended to tell Jackson *everything* about Pierce. But when Everleigh dropped the bomb about his ex-girlfriend, she realized if she was going to make him tell her the truth about his exes, she needed to do the same. And that meant ripping apart her past and telling him the truth. It was hypocritical, she understood that, expecting him to share the details while she held hers back.

He confessed about Ursula.

And she told him about Pierce.

They'd stayed up on the roof till the colors in the sky changed from dark blue to pink and orange. They dragged themselves back downstairs, stripped to their underwear and collapsed into her bed. With the truth off her chest, Ollie felt lighter. Sure, she was afraid Jackson wouldn't actually stick around now that he knew the truth, but she had to believe he wouldn't hurt her either.

When she woke up hours later, with the sun streaming through her open windows, Ollie felt Jackson's dick pressing against her back. He was still here. A soft smile brushed over her lips and she pressed back against him, eliciting a low growl from Jackson. The arm wrapped around her twitched and she felt him shift, pressing against her even more. Biting her lip, Ollie swallowed back a moan and rubbed her ass against him and when she heard Jackson curse, she laughed.

"Go back to sleep," he mumbled.

"Not when you're poking me like that."

Jackson grunted, his lips touching her bare shoulder. Ollie sighed, relaxing against him.

"Thank you for staying."

She felt him smile against her skin, "Nowhere else I'd rather be."

Ollie shifted so she could look over her shoulder at him. "Last night was heavy, I would have understood if you needed time."

"Would you really have understood?"

Ollie made a face. "Probably not."

"It *was* a lot," Jackson said softly, his breath whispering against her skin. "But I know how hard it was for you to talk about it. And I'm glad you did."

"Did I scare you?"

"No, I'm just angry you went through it at all."

Ollie sighed, pressing her back flush against his chest. "Me too. But, I'm slowly getting over it."

"You don't have to, you know."

"What?"

Ollie tilted her head back as Jackson moved around and looked down at her. "You don't have to get over it. And even if you do, there's no time frame in which you have to."

Ollie stared at him, impressed that he was being so understanding. He was younger than most people she spoke to and yet, Jackson seemed so much more mature. Their first meeting, she'd criticized his age. But now looking at her *boyfriend*, Ollie realized she had misjudged him.

"You okay?"

Ollie blinked and smiled. "Absolutely."

"Should we go see if there's any breakfast?"

"No."

"Why not?"

Ollie smiled and slid a hand between them, cupping Jackson through his boxers as she wiggled her eyebrows. Jackson grunted and shook his head, laughing as he lowered his head, their lips meeting for a kiss. Ollie moved her hand up to play with his hair, using her ass to create friction instead. Jackson moaned into the kiss and with deft hands he got her panties and his boxers off. He moved a hand over her stomach, pulling her back against him and slipped a hand between her thighs. Ollie gasped as Jackson ran his fingers through her folds and spread her legs, lifting one and setting her foot on his thigh as he continued to stroke her.

Without any conversation at all, Ollie stretched out for a condom, ripped a packet open and handed it to Jackson. His hand left her so he could roll it on and Ollie shuddered at the loss. But before she could complain, he was rubbing his cock through her wet folds and as she arched against him, he slid into her.

"Fuck, that's good."

Ollie cried out at Jackson's words and how deep he was inside her at this angle. Her fingers returned to his hair as Jackson moved his hips slowly, going deeper with every thrust. Her thighs quivered and Ollie pushed back against him. This position was different, new and it was definitely going on the list of ways in which she could enjoy being with Jackson.

"Harder, Jack." She growled the words, tugging on his hair and rolling her hips, wanting more. Wanting *everything* and Jackson chuckled low in her ear, making her realize he was going to drag this out. She changed the angle of her body and cried out when his cock rubbed against her sweet spot.

He grunted. "You have to be quiet."

"You need to move faster."

Jackson chuckled again. Instead of denying her what she

wanted, he moved his hand from her hip to between her thighs and teased her clit. But his fingers moved just as slow as his hips and Ollie was on the verge of screaming bloody murder.

"Jackson…"

"Is this not what you wanted?"

And then he *stopped* moving. Ollie growled and rocked against him, taking what *she* wanted. But he'd stopped rubbing her as well and that just wouldn't do.

"*Fuck me.*"

"Can I be in charge for once?"

"If you fuck me like I want, I'll let you be in charge next time."

Jackson chuckled and Ollie tugged on his hair a little harder, causing him to choke on his laugh before his fingers resumed what they were doing. And he gave her *exactly* what she wanted, pushing into her hard and fast, her hips rolling against his with every thrust, guiding him exactly where she wanted. Ollie felt her orgasm build and wrapped her hand around his wrist to stop him, but Jackson knew better than to do that. His lips moved from her shoulder to her neck and then her ear, nipping at her skin gently.

"I've got you, *Oleander*, let go."

That's all it took. She released his wrist, clenching around him as she came, her body shuddering hard at how intense the orgasm was. Jackson was right behind her, his chest pressed flush against her back as he jerked inside her. Ollie felt her hair flutter as Jackson let out a heavy sigh, his warm breath comforting against her cool shoulder.

"I think we need to do this more."

"Lazy morning sex or this position?"

Ollie giggled. "Both. Next time, we do it where I can be loud."

Jackson snorted and Ollie snuggled back into him some more. His arm stayed over her body and she closed her eyes for a moment as his lips brushed back and forth over her shoulder. As he softened inside her, she heard a phone buzz and stop, then start up again.

When it finally stopped, Ollie opened her mouth to say something, but *her* phone started ringing. She frowned as she reached for it on the nightstand. "It's Carson."

Jackson pulled out of her and took the phone, sliding to the edge of the bed.

"Hey man...what? Yeah, okay. Gimme a bit. No no, I'll meet you there."

Ollie sat up, tugging the sheets around her as Jackson hung up and dropped her phone on the bed. She watched the muscles on his back move as he removed the condom and shifted to face her as he tied it up.

"I have to go into work."

"I thought you had the weekend off?"

Jackson nodded. "I do...I *did*. It's a big pitch and it's all hands on deck."

Ollie pouted, but didn't stop Jackson from getting up to go dispose of the condom. Instead, she tugged on a large t-shirt and sat on the edge of the bed, watching as her boyfriend went about getting ready for his day.

OLLIE REALIZED NOW that in resisting him, she was taking back some control of those feelings. But that was ridiculous, she'd belonged to him whether they knew it or not. There was a part of her brain that was waiting for the other shoe to drop, but she also knew it was ridiculous expecting it when it could never happen at all.

Jackson had been an incredible boyfriend. Honestly, he was probably the best partner she'd had. He was attentive, generous in bed, adored her for reasons that still escaped her mind and he was always there for her. Plus, he got along with

Frankie and was slowly getting to know Lachlan better. Ollie looked forward to his texts and even had long phone calls with him, and she was someone who *hated* phone calls.

Not only did he make her happy, he made her feel *safe*. And that was in short supply these days. Even when she wasn't wrapped up in his arms, she knew he was there if she needed him. Ollie couldn't remember the last time she'd felt this light in a relationship. And while she was doing better mentally and physically, she made a mental note to get in touch with her therapist for a few more sessions. A new relationship definitely required some professional help.

"I'm really sorry, babe."

Ollie blinked as Jackson stepped out of the bathroom, towel wrapped around his waist and she shook her head. "It's not your fault."

"I know, but still, I promised you all weekend."

"There are more weekends in our future, I'll manage."

Jackson came up to where she was sitting and bent down to kiss her forehead. He pulled clothes out of his overnight bag and got dressed. Ollie watched him with a small smile on her face.

Their relationship wasn't just sex. Sure, they went at it like rabbits and even got caught by Lachlan a few times because they barely made it to the bedroom some nights. Jackson had the most incredible mouth and sometimes she wondered how she'd managed with exes when they hadn't made her come apart in seconds with their tongues and fingers. Jackson didn't ever try to pin her to the bed—they would fool around and he'd flip them over so she was straddling him. It took Ollie a while to realize he was doing it for her comfort and when she did, Ollie fell a little more in love with him.

Jackson looked over at her once he was dressed and Ollie smiled. He set his bag down and moved over, kneeling in front of her. Jackson's hands slid up her thighs, pushing the t-shirt up slightly before pulling away with a dramatic sigh.

"I'll call you."

Ollie leaned forward, her hands framing his face. "And text when you can."

"Send me nudes."

"Fuck no," Ollie laughed, smooshing his face. "But if you come home soon, I'll give you a proper show."

"Deal," he whispered and leaned in to kiss her, his hands moving to rest on the bed on either side of her.

"I love you, Jackson," she whispered.

He smiled and bumped his nose against hers. "I love you too. Go back to bed."

They kissed once more and Ollie reluctantly let Jackson go, chewing on her bottom lip as he grabbed his bag, phone and keys and walked out. She got to her feet and stood at her bedroom door and watched him. Jackson stopped at the front door, dropped his bag and came back towards her. Ollie flattened herself against the doorjamb and smiled as Jackson pressed against her gently and kissed her, his hands moving down to her ass to grab a handful. But he was pulling away just as fast and before she could make him change his mind, Jackson was walking out the front door.

TWENTY-NINE
Jackson

First, they said it would be just the weekend. Then they said two more days. And before Jackson knew it, he'd been working 18 hour days for a whole week, with no end in sight. It wasn't just the lack of sleep that made him miserable, it was also the lack of Oleander. It would be so easy to hate his job if he didn't like the pitch they were working on.

A group of women were launching a brand new IPA. Afocus Design was not only in charge of the branding, they had to come up with names for each beer. They had six flavored brews and every single one was great.

For Jackson, as a designer, being able to work on a project like this was a big deal. So he put a team together, they brainstormed and produced a bunch of sketches and presented them to the client. They picked the ones they liked and now the team needed to get together and crack the labels and the colors while the other team worked on names.

He knew this pitch was important simply because it was a brand and a marketing strategy that would change the face of their company. But it was also sucking up all of his time. The only time he got to talk to Oleander was before he went into work for another long day or between her dance lessons when he snuck off to the bathroom. They tried phone sex again, but it was clear Oleander couldn't multitask with the phone and her vibrator and they stopped trying. Instead, they spent the few minutes they could talking about what they missed.

There was one night when he thought the team would be able to take their work with them to the Barrel and he'd get to see Oleander. But the minute the project leader found out about this *grand plan*, they were forced to stay at work. And that little incident led to another working weekend. He'd been home once in that whole week and he'd been asleep almost as soon as his head hit the pillow. So any hope of him sneaking over to Oleander's apartment or inviting her to his for a late night cuddle session was pointless.

"We should definitely call this Berry Awesome," Trevor announced from where he was seated, tossing a baseball up in the air.

Jackson groaned and tossed a pencil at his friend. "They specifically said they don't want the flavor in the name."

"I know, but we should really *convince* them to change their minds."

"Trev, go back to your desk and do this without driving me insane." Jackson barely looked up from his screen, but he heard Trevor walk away, mumbling to himself.

Jackson was exhausted. They'd finished the designs, the branding and they had a basic plan for the strategy. The problem was, all the names they were coming up with were too cliché and boring, and Jackson was trying not to get involved in that process since he always ended up being the one who did most of the work—from basic design to name suggestions.

His phone buzzed and Jackson reached for it blindly as he scribbled more notes.

"What?"

"Is that any way to greet your girlfriend?" Oleander's husky voice put a smile on his face.

"Pray tell, how does one greet their girlfriend?"

Oleander cleared her throat. "By telling her you miss her and can't wait to see her…soon?"

He sighed. "I do miss you, terribly. But, I don't know what *soon* means."

"I know, I'm glad I got to talk to you before I went for my shift at the Barrel."

Jackson felt sad that he couldn't see her, so he repeated himself. "I miss you, Oleander."

"Aw, baby, I miss you too."

"What are you wearing?"

Oleander laughed and Jackson's heart raced at the sound of her voice, wishing he was wrapped up in her arms right then.

"At this very moment, I'm wearing nothing."

"Oleander…"

"Okay, I'm kidding, I'm wearing my usual—jeans and a tee."

Jackson groaned, because even that was enough to get him going. "What tee?"

"Today is Led Zeppelin."

"I've never listened to any of their non-popular songs."

Oleander gasped and Jackson got to his feet, attaching his earphones so he could put his phone in his pocket and go for a walk.

"I'm going to send you some of my favorite tracks and you're going to listen, so when we see each other again, we can discuss them."

Jackson laughed. "You're giving me an assignment?"

"Yes! You need to be educated on the greatest hits of the past."

"You're ridiculous."

"You love me," she whispered and Jackson smiled.

"Yeah, I guess I do."

The long silence on the other end made him chuckle as he walked to the pantry and made himself a cup of coffee.

"Oleander?"

"I'm trying to be offended by your response."

Jackson smirked. "So that means silence?"

"Yes, now stop distracting me from my silence."

Smiling, he took a sip of his coffee and walked towards the balcony. With Afocus Design on the 14th & 15th floor, they had one area dedicated to a balcony. It was most often used by smokers, but for Jackson, it was a place to go and think. Walking the length of the balcony helped clear his mind. And as he walked out onto the empty balcony with his coffee, he listened to Oleander shuffle around on the other end. They did this sometimes, stayed on call while the other went on with their day just to hear soft sounds and remind each other that one day, they could reconnect again.

Oleander was humming a song and Jackson was mid-sip when a scent hit him.

A scent he hadn't inhaled in a while.

"Hi, Jax."

Jackson swallowed the coffee in his mouth before turning to face the voice.

"Ursula. Why?" He stared at her, momentarily forgetting about Oleander on the other end of the phone call.

"That's no way to greet a friend."

Jackson frowned and cleared his throat before slapping on a fake smile, not bothering to hide his annoyance. "What the *fuck* are you doing here?"

"I came to see you, obviously."

"To return my clothes?"

"Oh, I tossed those out a while ago."

Jackson sighed, realizing Oleander was still listening and quickly disconnected the call.

"Why are you here?"

"I've got a proposition for you."

"Not interested." Jackson shook his head, tipping his cup at her in a 'thank you, goodbye' sign.

"This will benefit you greatly too."

He sighed. "I doubt that."

"You met someone new!"

"Where did you even get that idea?" He frowned.

"A year ago you would have dropped to your knees at the mention of a beneficial proposition, now you're not even looking at me."

Jackson tilted his head back, shoving his earphones into his pocket. "There are so many reasons why I wouldn't drop to my knees for you anymore, least of all because I met someone new."

"So you did meet someone new."

"Can you get to the point faster, because I'm busy trying to crack an idea," he said with as much patience as he could and frowned, realizing she wasn't supposed to be there. "How did you even get into the building at this hour?"

"The security downstairs still thinks we're together," Ursula said with a saccharine smile that made Jackson's stomach turn. "So, the proposition."

"Nope, not interested."

Ursula kept talking. "Ariadne's getting married and I'm the Maid of Honor, and I need a date."

"You have a date."

"Jax." Ursula was trying to reprimand him, but she was being coy and it was driving him insane. "Come with me."

"Why would I do that? We broke up, remember?"

"But we're still friends!"

"No, we're not. You said we're friends and closed the door. I never agreed to any of it."

"Now you're being dramatic."

"For the love of…" Jackson blew out a frustrated breath

and set his coffee down before turning to his ex-girlfriend. "No, I will not be your date. No, we weren't friends after you kicked me out of your life. No, I am not even remotely interested in getting back together with you. And yes, I have met someone new, not that it's any of your business."

"Wow, Jax, took you long enough to stand up to me."

"Please leave. Hand them your visitor's pass too, I'll let them know to take you off the list."

Ursula pouted. "I was really hoping you'd give me another chance."

"You had six months to come talk to me, Ursula. I don't owe you anything." He turned his back on her and focused on his breathing. This was why he so rarely talked about his exes and why he kept Ursula a *secret* from Oleander. *Shit.* She probably heard part of the conversation and Jackson hated that. He didn't expect Ursula to show up and he definitely didn't intend for Oleander to hear him saying her name.

He didn't care if she had left or not, Jackson pulled his phone out of his pocket and found a string of texts from Oleander with question marks and wide eyed emojis. Groaning, he quickly replied that it was nothing to worry about. But what was the point? She was worried. And after almost two weeks of barely seeing each other, Oleander heard him speaking to his ex. If the roles were reversed, Jackson would have felt the same. Or worse, really.

Fuck, he wanted to see Oleander again, even if it meant showing up and waiting in the parking lot until she finished her shift. He didn't want her to think he was doing it only because Ursula showed up, but because he wanted to see her. Ursula showing up speeded up the process.

As he walked back into the office, Jackson called Oleander and got her voicemail. He thought about leaving a message and changed his mind. At his desk, he tried her again and got her voicemail once more. Obviously she was ignoring him or she'd left for work already and had turned her phone off, which meant he wouldn't get to her until she was done.

Jackson started to pack up his things, because now he needed to go see her. He *needed* to make sure she was okay and wasn't thinking the worst of him. As he packed up, he called her again and when her voicemail answered, he knew heading to her place was the best thing.

THIRTY

Oleander

So here was the thing, Ollie wasn't angry. She was *disappointed*.

What was supposed to be a regular call before she went off to work had turned into a wake up call about how much time she and Jackson were not spending together. Ollie was fine when it was two days of not seeing him and she accepted the four extra days. But when it got to a week of no Jackson, she started to lose her mind. Because that week turned into two and there literally was no end in sight. Every time they spoke, Jackson sounded more tired and worn out and it was worrying her. Creative jobs like his always sucked the life out of you. It was why she had quit her desk job to find something a little more satisfying.

But working at the Barrel wasn't really satisfying anymore, not when your boyfriend was hanging out with his ex-girlfriend. The very same one who had broken his heart.

When she heard him say her name and stutter through the first part of the conversation, Ollie tried to get Jackson's attention. But he hung up on her. And that made her mad. After sending him texts about him hanging up on her, she finished getting ready and drove to work. Of course, that's when

Jackson decided to call her back. But Ollie wasn't in the mood. She was already feeling him slipping away with work and sure, their daily phone calls and texts were cute, but they were sporadic and sometimes enough to say 'hi' before he left his phone on his desk to go in for a meeting or something else. It was starting to feel like she was trying harder than he was and Ollie hated being *that* girl.

It was a regular shift at the Barrel, with all the lecherous customers and Cassie being absolutely useless by running out early for another 'emergency'. Ollie often wondered what would happen if she left this job to go find something else. Or, hell, she could teach dance full-time. It was definitely paying her more than this job was and Melody was constantly talking about adding more classes and bringing on more older kids.

Ollie was halfway through her shift when Frankie walked into the Barrel looking beautiful as always. Her best friend was most definitely oblivious to the effect her presence had on people, because she ignored every set of eyes that followed her as she approached the bar.

Frankie also knew that Ollie and Jackson had been apart for a few days, which meant that she was going to make a scene about it. Because that's just how Frankie rolled. Once she'd sat down and tapped her knuckles on the bar top, Frankie leaned in and used her *outside* voice.

"Please tell me Little John has been getting some action these past few weeks."

Ollie frowned. "Who the fuck named their vibrator *Little John*?"

"Wait, that wasn't you? Oh god, who was it?"

Snorting, she arched an eyebrow. "I'm sorry, you have other friends you discuss vibrators with?"

"Probably one of the brides, you know how open they are once you spend 24 hours discussing their dream wedding."

"I am *slightly* disgusted by the name, but it's very creative."

"That's why I thought it was you," Frankie said, narrowing

her eyes, like she was trying to make sure Ollie hadn't named her vibrator after a character in *Robin Hood*. "But that doesn't mean the question can be ignored."

"It is named *Grant*." Ollie rolled her eyes, pouring her friend a drink. "But since you asked so politely, yes."

"Hallelujah!" Frankie cheered so loud, startling the drunk man beside her.

"You're going to get me fired, Frank."

Frankie rolled her eyes. "Who cares? You're making the most of your vibrator while your boy toy is off bringing home the bacon."

"The word you're looking for is *boyfriend*." Ollie sighed. "And he's not bringing home anything considering he's barely home."

"I don't care what you call him, he's a boy toy," Frankie cackled, taking a sip of her drink and held the empty glass out. "Top me up, bar wench."

"I sometimes wonder why we're still friends."

Frankie gave her a sweet smile. "Because I make your life much more colorful."

"Not the term I would use, but sure."

"I'm proud of you, Anders," Frankie told her. "You deserve to have orgasms every night and that stupid smile on your face every day. Even when your boy toy is busy doing something else."

Ollie scrubbed her hands over her face. "That sentence has never been more accurate than it is right now."

"What happened?"

Ollie shook her head, trying to think of the best way to explain this.

Frankie frowned and gestured to her glass. "I'm going to need more booze for this, huh?"

"Most likely."

As Ollie topped up Frankie's glass, she explained the whole two weeks apart and the daily phone calls, and then she got to the part about Ursula. That made Frankie really angry. She made a fist and waved it around, like she was going to go find this offending woman and punch her face in. When Ollie finally finished her story, Frankie was halfway through a bottle of scotch and she was swaying slightly.

"I need to beat someone up."

"Easy there, Rocky Balboa."

Frankie giggled and steadied herself by grabbing the bar. "But seriously, Anders, you have to say something."

"Say what, exactly?"

"I dunno, he's *your* boyfriend."

Ollie sighed. "I don't know what happened, Frankie. Maybe it was nothing."

"Or maybe it was something. Sure, we like Jackson and we support your relationship," Frankie paused to burp, "but maybe this woman doesn't give a shit and wants your man."

"Okay, that's a tad dramatic."

"We know nothing about this girl outside of what Jackson told you, right?"

"Don't do that." Ollie made a face.

"Okay, fine, that was low. I trust Jackson to make the right choices, but also…"

Ollie sighed. "Yeah, I know what you mean."

"Talk to him, Anders. It's probably not as bad as we're making it out to be."

"I mean, it did take him a while to even tell me she existed."

Frankie shrugged. "I'm not going to tell everyone about Trent at the beginning of a relationship."

"That's different."

"How? Trent hurt me, he made me feel like shit and I had to pick myself up and move on."

Ollie groaned and put the bottle of scotch away. "No more alcohol for you, you make too much sense."

Frankie grinned and knocked back what was left of her

drink. Ollie handed her a glass of water and put in an order for wings and garlic bread so she could soak up all of the alcohol before she went home. But Frankie was right, Ollie needed to talk to Jackson. Maybe it was nothing. Maybe it wasn't anything to get worked up about.

But her trust issues were flaring up and Ollie hated that. Jackson had already kept Ursula from her for so long and now, he was hanging out with her? At the same time, she was worried about him. From everything Jackson told her, Ursula had really hurt him and seeing her again couldn't have been easy. Ollie knew that some heartbreaks hurt more than others and it didn't matter how it happened or what the impact was, it still hurt.

HOURS LATER, once she'd finished her shift and Frankie had inhaled all of the food in front of her, Ollie took her back to her apartment. With her best friend tucked into bed, water and Advil on her nightstand, Ollie drove back to her place. She was exhausted. While she hadn't danced that morning, the mental gymnastics she had done with the whole Jackson and Ursula thing had worn her out.

Letting herself into the apartment, she toed off her boots, dropped her jacket and bag by the door before dragging herself into the kitchen for some water. With a bottle in hand, she turned off all the lights and pushed open the door to her bedroom and found Jackson fast asleep in the middle of her bed. Quietly moving through the room, Ollie set the water down and fished out her phone to find a whole heap of texts from Jackson. She carried her phone to the bathroom, where she leaned against the counter and read them.

Jackson: *I'm sorry, I know how this looks, but I promise nothing happened.*

Jackson: *Oleander, please call me back.*

Jackson: *Babe, I can hear the wheels in your head turning, please don't think of the worst thing.*
Jackson: *I'm leaving work and coming to you.*
Jackson: *You're not here. Are you avoiding me?*
Jackson: *Oh wait, your shift isn't over for another few hours.*
Jackson: *Okay, I'll be here.*
Jackson: *I'm sorry.*
Jackson: *I love you.*

The first few came as she'd started her shift at the Barrel, then he texted when she was telling Frankie about what happened. And an hour ago, he'd sent her the last two texts. Ollie sighed and set her phone aside as she stripped down and had a quick shower.

She changed into an extra large nightshirt, grabbed her phone and quietly pulled open the bathroom door. And found Jackson sitting on the edge of the bed, rubbing his eyes.

"Why didn't you wake me up?"

Ollie walked around to her side of the bed. "Because you looked like you were dead."

"So you were going to let me be dead in the middle of your bed?"

A sigh escaped her lips. "What are you doing here, Jackson?"

He frowned and gestured to her phone. "I know you saw my texts and all my missed calls."

"And?"

"Come on, Ollie."

She shook her head and pointed at him. "No, do not *Ollie* me right now."

"Are you going to let me explain what happened?" Jackson huffed and came around to where she was standing, gently reaching for her hand.

Ollie dropped the covers and pulled her hand away, crossing her arms over her chest as she looked at him. "Fine, explain."

"She just showed up," he started and at the narrowed eyes she shot him, Jackson held his hands up. "A friend is getting married and she wanted a date for the wedding."

"So she thought she'd ask you?"

"Apparently I'm her only hope."

Ollie rolled her eyes and waved him off. "No *Star Wars* puns at a time like this."

"Sorry," Jackson sighed, rubbing his face. "I turned her down and she tried to get me to change my mind. I mentioned you *and* made her leave."

"What is wrong with this woman?"

"What do you mean?"

Ollie sighed and sat down on the bed. "She cheats on you, breaks up with you, leaves you high and dry for months and suddenly decides she needs you to be her date?"

"Ursula's always been flighty that way."

"There's flighty and there's selfish. And I'm frustrated that you stood there and listened."

Jackson frowned as he sat down beside her. "What was I supposed to do?"

"Tell her to go fuck herself."

"Well, that was an option."

Ollie shook her head. "These past few weeks have been hard without your ex-girlfriend showing up while I'm on the phone with you, but that? That was really frustrating."

"I'm sorry."

Ollie rubbed her face and looked at Jackson from the corner of her eyes—his hair was disheveled, there were dark circles under his eyes and you could see the exhaustion on his face. It wasn't fair to get so angry with him about something completely out of his control, even if she had been frustrated and stewing in it all evening. Plus, he looked so stupidly handsome in his dark blue Henley and khaki pants—seriously, how could he make khakis sexy?

She reached out and grabbed his hand, linking their

fingers together. When she glanced at him, he was staring at her with wide eyes.

"Are you okay?"

Jackson frowned. "I'm more worried about *us*."

Ollie ignored that for a beat. "Seeing her again must have been rough."

His eyes shuttered and Jackson nodded. "Definitely not what I wanted to be doing with my day."

"For the record, we're fine," Ollie said, turning to face him. "But I want to make sure you're okay."

"I mean...I'm okay *now*. But you're right, seeing her again was hard and also very unpleasant," Jackson said as he played with her fingers. "I told you saying her name out loud would conjure her."

Ollie rolled her eyes and pulled her hand away to smack his thigh. "That's ridiculous."

Jackson laughed, the sound filling up her bedroom and Ollie smiled. She scooted closer to him and ran her thumb under his eyes. A soft sigh escaped him and he leaned in to rest his forehead against hers. They stayed like that for a minute before Jackson pressed a kiss to the corner of her mouth.

"I'm sorry about today," he whispered against her skin.

"I know," Ollie responded, pulling back to look into his eyes. "But we both need sleep, so go shower."

Jackson nodded, kissed her fully on the mouth and then walked off to the bathroom, stripping his clothes off as he went. She crawled under the covers and curled up, waiting for him. While she believed him and everything that had happened, Ollie felt a twinge of something in her chest.

And it told her this was just the beginning of whatever was about to happen.

THIRTY-ONE

Oleander

Only Jackson would do something infuriating by inviting her to his sister's eighteenth birthday party days after *the incident*. And yet, Ollie couldn't refuse him. Now, a week later Ollie was nervous and very underprepared for what she was about to walk into.

As per her request, they weren't taking a gift, but Ollie insisted on flowers for his stepmother. So on their way to Middletown, they stopped at a florist and picked up a bouquet of lilies. She'd never met the family of the person she was dating—Ollie got so close to meeting Pierce's family, but then *everything* had happened.

When Jackson parked in front of a two-storied classic American home, Ollie let out a shaky breath and mentally coached herself to keep breathing. She got out, swapped her flip-flops for heels and nervously smiled at Jackson as he came around to take her hand.

"I won't leave your side," Jackson told her, clearly seeing the panic on her face.

"What if I need to pee?"

"We'll just have to go to the bathroom together."

Ollie laughed and using her free hand, poked Jackson in

the side. She'd never worn this off-white dress before, because she thought the large flowers made *her* look bigger. But the minute she'd tugged it on the night before during her display of clothes, Jackson had said *yes* emphatically. Not one to be undone, he'd pulled out all the stops with his clothes knowing it would drive her insane—cream Henley and dark pants that were tucked into his boots and his signature messy hair look.

"You look beautiful, Oleander." When he spoke, she realized that she'd been staring at him.

"I was just thinking the same about you."

Jackson smirked. "If you get tired, let me know. We'll hide in my old bedroom."

"I can't believe you had Ninja Turtles wallpaper."

"Now I'm sad that you'll never see it," Jackson said with a pout and gave her hand a gentle squeeze.

Okay, she could do this. It was a gathering of people and nothing else. Jackson led her into the house, sidestepping guests and smiling politely at people trying to get his attention.

But the minute they stepped through the front door, Ollie stopped breathing.

The Huxley house was gorgeous, it was like the house from *Father of the Bride*. The house was not only well maintained and clean, it also smelled amazing clearly thanks to the flowers set up everywhere. Ollie let her eyes wander over the gorgeous staircase and the polished banister as Jackson tugged on her and her visual treat was blocked off by a door.

"What...where are we?"

"I just wanted to put our bags down."

"This is a nice house, Jackson."

Jackson nodded, "Yeah, Mindy really did it up after she married my dad."

"I never asked, but how rich are you?"

"*I'm* not rich, my dad is. He's richer than this house, to be honest, but Mindy loved it so much she refused to let him move them into some gaudy mansion," Jackson explained.

Setting the bouquet down on the table, Ollie took a minute to look at the room they were in.

It was an office, most likely Mindy's judging by the flowers, paintings and photographs everywhere. Jackson was still speaking, but she tuned him out and surveyed the space. She had an incredible view of the front lawn and street where they'd parked from the windows behind the desk she was running her hand over.. It was neatly organized and color coded, and she appreciated Mindy for that alone.

"Oleander."

"Mmh?" She turned to look at Jackson. He was smiling at her in a way that told her he knew she wasn't listening to him at all.

"Ready to go out there and meet my family?"

"Sure. I put on this gorgeous dress and we drove all this way."

Jackson growled softly. "Don't talk about the dress. Because every time I look at you, I'm thinking of all the ways to take it off of you."

"You cannot destroy this dress, so you'll have to be patient."

"Now that's all I want to do."

Ollie laughed at the pained look on his face as he bit down on his fist. "Right now, we need to go meet your family."

Jackson sighed and Ollie stepped into his arms, sliding one hand up around the back of his neck to tug his mouth to hers. She felt Jackson's hand slide down to her ass and Ollie yelped when she realized that if she raised her arms too high, the dress would also ride up. Pulling away, she straightened her dress and frowned at Jackson.

"Behave."

IF SHE HADN'T STOPPED them, they would have spent the whole party in Mindy's office. Ollie adjusted her dress and brushed back her hair, Jackson kissed the side of her head as they stepped through the doors leading to the backyard and Ollie's eyes widened.

This is what she imagined garden parties at estates would be like. The amount of space that spread out behind the house was unreal. The back lawn was sprawling and there were pockets of garden chairs, tables loaded with food and drinks, a small stage with two acoustic musicians, and fairy lights draped over all the trees surrounding the property. It wasn't even a house at the end of a lane or in the middle of nowhere—there were houses on either side and further out beyond the back fence. Yet, the property never seemed to end.

Jackson led her through the crowd and she saw everyone glancing their way, sizing her up. When Jackson looked back at her with a smile, Ollie focused and felt her heart stop at the beautiful people in front of her.

She saw the same smile, the eyes and the lean build on the man standing before her. Where his son was a subtle kind of handsome, this man was all rugged cowboy handsome. Beside him stood an exquisite woman with high cheekbones and beautiful eyes that lit up with the smile aimed at her husband. Ollie appreciated men and women of all kinds, but this kind of attractiveness in one couple was truly unfair. She took a mental picture so she could describe them to Frankie later.

"Dad, Mindy," he started, tugging Ollie beside him. "I want you to meet my girlfriend. This is Oleander."

"Finally!" Mindy handed her glass to Jackson and clapped before stepping towards Ollie. Not knowing how to react, she let Mindy hug her, swaying as they held onto each other. When she pulled away, Ollie had to remember to blink and smile.

"You are beautiful. *No*...that's not enough of a word, stunning, gorgeous, totally out of Jackson's league even."

"I tell her that everyday," Jackson said and Ollie opened her mouth and closed it a few times before finally finding her voice.

"Thank you," she said fast and blushed.

Mindy gave her hand a squeeze and gestured to the man beside her. "This is my husband, Callum. Keleigh, our daughter is somewhere in this throng. And so are Lisbeth and Carrie. I'm sure Jackson will introduce you to the family eventually."

"Thank you for having me, I know we told you about me coming really last minute." Ollie smiled.

Mindy waved off her thank you. "I'm so glad to finally meet the woman making my boy happy."

"Okay, that's enough. We're going to go mingle," Jackson laughed, shaking hands with his dad and Ollie saw him wink, which made Jackson smile as he lead them away.

"What was that between you and your dad?"

"He approves, that's all."

Ollie smiled, glad that his parents liked her. "Speaking of which…do you know that your dad and stepmom are truly the most beautiful people I've ever seen?"

"I mean, they're all right. I know Mindy is out of my father's league, like you are out of mine."

"Obviously," Ollie teased, Jackson chuckled and tugged her into his side, his lips finding hers for a quick kiss. She curled her fingers into his shirt as they pulled away, their eyes locked till someone interrupted them.

"Okay, save it for later. It's *my* party, and that means you have to behave."

"Kel," Jackson said and pulled away from Ollie, turning to the beautiful young woman in front of them. Jackson hugged the brunette and turned to gesture to her.

"Keleigh, this is my girlfriend Oleander. This is my baby sister, Keleigh."

"Happy birthday," Ollie said as Keleigh did what her

mother did earlier and hugged her. "I've heard so much about you, but it's nice to finally put a face to the name."

"As you can probably tell, we haven't heard anything about you," Keleigh said with a pointed glare at Jackson. "But I was very excited when mom said he was bringing someone."

"We wouldn't miss it for the world," Jackson said. "Before we get caught up in festivities, I'm going to find Beth and Carrie. Any idea where they might be?"

"They've corralled all the kids into a room and decided to stay inside instead of enjoying this gorgeous weather."

"We'll go say our hellos and come find you later." Jackson said with a dramatic eye roll that made his stepsister laugh. Ollie smiled at the interaction.

"You didn't bring a gift, right?"

Ollie shook her head. "I got very strict instructions, so no gifts."

"Good! Beth seemed to ignore explicit instruction," Keleigh said with a roll of her eyes and wandered off, leaving Ollie watching her as Jackson sighed.

"On *that* note, it's time to meet my sister and sister-in-law. You ready?"

Ollie shook her head, both of them laughing as Jackson led them back into the house. And towards people she knew were going to completely change the course of this relationship.

MEETING PARENTS WAS ONE THING. Meeting siblings was another. Ollie knew that when Jackson met her brothers, they were going to stress him out. All three of them had gone into law enforcement of some kind, and while they no longer did background checks on the people she dated, she wouldn't put it past them to dig into Jackson just to scare the shit out of him. So far, Keleigh seemed great, but from the tension in

Jackson's shoulders, Ollie had a feeling meeting the next two people wasn't going to be as painless.

They moved through the house, heading for a room in the back. Jackson pushed the door open and Ollie's eyes widened. There were kids everywhere and in one corner, two blonde women were sitting on a couch drinking wine. Before she knew it, a round of high-pitched squeals followed by kids screaming *Uncle Jack* were charging towards them. Ollie gasped and stepped back as Jackson was tackled to the floor by these excited kids.

After more squealing and hugging, lots of playful grunting as he tickled some of the kids, Jackson sat up and gently moved kids aside.

"All right, let me breathe."

The kids giggled and climbed off him, and Ollie watched in fascination as Jackson stood up, and then noticed that all the kids were staring at *her*.

"Hi," one of the little girls said as she stepped closer.

"You're pretty," another one said and Ollie laughed softly as she looked at Jackson. Working with kids had made her a little more comfortable around them, but these were unknown kids and that was still going to make her nervous. Jackson's hand landed on her back as the kids finished their analysis and went back to what they were doing as the two women walked over.

Seriously, what was it with Jackson's family—why were they all stunning? Was it the water, the genetics?

"Jackson."

He smiled and turned to Ollie. "Oleander, this is my sister Lisbeth and my sister-in-law, Carrie. This is my girlfriend."

Ollie smiled, "It's really good to meet you."

"You too. *Oleander* was it?" The way her name sounded on Lisbeth's tongue felt weird, but she smiled anyway as she nodded. "So, where are you from, Oleander?"

"West Virginia."

"Born and raised?"

"Beth..." Jackson growled, but she faked looking confused by his displeasure.

"Yeah." Ollie kept going and she could feel Jackson tense up beside her. "My brothers and I are second generation Indian-American."

"Ah, of course."

"What about you, Lisbeth, where are *you* from?" She asked it with a straight face, Jackson snorted and coughed loudly. And because Ollie wasn't going to be undone by this woman, she smiled sweetly and added, "It was *great* meeting you."

Ollie walked out of the room and once they were out of earshot, Jackson chuckled. "That was brilliant."

"Ugh, I hate doing that."

"Well, she deserved it."

Ollie sighed. "It's not *my* job to school her on her racism."

"But you put her in her place, which is more than can be said for any of us in this family."

There was always one member of every family that had a tendency to say stupid shit and behave like an idiot. Ollie was glad she'd finally gotten through the interaction, but she *knew* someone like Lisbeth wouldn't let it go that easily.

"I'm sorry you had to deal with that."

"I'll just stay clear of her."

"Good plan," Jackson nodded and Ollie sighed. "Come on, let's get some booze in you."

THIRTY-TWO
Oleander

Between Lisbeth's words and the large number of people around her, she felt lost. Jackson held onto her for as long as he could, but when his father asked for help, he was gone. She didn't blame him; he had a responsibility.

As if hearing her worrisome thoughts, Jackson's nieces dragged her towards the stage and insisted she dance with them. For one song, she twirled and bounced, letting her hair down and ignored everyone else. But the whispers started to get louder than the music and Ollie freaked out. She hadn't danced in front of people she didn't know for this reason, because sometimes just letting go was frowned upon in some way.

After thanking the kids for the dance, Ollie walked back into the house to cool down. She found a wall of photographs, smiling as she traced Jackson's growth. He truly had been an awkward kid and she could see the point in his life where things had gone wrong for him. Then there were smiles, because Mindy happened. Ollie brushed her fingers over the baby face of her boyfriend and smiled to herself.

Callum and Mindy were perfection, right from their looks

to their kind hearts, and Ollie was glad that despite his father not being around for a few years, Jackson got to have him back and to build a relationship with him.

The wandering took her to another office that looked like Callum's—from the dark colors to the leather chair and the lack of personal touches. Stepping through the open door, Ollie took in the tall bookshelves, lined with leather-bound books she'd never heard of. The office was in such good condition, she wondered if he even used this space anymore. She traced the spines of the books and sat in the large leather chair behind a big desk.

Her family wasn't wealthy like this, but her parents had made enough money over the years to give the kids a good life. Ollie never had to wonder if she was going to miss a meal, she had good clothes, and every year her mother took her stationery shopping before the first day of school. They'd gone on family holidays every single summer and once in a while, they went somewhere during Christmas. She'd been to both Disneyland and Disney World at least once in her life and grew up watching movies at the cinema regularly. But this kind of luxury was something Ollie had never imagined for herself.

And by looking at Jackson, you'd never even realize he came from money.

Sitting there, Ollie remembered the flowers she'd picked up for Mindy. So she went to get it and then slowly navigated her way to what she hoped was the kitchen. She got lost once and turned a corner in time to hear someone say her name. Frowning, Ollie hugged the bouquet to her chest and walked in the direction of the voice. Not only did she find the kitchen, she found Lisbeth standing at the center island, phone to her ear.

"...and to top it off, she's *Indian*...yeah, Indian food is fine, but an Indian in the family? Can you even imagine... God, no, I'm not going to play nice. Jackson can pretend all he wants, but she doesn't fit...No, I can't *fake* it for Jackson. He should have warned us he was bringing this...did I mention that she's much older? Close to your age...That makes her *old*. Jackson is still a kid."

Ollie rolled her eyes. She'd faced off with lots of racist people, but this was ridiculous. While confronting Lisbeth would only make the situation worse, Ollie needed to end this now. She stepped into the kitchen and *accidentally* bumped into a lower cabinet. Lisbeth turned around and narrowed her eyes.

"Can I help you?"

"I'm looking for a vase to put these into."

Lisbeth hung up the phone and waved Ollie off. "Leave them there, Mindy will do it later."

"I'd rather do it myself."

"So, we're going to pretend like you didn't eavesdrop on my entire conversation?"

Ollie pulled open cabinets, looking for a vase. "I'm not pretending. You don't like me, I don't like you, it's simple."

"You don't belong with Jackson."

"Why not?"

Lisbeth sighed as Ollie finally pulled out a vase and set it on the counter. They turned to face each other, like they were preparing for war.

"My brother is naïve, young and impressionable. You're not from here and even if you are, you've got your customs and your beliefs and I don't want you brainwashing Jackson."

Ollie snorted. "Why are you treating Jackson like he's incapable of making his own decisions?"

"Ever since our mother left, he's been making terrible decisions and you're another one."

"I don't think you actually know your brother as well as you claim."

"It doesn't matter what I do or do not know," Lisbeth said. "The point is, you come from a different culture. Don't you have enough Indian men you can get into an arranged marriage with and leave our men alone?"

"Wow, *our men*," Ollie snorted, shaking her head as she filled the vase with water and arranged the flowers.

There was a loud cheer from outside and Ollie wasn't sure if she was glad for the high volume drowning out this conversation or if she wished someone was able to hear what was happening.

Speaking of which, Ollie was so enraged about the whole *our men* nonsense and the way people used arranged marriages as an insult. On the other hand, she hated the way Bollywood romanticized it, because it wasn't always successful. Her parents fell in love, so did Baby and her grandfather. Her brothers all fell in love with their wives, some of her cousins were lucky. But most of her family in India had arranged marriages, some of them were unhappy, some were divorced and a tiny portion were in love with their partners.

And after everything she went through with those ridiculous *meetings* her grandmother set up, Ollie wasn't going to stand around and let someone make arranged marriages be a reason why she was unworthy of Jackson. Or anyone, really.

"Your family believes in arranged marriages, do they not?"

Ollie sighed. "So what?"

Lisbeth put her hands on her hips. "I've seen Bollywood movies."

"Real life isn't like a Bollywood movie, Beth."

"*Lis*beth," she corrected her and Ollie held her hands up in silent apology. "My point is, you can go back to your Bollywood life and we'll go back to ours."

"Does it even matter to you what your brother wants?"

"Obviously you've brainwashed him."

Ollie frowned, because Lisbeth had said that once already. "Being Brown means I have brainwashing powers and live a Bollywood life?"

"I don't have to explain myself to you. You come from a

different country and you sweep in and take all of our jobs, marry all of our men and…you know."

"Is stereotyping part of the racism class you take?"

Lisbeth's eyes widened at the word 'racism', her face turning red as she shrieked, "Get out of my house!"

Almost as if the universe didn't want anyone to know what was happening in the kitchen, the music changed to something upbeat that caused everyone outside to get really excited. Ollie wanted to roll her eyes to the ceiling and ask the person up there what the fuck they were doing to help her out of this situation.

"This isn't your house, *Lis*beth, and quite honestly your hostility is unwarranted."

Lisbeth was still going. "This isn't your home. You can't walk into our lives and try to upset the balance of everything."

"I was born and raised here, just like you. So if I go, so should you. I bet your ancestors aren't even American."

"Of course they are. You're not welcome here, *Oleander*."

Ollie stood firm. "I'll let Mindy and Callum decide that for me."

"We don't want your *kind* here."

"And what kind is that?"

"Illegal."

Ollie scoffed out a laugh, wishing Lisbeth had used a different term. Something more original, and a little more *impactful*. As a Brown woman living in a small town, Ollie got called *illegal* quite often. It wasn't new. She'd even been called a terrorist once and she'd argued with the man that she was Christian, born and raised in America and still nothing happened.

Much like that, arguing with Lisbeth was about as useful as a hole in the head.

There was a smart comeback on her tongue when Jackson suddenly appeared. He looked angry and Ollie blew out a breath as she tried to center herself. It was one thing to be attacked by a stranger, but a whole other thing to have someone related to the man you loved attack you this way. Ollie wondered how much Jackson had heard, but by the way he was moving towards Lisbeth, she figured he'd heard *enough*.

"What the fuck is wrong with you?"

Lisbeth scoffed. "She's *using* you, Jackson."

"For what?"

"Money and everything that comes with it."

Jackson looked as exasperated as Ollie felt. "Jesus, you've completely lost your mind."

"You broke up with amazing women for this *pathetic* excuse of a girlfriend. And for what?"

"Excuse me?" Ollie stepped forward, glaring at Lisbeth who smartly took a step back.

"Jackson." Lisbeth turned to her brother, her eyes taking on a fearful expression. "You know as well as I do that she is not the right person for you."

"And what are you basing all of this on?"

"Seriously?" Ollie glared at her boyfriend and Lisbeth laughed.

"What do you do for a living, Oleander?"

Jackson shook his head as Ollie opened her mouth. He spoke instead. "How is that relevant here?"

"So her job isn't great and she's definitely not doing well in the men department, so what, she picked you and you just accepted her?"

Ollie backed up, leaning against the counter as she stared between the two of them. What was it with people and bitching about her career choices? Ollie waited for Jackson to say something in response, but he stayed silent for so long she felt like he was not going to contribute anything useful. As she started to speak, Jackson filled the silence.

"Oleander's damn good at her job and looking after herself. If anything she's probably looking after me," Jackson said, moving closer to his sister. "And it's not like she's the only one with bad relationship experiences, I've had my fair share."

"Oh honey." Lisbeth gave him a fake sad face and Ollie wanted to punch her. "She's using you to fix everything that's wrong in her life and you don't even see it."

"Jesus, Beth, you're reaching."

"I'm not even going to pretend to like her," Lisbeth countered, glaring at Ollie. "She doesn't belong in this family and the sooner you see that, the better for everyone."

Ollie was done. She was exhausted, worn out from this conversation and done defending herself constantly. Ollie tugged on Jackson's arm to get his attention.

"I think I should go."

Lisbeth clapped slowly. "You should. I'll let dad and Mindy know you were *so* happy to be invited."

"Shut the fuck up, Beth," Jackson snapped and Ollie took his hand, heart racing at the anger on his face. This was a whole new side of Jackson and it scared her while also comforting her. Instead of saying anything else, Jackson led her out of the kitchen and to get their bags.

Ollie stepped in front of him. "You should stay. I'll get myself a ride."

Jackson shook his head. "No way, I'll take you home."

"Jackson...this is an important party for Keleigh."

"And *you're* important to me." He cupped her face and brushed his thumb over her cheek.

Ollie realized she was crying. "Are you sure?"

"Absolutely, I'd rather be with you anyway."

Jackson grabbed their overnight bag from Mindy's office and Ollie followed him to the car. She looked over her shoulder and found a grinning Beth watching them. It made her want to go back and smack the smile off her face. For Jackson's sake, she climbed into the car once he had it unlocked and slipped off her heels, tucking her feet under her butt. When Jackson got in and started the engine, Ollie sank into the seat and rested her head against the window with a heavy sigh.

The tears came faster now. Ollie hated crying when she was trying to make a point, because the minute you started crying, people would treat you like you were weak. It wasn't Ollie's fault her emotions got heightened when she was angry. Beth didn't need another reason to fuck with her. She felt bad for not telling Mindy and Callum she was leaving, but Ollie knew that if she went back into the house, she would *most definitely* kick Beth in the face.

Glancing at him as he drove, Ollie wondered if Jackson was aware of *how* horrible his sister was. Being racist was one thing, but attacking someone for being a different skin color was a whole other level. Ollie winced as she replayed the entire conversation and then Jackson walking in and getting angry. He didn't seem surprised, but he was definitely angry.

Which was good, but was it enough?

THIRTY-THREE
Jackson

This meeting with his family hadn't gone the way Jackson thought it would. Oleander was supposed to meet his parents, his siblings and let everyone see he'd found the most amazing woman.

Except *everything* had gone to shit.

They'd grown up in an affluent white neighborhood and Jackson knew most families in the area had nannies and a lot of them were Hispanic women who did everything for the kids. All his closest friends were white, most of the people he went to school with were white—there were so few instances where they interacted with someone of color. Maybe it was that upbringing that made Beth the way she was, but he knew his parents and even Brandon didn't look at race the same way. None of them, except Beth, had voted for He Who Shall Not Be Named—that was enough proof.

Oleander was silent the whole way back to Wildes. She was curled up in her seat and her head was turned towards the window, so he couldn't even catch her eye. He kept both hands on the wheel, even though he wanted to reach over and put one hand on her thigh to let her know he was right there through it all, and drove straight to her place.

He parked his car and watched Oleander climb out, taking her heels and purse with her, leaving him alone. Sighing heavily, he grabbed their bag from the back and followed his girlfriend up to her apartment. She'd left the door open, so Jackson walked in and locked it behind him. He found Oleander in the kitchen, staring into the open fridge, tears leaking down her face.

"Oleander."

"I think I want to be alone, Jackson."

"I'm really sorry about what happened today."

"I know." She sighed and closed the fridge, a bottle of wine in one hand as she used the other to wipe her face.

"We need to talk about this."

"Nope."

"Oleander."

"Stop." Oleander said firmly. "As much as I want to pretend like all of *that* didn't happen, we both know I can't. I don't even know what to do because I'm in shock and angry, but I'm so…lost."

"I didn't know Beth was going to be *that* kind of person," he said softly, like he needed to unload his guilt and apologize for his part in this.

"What kind of person did you think she was?"

Jackson frowned, unable to comprehend what she was saying. He'd known Beth his whole life and sure, she was a bit of a bitch and she drove him absolutely insane most of the time, but was Oleander implying his sister was a bad person? Beth had said ugly things and *definitely* meant them. Which didn't help either of their cases at all.

"I dunno? I'm sorry."

"Stop apologizing!" Oleander yelled, then covered her mouth with both hands as she stared at him. Jackson knew her well enough to know yelling wasn't her style. She looked surprised at the volume and tone of her voice, but he didn't move.

Oleander's shoulders slumped and it looked like the fight went out of her completely. Jackson wanted to hold her, but he knew if he moved, he would regret it. His own feelings were so conflicted—he was angry with Beth, but he was also confused about Oleander. He'd never been in a situation like this before and he didn't know what the right thing to say or do was. All he could do was hope that every word that came out of his mouth didn't make Oleander's body tighten with tension.

He blew out a breath. "I wish we could redo today."

Oleander sighed and poured herself a really big glass of wine. He watched her take a large gulp before setting the glass down. If she was going to be drinking the whole glass, he needed to be prepared for what was about to unfold.

"I don't want this to go away. I want you to remember and understand how the world sees me."

"It's not the whole world, just my asshole sister."

Oleander let out a frustrated laugh and shook her head as she tugged on her hair. She was really angry, her body was vibrating. "My whole life, I've been told I'm all kinds of things. I'm too tan to be white, when really I'm *brown*. Or I would be so much more beautiful if I lost all my weight. Or if I put a little more effort into my clothes and my makeup and my hair, I could win the affections of any *man* in the world.

"You're a cisgender white male who grew up in wealth and luxury. You had the best education money could buy, you had a good life," Oleander explained and Jackson hated that she'd seen that side of his life. "Not to say I didn't have a good life, but I'm a woman of color in a country where the color of my skin is instantly a reason to hate me.

"Let's not forget that I'm not the ideal size for women in this world and I am bisexual. And of course, in *your world*, my jobs aren't exactly glamorous." She moved closer to him and Jackson tensed. "But when others call me out on all these things to use them as insults, slurs and a way to break me down, it *hurts*.

Because to me, being brown, bisexual and fat is not a bad thing. I love who I am, but I don't like how other people make me feel."

"None of that matters, I love you the way you are."

Oleander stared at him and Jackson saw something new pass over her eyes—she was *disappointed* in him. She was standing so still, except for her chest rising and falling fast. Looking at her made him feel ashamed, so Jackson looked away.

The problem was, he didn't know *what* she was angry about. Beth had said some horrible things and she'd insulted his girlfriend, but what was it that made her feel like she wasn't good enough?

"I feel like some things were lost in translation?"

Even as the words came out of his mouth, Jackson knew he'd made a mistake. The problem with saying words out loud was that you couldn't take them back. There was no rewind button in real life.

When she spoke, it was slow and measured, which only made it so much worse. "Was your sister speaking in a different language?"

"No, that's not..." He hesitated and rubbed his elbow, the back of his neck, anything that would give him time to get his words together. "She was talking about stereotypes and using it to piss you off."

"Wow."

That one word said everything.

Jackson chewed on his lip, watching Oleander as she started pacing. How did he end up saying the wrong thing every single time? He took a deep breath and tried to piece his thoughts and words together. So far, everything he said had upset Oleander. Which meant whatever came out of his mouth next needed to be better.

Oleander spoke, interrupting his thoughts, "You do know what she said to me was wrong, right?"

"It's just Beth talking shit. She doesn't mean anything by it."

Oleander laughed and Jackson winced, because it wasn't an *oh my god you're so funny* laugh. It was a *wow you're an idiot* laugh.

"I can't believe you're defending the woman that attacked me."

"Whoa. Attacked you? She…"

"She *what*, Jackson?" Oleander was almost in his space. "Words hurt almost as much as actions and if you think you can brush her hateful words aside like it meant nothing, you're in for a treat."

"You're being silly, Oleander."

Oleander went still and Jackson's eyes widened when she put her entire focus on him. He backed up, bumping into a counter as he stared at her. It seemed like his brain was a million steps behind his mouth, because he replayed his words and he could see *why* that would upset her so much. Actually, *upset* was an understatement. Oleander had been angry before, now she was livid. And Jackson was so thrown by the look on her face, he didn't know what to say or how to respond.

"I can't tell if I've been stupid to think you're not like everyone else or if you've been putting on an act this whole time." She said the words slowly and Jackson found himself frozen on the spot. "Because the guy who took me to the food truck festival wanted to protect me from guys who grabbed my ass, but this guy in front of me is calling me silly and asking me to ignore his sister's racist and hurtful words."

"Oleander… that's not…"

"Don't," she whispered and Jackson saw the tears in her eyes. "I've been here before. I've been called silly, that I'm overreacting and misunderstood what the person said. But we both know I'm not wrong. We know what your sister said to me is the worst kind of insult. And you know what stings?"

Jackson's heart broke at her words, realizing he'd said those things to her.

"You're not listening to me. Instead, you're defending your sister, who is a horrible person, by the way. I know you love her, but Jackson, there is literally nothing nice about her and you know it."

"I…" Jackson paused when Oleander held up a hand and shook her head.

"Whatever you have to say next, I want you to think about it carefully."

Jackson pursed his lips. He understood what he *needed* to say, but he didn't know how to say it. He took her advice and thought about it. Nothing he could say now would fix the situation. He'd hurt her, he'd used words he didn't mean, but he'd said them and there was no turning back. He wanted to undo everything, but here lay the problem—he didn't know what he wanted to say. Other than 'sorry'. And it was very clear that Oleander didn't want to hear the word ever again.

"That's what I thought." Oleander's words broke through his inner monolog and Jackson sighed. "I know you love me, but you've never been with a woman who looks like me. This can be a learning opportunity for you."

"What?"

Oleander shrugged and Jackson's eyes widened. It sounded a lot like she was done with him. Jackson's heart cracked, his chest ached and his entire body felt like it was falling apart. She wasn't meeting his eyes and that said everything. She didn't look angry anymore—she looked tired. Jackson wanted to go to her, wrap her up in his arms and make everything okay again.

"Oleander, *what are you saying?*" He repeated, pleading with her. The words were shaky as he clenched his fists to stop the rest of his body from shaking as well.

"You should probably leave, Jackson."

"No…"

"I *need* you to leave."

"No, that's not good enough," Jackson told her, moving closer as he spoke. "I do understand what you're saying and I know her words hurt you, but what about me? I don't want to be an asshole and say my feelings are important too, but you're being ridiculous by throwing away the last eight months because of something my sister said."

Oleander scoffed, then looked shocked at how close he'd gotten. Jackson realized his mistake too late, because she put her hands on his chest and pushed him back. "You *are* being an asshole."

"Come on, Ollie, we can't end like this."

"How else should we end? When your sister calls me a terrorist?"

Jackson frowned. "That's not fair."

"You know what's really not fair? My *boyfriend* not being able to understand a simple request because he's crossed a line."

"*Fuck*, what does that mean!?"

Oleander let out a growl. Except, this wasn't sexy or attractive. This was an angry growl. She was back to vibrating, with her eyes dark and angry.

"Jackson." She said his name firmly and he stiffened. "You're walking out of this apartment and we're going to take some time to really think about what happened."

"That's it? We're walking away from each other because of *one person*?"

"Yes." Her voice shook slightly and Jackson sighed when she didn't say anything else.

"Oleander, *please*."

She shook her head and turned away from him. Taking the wine with her, Oleander walked towards her bedroom and looked over her shoulder at him.

"This is for the best, Jackson."

She stepped into her room, pushed the door shut and left

him there alone. Standing in the middle of her apartment, Jackson inhaled deeply and released the breath, unable to focus on the fact he'd been broken up with.

At least this time it wasn't because someone was cheating on someone else. But this hurt more. His sister had done some serious damage and Jackson couldn't do anything about it. She had unleashed her ugly colors and Oleander was collateral damage. He'd seen the light go out in her eyes and wished he could make it better. But there was literally nothing he could do to help. His words weren't helping, his actions weren't helping either. It was a mess.

With one last look at her closed bedroom door, Jackson walked out of the apartment.

THIRTY-FOUR
Oleander

Ollie was tired. After she closed the door on her relationship with Jackson, she'd inhaled the entire bottle of wine and woke up the next morning feeling like shit. She missed her class at Tiny Dancers and her shift at the Barrel because she stayed in bed the whole time. Sure, she was getting paid to show up to both jobs, but when your heart was broken, it was impossible to do anything.

Let alone get out of bed.

Her phone rang constantly. She read every text, listened to every voicemail, but didn't respond. And ghosting everyone was definitely *healthy*. She knew it was ridiculous, but Ollie was hurting.

The conversation with Lisbeth was totally predictable. She knew right from the moment they met, Jackson's sister was going to attack her in every way possible. Pierce might not have been so forward, but he'd done it. Chipping away at her strength and her confidence because she never reacted. Almost everything Lisbeth said, Pierce had said once or twice. The difference was, Pierce said it with a joking tone as they cuddled on the couch or lay in bed. Until they broke up, she didn't realize how terrible he was. He obviously kept saying it because Ollie hadn't been reacting the way he hoped.

And the opposite happened with Lisbeth.

She said something horrible and instead of cowering and running away, Ollie snapped. She hadn't spent her whole life in America to have some high and mighty white girl tell her she didn't belong there. Lisbeth was just one of the many racist assholes in the country and she could handle her.

What she couldn't handle was Jackson.

The whole time they'd been dating, they'd never once talked about her race. Because it had never seemed important —she was a woman who was dating a man and that was it. Sure, they talked about her sexuality and her family, but it had never occurred to her that Jackson might not *understand*.

He stood there and listened to her speak, and instead of trying to learn or understand, Jackson kept repeating the same things over and over again. And worse, he used words Pierce did when Ollie was trying to make a point.

Jackson and Pierce weren't the same, not even by a long shot, but it was triggering enough that she ended it. She'd spent three years with Pierce and he'd basically tortured and hurt her till she was unable to function. But she wasn't going to let that happen with Jackson. She loved him. But, she could not be with him until he understood where Beth went wrong.

Jackson's lack of knowledge about racial issues was their undoing. Ollie wasn't going to educate him. If he couldn't learn on his own, then she wasn't going to spend all her time trying to teach him.

Just thinking about him, about the conversation and how he barely even fought to understand what was going on brought tears to her eyes. Ollie appreciated that Jackson understood her words were final and she wasn't in the mood to argue, but at the same time—why didn't he try harder?

STARTLING AWAKE when her phone rang, Ollie groaned and reached for it, only for it to stop suddenly as the screen went black. Cursing under her breath, she carefully got out of bed, tripping over her shoes and the bottle of wine she'd emptied and plugged her phone in to charge. The apartment was silent, which meant Lachlan was gone again. Ollie didn't care. She watched her phone come back to life and sighed when it started ringing again.

"What?" She spat out the word as she answered it.

"Good morning to you too."

"What do you want, Frankie?"

"To see your face, really."

Ollie sighed. "Nothing has ever stopped you from showing up at my front door before."

"Well, you seem to be in such a wonderful mood, I didn't want to take any chances."

"I'm fine." She forced a little pep in her voice.

"Said everyone who was ever not fine."

"Frankie…" Trailing off, Ollie closed her eyes and rubbed them with the heel of her free hand.

"Look, your parents are worried—they've been calling me constantly."

"It's been like a day."

Frankie chuckled. "Anders, you've been MIA for four days."

"*What?*"

"Exactly! You tuned out for four whole days and your family is worried."

"What the actual fuck?"

Frankie sighed. "I'm coming over, so you better be decent, because I have food and more booze, not that you need any. And we're going to talk."

"I'll take the food and booze, but I'm good on the talking."

"Oh honey, *I'm* going to do the talking. As always."

Frankie hung up before Ollie could speak, so she set her phone down and flopped back onto her bed.

Four days.

No wonder everyone got worked up. A part of her was curious if Jackson had called, but she decided she didn't want to know. They were broken up, she'd made her decision and that was the end of that.

Forcing herself out of bed, Ollie stripped off her clothes. She turned on the shower and her eyes snagged on her vibrator on the edge of the sink. The last time she'd used it had been with Jackson—they'd spent an evening in her tub and he watched her get off with it.

Ollie shook her head, growling at the image in her mind. Forced herself to focus on the matter at hand—she needed to shower, smell presentable and spend some time with Frankie. Being with her best friend would be a good distraction.

The water was scalding, but it helped numb everything. Ollie adjusted the taps until she had the right temperature and washed her hair, scrubbed her body—behind her knees, her elbows, behind her ears, her neck—and when she was smelling like herself again, she dried off and changed into fresh clothes.

Once she felt more human, she texted her parents and let them know she was okay. And even though they asked what was wrong and why she was out of contact, Ollie kept the information to herself. There were some things her parents didn't need to know. Given that they didn't even know about Jackson yet meant breaking the news to them now would only make them dislike him more. She wanted to get her life together and everything straightened out before she brought up Jackson.

Ollie heard the front door open and close and turned the volume up on her phone before walking out to meet Frankie in the kitchen.

"Look at you, pretty as a daisy."

"*Fresh* as a daisy."

Frankie shrugged, "Potato, potahto."

"What did you bring me?"

"Nachos, guac, ice cream, lots of wine and your favorite Chinese food."

Ollie stared at the pile of food Frankie was unloading onto the kitchen counter and shook her head. There was so much and yet, she knew between the two of them, they'd finish everything off before Frankie left. *If* she left.

"Thank you."

"Oh please, all of this is mostly for me."

Ollie smiled. "For coming here."

Frankie turned to her. "You're my soulmate and if you're hurting, I'm hurting."

"You don't even know what happened."

"I know." Frankie sighed and Ollie frowned. "Jackson's been miserable and talking Milo's ear off."

In all of her love and then rage haze, she forgot about Frankie and Milo being together. But what bothered her more was knowing that Jackson was miserable. It comforted her to know that he was as broken up about this as she was, but it still made her sad.

"Speaking of…how are things with Milo?"

Frankie lifted a shoulder in a shrug, "They're good. I'm happy."

Ollie smiled, "I can tell by the fact that you're fighting the urge to grin at me."

Laughing loudly, Frankie covered her face. Ollie was glad for her, because her best friend worked too much and didn't have enough fun. By the looks of it, she and Milo were still having fun and that's all that mattered.

"I'm happy for you, Frank. You deserve someone good."

Frankie grinned, a light blush covering her face. "And *hot as fuck*."

Ollie laughed as she reached for a bag of nachos.

"But seriously, Anders, I'm sorry about what happened."

"It was inevitable." Ollie sighed.

"What do you mean?"

Ollie leaned against the counter and kept eating nachos, getting dust all over her fingers and the front of her clean t-shirt. But she didn't care, she was so hungry.

"Not only am I the first person of color Jackson has dated, but I'm the *first* person of color in his life," Ollie explained. "Jackson's sister is the perfect example of being intolerant even though she was raised by two great people."

"Is it normal for me to be confused right now?"

Sighing heavily, Ollie glanced at her best friend. "Jackson's closest circle is made up of white people, but he wasn't taught to be racist. He's never had the opportunity to be around people of color and know what it meant to…understand where they came from."

Frankie nodded and Ollie ate more nachos, needing to catch her breath.

"And if you've never had people of color around, you're never going to know how that feels."

"I was taught how to not be racist," Frankie argued.

Ollie nodded. "By *our* grandmothers. Well, more by Baby than anyone else, because she doesn't take shit from anyone. But that's exactly my point."

Frankie frowned and nodded, prompting Ollie to keep going.

"You spent time with an Indian family as a kid and you spent most of your life around my Indian family, so you *know* how to behave in those situations, what to say and what not to say. But it's not like everyone has that same experience." Ollie set the bag of nachos aside. "Jackson has never faced a situation like this before and it *definitely* made him uncomfortable, but also made me aware of how much he doesn't know."

"So what did Jackson say?"

"Mostly what he did *not* say," Ollie sighed. "He kept

defending his sister, like her words shouldn't offend me. I couldn't understand why he wasn't getting it.

"Then I realized he's never had a reason to deal with a conversation about race. But, it's on him to rectify it and *that* means learning about everything related to race and how America sees those of us with different skin color. And I can't be the one who teaches him, he needs to learn on his own."

"Wow," Frankie whispered.

In their entire friendship, Ollie and Frankie had never talked about anything like this. That made her realize they didn't have to because Frankie had seen it first hand. Between Baby and Nana Willows, Frankie's grandmother, they had been taught the right and wrong things when it came to race. It didn't matter if the person was white, Brown or Black—you showed them respect, you understood where they were coming from and you *did not* belittle their situation.

It was definitely Jackson's responsibility to learn about this and to fully comprehend the damage Beth's words had done. But more importantly, how to be an ally. Everyone put on airs of being an ally, of being someone who supported the oppressed or the minorities, but actions spoke louder than words. And right now, Jackson's actions and words were still hurting her.

"I love him, I do. But this reminds me of Pierce's tiny digs and how he brushed them off as jokes."

Frankie gave her arm a gentle squeeze. "If anyone reminds you of Pierce, they've got to go."

Ollie smiled sadly. "I thought I was past it, you know? I was past the whole 'men trying to make me feel small because I didn't understand where they were coming from' thing."

"But Jackson is different," Frankie argued. "Jackson doesn't think you're pathetic or disgusting because you've been with women."

"I know."

"Anders, that boy went out of his way to take you on the

best dates of your life; he is *nothing* like Pierce. Even if there are things he said or did that *reminds* you of the asswipe, that's not who Jackson is. Right?"

"You went from 'he's got to go' to defending Jackson pretty fast."

Frankie shrugged. "These past few months, you've smiled more than you have in any relationship. And I've known you most of your life."

Ollie nodded, offering her friend a small smile. "You're right, that's not who Jackson is. He *is* different. But that night...it triggered me. And the more he said and the less he paid attention, the angrier I got. And before I knew it, I was asking him to leave."

"Hear me out," Frankie started and Ollie narrowed her eyes. "Do you think you were *waiting* for something like this to happen?"

"Yes." The word came out without even hesitation.

"Oh, that was easy."

Ollie shrugged. "I was waiting doesn't mean I wanted it to happen. If it could have been avoided, I'd have been happy as fuck. But, it happened."

Frankie opened two pints of ice cream and slid the Rocky Road over to Ollie. "Are you going to be okay?"

"Eventually. Right now... I think we need this space. Or maybe *I* need this space to really see if this is what I want and if it's all worth it, right?"

"But you love him."

"Love is easy. I loved Pierce, too. Look how that turned out," Ollie said with a smile. "But it's less about love and more about what goes with it."

Frankie nodded and they lapsed into silence as they dug into their pints, eating the ice cream quietly. Frankie made some good points, but Ollie knew they needed this time apart. This was the most crucial part of their relationship. It hurt more because it was someone related to Jackson, but it could have happened in any situation. Until Beth's outrage, neither of them were even aware this was something that could upset the balance of their relationship.

Ollie heard her phone ring from the bedroom and the soft sounds of the ringtone she set for Jackson made her heart ache. She wasn't ready to hear his voice or speak to him.

It might have been four days, but it felt like yesterday and she was still recovering from the hurt.

THIRTY-FIVE

Jackson

THREE WEEKS LATER

Oleander was avoiding him. So he accepted that she was officially done with him. But Jackson wasn't done with her, or them. He knew what he needed to do to get her back.

But for now, the only thing keeping him sane was work.

Days after Keleigh's party and *the conversation*, Jackson had been given an incredible opportunity at work. With the success of the last pitch and the work he put into it, the higher ups believed he was ready for something more, *something bigger*. And that meant leading an entire team for a new campaign.

Much like the weeks before they broke up, Jackson worked for close to 18 hours every day. But unlike that time, he was glad for the long hours. It kept him busy and focused on the task at hand and not thinking about Oleander every chance he got. He barely even had time to catch up with Milo and Gavin.

The project was important, like almost every other one he worked on. He wanted this promotion; he'd worked his ass off for the last five years to get to this place.

And while getting Oleander back was just as important, he knew she needed the space. She was right, he needed to *learn* about racism and about how it affected the lives of people. Jackson had a privileged upbringing and wasn't going to pretend otherwise. Even if he lived a simpler life now, he still had everything accessible to him and he'd taken it for granted.

It took him a few days to really gather his strength to do some research. If you typed in 'racism in America' into Google, there were not only 100 news articles about how the country was falling apart after the last presidential term, but there were essays and studies done about the same thing. Jackson opened every link he could find, he did more research on books he should read and it was *overwhelming*. While most of the stories were about racism Black people faced, there were still quite a few about racism towards Asians.

It was actually more than plain racism, it was *hate*. It was propaganda.

It was systemic racism.

And Oleander was right—it was ugly.

The weekend before he was sucked into work, Jackson drowned himself in all the learning and reading. He ignored the guys, ignored his phone and soaked it all up. Racism meant different things to different people and that's where the problem rested with him. He knew Beth was racist—*everyone* knew it—but he believed she was joining the masses about people taking their jobs and building the wall. Accepting those as her form of racism was bad in itself, but Jackson hadn't even thought twice about how deep it ran. Until she was standing there, shouting at his girlfriend, Jackson had been ignorant of her ugliness.

When he replayed the entire conversation he had with Oleander and thought back to whatever he heard Beth say, Jackson realized *where* he'd gone wrong.

His sister had used Oleander's heritage and her ancestral culture to make her feel small, to make her feel like she didn't *belong*. Sure, she changed her tune when he showed up. Accusing Oleander of wanting to be with him for his money and his status, but that wasn't even close to the truth. Until he pulled up in front of his childhood home, Oleander didn't know Jackson came from money. Beth played on all the things people had poked Oleander about—including her disastrous ex—and Jackson hadn't realized it. He'd argued with Oleander about how she was misunderstanding Beth's words or taking it too personally, when the truth was, it *was* a personal attack and Jackson had been stupid not to see it.

Losing Oleander had been hard, but realizing *why* he lost her was worse. Jackson barely got any sleep before his first day of long weeks, because he stayed up till the sun came up reading. And when he wasn't reading, he was making notes and berating himself for not being an *ally*.

Oleander deserved better than him; but that didn't mean he was going to let go without a fight.

JACKSON and his team were six days into planning when he got a call from Mindy. She sounded panicky and worried, and instead of asking her what was wrong, Jackson drove to his childhood home. He should have probably talked to her first, because when he pulled up in front of the house, he found every car there—Brandon, his father and *Lisbeth*.

Jackson didn't want to see his sister.

Just as he was about to reverse and go back to Wildes, the front door opened and Mindy appeared. Jackson knew there was no running away now, so he met her on the front stoop.

"Sorry I tricked you, but it was the only way I could get you all in the same room."

Jackson gave Mindy a hug and followed her into the house. It was a *Huxley Family Meeting*. After Mindy joined the family, they had these meetings. It started out weekly, but then everyone got really busy, so it became monthly and now they only happened when there was something important to discuss or a family emergency. And clearly this was an emergency.

He hadn't told Mindy or his father what had happened, because he didn't want them to know he'd ruined things with Oleander. When they left early, Mindy had texted to find out what happened once he got home and Jackson made up some excuse about Oleander being unwell. But clearly the truth got to them somehow.

Walking into the kitchen, Jackson avoided meeting Beth's eyes. Instead, he looked at his father and his brother and saw disappointment reflected at him. He'd run away from a big project for a family meeting, so whatever it was, it needed to be fucking good.

"What's going on?"

"You've been keeping secrets," Mindy started, pointing at him and then at Beth.

Beth rolled her eyes. "I'm *allowed* to have secrets."

"Not when they're harmful," his father contributed.

"Can someone please tell me what's happening, or I'm going to head back."

"This is an intervention, Jack," Brandon said and Jackson watched as his brother looked past him to Beth. "To stop our sister from being a complete asshole all the time."

"What the fuck, Brandon? Excuse you."

"Lisbeth Catherine Huxley, you will not use that language in my house." His father's booming voice echoed through the room and Jackson shrank back.

"Jeez, dad, way to be an asshole yourself."

"Lisbeth," Mindy started and Jackson watched as the two women faced off. "We do not allow racist behavior in this house. We do not tolerate your brand of mean and we will not stand by as you hurt people that are important to us."

Jackson felt the air leave his lungs. They *knew* and they were calling Beth out on it. He hadn't expected everyone to step up, but looking at his family, he could see they were angry.

It wasn't just disappointment, it was a whole other level and it was shocking. But also satisfying, especially given the look on Beth's face as she glanced at every single person in the room.

"What are you talking about?"

"Seriously, Beth, you're going to play innocent now?" Jackson finally found his voice and stepped towards her.

"Oh please, you should be *thanking* me."

His father came around the counter so he was looking directly at Lisbeth. "If you cannot keep your mouth shut about your ugly opinions, you are no longer welcome in this house."

"Daddy…" Lisbeth's eyes widened and Jackson watched as his big sister became a little girl again. "I didn't do anything."

Jackson opened his mouth, but Mindy held her hand up to stop him. "Keleigh recorded the entire conversation. We know what you said to Oleander, how you treated her and we are done letting you get away with it."

"Daddy, you know that's not who I am."

His father shook his head. "I've seen the video, honey. You can't charm your way out of this one."

"Brandon," his sister pleaded, hoping someone would be on her side. "You agreed with me."

His brother frowned. "I barely know this woman."

Jackson stepped forward and looked his sister in the eyes. After everything he'd learned, he understood what was happening. Beth was gaslighting them and it made him realize he'd done the same thing to Oleander.

Because she was saying so many things Jackson had said to his girlfriend.

He kept his voice soft, trying not to agitate her, like she was a caged and rabid animal that would lunge for him. "What was the point of the showdown, Beth? Were you trying to show your strength over Oleander or just behave like an asshole?"

Beth's face changed, a sneer and a growl taking the place of the innocent act she'd put on for their father. Jackson sucked in a sharp breath as his sister leaned forward. "She broke up with you, didn't she? That's why you're so angry. You didn't care when I was talking to her."

"Lisbeth, enough."

"No, Daddy, Jackson stood there and growled at me, but he never said anything to defend his little girlfriend. So clearly he believes everything I said."

Fucking Beth. She was right, and Jackson hated how right she was. He hadn't defended Oleander. He'd told Beth she was being an idiot and then they'd left. The issue was, none of them knew how to deal with a racist family member the right way, and by not defending his girlfriend, he'd made it look like he was on Beth's side.

But he wasn't.

"I do not," Jackson responded, gritting his teeth as he glared at Beth.

Beth giggled and patted his arm. "It's okay, Jack, she's not worth it and you deserve better."

"Beth…" Her name came out a growl from their father and Jackson laughed as he backed up.

"You're right, I didn't defend her properly and I'm paying for it dearly. I lost her because you decided your petty issues were more important. And because I didn't understand how deep your dislike for those who are different runs. You're not opinionated, Beth; you're *racist*. What you don't and will never understand is that Oleander is worth more to me than you'll ever be."

Beth rolled her eyes and Jackson looked at his parents and sighed.

"We're all allowed to have our opinions about everything in the world, but what we're not allowed to do is belittle someone because they don't fit into our box," he explained, looking at Beth. "And I lost Oleander because I wasn't listening or paying attention. I lost her because I didn't *understand*. But if Beth gets to stay in this family, I'm gone."

"Jackson…" Mindy reached for him and Jackson shook his head. He glanced at his father, nodded once and did the same with Brandon before walking out of the house. He moved at a normal pace and slid into his car and leaned forward to rest his forehead against the steering wheel.

His head ached and his heart longed for Oleander. He could love her from a distance, that feeling would take years to fade away. But being in the same room as his family and knowing he could lose whatever was left of his life exhausted him. Jackson knew learning about racism had come really late, but he also believed it was better late than never. It made him wonder how often this happened to Oleander, because she fought back without even hesitating. It hurt to think she'd had to go through this more than once and it had numbed her to the way people behaved.

Blowing out a breath, Jackson shook his head and counted backwards from 50. It was a tactic his sensei taught him when he showed up to karate with a dark cloud over his head. It might have only been three weeks, but it felt like three years. He'd spent the whole time learning about where he went wrong and how to fix what he'd done. Jackson felt like maybe it was too late to fix things with Oleander.

But fuck, he wanted to try.

The passenger door of his car opened and he opened his eyes to find Mindy sliding in beside him. Jackson shook his head, silently letting his stepmother know that he didn't want to talk about it. But this was like high school all over again—Mindy knew he needed the help, so she was going to sit there until he listened and did whatever needed to be done to fix the situation.

What Mindy didn't know yet was that Oleander had ended things.

And like he predicted, he did something to fuck it all up.

"I'm sure that was hard."

Jackson huffed. "The ultimatum or admitting I was wrong?"

"Both." Mindy gave his arm a squeeze and Jackson relaxed back in his seat.

"I just stood there and did nothing. Even after we got home, she said all these things and I kept defending Beth. Or at least I kept ignoring all the things that were wrong with what Beth said. And it hurt Oleander."

"But you understand what you did wrong?"

"At the time, I didn't know why Oleander was getting so angry with me," Jackson sighed. "But, I get it now. I told her she was overreacting. I made it seem like I believed in what Beth was saying and kept making it worse every time I opened my mouth."

Mindy winced and Jackson groaned. She squeezed his arm again and Jackson shook his head. "I basically shut her down, and instead of supporting her, I kept insisting she ignore it."

"Oh honey," Mindy said softly. "Nobody, woman or man, wants someone they're leaning on to brush things aside."

"I didn't even realize what I was doing. Oleander was right to leave me. What kind of partner does it make me if I don't know what my girlfriend is going through and I can't defend her when someone says the shit Beth did?"

Jackson heard Mindy sigh at his words, but he continued. "And I called her *silly*. Her ex…he hurt her so much, Mindy. And he called her silly and pathetic, and more I don't wish to repeat. I dismissed her and her struggles the way he did and I didn't even realize it till later."

A low whistle came from the passenger seat and Jackson clenched his fists as he glanced at Mindy, smiling sadly at the look on her face. She sat quietly, hand still on Jackson's arm and after a long moment, she spoke.

"Soon after we got married, your father called me childish

and sensitive because I was getting worked up over something related to you. He kept saying you had to fend for yourself and I refused to listen. But you know your father, he insisted he was right and I was wrong. I left the house and stayed with a friend for the night." Mindy paused and Jackson realized he'd never known about this. "The next day, your father showed up at my friend's house with my favorite coffee and a breakfast pastry. We sat on the porch and he apologized. But more importantly, he admitted where he was wrong, and he accepted he'd overstepped and said awful things to me.

"You can't undo what Beth has done, you can't take her words back and make Oleander feel better. But what you can do is apologize for where you went wrong." Mindy nodded at Jackson's pained expression. "I know your issue is not admitting you were wrong, but what comes after. And that's good—you should be worried. She might not take you back, she might forgive you or she'll tell you everything is fine and you can be friends. But whatever she decides, Jackson, you have to accept it. Because you hurt her and it's going to take more than an apology to make up for it."

Jackson nodded, blinking back the tears. If his father and Mindy could sort through their issues, he and Oleander could as well. He glanced at Mindy and she smiled at the expression on his face.

"I believe you and Oleander can sort through this, and if nothing else, you'll be able to have her in your life again in some way or the other. Isn't that enough?"

"I'll take what I can get."

Mindy laughed softly, "You love this girl, Jackson, so go and get her."

THIRTY-SIX
Oleander

After her day of indulging with Frankie, Ollie made *big* decisions.

First, quit her job at the Barrel.

Working at the Barrel had been fun at first. Frankie got to drink for free and Ollie always ate great food, met fun people and got laid quite often. But was that enough to keep a job? With how little she was getting paid or cared about the job itself, it made no sense to stay when it frustrated her. Plus, as much as Ollie didn't want that to be a reason, she was constantly afraid she would run into Jackson or his friends. And for the time being, that excuse was going to have to be enough.

Second, devote herself to teaching dance full time.

This was the easiest decision to make. She'd thought about taking on more classes for years, but knew that she needed *me time* between working the bar and dancing. Ollie knew most people would work back-to-back jobs, but that was never going to be okay for her.

Third, tell her parents about Jackson.

The first two were easier than the third, so Ollie decided to tackle it last. She might have been raised to always do the difficult things first, but this one required patience and finesse, and she didn't want to wing it.

So she did the first two things.

After skipping out on work for four days, Killian was gunning for Ollie. She showed up on time for her shift the day after Frankie came to her apartment and spent close to 30 minutes listening to Killian go on about how irresponsible she was.

When he paused to take a breath, Ollie dropped the bomb. "I quit."

"*What?*" Killian looked surprised.

"You treat everyone like shit and I'm one of your oldest employees," she explained, gesturing with her hands, "*and* you pay me crap, even though I do more than anyone else and work all the late shifts."

"Okay, you're being dramatic."

"One more thing," she said, ignoring his remark. "Start treating your female staff better or I'll make sure they all quit and file sexual harassment lawsuits against you and your patrons."

His eyes widened. "You wouldn't."

"Don't tempt me. I have *nothing* to lose," Ollie said with a sweet smile. "I'll finish my shift tonight, then I'm done."

Killian was flustered for the rest of the evening. Ollie worked her shift like usual and when her time was up, she clocked out for the last time and walked away from the Barrel knowing she was making the right decision.

While her parents had kept insisting Ollie didn't have to pay them back for college and everything else, Ollie wanted to do that at some point. Now was better than never. And working at Tiny Dancers would definitely make her more money.

The next day, she went in to see Melody about coming on full time and taking on more classes. Other than the sessions she had, she knew Melody was looking to expand her classes and add more to the schedule. Maybe this was her chance to dance because it made her *happy*, instead of dancing because it paid the bills.

"You're in a very chipper mood this morning," Melody said in lieu of a greeting as Ollie walked into her office.

"I come bearing great news!" Ollie grinned.

"Well, I've got some great news too, so do you want to go first?"

Ollie nodded and sat down, straightening her back as she smiled at her. "I want to come on as a full time dance teacher."

Melody smiled, but stayed silent. Ollie frowned as they stared at each other. She opened her notebook and pushed it towards Ollie.

"These are the new classes we're thinking of adding to our schedule."

"Whoa." Ollie's eyes widened as she looked at the hand-drawn table in front of her. She couldn't count fast enough, but it looked like there were more people looking for dance lessons than either of them expected.

"So your decision to go full time could not come on a better day."

"Holy shit, Mel, this is incredible," Ollie laughed and brushed the tip of her finger over the list. "Hold on, how is this going to work?"

"We're bringing on two more teachers, obviously. So along with the classes you already have, you could probably take on two more. Which means you'll start your day at 9AM and finish up by 8PM."

Ollie nodded, processing the new schedule. While it was a lot of hours of dancing, she knew there would be at least four hours in the course of the day she'd be free. She could use the time to sleep or get out for a bit, as long as she came back on time for her next class. *And*, it freed up her evenings.

"And, there's one more bit of good news."

"No more dance moms in the studio?" Ollie said with an arched eyebrow and Mel laughed. "Hey, a girl can dream, okay."

"Nice try, but what I was going to say was you don't have to work weekends. I'd like to start the new teachers off on the weekends."

"Seriously?"

Mel nodded. "Absolutely. You've been with me for years and you've given up your weekends and a lot of your days to fill up slots. I don't want to put you through that for much longer."

"Mel...that's," Ollie shook her head, shocked that this was actually happening. "This brings up the big question."

"Yes, you'll get paid more," Mel smiled. "With more registrations, I can definitely afford it. Besides, you're now a full time teacher, you'll get paid as such."

"While we're on this subject," Ollie said as she leaned forward, offering Melody her most charming smile. It was not charming at all. She probably gave Pennywise a run for his money. "Can we implement a new rule?"

"You think that smile is attractive, but it's actually quite unsettling."

"I know." Ollie smiled wider, tilting her head to the side. "Parents, friends and boyfriends of older kids can't hang around inside the studio during classes."

"You know it won't work."

"The kids are so unmotivated when their moms are yelling from the sidelines."

Mel sighed. "I've had my fair share of it; I know what you mean."

"It's just for the sessions with kids above the age of 10. The younger kids are there for the fun of it and the moms can be as neurotic as they want."

"Let me think about it? I'm sure we'll have to find somewhere for all of them to hang out during class and Kris will *kill* me if I insist they stay in the reception."

"As long as she never knows it was my idea, I don't think she'd mind." Ollie finally unscrewed her creepy smile and got to her feet.

'I'll put together the new schedule and we can start you off in a few days, how does that sound?"

Ollie grinned. "Absolutely. Thanks Mel, I needed this."

Mel stood up and they shared a quick hug. When Ollie walked out, she felt lighter and happier.

THE LAST THING she had to do was talk to her parents. Of course, she wanted to do it in person, but flying out to Huntington for a weekend was ridiculous. And then there was the whole thing about physically looking Baby in the eyes and explaining the truth. The easier thing was to do it via FaceTime and get the conversation done with.

The call went about as well as Ollie thought it would—it took 15 minutes to get everyone in the frame and by the time Baby could hear everyone, Ollie felt like she'd aged a million years. Frankie sat by her side, being the supportive best friend and held her hand as she told her family about everything.

Which included telling Baby the boys she kept introducing Ollie to were duds.

When she finally told them about Jackson, her grandmother looked unhappy. But her parents seemed to be dealing with it better. Ollie knew her family would support her, like they did when she came out, but this was different. She wasn't with Jackson anymore, so it was strange to be talking about him like he was still in her life. Sure, the call had two important topics and both of them were received with mixed reactions.

"So, when are we meeting this boy?"

Ollie looked at Frankie at her father's question. "I don't know, we're a bit of a mess."

Baby mumbled in broken English, "You cannot trust these *Americans*."

Frankie scoffed and pointed at herself, which made Baby roll her eyes and Ollie chuckled, "Ammachi, that's not entirely true."

Baby shrugged it off and her mother stepped in. "What happened?"

"Let's just say his sister isn't as kind as Jackson is and she made a bit of a scene."

Her father frowned. "So you broke up with him?"

"Look, it's a long story and one I'm not really enthused about rehashing right now."

"Annie, why are you telling us about this boy if he is no longer in your life?"

"Because, mom," Ollie sighed, "I want all of you to know I'm not interested in meeting a *very eligible Indian boy*. I want to meet my own partner, I want to get to know them, have them get to know me and like me for who I am. Not what's written on a piece of paper."

Baby *tsked* and Frankie snorted at her side, which made Ollie smile.

"And Ammachi, every boy you've found for me has issues with who I am. And honestly, it's very demotivating to meet someone and think you've hit it off when they end up pointing out all your flaws."

"There's a right person out there for you somewhere," Baby said in her rough English.

"I found that person, that's what I'm trying to say," Ollie added, noticing everyone's eyes widening. They clearly didn't expect her to drop *that* bomb. It was one thing to tell them about Jackson, but a whole other thing to talk about him like he was *the one*. But he was. He had been. "He might have hurt me and his sister might have said things I will never forgive her for, but Jackson is the best kind of person."

"You were never this sure about that Pierce," her mother pointed out. Ollie shuddered and so did Frankie, and if her family noticed, they didn't bring it up.

"Pierce was wrong for me, on so many levels. For all his faults, Jackson is great. He loves me for who I am."

"So you will marry this Jack-*son*," Baby said firmly and Ollie laughed.

"We're not even together, so no talking about marriage."

She muttered on about *kids these days* in her mother tongue of Malayalam and Ollie saw her parents smile.

Baby cleared her throat. "Do you love this Jackson?"

Ollie swallowed and nodded, blinking back tears. "I do. I didn't want to, but you know how it goes. He basically bulldozed his way into my life and made me love him."

Her father's eyes misted and Ollie gave Frankie's hand a squeeze as she glanced at her best friend, who was also teary eyed. This was turning out to be a lot more emotional than she expected, but Ollie was glad she was finally having this conversation, because it was important that her parents know she had met someone. Even through his complicated situation, he was the one for her.

Except, Ollie wasn't ready for him again. Not yet.

"All right, guys, Frankie and I are going out this evening. And we need to go g—"

Baby disconnected the call before anybody else could say anything. Ollie laughed, collapsing back against her couch as Frankie did the same.

"Baby is still such a riot. I would have been disappointed if she'd changed."

Ollie snorted. "That woman is going to drive everyone crazy even after she's dead."

"That's how I want to be when I get to her age," Frankie said with a grin. "Sassy and unstoppable."

"You're already those things, more of it for the rest of our lives? God help us."

"God can't help you now, Anders, you're stuck with me."

THIRTY-SEVEN
Jackson

After the family meeting, Jackson went back to research some more. His learning was never going to be done and he knew it was going to take a really long time before he was fully ready to give Oleander what she deserved. Being a supportive partner was one thing, but it was also about being an understanding partner and someone who would be willing to learn from his mistakes.

His brain played the greatest hits of that day and the look on Oleander's face when she'd pulled away from him. Jackson had spent most of his childhood crying, but as an adult, he didn't shed too many tears. But the more he thought about Oleander and how badly things had turned out, he found himself crying in the shower.

Beth was finally given an ultimatum with the family and Jackson heard all about it from Brandon a few days after the family meeting. It had been ugly, as predicted, but at least now everyone was completely aware of where Beth stood. She had made her choice too, by cutting out the family and doing her own thing. Jackson was worried for her kids, because they would grow up the way Beth wanted them to and that included being racist, ugly and horrible. And those kids were too young to be molded that way.

While he was wallowing, Milo and Frankie seemed to form some kind of bond. They weren't seen in public together, but Jackson had seen Milo's phone ringing a few times, with Frankie's face on the screen. It only made him long for the days when he had that kind of relationship with Oleander.

When some friends from college invited them to a party, Milo said he was inviting Frankie. Jackson hoped that Oleander would also show up. But they hadn't spoken at all and Jackson didn't know where he stood in her life. His head was so full of questions and desires, and wanting to see Oleander that he stopped trying to make sense of everything else.

"Who invited these three good looking motherfuckers to my party?!" someone yelled as Jackson walked into the apartment with Milo and Gavin. That was always the greeting *they* got, but Jackson had never felt like they meant it till that night. Thanks to Oleander, he found greater appreciation for himself. She helped him see that he was worth a second look and he had other redeeming qualities to focus on too. The three of them shook hands, bumped shoulders with their friends and moved around until they had drinks in their hands.

Jackson was catching up with a friend when he heard Frankie's voice, followed by Milo greeting her. His eyes moved around the room and froze at the sight of Oleander. She looked incredible. It had been so long since he'd seen her, but Jackson hadn't forgotten how beautiful she was.

It felt like he was seeing for the first time. When their eyes met, he smiled and got one in return. But he didn't move, he let his eyes move over her body, his dick stirring in his pants as he took her in.

Oleander was wearing a white swishy skirt that stopped above her knees with a black strappy top. It dipped low in the front, hugging her beautiful breasts. Her hair was loose and flowing, making him miss sliding his fingers through the soft strands. She was wearing Chucks this time, but her legs still looked so long and firm. His eyes moving back up her body, smiling at the hint of her tattoo between the top and the waistband of her skirt. When their eyes locked again, Jackson saw heat in Oleander's eyes and he wondered if she saw the same in his.

Seeing her was like a breath of fresh air and he didn't know how he'd breathed all this time without her. Beyond her beauty, his heart ached for her. His arms hadn't forgotten what it felt like to hold her, his lips didn't forget the way hers fit against his, but his brain was happy to remind him of the look on Oleander's face the last time they saw each other.

She was breathtaking. He had never felt this way about anyone else before, and watching her as she smiled at people Milo introduced them to, Jackson felt like they were so far apart. He'd done this, he'd put this space between them and he'd broken them by being himself.

She stayed with Frankie and Milo as Jackson made his rounds, their eyes meeting every time he glanced her way. He knew he needed to go over and say hi, but he was also worried that once he got close enough to her, he wouldn't be able to walk away. And Jackson wasn't sure if she was ready for him. The last time they'd seen each other was almost a month ago, and he'd hurt her to the point of her kicking him out. Oleander had every right to make him leave. And it took him facing off with his sister to realize where he'd gone wrong.

Milo found him standing in a corner by himself and nudged him forward. By the time Jackson reached Oleander, Milo was tugging Frankie away and leaving them alone.

"Oleander."

The scent of her perfume swirled around him and Jackson had to resist the urge to close his eyes. They came together and he hugged her, his free hand sliding around her waist to hold her against him a minute longer.

"Jackson." She said his name softly, pulling back.

"You're so beautiful." She *looked* beautiful, but Oleander radiated beauty all the time.

"You don't look too bad yourself," she said softly, brushing her hand over the front of his blue Henley.

That simple action made his body lean towards hers. He missed the way she touched him, the way she smiled, the way her eyes twinkled when she was being silly and naughty in bed. He missed the sound of her saying his name too and he let it replay over and over again, because it was now going to be the soundtrack to his life.

Jackson knew how much Oleander liked these shirts, so he'd gone out and bought a whole new set in different colors. And tonight, he'd chosen a slightly brighter blue and paired it with jeans and his usual sneakers. His hair was messier than usual and he'd let his facial fuzz grow out. Milo had made him trim it before leaving and Jackson was glad. Because looking at Oleander, he could see she was cataloging all of those things too.

"Can I get you a drink?"

She laughed softly. "It's weird being served drinks."

"That's right, I heard you quit."

"And I heard you haven't been back since."

Jackson blushed as he moved to the kitchen. "I didn't have a reason to go back anymore."

"Where are you guys going now?"

"A sports bar close to work. It's missing hot girls in band tees, though."

"That's a shame."

Oleander smiled and Jackson gestured to the makeshift bar. She tapped her finger against her lips and Jackson's eyes drifted to her mouth, his mind filled with memories of them kissing, nibbling on her plump bottom lip as she pushed her hands into his hair.

"Jackson?"

He blinked. "Yeah, sorry."

"Scotch on the rocks?"

Jackson nodded and poured out Oleander's drink. He handed it to her and grabbed himself a fresh beer. "Wanna go somewhere a little less…this?"

"Yes." She said it almost as soon as he finished his question and Jackson smiled, holding his hand out to Oleander.

She slid her hand into his and Jackson led the way out to the large balcony. This felt so easy, because they'd done it so many times before. There were a few people scattered around, but he kept moving until they got to the other end. Jackson watched as she smoothed her skirt and sat down, crossing one leg over the other before he sat opposite her.

They were silent for a moment, the sounds of music and conversations from around them filling the space. Jackson had so many questions and so many things to say, but he didn't want to overwhelm her. He wanted to give her time to get comfortable talking to him again.

"What made you quit?" Jackson asked the question as Oleander said, "How have you been?"

They laughed, shaking their heads. Oleander gestured for him to go as she took a sip of her drink.

"Why did you quit?"

"I was exhausted all the time. Besides, dancing is more fun and I make more money too."

Jackson nodded. "I'm happy to hear that. I'm sure everyone at the Barrel misses you."

"I doubt it," Oleander told him with a tight smile.

"So, Frankie and Milo."

Oleander snorted and Jackson glanced at her. "I should've known they'd fall into bed together."

"He's constantly attached to his phone too, it's impossible to have a conversation with him."

"She indulges me in all the sex she's having, so…" Oleander shuddered.

"I'm sorry." The words came out in a rush and Jackson was confused how it had come out of his mouth without his knowledge. But obviously he didn't want to talk about Frankie and Milo. Not when he finally had time with Oleander. This was about *them*, not their friends.

"Neither of us can stop Frankie from talking about her sex life—"

"Not about that." Jackson interrupted with a shake of his head. "I *am* happy for them. But, I'm sorry for the way I behaved *that night*."

Oleander went still and Jackson watched her hand tighten around her glass. He looked up and found her watching him, and all he wanted to do was hold her. Assure her that he wasn't going to hurt her, but he knew he had so much more to say before he did anything. The way she was staring at him made him feel like she could see his soul and Jackson felt unsettled.

But this was good, he needed to be uncomfortable. It was the only way he would say everything and admit to Oleander he was wrong.

"You were right, about everything. About Beth's behavior, about my lack of support, about…fuck, *everything*." He sighed. "While I don't support my sister's words or her behavior, I brushed it off like it meant nothing. Even though she was hurting you."

Oleander cleared her throat, but Jackson kept going.

"We had a family meeting and we confronted Beth," Jackson explained, glancing at Oleander and saw her eyes widen. "Keleigh filmed the entire thing and shared it with my parents, who then gave Beth a piece of their mind. Brandon did too and I've never seen him so angry with Beth before."

Jackson was still so amazed that Keleigh had caught it all.

Because it was enough proof for the family and the push Jackson needed to make sure he never made that mistake again.

"And I did, as well," he added softly. "I'd been reading about racism and learning about it before I saw my family. When Beth accused me of standing there and doing nothing, I realized she was right. I didn't stand up for you, but I finally found my voice and it was a lot. I walked out of the house because I was so angry with her for brushing it all off like it meant nothing."

A weird sound came out of Oleander. "Oh god, I broke your family."

Jackson shook his head. "We did this to ourselves. It's not like we've been oblivious to Beth's leanings, we got comfortable ignoring it. Because it wasn't affecting anyone we knew. Which is worse. We were *enabling* her racism and I hate that we let it get this far."

"Now what?"

"My dad gave her an ultimatum. She needs to apologize to you for everything she said, or she can step away from the family," Jackson said.

"Jesus."

"But this isn't about Beth, this is about me," Jackson insisted and turned to face her. "I was not being the supportive boyfriend I thought I was or who you deserved. I brushed off your concerns, I ignored your feelings and I focused on trying to make it all go away. I couldn't see past the frustrations of Beth being *Beth* and seeing you cry. I never meant to hurt you or make you feel like you didn't have anyone on your side."

Oleander stared at him and Jackson saw her eyes shine with unshed tears. He wanted to pull her into his lap and kiss her, but he wasn't done.

"It's not an excuse, but I've never encountered a situation like this outside of what happens in the news, and I didn't know how to behave. I might be old enough to experience these things, but I haven't. I *have* lived a very privileged and sheltered life and I hate that my behavior and my lack of response hurt you even more."

Instead of saying anything, Oleander stood up and moved away. Jackson sighed heavily and stared into his drink, listening to the soft swishing of her skirt as she moved. After a long moment, he stood up, but Oleander turned to face him at the same time.

"Thank you," she whispered. "For being honest, for admitting your privilege and your mistakes."

"I'm sorry it took me so long." He breathed out. "That night, you were telling me so much through your body language, through your frustrations and your anger, and I ignored all of it. I can see how tense you are right now and I hate that I make you feel that way around me."

Oleander shook her head and a tear slipped down her cheek. "I know what I'm going through or what happened is not something you're used to or even aware of, but I appreciate that you took the time to learn."

Jackson nodded. "I did. I know my learning about racism is nowhere near done and it never will be, but I'm so angry that I've been ignoring it and how in doing that, I hurt you even more."

He took a step forward, itching to wipe away the tears and Oleander sighed, so he didn't move again. He felt so distraught and helpless. The fact that Oleander had given him a chance to talk didn't mean anything more than that. Yes, they were saying the right things to each other and there was promise of things getting better, but Jackson knew he'd fucked up so bad that she would need more time.

"I need you to know I never stopped loving you," Oleander said softly, making his chest ache. "But this time apart was important. For both of us."

He nodded. "I agree, because it helped me see what I had

done wrong."

"I missed you, Jackson."

"Fuck," he mumbled, blinking back tears. "I missed you too. More than I can put into words."

"But..." she added and he nodded, knowing it was coming, "I'm still going to need some time."

"I get it."

"There's more to learn, for your family to wrap their heads around and for me to process."

Jackson nodded. "I know."

"But we'll see each other again soon."

"I love you." The words came out of him in a rush and Oleander smiled.

"I don't think we could stop even if we tried."

He nodded with a small smile. "It was good seeing you tonight."

"Stay out of trouble, Jackson."

"I'll do my best," he whispered, his eyes trailing her as she walked off. Oleander stopped at the entrance into the apartment and glanced back at him and Jackson's heart pounded so loud. She blew him a kiss and vanished into the apartment, leaving him there alone.

But at least now, he had hope and he knew if he found a way to remind her how good they were together, they could get back there eventually.

THIRTY-EIGHT

It had been a week since the party where he spoke and apologized to Oleander. He didn't *want* the time away from Oleander, but *she* needed it. And that meant he would give it to her. All he wanted was for Oleander to step back into his life and never leave. In order to make it happen, he needed to trust her process and take the time to appreciate what he had with her. Even if she loved him, there was no guarantee she would come back.

According to Frankie and Lachlan there was a thing called *grand gestures* and it was Jackson's only hope of winning Oleander back. As someone who had watched romantic comedies most of his life, Jackson was ashamed he didn't know that's what they were called.

And since the conversation with her friends, Oleander had started texting him. A few messages here and there, sending him pictures that reminded her of his two weeks of wooing. That told him he had *hope*. Jackson had been thinking about making the first move, but she clearly beat him to it.

At least she was talking to him and Jackson was going to take the win.

On the first day he was free, Frankie dragged him out of

bed. She put him on speaker phone as Lachlan lectured him about the infamous grand gesture. The two of them asked him questions and jotted down answers. Given that he was completely confused by everything, he asked Frankie for help. As someone who got off on planning every celebration, she was more than happy to help. And spent the following week putting everything together.

Frankie enlisted Milo and Gavin to help and insisted on bringing his parents in as well. Jackson hadn't spoken to his parents since the family meeting with Beth. Mindy seemed impressed; his father was still upset with Beth, but showed up for moral support.

Phone calls were made, credit cards were swiped and Jackson crossed things off his list. While Frankie was organizing everything, Jackson was planning it. And he knew exactly what he needed to do in order to win his girl back.

SUMMER HAD SHIFTED into fall and it was getting cold enough to make Ollie hate everything about winter. The additional whining was because Frankie made her leave her apartment on her one day off. That included wearing jeans and sneakers and her long coat, because it was nippy. Ollie had intended to stay wrapped up in her onesie. Instead she was on her way to meet her best friend at the park. Apparently there was a mini food truck festival and since she didn't take Frankie to the last one, she had to make the trip now.

Ollie parked her car in the unusually empty lot and walked towards the park entrance. When she got there and didn't see a single food truck, she pulled out her phone to call Frankie. She was sent directly to voicemail. Ollie tried Lachlan and got the same response. Growling, she started to write a text in their group chat when music began to play. It was faint at first, but it started coming into focus.

Looking around in confusion, Ollie tried to figure out where it was coming from and saw four human shaped balloons. Unable to see them clearly, Ollie shielded her eyes with one hand as they got closer and gasped when she recognized the Ninja Turtles. The music got louder and she recognized the Ninja Turtles theme song immediately. Before she could even try to understand what was happening, a food truck was headed her way.

Ollie's eyes widened as she took in the line of food trucks coming towards her, the Ninja Turtles balloons moving with them. The song changed and Ollie tilted her head till she recognized the song from the bar the night she and Jackson went out. She smiled as the trucks formed a large circle around her.

"Hello there, lovely lady."

Ollie laughed when Niles hopped out of his truck with a drink in his hand. "Niles."

"I find myself willing to go to the ends of the earth for both of you and something tells me this is just the beginning."

"I honestly hope so," Ollie told him, taking a sip of the drink. It was exactly what she had the first time they visited Niles' truck. Niles stepped back as a pile of tulle and pink shoved their way through the gaps between the trucks. Her tiny dancers!

They lined up perfectly and grinned at her as the song changed. They executed their dance routine without a single mistake. Ollie was in shock, staring at them as they moved in synchronization and finished with a flourish.

"What!"

"We've been practicing, Miss Bowen."

Ollie shook her head. "You guys have been lying to me every day in class?"

Claire huffed, like it was obvious. "It was a secret, and we didn't want to spoil the surprise."

"Who told you to keep it a secret?"

Claire grinned proudly and turned to point upwards. Ollie lifted her head to find Jackson standing on top of a food truck dressed up like Master Splinter. Ollie covered her mouth with one hand and stared at him, shaking her head at how ridiculous he looked. He'd put so much effort into his costume and she had to admit it was blowing her mind.

"Oleander."

"What are you doing, Jackson?"

"This," he said with a sweep of his arms, "is a public declaration of my love for you."

Ollie shook her head and watched as he vanished from sight. Frowning, she looked over her shoulder and found Frankie, Lachlan, Milo, Gavin, Everleigh, and Jackson's family standing there. Mindy looked so excited and Ollie couldn't help but laugh at the happiness. They all started pointing behind her and Ollie turned back in time to see Jackson walk towards her.

Seeing this Master Splinter costume up close and personal was a treat. His strong arms were bare and his tattoo was clearly visible, and the soft hair on his chest peeked out through the V in his top, making her want to run her fingers through it.

Instead, she smiled, "Hi."

He smiled. "Did you know grand gestures are a thing that exist?"

"Is that what this is, a grand gesture?"

"A declaration, actually," he said with a firm nod. "But it's the same thing."

"Now what?"

Jackson cleared his throat and took a step back. "I'm declaring my love for you."

"I thought you already did that once."

"No, this is different," he told her, a stupid smile on his face. "I wanted to recreate our first date, I wanted to remind you of all the good times we had when we first went out together. I wanted to show you that you always come first."

Ollie blinked back tears, smiling at him. "We didn't have Ninja Turtles on our first date."

"No, that came much later."

"Speaking of which, I'm wearing them today," she told him, because of course she was wearing her famous TMNT undies.

"You're killing me, babe," Jackson groaned and Ollie smirked.

"So, your declaration, let's hear it."

"Right." He straightened up and smiled. "I wanted to bring all of the important people in our lives to remind *us* about why we got together in the first place."

"And why is that?"

Jackson smiled. "Because of the Turtles, of course."

"And my shakes!" Niles called out from his truck.

"And Niles' shakes," Jackson added, waving a hand at their friend while keeping his eyes on her. "But also because we both felt more like ourselves with each other than we did with any other partner we've ever had. Because when we're together, everything else fades away."

"And we come into focus."

Jackson nodded. "And the only thing I see is you. It's been you since the day we met and it'll be you till the day I die."

"Oh my, was that a proposal?"

Ollie laughed at Mindy's interruption, which got a glare from Jackson. "I'm not rushing us into marriage yet, but I hope in the distant future, you might be open to marrying me."

"I've got conditions."

"Of course you do," Jackson teased. "Let's hear them."

Ollie chuckled, not really having any serious conditions, but she wasn't going to back out now. "We must woo each other once a month. You need to learn how to make me pancakes. I will spoil you constantly. We'll also learn how to make pizza the right way. But most importantly, some days, I won't feel like being a human and you'll have to deal with that."

Jackson nodded. "Deal."

Ollie grinned and they stared at each other till Jackson stepped forward.

"I didn't want to do this in front of the whole world, but apparently they don't like being left out of the good stuff, so here we go." Jackson took another step closer. "I love you, Oleander Bowen. I know these last few months have been rough and I've not made it any easier. But I also know that my life without you is empty, there hasn't been a single day when I've felt like myself. I am *nothing* without you." Ollie smiled and Jackson continued. "I vow, for the rest of our lives, to be more receptive and spend every single day learning about being the man you deserve."

Ollie sniffled, nodding as she looked at Jackson.

"So I have one last thing to say, a question if you will." Jackson cleared his throat and dipped his head to look at her properly. "Oleander…will you let me woo you again?"

She laughed loudly and nodded. The smile on his face was *everything*.

"I always promise you more wooing, food trucks, lots of dancing and our friends."

"Jackson?"

He nodded, still smiling. "Yes, Oleander?"

"Will you let me love *you* for the rest of your life?"

Jackson frowned. "No."

"Why not?"

"This is *my* declaration. You can't hijack it."

Ollie rolled her eyes. "It's not an official proposal."

"Then what was that?"

"A promise?"

"Are you not sure what that was supposed to be?"

She shrugged. "It was a reflex. I didn't want to feel like I didn't want to bring anything to this...*declaration*."

"It's not a potluck."

"So..."

Jackson made a face. "Ugh."

Ollie laughed and moved forward. His face lit up as he stepped closer and slid an arm around her waist. "I love you, Jackson Huxley."

"Damn right you do," he grinned and dipped his head to kiss her. Ollie wound her arms around his neck and kissed him back, moaning softly against his mouth as his tongue brushed over her bottom lip. Ollie's fingers curled into Jackson's hair as she pressed herself closer, his arms tightening around her waist.

"For *fudge's* sake, there are children here!" Frankie's laughter filled voice burst through the space and Ollie broke the kiss to groan, pressing her face into Jackson's chest.

"Thank you, trouble, for ruining this wonderful moment," Jackson chuckled.

Frankie took a bow. "You are most welcome. If you two are done, I'd like to get my grub on."

Jackson still had his arms wrapped around her, but he nodded at Niles, who whistled really loudly. All the food trucks started opening up their service windows and everyone who had come out to support them scattered to go get their food. Ollie nuzzled into Jackson, her arms moving around his waist as she inhaled the scent of him.

Their relationship had gone through every stage at this point and she was impressed with how far they'd come and where their relationship was going. In her arms was the only man she could see herself marrying.

And the crazy part was, Ollie didn't even know she wanted to get married until Jackson was telling her he hoped it would happen one day.

THIRTY-NINE
Oleander

She was floating. Her heart was full and so was her stomach. Between the shake Niles gave her and all the food she consumed, Ollie was happy as shit. They were surrounded by their favorite people and food trucks that she had been obsessed with on their first date. Ollie looked around at everyone and then at her boyfriend and realized she had everything she always wanted. This was her *family* and they were willing to stick it out with her through everything.

When she broke up with Jackson, she knew it was going to kill her to be away from him. But it was the right thing to do at the time. Both of them needed space and she needed Jackson to realize where he'd gone wrong. Obviously everything that had happened with the family meeting and coming to terms with what he'd learned about his sister had made things clearer for him. And she could tell that Jackson was serious about making a change, which was all she could ask for.

Someone had set up benches and chairs and their entire group of friends and family sat down and dug into the food. Niles kept everyone's shakes filled, there was a steady stream of tacos, donuts and waffles.

"What's going through that pretty head of yours?"

Ollie glanced at Jackson, who was watching her curiously. "I'm happy for Frankie."

Jackson looked over at their friends and smiled. "I think Milo's in love with her."

"Well, good for Milo."

"Are *you* good?"

She nodded. "I am. I'm *really* good."

"You look pensive."

"Just thinking…"

Jackson tucked her hair behind her ear. "About us?"

"Obviously," she smiled and leaned into his hand. "A year ago, I kept telling myself I wasn't ready to meet anyone or have a serious relationship. And you appeared almost like the universe was telling me to get over myself."

"I know you don't have regrets, because you're here, but there is a *but*…"

Ollie smiled. "But…I've been scared this whole time. I love you and I love what we have, but I feel like I was *waiting* for something to go wrong. When your sister laid into me I felt like it was my *aha moment*. Like there's the other shoe falling."

"You think you willed this into existence?"

"No, but I was waiting for it," Ollie sighed.

"We pushed through it and look where we are now."

Ollie nodded, because he was right. They *had* pushed through it, talked about it and learned from everything that had gone wrong. And he'd fought for her, which was enough.

"Jackson."

"Oleander," he smiled as he looked at her.

"I think it's time for us to go *home*."

He got to his feet and held out a hand. "All right."

The short ride home was quiet as she watched Jackson drive, his hand on her thigh, thumb stroking against her jeans-clad leg. Discounting the time they'd been *broken up*, they'd been together for nine months and she'd connected more with Jackson in that short time than she had with any of her past relationships. She'd found someone she could spend her life with and it was the last person she expected it to be.

Since Lachlan was still at the park, the apartment was empty. A few lamps were on and Ollie sighed happily as she stepped into the warm apartment and shed her coat. She offered him something to drink and Jackson agreed on a glass of wine before going to get out of his outfit.

The last time they'd been in this apartment together, Ollie had been angry. They were different people now—she was stronger and he was learning. They still loved each other, but there was a different kind of charge in the apartment. Ollie shook her head, trying not to get too caught up in the past. It had changed the course of their relationship, but loving Jackson was the easiest thing she'd ever done.

Having Jackson in her apartment could have been a trigger, but it was comforting. Their love for each other was bigger than the fight, bigger than the pain they'd struggled through. Ollie wondered if Jackson could feel it too, because it was crackling and goosebumps exploded across her skin.

In the kitchen, she pulled out her last remaining bottle of wine along with the corkscrew. Ollie also set the glasses on the counter and worked to open the bottle. The corkscrew didn't go in straight and in her frustration, Ollie yanked it out. Her hand smacked into one of the glasses, which shattered on contact and knocked the other one over, shattering on the floor.

And *of course*, in all of that, she hurt herself.

"Babe? What happened?" Jackson appeared in the kitchen in gray sweatpants, t-shirt in hand.

Ollie was temporarily distracted by his state of undress

and choice of clothes, before she lifted her bleeding hand. "I broke the glass."

"You know what this reminds me of?"

She narrowed her eyes at him. "First aid kit is under the sink in my bathroom."

Jackson laughed and went to get it while Ollie rinsed the blood off her hand. Using her other hand, she grabbed the broom and started sweeping up the glass when Jackson came back with his shirt on.

"Stop it, come sit down."

"Ugh, you're enjoying this."

Jackson smirked, pulling out a chair for her. "It's poetic that this happened tonight."

Ollie held her hand out and Jackson wiped the blood off before checking to make sure there were no glass pieces stuck in her skin. She smiled, watching him. Because he was right, it was poetic. While it wasn't their first meeting, the crash had been what put them in each other's lives forever. She still remembered how distracted she was by his strong forearms, messy hair and sparkling eyes.

It felt surreal to have him there. Ollie wanted to forget about her hand and crawl into his lap. He was there, he came back for her. Even though Ollie told him she needed time, both of them knew it wasn't going to be forever. She could have walked away, but she would have regretted it every single day. This was where they were meant to be.

"Ouch!" She yelped when her hand burned.

"It's just a little alcohol."

Ollie smacked Jackson with her free hand. "I didn't do this to you!"

"No, but you probably should have." Jackson chuckled. She liked that *he* was playing nurse, cleaning and wrapping up her hand.

"There you go," he said.

"You'll need to open the wine."

Jackson lifted her injured hand to his lips and kissed the gauze. "Anything for you, my love."

Ollie swooned a little and focused on packing up the kit before joining him in the kitchen. He managed to open the wine without any accidents and poured it into two glasses. Ollie came around the counter and wrapped her arms around his waist and pressed her lips against his bicep, resting her chin on his shoulder.

"I'm glad you're here."

Jackson kissed the top of her head. "Now that I'm back, I'm not leaving."

"The horror!"

"True story, you better be prepared for me to drive you insane."

"More than you already do?" Ollie quirked an eyebrow.

"I drive you insane *with love*."

"Okay, hot stuff."

Jackson smirked. "I appreciate the evolution from cutie to hot stuff."

"You're a regular Pokémon."

"Wait, you know what Pokémon are?"

Ollie gasped and moved to smack him, but realized she was using her injured hand and changed her mind. Jackson laughed and tugged her into him. Their lips met in a slow kiss, wine and injured hand forgotten.

And there it was—the electric charge she was worried wouldn't come back. Jackson had always set her body on fire with a kiss or touch. Sure, they were still *Ollie and Jackson*, but that kiss was deeper and more passionate. It held everything they felt for each other and Ollie was so overwhelmed by the feelings she had for this man.

Jackson pulled her closer and pressed her against the counter. His hands wandered down to squeeze her ass through her jeans. Ollie whimpered, her lips parting as Jackson's tongue swept over her bottom lip and into her mouth. With her uninjured hand, she grabbed at his hair and moaned, her tongue dancing with his as he pressed himself against her.

Ollie didn't think as she dragged her injured hand down to the front of Jackson's sweatpants, moaning when she felt how hard he was. But when she tried to wrap her hand around him, pain shot through her arm. Yelping softly, she broke the kiss and frowned at her offending hand.

"This is ruining the sexy vibe I'm trying to set."

Jackson chuckled against her skin as he dragged his mouth down her neck. "You're fucking sexy all the time."

Ollie hummed happily at that statement and set her injured hand on his shoulder as she dropped the other one to cup him through his pants. Jackson groaned into her neck, his fingers digging into her ass. Palming him, Ollie gently nipped at Jackson's earlobe and added a little pressure to her grip. Jackson let out an unidentifiable sound, which encouraged her to slide her hand into his pants and dragged her fingers along the length of his hardening dick.

"*Oleander...*"

"Take them off," she whispered, tugging on his earlobe as she wrapped her hand around his dick.

Jackson complied, hands leaving her body to untie and push off his sweatpants and Ollie smiled as she leaned back to stare at him. She could feel his warm breath ruffling her hair as his chest heaved, so Ollie wrapped her hand around him again and this time she stroked him from base to tip slowly.

"You're killing me, babe."

Flicking her eyes up to meet his, Ollie gently pushed Jackson back a step and then dropped to her knees before he could stop her. She heard him growl when she walked the tips of her fingers along his dick, smiling at how he twitched. Ollie lifted her eyes to his as she leaned in and licked the bead of moisture off his tip, humming as she shifted on her knees till she was comfortable on the floor. Then wrapped her uninjured hand around him and rested the injured hand against his hip, and slowly took him into her mouth. Jackson's groan echoed through the kitchen and Ollie closed her eyes as she took him deeper, her hand stroking his base *slowly*.

Jackson's hips jerked, sliding him deeper into her mouth and Ollie opened her eyes to look up at him. His hazel eyes were a dark brown as he watched, both hands pressed to the counter behind her and his jaw was clenched so tight, she was afraid he'd hurt himself.

"You okay?" His voice came out strangled and Ollie nodded, humming around him in response. Taking him as deep as she could, Ollie hollowed her cheeks and sucked, distantly hearing Jackson let out a string of curses. She felt his fingers in her hair, tangling and tugging as she gripped his base and then dragged her mouth all the way off. Sucking on his tip, she twirled her tongue around his cock and at another strange sound from Jackson, she pulled off him completely.

Ollie looked up at Jackson as she licked the underside of his cock first, and then every inch of him before taking him back into her mouth. With the way he was gripping her hair, Ollie knew that Jackson was getting close, so held his hips steady as she moved her mouth along his cock. As she reached his tip once, Ollie gently scraped her teeth over his skin and Jackson growled loudly and pulled on her hair. She stored that information away for later as she used her uninjured hand to cup and massage him.

And that was all it took.

Jackson slapped the counter with one hand and tightened the fist in her hair as she took him deep enough that he hit the back of her throat. She heard him mumble something, but Ollie barely cared because his hips jerked again and he was coming; warm, salty liquid filling her mouth and throat. Ollie pulled back slightly and swallowed, her body quivering as she tasted him. When his hand relaxed in her hair, Ollie pulled off Jackson fully and sat back on her haunches with a proud smile.

"Fuck, that was good." He breathed out and Ollie beamed.

Jackson held a hand as his chest heaved and Ollie shook her head, hooking a finger to call him down to the floor with her. He hesitated for a second before kicking his sweats aside and dropped to his knees in front of her. She wound an arm around his neck and Jackson slid one around her waist, pulling her closer to him as their lips met for a kiss that sent shivers up her spine.

She could feel his still-hard cock pressed against her and Ollie realized that she was still fully dressed, so she broke away to tug off her t-shirt. Jackson's eyes dropped to her pink lace-clad breasts and he licked his lips, lifting one hand to cup her. Ollie smiled, unbuttoning and unzipping her jeans to push them off. She stretched her legs out and Jackson helped get them off, running his hands up her thighs as he smiled at her.

"I'm gonna need a minute, babe."

Ollie nodded, running her fingers through his hair. "You can help me out of the rest of my things."

Jackson leaned back to take off his shirt and Ollie shifted the floor, laying on her back. Their eyes met as she unhooked her bra and tossed it aside and Jackson frowned.

"I could have done that."

Ollie chuckled and gestured to her Ninja Turtle panties. "I even wore the right day this time."

Jackson smiled as his eyes locked onto her underwear then he grabbed the waistband and slid it down her legs. She smiled at the look of love and adoration mingling with desire in his eyes as he stared at her.

"I want you on top of me," Ollie said softly.

Jackson's eyes widened. "Are you sure?"

She nodded and he crawled over her, his knees on either side of her legs and hands pressed against the floor on either side of her head. Ollie smiled up at him and the tension on Jackson's face eased. She grabbed the back of his neck with her uninjured hand and pulled his mouth to hers while the fingers of her other hand brushed along his hardening cock. Jackson shuddered and carefully lowered himself on top of her.

A growl escaped Jackson, but Ollie didn't stop touching him. He rocked into her hand and Ollie smiled into the kiss. Jackson pulled back to look at her properly. It was only then that she realized she hadn't freaked out at all—not when he put most of his weight on her, or when he hovered over her like that.

"I'm okay," she assured him.

"We can go to the bedroom."

Ollie shook her head. "I want to cross kitchen sex off my bucket list."

Jackson laughed, shaking his head as he sat up on his haunches and ran his hands down her sides. Ollie bit her lip, squirming at his wandering touch and spread her legs as he moved so that he was between her legs. Ollie licked her lips and bent her legs at the knees, watching Jackson stare at her.

He started to get up. "Let me get a condom."

Ollie shook her head, putting one foot on his thigh. "I haven't been with anyone else and I got tested before we started dating. I'm also on the pill."

"Same," Jackson whispered, his eyes wide. "Not the pill, but I got tested recently and you're the only woman I've been with in a year."

She smiled, pushing her hips against him and felt his dick rub against her. Ollie bit down on her lip and wiggled her eyebrows. Jackson seemed to center himself before he pressed a hand between her thighs and cupped her. Ollie whimpered, rocking against his hand, her eyes never leaving his.

"Can you fuck me now?"

Jackson snorted, but returned to hovering over her as his hips pressed against hers. Squirming under him, Ollie wrapped her legs around Jackson's waist and one arm around his neck as they stared at each other. He reached between them and she felt his hand rub against her wetness as he stroked himself. Ollie lifted her hips and looked down the length of their bodies as Jackson guided himself inside her.

The first contact made her hips jerk and Jackson filled her in one hard thrust. Ollie's back arched off the floor, her fingers curling into his hair as their bare chests pressed together. Giving Jackson the blow job had gotten her so worked up, she was already at the edge of her own orgasm as he thrust into her slowly, building a steady rhythm.

His mouth found hers in a hot kiss that made Ollie's toes curl. She wrapped her other arm around his neck as Jackson's thrusts got harder, the sound of their skin slapping filling the kitchen. Jackson's arms settled on either side of her head as he rocked faster, taking Ollie to a whole new level.

As she grabbed his hair, pulling his head back so she could look into his eyes, Ollie felt a sense of calm wash over her. In the past, being pinned under a man as she was fucked would have made her panic. With Jackson, it was the opposite. She was breathless and her heart was racing, not out of fear or panic but because she felt *good*.

Jackson smiled, clearly reading the pure ecstasy in her eyes and kissed her again. Ollie moaned into the kiss till Jackson pulled out of her almost all the way and before she could react, he pushed back into her hard enough that she saw stars.

"*Fuck*, do that again."

Jackson obliged and pulled out, but this time he pulled out fully and rubbed his tip through her wet folds. Ollie touched herself, spreading her folds and growled as Jackson pushed back into her, making her body bow.

She clenched around him and Jackson's thrusts turned shallow as they kissed. He ran a hand down her body and played with her clit, making her walls flutter around his cock. Ollie had never felt someone so deep inside her before, and it felt *incredible*. Jackson pressed her clit and a gasp fell from her lips as she rocked up against him and fell apart, soaking his cock as her body shuddered under his.

Jackson continued to thrust into her, his grunts and groans echoing through the kitchen as he came as well, spilling into her. Ollie shivered at the feeling of him emptying into her hot and desperately, her mouth and fingers clinging to him. Jackson half-collapsed on top of her and Ollie laughed softly, brushing a hand down his back.

As their breathing regulated, Jackson pulled out and lay down beside her. Ollie turned onto her side, wincing at the bruises she was sure were forming on her back and smiled at her boyfriend.

"You still doing okay?"

Ollie nodded, smiling at the concern in his voice. "I'm doing *great*. You are the only person I could have done that with."

Jackson turned to face her and Ollie cupped his face, rubbing her thumb over his bottom lip. He pressed a soft kiss to her thumb and she grinned, looking into his eyes—she saw love and trust.

"I know."

"I didn't say anything," Jackson chuckled.

Ollie grinned. "Your eyes said it all."

"And then you Han Solo'd me."

"It seemed appropriate."

Jackson leaned in and Ollie pressed her mouth to his as his arm snaked around her waist. They held each other and she realized that in some part of her mind, she'd given up hope of ever being loved or feeling safe again. Now, she had it all and she couldn't imagine life without him.

Oleander

EPILOGUE

THREE MONTHS LATER

Jackson might have jokingly *suggested* they get married during his public declaration, but Ollie knew that he was serious about it. But still, she wasn't ready to take that step yet. She wanted to be fully established at Tiny Dancers and on top of that, she was getting offers from dance teams across the state to choreograph their competitions. She didn't want to run off, get married and go on her honeymoon when she could be making a name for herself.

Then there was the whole meeting her family properly thing. She'd introduced him to her parents and Baby via FaceTime once, but it was about as awkward as one can imagine.

Ollie and Jackson spent Thanksgiving with the Huxley family—sans Beth and her family—and it had been great. Mindy and Callum kept dropping hints about a wedding, but Ollie and Jackson kept brushing them off.

After which the plan was to fly down to Huntington for Baby's birthday and fly home for Christmas with their friends. Plus, her brothers and their families were going to be there. So Jackson was going to get the full Bowen family experience. And he was nervous, as he had been for days leading up to their trip.

"Okay, time to quiz me."

Ollie groaned. "Not again."

"I can't remember your brothers' names or what they do."

"Thomas, James and Matthew," Ollie said, stretching an arm over the console to stroke her fingers through his hair. "Lawyer, FBI and CEO, respectively."

"Right, James is the one I need to be wary of."

"James is harmless, he carries a badge to be an asshole."

Jackson took his eyes off the road for a moment. "He has a *gun*."

"It's an intimidation tactic."

"It works!"

"Jackson." Ollie rubbed his scalp and saw him visibly relax. "They're my brothers, they're bound to be protective. I'm their *baby* sister and always will be."

"What if they hate me?"

"I think it's physically impossible to hate you."

"I can think of tons of people who hate me."

Ollie rolled her eyes. "People at work don't hate you."

"I still can't believe they gave me a new title."

"I'm so proud of you," Ollie grinned, remembering the day Jackson came home with the promotion and now he was the Assistant Creative Director for design.

"Thanks, babe. Even if it means more stress."

"You're going to do so great. You earned this, like everything else in life."

Jackson smiled. "Like you?"

Ollie laughed. "I think I'm the best reward for all your hard work."

"I will pull over and show you how much of a reward you are."

"If we show up to my parents house late, my brothers are going to definitely kill you."

"Jesus." Jackson growled, putting both of his hands on the steering wheel and focusing on the road. They were about 20 minutes out and she could see the tension creep back into his body. Ollie smiled, unable to take her eyes off of her boyfriend.

When they turned onto her parents' street, Ollie straightened up and looked at herself in the tiny mirror she fished out of her bag. They'd gotten ready at the airport, not having enough time to get to Huntington and change for dinner. Jackson was wearing her favorite combination of dark blue trousers and a deep burgundy long sleeved sweater, paired with his messy hair, the right amount of scruff and her favorite cologne. Ollie was wearing a burnt orange dress that fell mid-calf and had a deep neck. She'd wrapped a bunch of necklaces that distracted from her cleavage and would also make Baby happy. She was wearing a bit of makeup, and Jackson's favorite heels. And they both had their coats and scarves, because it was fucking cold.

"Here we go," Ollie whispered as Jackson pulled into the driveway of her childhood home. Once he'd parked, she found him forcing his hands off of the steering wheel with a heavy sigh. "Stick with me, kid, they're gonna love you."

"If I start rambling, slap me."

"I've got other ways to stop you from rambling."

"Don't flash me, that would be awkward."

Ollie laughed and gently shoved Jackson. "Get out of the car, weirdo."

Jackson grinned and got out, grabbing their jackets. Coming around the car, she slipped her hand into Jackson's as the front door swung open and her family poured out. Jackson squeezed her hand and Ollie smiled up at him, silently promising to be there for him no matter what.

THERE WAS A FLURRY OF ACTIVITY. Jackson was introduced to everyone and Ollie stood by his side, rubbing his back when she felt him panic or tense up. He relaxed in the presence of her nieces and nephews and Ollie was glad, because Baby beckoned for her.

Walking over, Ollie's heart raced at what her grandmother would have to say. When she introduced Jackson earlier, all Baby did was pat him on the arm.

"Are you serious about this boy?"

Ollie nodded, squatting beside her grandmother. "Yes, I am."

"He makes you smile." Baby said, gesturing to where Jackson was making the kids squeal with joy. "And I haven't seen you smile like this in a long time."

Ollie looked at her grandmother. "He makes me feel how you said Achachan made you feel."

At the mention of her grandfather, Baby's eyes softened. "Then he is special, because I believe that kind of love is rare and comes along only once."

"You were very dismissive of this when I told you about him."

"I only want you to be happy, *ponnumole*." Baby refused to call her by her first name, instead she used an affectionate Malayalam term that literally translated to *gold daughter*. Every time Baby called her that, Ollie's eyes filled with tears. "I was always worried you would find someone who wouldn't see your worth."

"I did find some of those people along the way to Jackson."

Baby pointed at Jackson. "But he sees *you* and loves you, like your Achachan made me feel."

"I never wanted to hurt you or disappoint you, Ammachi."

Baby put her hand on Ollie's cheek and smiled. "You and me? We are so alike. I knew it would take you time to find the love of your life. And it doesn't matter how old he is or the color of his skin. As long as he makes you feel the way you do right now, as long as he continues to put a smile on your face and says you're worth it every day."

Ollie sniffled, wiping away the tears streaming down her face as Baby continued. "I knew about all those bad people you dated, they were not the ones for you. But it was *your* journey."

"You knew?"

Baby shrugged. "I have the Facebook. I don't understand it, but I see pictures."

"*Oh my god*, you never said anything!"

"Because you had to find yourself," Baby told her and laughed. "I also knew if I said anything, you'd never come home to see me again."

Ollie snorted. "Not forever, but for a bit."

"But you found someone who puts that smile in your heart and love in your soul."

"Is this what it felt like with Achachan?"

"Exactly how it felt." Baby rummaged around in the armrest of her chair before lifting a closed fist and holding her hand out to Ollie. "And that is why you need this."

Ollie held her hand out and Baby dropped her diamond encased wedding ring into her palm. Gasping softly, she looked at the ring and at her grandmother. "I can't take this."

"It has always been yours. In your Achachan's will and mine, it belongs to you."

"But this is all you have left of him."

"I don't need anything of his when I lived a good life with his love. Now you must make your own memories."

Ollie blinked back tears. "Ammachi…I don't know what to say."

"There's nothing to say. You are exactly where you need to be, with the person you need to be with."

Ollie slipped the ring onto her finger and covered her

mouth with one hand, tears streaming down her face at how perfectly it fit. "Thank you."

"I am sorry if I ever made you feel like you weren't good enough." Baby shook her head. "I know I pushed you very hard and expected so much from you, but it's what I believe you are capable of. What I believed you deserved. And after lectures from your parents, I know I was hurting you more."

"I always felt like I wasn't good enough."

"I have watched you grow up and become this wonderful woman and I am so proud of you."

Ollie blew out a breath. "I love you, Ammachi."

"I love you too." Baby kissed her forehead, wiping away Ollie's tears. "Now go save that boy from those rascal children before they scare him away."

For the first time in her life, everything lined up.

Her family loved Jackson, her grandmother was proud of her and Jackson held onto her through everything. They returned to Wildes and didn't tell anyone about the ring or the unofficial engagement, even Frankie. Because she wasn't ready to share that with the world just yet.

JACKSON CONTINUED to prove he was worthy of his promotion and earning more money, and Ollie slowly built a reputation as a choreographer for dance competitions. And in the process, they decided to move in together—it took them a week to find the perfect place.

Ollie moved out of the apartment she shared with Lachlan in time for Everleigh to need somewhere to stay because her building caught fire and almost burned everyone alive.

And after lots of back and forth, Frankie and Milo were finally in a good place with their relationship. After all, he'd moved in with his best friend.

After years of trying to make sense of her life, Ollie finally found it in the unlikeliest places.

And she's never letting go.

THE END

THANK YOU!

Seriously, thank you for taking a chance on a brand new indie author. I've spent a little over a year writing this story and perfecting it. And now it's finally in your hands and I sincerely appreciate the time you've taken to read this story.

As an indie author, reviews make the world go round. I'd appreciate it if you could leave a review on Goodreads and Amazon—it doesn't have to be a long one, even a short review about how it made you feel would be enough!

NEXT UP...

If you hadn't guessed it yet, **Frankie and Milo** are coming this winter!

Theirs is a fake relationship, friends with benefits, age gap romance and I can't wait for you to meet these two super sex positive and passionate humans.

ACKNOWLEDGMENTS

Like a lot of 2022 debut authors, I started writing this book during quarantine. I was working 18 hour days and this story came to me during sleep and meetings. And I finally decided to take the plunge and just do it. But then, I didn't know I would get to this point in my life. Brace yourself, this is a long list.

My parents and brother, for always being so damn proud of me. Even when I wasn't sure about this journey, they cheered me on. I also want to apologize to my parents for the explicit scenes. I warned you that it would be more than you could handle! They've been so generous with their time and love and I am the most fortunate human to be *theirs*.

My best friends—Alpa and Akshaya—who've seen me at my best and worst through this writing process. Who've assured me that this story is necessary for the world! Alpa who has been so supporting and excited, even though we're no longer in the same city. Akshaya for being my constant hype woman even when I don't always feel comfortable telling people I'm a published author. Plus, Akshaya gets all the brownies for this GORGEOUS cover!

My Romance Boos! ♥ Lila Dawes, you are my favorite

crumpet in the whole world. I am so lucky to be your friend and have you as my critique partner. Thank you for never giving up on me even when I sometimes gave up on myself. Thank you for reading my stories and ensuring that they are good enough for other people to read. I promise I'll get better at replying to your voice notes on time. ♥ Chula Gonzalez! Babe, you are the reason this book is being published. From the moment we exchanged our first DMs you've been the best writing partner a person could ask for. I don't think I have enough words to express just what you've done for me on this writing journey. I can't wait for the world to read your stories, because you're going to rock their socks off! I love you both so much!

My editor, Sarah. ♥ You are a saint. You are a joy. I've lost track of how long we've been friends, but these past few years of talking to you literally every day has made my life better. Thank you for finding every comma, dismissing them and me in the process. I am so grateful to you and our friendship. PS. If you find more chaotic commas, feel free to keyboard smash me about it.

My alpha and beta readers—Natasha, Michelle, Marianne, Unnati and Carly—thank you so very much for taking time out of your lives to read my words and give me the best kind of feedback. My writing and my stories have improved only because you took the time to help me through this process.

Kiira Kalmi! What would I have done without your friendship, support and guidance? Thank you for pushing through the Amazon and Goodreads struggles so I could just coast through it. More than that, thank you for just being truly awesome. Our conversations are some of my favourites and I know that your friendship is one I'm going to treasure forever. One day, we'll go on that Party Cruise and drink from wine taps while taking in the views.

Amy Wuertz. I know you weren't expecting this, but we've

been writing together for more than 10 years and I know that one of the reasons I had the courage and creativity to do this is because of that. I am so lucky to have met you through Perfect Ending and for us to keep this friendship and all of our characters intact since then is a gift. We owe ourselves that California wine trip now. ♥

Special thanks to Jen Morris who read the very first and messy draft of this book and spent a few hours giving incredible feedback that turned that pile of junk into a story I'm finally so damn proud of. I've said it before and I'll say it again, you writing about Alex and Michael in your debut is what prompted me to finally get off my butt and write this story. So thank you!

To all of my favorite authors who've supported me and been excited for me, who've believed in me even when I wasn't sure I believed in myself. THANK YOU.

Most importantly, thank you! Yes, all of you who are reading this book right now. Thank you for taking a chance on this indie author who has been dreaming about this since she was 25 and didn't have the courage to make it happen.

♥ **Anna**

ABOUT THE AUTHOR

Since she was a child, Anna has lived in a world of imagination. From teaching an imaginary classroom to being an astronaut, she's found ways to tell stories to keep herself entertained.

Anna studied journalism and has a Masters in Creative Writing, and a love for music and writing got her jobs with Rolling Stone India and Sony Music, and after a couple of years of selling her soul to advertising, she's finally following her childhood dream of writing books.

Anna lives in South India, where she spends her day rocking out to Foo Fighters and reading 300 books a year. She's currently working as a freelance copywriter and book editor, while sipping on copious amounts of black tea and white wine. When she's not writing books, she's making up languages with her best friend and spending time with her family.

Connect with Anna on Instagram: @annawriteshere